To Howard
Many Merry Christmases to Come
Alan Montgomery

FIFTEEN TALES
for
Christmastide

ALAN MONTGOMERY

Order this book online at www.trafford.com
or email orders@trafford.com

Most Trafford titles are also available at major online book retailers.

© Copyright 2012 Alan Montgomery.
All rights reserved. No part of this publication may be reproduced, stored in a retrieval system, or transmitted, in any form or by any means, electronic, mechanical, photocopying, recording, or otherwise, without the written prior permission of the author.

Printed in the United States of America.

ISBN: 978-1-4669-5951-4 (sc)
ISBN: 978-1-4669-5953-8 (hc)
ISBN: 978-1-4669-5952-1 (e)

Library of Congress Control Number: 2012917342

Trafford rev. 09/18/2012

 www.trafford.com

North America & international
toll-free: 1 888 232 4444 (USA & Canada)
phone: 250 383 6864 ♦ fax: 812 355 4082

CONTENTS

Author's Note vii
Tale 1—The Candlelight Service 1
Tale 2—In the Attic 17
Tale 3—Celestial Greeting 36
Tale 4—Christmas in Baghdad 57
Tale 5—25 Percent Off: Just in Time for Christmas 82
Tale 6—The Spirit of Love 95
Tale 7—Escape Button 111
Tale 8—The Sled 134
Tale 9—The Chimney Visitor 150
Tale 10—The Matchmaker 174
Tale 11—The Christmas Punch 188
Tale 12—Christmas Vacation 210
Tale 13—A Day of Hope 229
Tale 14—The Orphan at Christmas 242
Tale 15—New Road, Old Destination 272

AUTHOR'S NOTE

This series of fifteen short stories began as a group of ten. Those ten were in a different order and have each been improved in the editing process. Two of those were eliminated entirely—they didn't "fit." Only one of the stories is based on a previously known story, and I hope that in adapting that story for this series, I have been able to give it new meaning and charm.

The reason for this volume is simple. I have always taken an element of seasonal joy from Charles Dickens's ***A Christmas Carol***. Stories about the season of Nativity can convey elements of wonder and joy that wipe away the cynicism that pervades too many people most of the year. This series deals with the inner joy that many of us feel. Several of the stories, like the Dickens story, deal with a restoration of that seasonal spirit.

This series of tales doesn't begin to scratch the surface of what the season *can* mean. The names of a few real people are used for realism. It is hoped that the people concerned (or their relatives) will consider these portraits flattering. Only Bob Hope actually appears, though others are mentioned in passing.

To my readers, let me simply say that I hope you enjoy the groups of stories. Writing them has given me great joy.

Alan Montgomery

TALE 1
The Candlelight Service

The Reverend Mr. Bertrand R. Coleman had only been in the church for eight years. His predecessor, Rev. Harold Martin, had remained in that post for twenty years, and most of the parishioners said that had been too long. It was an amazingly long time for a Methodist Church! Reverend Bert, as he was normally called, was most happy in his current position and felt he had at least two years of things he needed to do to improve things with the congregation. He had no intention of staying even approaching twenty years. This had been discussed with the district bishop who had concurred. Reverend Bert was still young enough to move on to another post and do wonderful things in at least one more church.

His personal life had never entered into the consciousness of the congregation. That he was unmarried was never questioned. Several parishioners knew he had been close once, but events had occurred that had derailed that relationship. Reverend Bert passed it off gently. "I live for my congregation, and I think God has always intended it that way." So he stayed on, securely loved by all.

An unfortunate thing happened, however, in the last two weeks before Christmas, and it had shaken the congregation to the very roots. As one parishioner put it, "One expects this in some parishes and congregations, in some denominations. Methodists were just not *that kind* of a church." The person had not gone into just what "that kind of a church" was, but it seemed everyone guessed at and knew what the parishioner meant.

The crux of the problem stemmed from Michael Derringer, an acolyte of long standing. Reverend Bert had caught him taking some money from the collection plate as he returned the plates back to the vestibule. It had been considered a possibility for several months, but only when a marked bill ended up in Michael's pocket was the young man chastised and removed from his duties as an acolyte. His removal had caused quite a few tongues to wag since Michael had such a good attendance record. His parents were also well-respected members of the congregation. Charges were not going to be pressed, but the boy was told that he would light candles no longer. Michael's father had believed the pastor, but his mother had believed Reverend Bert was lying to cover up an indiscretion.

That was when the charges came out. In retaliation for being humiliated, Michael Derringer insisted that Reverend Bert had taken sexual advantage of the young man over a period of the last four years. Reverend Bert knew why Michael Derringer had said those things, but he felt powerless to negate the charges the boy had made. Denying the charges only made him seem desperate. Yet he couldn't just ignore them.

The charges were devastating for Reverend Bert. It made the last two Sundays before Christmas quite difficult. His sermons, always models of logic and passionate reasoning, had become disjunctive and rambling. Now it was Christmas Eve, and he was supposed to give a wonderful and inspiring message. Yet he knew that the congregation, including Michael Derringer, would be ready to pounce on his message and turn it into a free-for-all, never mind the solemn evening.

Reverend Bert was just opening the box of new candles for the service when Joshua Huff came in the side door of the church. Joshua—he was always known as Josh—was another acolyte, and his cheerful disposition had helped get Reverend Bert through the last two weeks. "Good afternoon, Reverend Bert, and Merry Christmas."

"Thanks, Josh. Help me put the collars on these candles." They were the paper collars, some of them recycled from the year before, that kept the candle from dripping painfully hot wax on the hands on the congregation. "What's that you've got there?"

Josh placed the package he was carrying down on the desk. "That's the communion bread. Mrs. Wilkerson sent it over. She won't be in church. She said that there was bad weather predicted."

"What she meant was that her grandson Michael wants to make a scene and she doesn't want to be here." Reverend Bert looked at the bread. "She must be feeling really upset or something because she *never* misses a communion service. You'd think *she* was the minister! I'm sorry, Josh, I should not have said that."

Josh just laughed. "Why not? Everyone thinks it. She firmly believes that no one can set up communion but her. Last time all she did was stand over there and point, squawking out, 'Put that there. Pour that in there. Don't wrinkle the doily.' You'd think I had never prepared communion before." Josh paused a minute. "Pastor Bert, I've heard what Mike has said. He's making sure the school and everyone else knows. I even got a phone call today from the bishop, just asking a question or two, you understand."

Reverend Bert looked a moment at Joshua. "Well? And what did you tell him?"

"I told him that you had never done anything to me, and I was positive that you had never done anything to Mike either. I even told him that the only reason Mike was charging you for having done things was that he had been caught with his fingers in the collection plate and didn't like being called for it." Josh finished up the candles and went on to opening the bottles of grape juice. "I assume you don't want to switch to wine."

"I'd love to, but that might just fan the flames." Reverend Bert walked to the other side of the desk and handed the other bottles of juice to Joshua. "You might as well make it a large amount. The gossip will ensure a full house tonight." He paused. "Thanks for the vote of confidence with the bishop."

Josh started putting the cups into little holes in the tray. "That's okay. He and I met last summer at camp. I also told him that Mike's attitude had shown no signs of the Christmas spirit. Of course, *I'm* going to divinity school after college, and *he's* going to be a mechanic, if his uncle will have him. By the way, the bishop said he would be here tonight." Reverend Bert didn't need that news.

After fifteen minutes, a young girl, Marietta Simpson, stuck her head in the door. "I'm here, if you have anything for me to do." She made a point of not coming in.

Josh spoke up. "Well, you can't get anything done out there. Why don't you take these candles to the front of the church?"

Marietta came in and grabbed one of the baskets of candles. "Why don't you bring the other one? I don't know where the light switches are." Josh took the other basket with a sigh. He knew Marietta could have done this alone, but something told him she had something to say.

Halfway down the center aisle, she proved him right. "I heard that the bishop is going to be here tonight. Do you think Mike Derringer will make a big stink?"

Josh placed his candles on the floor and started setting up two card tables. "He'd better not. He may think no one knows the truth about what he's been saying, but I know better."

Marietta helped Josh set the tables upright and then placed her basket on one as Josh placed his on the other. "Maybe you think you do. But you won't be in a position to speak, and Mike will. He told me that he intends to make it impossible for Reverend Bert to speak a sermon." She seemed somehow happy about that. "What do you think about that?"

"That's certain to improve the Christmas spirit, isn't it?"

They checked the front door to make certain it was unlocked. Then they set the sanctuary for the usual night service lighting. They were back with Reverend Bert within ten minutes.

He was just starting to put on his robes. "By the way, Josh, did you get your car out of the shed? With the storm coming tonight—ice and then eight to ten inches of snow—I'd sort of like my car to be sitting inside."

Marietta stood rather uncertainly, doing nothing. She knew there were things to do, but she didn't want to commit to anything. Josh reached for his acolyte robe. "I moved it this morning. Dad cleaned out his half of the garage at home so there's room for my car too." He was buttoning the top button when he had an idea. "Reverend Bert, you know you once said that maybe I should do a trial sermon to see if I really want to become a minister. How about doing it tonight?"

Reverend Bert paused, as did a shocked Marietta. Bert had stopped at first to negate the whole idea and then decided to think about it. He knew that he shouldn't, but the whole accusation thing had him rattled. Marietta answered a little too quickly. "I think that is the silliest idea I have ever heard."

Reverend Bert turned to her. "Why is it, Marietta?"

Marietta huffed. "Well, he's only sixteen. Who's gonna take a sermon from someone like him?"

Reverend Bert thought about that a moment, but it was Josh who answered. "Do you think people won't believe me? They believe Mike Derringer, who is only a year older, and what he says makes no sense at all."

"I believe Mike!" Marietta said it with a stern and pouty face. "He has no reason to lie, does he? I believe him."

Josh answered before Reverend Bert could. "Well, don't believe something until you know all the facts. He might have several reasons to lie." He stopped suddenly and looked first to the right and then to the left, trying to clear his head. Then he turned abruptly to Reverend Bert. "I *want* to give the sermon tonight. It all just came to me, exactly what I should say."

Reverend Bert shook his head. "I don't think so, Josh. It is too hostile around here as it is. Marietta, are you going to acolyte tonight or not?"

Marietta scowled. "No. I'll sit with my mother and listen to the service." She flounced out, leaving Reverend Bert and Josh alone. They both knew she meant that she would listen to the wrangling arguments, which would be abundant. Marietta wasn't there to hear an uplifting service; she would come to the service to experience a fight, one sure to fill coffee circles for weeks.

Josh put his hand on the preacher's shoulder. "Will the usual elders serve communion and take up the offering?" Reverend Bert just nodded.

He was quite upset and didn't want to think about anything else. "Well, Reverend Bert, if you want, I can read the scriptures." Josh zipped up his acolyte robe. "And you just remember my offer, both for the scriptures and the sermon."

Reverend Bert smiled. "I'll let you read the first two scriptures. How's that?"

At that moment, the choir all started filing in, led by Florence Williams, the organist, and Craig Knowles, the choir director. They went to the choir room for a brief warm-up.

Joshua knew he wasn't going to give the sermon. Reverend Bert was probably right. It would create too much controversy. But he kept thinking about the idea he had had. He picked up the acolyte's wick and went out into the sanctuary.

Each window of the church had a real candle sitting in a holder, the holders having a drip catcher and a firm grip on the candles. Along the central aisle of the church, on the end of every other pew, a beautiful candleholder was affixed, with a hurricane lamp glass cover to protect the flame. It was Joshua's job to light each of these candles.

It was already 7:20 p.m., and the congregation was filing in. Joshua began lighting the window candles first. He would then proceed to the other side of the church and then down the central aisle, alternating from side to side, lighting those candles. He couldn't help hearing the conversation of the congregation as he lit the candles.

"I suppose he just thinks he can get away with anything. Preachers can be like that." "Imagine what the Derringer boy has had to go through." "I can't imagine why none of us ever suspected or tried to help." "If that's how he acts, we have to hope he gets what's coming to him." "Did he think a smoke screen about money would get by? Really!"

Joshua became more and more upset. He was almost shaking when he lit the final candle. He pulled his wick back into the tube and looked up directly into the eyes of an older lady. "Mrs. Wilkerson! I thought you weren't coming!"

"Never mind, Josh, I decided I should be here after all. I've been quite upset all day, and I think I need to be here to get my spiritual reawakening. Now where is my family sitting?" Joshua pointed out Mike Derringer, his mother, and his father. He even ushered Mrs. Wilkerson to her seat by them, and then he went on back to Reverend Bert. Just as Joshua entered the preparation area, the organist began the prelude. Joshua almost felt it was fittingly right for the occasion—"God Rest Ye Merry, Gentlemen."

The service was a traditional sort of service. After the prelude came the welcome. This Reverend Bert did quite well. He looked nervous and even a bit haggard to Josh, but his voice was steady and his manner close enough to normal that most people wouldn't notice. Josh could see Mike Derringer all the time, and although Mike kept his head down, Josh noticed an uncomfortable kind of smile on his face and even a furtive look up once or twice.

After the *welcome*, the congregation stood and sang "Joy to the World." This was followed by an alteration of scriptures and more hymns. There were passages of prophecy from the Old Testament, which Josh read, and passages from Matthew and Luke, which Reverend Bert read. So the congregation would not get tired of singing a lot of hymns, the choir had two anthems. One was all about Bethlehem being the birthplace of Jesus, and the other was one about the message of the angels to the shepherds. It was a particularly rousing anthem. Mary Durham, a classmate of Joshua, played a lovely viola solo. Joel Baumhart sang two German Christmas carols in German for which the bulletins had the translations. They were not unknown carols to Joshua, but he didn't know the German. Josh liked the songs a lot, and he felt they set a beautiful mood for the sermon.

Josh looked over to Reverend Bert, who was now supposed to stand and begin the message for the evening. Josh also glanced out at Mike Derringer, who, despite the solemn and beautiful service so far, showed signs that he was just possibly ready to cause a big stink.

Josh looked back at Reverend Bert, who was frozen to his seat. The nerves that the pastor had held so completely under control before this moment had taken over. Reverend Bert was almost deathly pale and shaking a bit. Josh wanted to say something to him, but Josh knew that any movement would be seen and condemned by the whole congregation. What to do? The congregation waited, some with fire in their hearts instead of the Christmas spirit.

It was a split-second decision. Josh Huff suddenly stood up and went to the pulpit. Reverend Bert didn't even realize Josh had stood up until he heard his voice sounding clean and clear over the speaker system. "As some of you know, I made a decision three months ago to enter the ministry. I know I still have college and seminary to attend, but Reverend Bert suggested that it might be a good idea for me to preach a trial sermon sometime. When he told me earlier tonight that he was having trouble coming up with yet another new angle for the Christmas service, I said that I could do my maiden flight tonight. He didn't think it was probably a good idea, but just before we came out here, he said that I could if I wanted to. Now I feel that . . ."

Josh didn't get much beyond that. It wasn't that he faltered, nor was it a fact that Reverend Bert intervened. It wasn't an interruption from some parishioner either. It was the back door of the church opening that stopped the sermon. Captain Jim Buckland of the city police came into the church, helping to hold up a woman whose husband was on the other side of her.

Captain Jim's voice was strong and gravelly. He sometimes attended this Methodist Church, and any time he spoke, you could always hear his voice cutting through even the loudest prelude. "Folks, I am going around to the various churches to give you all warnings. The weather outside has badly declined in the last forty minutes or so. The rain has frozen on everything, and it's now changed to snow—hard and driving snow—and the police are asking that you don't even try to leave here tonight until we come around and give an all clear. The temperature is falling right now but should rise again in the overnight. As an example of the problem, this couple was trying to get to Richmond, and they just slid off the road into McMahon's maple tree. Our one and only motel is closed for the season. I hope you can take care of them. Uh, she's about to have a baby—she may be in labor now." Captain Jim stood quiet for a moment.

Joshua was still standing openmouthed at the pulpit. He could see that the woman was really pregnant, and, from his high school classes, he could tell that the baby was riding quite low. In other words, she could deliver any minute. Josh looked around the congregation. "Dr. Bothast, could you please go and help? Emily Bennett, you're a registered nurse, could you help, too? Reverend Bert, could you go and help them get the woman into the fellowship room? Dale and Carl, could you help, too?"

Janice Derringer spoke up. "We're set up for the Christmas Eve party in the fellowship room. It follows the service. Isn't there someplace else they could go?"

"Mrs. Derringer, they'll need hot water and towels, and those are in the kitchen off the fellowship room. They may need a table too. It's the best location for them to go. Besides, should we not do everything we can to help someone give birth on the greatest birthday our faith tells us ever was?"

Mrs. Wilkerson turned to her daughter. "He's exactly right, Janice. The birth is more important." Mike clearly did not like his grandmother siding with Josh.

Josh spoke even more decisively. "While they're doing that, let's sing number 219, 'What Child Is This?' Mrs. Williams, if you would, please."

Everyone did as they were told. After the hymn, Joshua had cleared his mind and stood confidently ready for his sermon. "One kind of sermon that can be very effective, if used sparingly, is the drama sermon. In that sermon, the preacher takes on the persona of someone else. I have opted to do just that tonight. The persona I will take on should not be too much of a stretch for me. You see, I'm going to portray Joshua. No, I'm not playing myself, nor am I Moses's right-hand man, but a Joshua who lived, I should imagine, about two thousand years ago."

Joshua took the handheld microphone and stepped down the three steps to the main floor of the sanctuary. He stood at the end of the central aisle. "My name is Joshua. I am a shepherd. My father Benjamin and a friend named Yitzhak own a large flock of sheep. My brother Jeremiah and I help watch the sheep. I also like to help Uncle Nahum with his inn. There are three inns in Bethlehem. A couple of people rent out rooms too. Relatives, when they come to town, stay with relatives if any still remain in town. Uncle Nahum's is not the biggest inn, but it is certainly big enough—normally. He has fourteen rooms he can rent out. Once, two years ago, he had to use two storage rooms as extra sleeping room. But nothing has ever been like it is right now.

"You see, the Romans have set up this ridiculous idea of having a big census, with added-on taxation while they're at it. It has been a major headache all the way around. Bethlehem is a town where people come *from*, but very few people stay here. So everyone has to come back here. Our population has at least tripled in the last two weeks, and Uncle Nahum has been booked solid for those two weeks. It brings in a lot of gold, but it is such a hassle. Mother helps my aunt bake enough bread and cook enough food to keep the travelers fed, but it is really difficult.

"My uncle had a great idea about six months ago. He and the other innkeepers, along with the blacksmith and the cobbler, have taken to lighting lights in certain places all over town. They are torches in prominent places, with good mounts to hold them to the walls. This plan has cut down on the number of robberies and beatings. Some street thugs used to roam the streets and beat up people who 'challenged' them. Not anymore! Someone ***did*** take money from the collection plate at the synagogue a month ago. But that was in broad daylight. The brightest lights would not have stopped him.

"Tonight, the air is just a little bit nippy. It isn't that it's cold, but I don't want to dawdle outside. My uncle is so busy with the inn that he has asked me to light the new lights all over town. So that's what I'm doing. As I stepped from the inn, I almost ran into a man and his wife. She was riding a donkey and was pretty sick. I don't think it was that she was ill exactly, but she was ready to give birth, and I do mean ***ready*** any moment. I pointed them toward my uncle's inn and went on.

"I was just lighting my first light when I was accosted by a woman, who was sitting under the next archway. 'Young man,' she said, '*don't* light that torch. The sky is so clear and the moon so full, we won't need the torches tonight.'

"I had to explain to her that it was a safety concern, but she didn't want to hear it. Shrugging, I went on, ignoring her constant complaining. When I got to the next light, a rich man was talking hurriedly to a Roman centurion. The rich man was indignant. Even though I wasn't trying to listen, I heard them mention Uncle Nahum. 'If that's how he acts, we have to hope he gets what's coming to him,' the rich man said.

"The centurion nodded. 'I'm sure I don't know all there is to it, but I'll investigate. I can't imagine that the kid lied.' The centurion went off, and the rich man, rather proud of his own cleverness, sat down with a bottle of wine. 'I hope the rabbi gets his comeuppance.'

"That worried me a little bit. I didn't know what it was about, but I was sure Uncle Nahum was innocent of anything important. I lit three more torches and came across a couple of women sitting under an awning. They were combing wool. The tall and skinny woman said, 'I suppose he just thinks he can get away with anything. Rabbis can be like that.' Uncle Nahum was an ordained rabbi, although he seldom served at temple. Still everyone called him Rabbi. I decided I was being silly. I'm not usually this paranoid about what I hear.

"Then the other woman, a squat and sweaty woman, clucked her tongue and said, 'Rabbi Nahum will have a lot to answer for.'

"I couldn't stand it. 'What did he do?' I asked, but the two women just said, 'Humph!' together and said nothing more.

"Now Uncle Nahum had a boy working for him. His name was Micah, and, although he's a nice fellow, he was, well, not blessed with lots of smarts. So I was almost panicked when another man, the blacksmith, said, 'Imagine what that Micah boy has had to go through working with him.'

"I still had two lights to go, and I lit them in a panic. I thought that I had better be getting back to Uncle Nahum at once. What I heard on the way back was even worse. Three men were standing across the square from my uncle's inn, and one of them clearly said, 'That Nahum. I can't imagine why none of us ever suspected or tried to help.'

"The second man answered, 'Did he think a smoke screen about money would get by? Really?'

"I ran across the square and into the inn. As I entered, that centurion I had seen earlier was leaving, laughing and quite sensibly amused. I ran to find Uncle Nahum, but Aunt Deidre intercepted me. 'Your uncle is busy now. What is so important?'

"I told her what I had heard. She listened quite solemnly, but then she just smiled. 'Haven't I told you a few times not to put your trust in gossip? The centurion will start spreading the correct facts as well as he can. It was just a misunderstanding. There was a man, Rabbi Joseph, came here with his wife, who was ready to give birth.'

"I nodded. 'I know, I pointed them this direction.'

"My aunt continued, 'Well, we had no room. I guess you know that too. They needed help and a place to stay at once. I cornered your uncle and told him that he was not to send them away without a place to stay. He didn't know what to do. I mean, we have no room. So I sent him after them—they were still out front and getting desperate—and he took them back to our stable in the cave. It is warm enough. It would keep the night air off of them, and, most important, they could have a little privacy. I then sent Miranda, the midwife, to help them. We'll pay her fees. She's with them now. Here,' she continued, grabbing some of our older blankets and furs, 'I want you to take these back to them. Did you get the lights all lit?'

"I nodded and, without saying another word, took the blankets and furs out the back of the inn. It was several hundred yards back to the three caves that we considered ours. We kept one of them for storage—particularly when we had to take the normal storage rooms for guests. The second was where we could keep our sheep when the storms came. The third one, the biggest one, was where we kept our other livestock—three cows, a pair of goats, an old horse, and an old donkey.

"Just as I stepped into the third cave, I heard the first cry of a baby being born. Although I had never seen a birth before, I also knew Miranda could be pretty particular about who she allowed to help. 'Miranda, it's Joshua. I have some things to keep the couple—and baby—warm and comfortable.'

"A young man came out and shook my hand, introducing himself as Joseph. He took the blankets and furs and thanked me very much. I turned to go, but he stopped me. 'Would you like to see my new son? The midwife is about finished cleaning him and wiping the sweat from Mary, my wife. If you would like to see him, you'll only have to wait a moment.' He was beaming, as only new fathers can, with joy and excitement.

"Sure enough it was only five minutes, and Joseph motioned me farther into the cave. His wife was holding the baby. He was so sweet and small, and he had such a mop of dark, wet hair that I had to giggle. I was filled with such joy. I wished them well and turned to go, but as I got to the mouth of the cave, I ran into my father and Jeremiah along with several shepherds from the area.

"My father briefly told me why they were there. If my aunt told me not to believe gossip, most of which was untrue, what was I to make of my father's tale? I almost thought that he might have been drinking to ward off the cold. But Jeremiah was convinced that everything my father said was true. Heavens! There had been an angel and then an angel choir? How could I believe all of that? It was crazy! And yet I knew that if my papa had said it, it was true. I just wish I had been there too instead of running around the place lighting town lights. The gossip I had heard about Uncle Nahum could have been heard in any town in any year, but the gossip that spread after that night is still causing people to shake their heads in awe."

Joshua paused a moment to take a drink of water. As he was placing the glass down, he noticed Reverend Bert was standing back in the vestibule, smiling. The pastor made a rocking motion and mouthed the word "boy."

Smiling, Joshua nodded and continued. "So the town of Bethlehem soon learned that my uncle, Rabbi Nahum, was not anything near as awful and unfeeling as the gossip had said. Besides, the town had a lot more important things to talk about. Everyone was buzzing about what the shepherds said. There were doubters, of course, but they were far outnumbered. My uncle is happy to say that the couple moved into the inn two nights later and went on their way after about a month. He is rather hushed mouth, though, about three men, quite richly attired, who came to see the baby about ten days later."

Joshua was about to sit down, but then he remembered one more thing. "Oh, yes, that birth has been reenacted tonight here in our church. A boy was born a few minutes ago. While they rest, I'll ask Reverend Bert to come forward and serve communion. Then Millicent Thomas will sing 'O Holy Night' as we prepare for Joel Baumhart to sing the first verse of 'Silent Night' in German. As he does so, those on the inner end of the rows, dip your candles into the flame of the candle nearest you. Then each person should dip their unlighted candle into the lighted candle—that keeps hot wax from dripping."

Mike Derringer stood up. He alone of the entire congregation had not been moved by Joshua's sermon. "Hey, Josh, what happened to the guy who stole from the synagogue? Was he ever caught, or did the rabbi just make him pay in other ways?"

Surprisingly, it was Mrs. Wilkerson who answered. She stood and shoved Mike back down into his seat. "The rabbi had nothing to do with it, Mike." she began. "The criminal was caught and, according to the laws of the time, he had his left hand cut off! That might be a fitting punishment at that, don't you think so, Mike?"

Reverend Bert tried not to smile. Communion (and Christmas) was filled with new meaning that night. Collection followed. Extra envelopes were filled heavily and labeled "The new parents in the fellowship hall" or something like that. During the singing of "Silent Night," the people slowly raised their candles higher with each verse. At the end, they did not blow the candles out, as they normally did, but without being told, they all filed out, humming the German carol, and made their way to see the newborn. The mood would not be broken for several minutes.

As Joshua came down from the altar area, his head still swimming that he had actually pulled off an impromptu sermon, a hand gently tapped him on the arm. It was the bishop, whom Joshua had mercifully forgotten was even in the service. "Young man, may I ask you to tell me truthfully how long you planned that sermon?"

Josh looked at his watch. "I started thinking about it around 7:20 tonight. I will have to confess that the little interruption by Captain Jim was quite helpful."

The bishop smiled broadly. "Well, I was quite impressed. When it comes time, you contact me and I can give you a good recommendation for seminary."

The Christmas party was held (quietly) and, by the end, the driving conditions had still not improved, so people slept in the sanctuary, the garage (now empty of Josh's car) and even in the parlor and classrooms. Reverend Bert actually slept in the chair in his office.

Early the next morning, everyone went their own way, each person being aware that the night had been really special. "Merry Christmas" rang throughout the church as people went home to their presents. The bell, which had for some reason not been rung in at least five years, was rung joyfully. The treasurer, after separating out the special envelopes, took the collection and went home too, surprised to find a check in it for $50 dollars from Michael Derringer.

Joshua received many good comments on his sermon, most warmly from Reverend Bert, who was surprised at the many expressions of warmth and praise he had heard about the protégé. Mike Derringer even cornered Joshua coming out of the bathroom and said, not at all grudgingly, "That was a pretty darn good first sermon, Josh."

Josh warmly shook Mike's hand. "Thanks. I'll try to remember it and maybe right it down. I'll check the wording on the recording. It won't ever be as special as it was last night, what with all the extra stuff going on."

Mike sheepishly lowered his head. "You mean me?"

Josh laughed. "Heavens no. I knew the turmoil around you would die down soon enough. I meant the amazing birth we had here—on Christmas no less. That will always make last night special to me."

Mike looked cheerfully at his friend. "Did you hear what the couple called their new kid?"

Joshua had been so busy that he had to admit he had not even thought about it. The couple was gone to the hospital now, so he couldn't ask them.

Mike just poked Josh in the stomach. "Well, you have something else to live up to, Josh. They named him Joshua Noel Woodard."

TALE 2

In the Attic

Marjorie Billingsley was in her midseventies and proud of it. One could say, truthfully, that Marjorie was a proud woman about many things. One of her proudest attitudes was that she always charted a keen and even course, and that she did not get caught up in the hoopla that surrounds various events. Whether the religious holidays (Easter, Christmas, etc.) or the national observances (the Fourth of July, Memorial Day, Martin Luther King Day, President's Day, etc.), it did not matter to her. She had her own private way of ignoring such events, and no one needed to tell her that she could ***possibly*** be wrong for ignoring them. She didn't even acknowledge the birthdays or holidays in her own family. She was certainly not going to consider non-Christian holidays.

Her niece had tried on numerous occasions to get Marjorie Billingsley to join the family for Thanksgiving, but the elderly woman had always demurred, with the usual reply of "You know I don't like going to gatherings like that." The even more advanced idea of joining the family for Christmas or other traditionally family gatherings was anathema to her. She didn't even go to visit relatives for an evening meal.

Some thought it had to do with losing her sister, Theresa, when they were both in their thirties. But, Freddy, the husband of Marjorie's sister, would deny it. "She was an isolationist from way before that. When she was alive, Theresa tried to get her to come over at least for dinner, but she wouldn't do that at any time, holiday or not."

The thought sometimes crept into the collective minds of the family—Freddy, Margie (Marjorie's niece), her husband Mike, and their two children, Mike Jr. and Clara Marjorie—that Aunt Marjorie Billingsley was only keeping her distance so she would not have to buy gifts or go shopping (something she hated doing, even for food).

When Mrs. Pennington suggested that she shop for food for Ms. Billingsley, Ms. Billingsley took her up on the idea. Mrs. Pennington was normally her cleaning lady, but she also cooked for the elderly Ms. Billingsley, as often as not, making certain that there was enough food in the refrigerator to hold the woman over until Mrs. Pennington would come again. It was never more than five days, and the salads, soups, breads, and vegetables were either long lasting or frozen and easy to thaw out. It never occurred to either woman that Mrs. Pennington might not be able to get back for more than a week. She only lived two blocks away, and she never took vacations.

Three years ago, in the weekend just ahead of Christmas, Mrs. Pennington, however, was most ecstatic. She was going to Oregon to visit her sister, whom she had not seen in over six years. Her sister had children who were now in their midteens, and Mrs. Pennington felt she was losing out on her own kin. So on the twenty-first, Sharon and Jeffrey Pennington bid Ms. Billingsley a Merry Christmas and went by taxi to the airport, flying off to Oregon.

Marjorie Billingsley was most cordial and wished them both a fond farewell and Merry Christmas as well. Don't get me wrong! It wasn't that Marjorie Billingsley was against Christmas. She was not against **any** holiday. She just did not want to celebrate.

The day they left had been dark all day, and by four o'clock it was actually getting darker. Rain had held off most of the day, but now it was coming down in cold sheets. The outside temperature was about freezing, and Marjorie Billingsley soon noticed that the trees were getting ice on them. She called Freddy. She wanted him to check in on her every three or four hours, at the very least. She was afraid lines would fall and no one would know. She didn't want to freeze to death in her own house.

Freddy comforted her. "Marjorie, I know you have an ample supply of wood. If for some reason you lose power, use the wood and light a fire in the fireplace."

"Freddy, you know I haven't had a fire in there for five years." She was unyielding.

"I know, but the last time you used it was just before you had the sweeps come in. You ought to be fine. Of course I'll check in on you. And if you lose power, please call me. I can come get you and bring you here. I have a wood-burning stove." He knew she would rather freeze to death than call her brother-in-law.

The evening news came on at 6:00 p.m. A winter advisory had been posted. She looked out at the streetlight. By that light, she could see that the ice was clinging to the trees about a quarter-inch thick, or so she estimated, and the rain had turned to heavy, wet snow. Her programs were all preempted by holiday programming, most of which consisted of cartoons or pop and rock singers. "And they call that Christmas music?"

Marjorie shut the TV off at 8:30 p.m., despairing of anything worth watching. She caught up on her diary. It wasn't till 9:15 p.m. that she noticed that the house seemed cold. The thermostat read as normal, and the furnace was not running. The lights were still working—"At least for the moment!"—and she couldn't decide what was wrong. She put her hand under the lip of the fireplace. Was it just possible that the flu had blown open? The wind **was** rather strong. But that was not it.

After further investigation, she finally realized that the coldest drafts were coming from upstairs. "Oh, dear, I hope there isn't a broken window or something. I'll check, and if there is, I'll just have to call Freddy or Mike to come over to see about fixing it."

As she started to ascend the stairs, she checked the thermostat again. It said everything was all right. It was seventy degrees. She even went into the dining room, where she had a small thermometer. It said seventy degrees too. "That's ridiculous! Why, I can almost see my breath."

She went up the stairs. She was tired enough, she thought, she might just go to bed. She knew that her niece would call again the next morning to invite her to Christmas dinner, and she had to be rested enough to resist.

The bathroom was fine. The window there was tightly shut. There weren't any trees outside there anyway that could break it. She checked the laundry chute that went to the basement. There was no cold air coming from there either.

Her bedroom seemed fine too. The huge maple tree outside the window was not too close to the house, and, in any case, it was still sturdy and strong. There was no problem there. The closet doors were shut. When she opened them, there was no draft from anywhere. The heat ducts all seemed to be fine. Nothing cold was pouring out of them.

The second bedroom was like everywhere else. An elm tree, half dead, was outside the window, and it had a limb that was newly broken off, but nothing seemed out of place. Marjorie Billingsley was at a loss.

The hallway was coldest. So she looked into the utility closet and the linen closet. Nothing there. "How could there be?" Then she thought about the third bedroom. The door to that room was ajar, and it seemed that the cold was coming from there. She went hesitatingly into the room, flicking on a light on the bed stand.

The bedroom was fine. This was the largest room; it was the room where Marjorie and Theresa had been children together. She had not been into this room for several years. She normally kept the door shut and locked. In fact, she could not remember when she might have opened the outer door to the room. Yet it stood open and more than a little cold air was flowing from the room.

As she started to leave the room, she noticed that the door in the corner was open too. This door led to a stairway that went between two bedrooms and up into the attic. This door, she was certain, had been locked. She had not been up in the attic in at least ten years, and she saw no reason for the door to be open. She had definitely ***not*** opened it. Common sense, she told herself, said that she should call Freddy at once. But he might get pretty bent out of shape if she called him and it was nothing.

She went back to her bedroom and got her old gray sweater and put it on. "I'll just check up in the attic. If a window has blown open, or if an eave has somehow sprung a leak, I'll call Freddy. He'll know what to do about it. I don't want birds or bats getting in after all."

She reached inside the door and flicked the light switch. The cold air drifting down the stairwell was somehow extremely cold. The lights—one at the bottom of the stairs and three up in the attic—were large wattage and cast strange shadows everywhere. Marjorie Billingsley slowly climbed the stairs.

At the top of the steps, she turned on her flashlight too. "No use peering into shadows that the electrics don't penetrate." She was talking to herself, and she pooh-poohed the idea that she was doing that. "Silly! Only crazy people talk to themselves." This she spoke out loud, and she was surprised to hear what she thought was an answer.

"Not necessarily."

Her back went straight, a cold chill shooting up her spine. She looked around, sure that somehow someone had broken into the attic. The attic windows were closed tight, no panes broken or even cracked. The chimney from the furnace went up through the attic, but it too seemed to be fine. She started flashing her light around with very steady purpose. Although she had not been in the attic for years, it was exactly as she remembered it to have been, except for the larger quantity of dust. The walls all seemed to be fine, no openings anywhere. There was nothing flying around to bother her. Still the attic was extremely cold and drafty. "I might expect it to be a little cold up here, since I don't heat the attic, but this is too cold. And I want to know where that draft is coming from."

Marjorie noticed an old candle and matches sitting on the top of a chest. "If I light the candle, the flickering flame will tell me from what direction the draft is coming." She sat down on the chest and opened the box of matches. She felt them to see if they were at all damp or rotten. "It won't do to try to light old matches. I could strike and strike and get nowhere."

"A candle won't necessarily show you what you want to know."

This time Marjorie Billingsley, sitting uneasily on the old chest, was certain that she had heard a real voice. She looked around again. Where was the voice coming from? It sounded both close and miles away, as if it was beside her or in her memory. She held up the lighted candle and walked around the attic, searching for a source to the breeze.

The flickering flame danced around, blowing first one way and then another, but it showed no single source of the breeze. Then just as Marjorie was about to give up, she heard the door at the bottom of the stairs slam shut. She sat the candle down, still lit, on the top of the chest and walked carefully down the stairs. The door would not open. It would budge—so it wasn't locked—but something was holding it shut.

She went back up into the attic and was just reaching for the candle when the electric lights went out. As Marjorie reached for the candle, she saw a pale gray hand come up out of the chest and smother the candle's light. Marjorie was in total darkness.

Her eyes took a while to adjust. She could see where the windows were due to the light from the streetlights. Inside the attic, however, everything was dark. She started to sit on the chest, but just as she began to sit, the chest opened up. At first Marjorie could make out nothing inside, but then, slowly but very surely, the attic took on a strange, bluish glow, and from the chest arose a spirit, shrouded in heavy veils and moving slowly to a spot three feet in front of Marjorie. Marjorie was too scared to scream, but she tried.

The figure stood looking at Marjorie, and the elderly lady felt, somehow, that the ghostly apparition was sizing her up. She also felt that the figure carried an aura of sadness that was impossible to understand.

The spirit spoke quietly, each syllable coming slowly from her mouth. "Marjorie. Marjorie? Why are you here on Christmas Eve?"

Marjorie shook herself out of a kind of trance. "What do you mean? I'm up here because . . . well, because I felt a draft and traced it to the attic. In fact I think it's coming from you. So maybe I should ask you what you are doing here." The words sounded more challenging than Marjorie intended. She was too frightened to challenge a spider, let alone an apparition that might stand before her, exuding a cold aura that went right through to Marjorie's bones.

The spirit stood a moment and then said, in a somewhat more commanding voice, "Sit in the rocking chair." The spirit watched as Marjorie moved to the chair and sat. An afghan lay folded up beside her. This she picked up and draped over her legs. "Are you cold, Marjorie?"

"I told you. You've brought a cold wind into this house, whatever you are, and it chills down to my bones. My knees don't like cold weather." Marjorie would always be a little argumentative.

The spirit stood looking at Marjorie for about a minute, saying nothing, and yet always engaged in observing Marjorie. Suddenly, without a word of warning, the spirit reached up and lifted the veil which covered her face, draping it back down her back with the practiced grace of a bride.

Marjorie looked up and gasped. "Theresa! Theresa, is that you?"

Theresa's spirit nodded and smiled. "Yes, Marjorie. I came back here to look in on you. I'm glad I came. I've been here many times before, but you've never noticed. This time, I found you sad and alone. That worried me, so I decided to let you know that I was here."

Marjorie Billingsley shuddered, but it wasn't because of the lack of heat. "Do you by any chance . . . do you happen to have any particular reason that you look in on me?"

Theresa stretched out her hand, and the lid to the chest closed with a gentle thud. She sat on the chest. "Yes, there is a reason." Her eyes stared gently at Marjorie. "You're my sister, and I am concerned about you."

Marjorie's face softened at first, but then a curious hardness came into it. "If you are concerned about me," she began, "then why did you leave me? I've gone through so many Christmases and Easters and Thanksgivings without you."

Theresa laughed. "Oh, heavens, Marjorie, I've been out with Freddy and the children. They need me too, you know. Oh, I haven't made my presence known to them, not like this at least. They still miss me, and I try to whisper words of comfort into their ears. They need them."

Marjorie shifted in the rocking chair, pulling the afghan around her legs more tightly. "Well, I need you too. It's been years since you . . . since you died."

"I know, Marjorie, and I've counted every second and every minute." Theresa's voice was almost musical in its gentle persuasiveness. "But, Marjorie, why do you think I came to you this year?"

"You died on this date. Is it anniversary guilt?" Marjorie was uncertain how to answer, so that was what she came up with. Whatever she might have thought would be Theresa's response, it was not what she received.

Theresa tilted her head back and let out a howl, a primal, guttural sound, half groan and half scream. It sent chills down Marjorie's back once again. "Guilt? Guilt! What do I have to feel guilty about? Why should I think that anything I have done should cause a feeling of guilt in me? I died a natural death. I had pneumonia, and Freddy almost died trying to nurse me through it. It was my family in marriage that concerned me, as it does today. I have no guilt about leaving you. My death was from natural causes. I left my daughter without a mother and my husband without a loving wife. My grandchildren never knew me. I've never known them."

Marjorie's chin jutted out a little in self-defense. "You left me too. We weren't only sisters, but we were the best of friends as children. There wasn't anything we didn't do together. Even when you married, I could call you to ask for a recipe, to garner an opinion—even if I didn't always agree with it—and talk about our friends and relatives. You left me alone without that wonderful attachment to family and friends."

Theresa sat quietly for several minutes. Then she rose and put her hand on Marjorie's arm. The attic seemed to vanish. It seemed almost at once that they were standing at the bottom of the attic stairs, looking into the bedroom and watching two young girls playing. The two girls were having a wonderful time. Then a young boy came in. Almost at once, the younger girl, the one with auburn hair with a big red bow in it, called out to the young man. "Hi, Freddy. Merry Christmas. Do you like the doll I got? It actually says 'momma' if you tilt it right."

Freddy didn't seem too concerned with the doll. He was twelve, and dolls were too feminine a thing for him to care about. In the corner, the other girl, whose hair was lighter brown, sat apart, playing with her doll and yet paying no attention to Freddy. This scene went on for a few more minutes and then faded.

Theresa and Marjorie were once again in the attic. "You never liked Freddy, did you? I could tell, and you just saw it too. You thought Freddy was somehow coming between the two of us. That's why, when we were adults, you would call me, but you never came over. I wanted you to enjoy my family so much. They wanted to enjoy the love and affection of Aunt Marjorie. You would not come over. You would not give my children even a little bit of the love that Aunt Marjorie had to offer. You kept it to yourself. I knew that then, and I tell it to you now." Theresa touched Marjorie's arm once again.

In the corner of the attic, there suddenly appeared a much younger image of the adult woman Marjorie. Her hair was somewhat untidy, and she was putting clothing and books into a large trunk. Her eyes showed clearly that she had been crying. Hurried footsteps came noisily up the stairs.

It was the younger Theresa. She still had on her outer winter coat. "Oh, Marjorie, I came over as soon as I could. I only heard a half hour ago. What happened?"

Marjorie looked at her sister. The two observers noticed that an engagement ring glistened on the finger of the younger Theresa. The younger Marjorie pushed a stray strand of hair back from her forehead. "Paul was too impetuous anyway. I guess it's for the best."

This did not answer Theresa's question to such an extent that the younger woman stood and stomped her feet, real anger flaring out. "What do you mean he was too impetuous? He loved you. He asked you three times to marry him. You even went with him to look at a house. I was expecting wonderful news this Christmas, and instead I hear that you said no again, and that he went off to New York City. I was coming over today anyway, but to have that news followed by the news of the bus wreck and of his dying. Marjorie, it was **not** at all for the best. Why wouldn't you love him? He was a handsome man, outwardly and inwardly. When we were children, you swore you knew exactly what sort of a man you wanted to marry. I still have your written avowal, and it matched Paul to a T. Why couldn't you let yourself love?"

The younger Marjorie slammed the trunk shut and was about to answer. She stood and faced her sister, nostrils flaring hotly. Then as suddenly as it had come, the image vanished. The two sisters were alone in the attic, one alive and the other dead. It was, at that moment, not so easy to tell which was which.

Theresa brushed gently at Marjorie's hair. It rustled lightly in the gossamer touch. "You know, of course, that you never ***did*** give me a good answer. I would like to hear it now."

Marjorie at first tried to make up something that she thought might appease her sister, but the words froze in her mouth, unable to tumble out with any meaning or consideration of reality. Then she thought an excuse would work. The first two words attempted to slip out of her mouth, but they too caught in her throat and died away before they had approached a full thought.

Marjorie then stood and folded the afghan, placing it on the seat of the rocker. "I think I'll have Freddy bring this afghan and rocker downstairs. I had forgotten how nice they could be."

Theresa was sure that her sister would not say anything more and stood up, ready to plead once again for an answer. Instead, Marjorie held up her left hand, one finger slightly more prominent than the others, a gesture meant to say, "Wait a second, and I'll tell you."

Marjorie started over to the corner of the attic. "You know, Theresa, a little brighter light up here would help a great deal." Theresa nodded, and the attic lights all came back on. The corner seemed even brighter as if a special light had been brought up there too.

Marjorie went to the corner of the attic and lifted an old horse blanket from its place as cover to a large trunk. It was the large trunk that they had seen in the vision. "I had almost forgotten that this trunk was still here." Marjorie began fumbling with the lock. "I don't have the key with me." The desired key floated up the stairwell and into Marjorie's hands. "You know, Theresa, I could probably get a pile of cash for some of this junk up here. I've seen that antique show on TV. Why, that frame alone is probably worth $300. And that filthy painting in the corner of our old cabin at the lake would probably fetch $5,000. The artist is famous now and highly sought after."

Theresa just smiled, her soft voice drifting through the attic. "The trunk, Marjorie!"

Marjorie nodded and opened the trunk. On the top was a tray of what had once been moth crystals. Very little was left of them. Marjorie lifted that tray, so carefully perched on top of the contents, slowly out and placed it on an old table beside her. "I know Mother loved this table, but I hated it. It's too high."

Her sister's glare did not falter, so Marjorie went further into the trunk. She brought out some schoolbooks, some written papers, and, when she reached in again, she brought out the large package she was placing inside the trunk in the vision. Marjorie looked at the closely wrapped package with almost fearful eyes. She started to put it aside, as if it was not the source of the troublesome vision. But Marjorie had barely put the package down, when she picked it up again with some determination and carefully pulled the string that held the paper covering in place.

The old newspaper and tissue coverings fell aside, revealing a beautiful blue and white sweater and a pale blue blouse. Marjorie unfolded them so the ghost of Theresa could see. "Did you know these were in here?"

Theresa shook her head. "We aren't allowed into secret places like a locked trunk. We are only allowed into unlocked ones, those with nothing in them."

Marjorie held up the blouse. "It looks a little old fashioned now, doesn't it? The sweater could still be nice." She examined it. "Not a hole in it. The moth crystals did a good job. It was either that or else the cedar lining of the trunk." She put the two things aside, planning to take them downstairs. Under them, still on her lap, was a large picture book. "Mother insisted that we keep our pictures in books, carefully labeled. Do you remember her always saying, 'Pictures don't tell a story if, ten years down the line, you can't tell who the people in them are.' I'll take the book down with me."

Theresa brought up a little more light in the corner. "You were going to show me something important, Marjorie. I still don't know what it is, and I've been waiting for decades. Why did you send Paul away?" Her tone was soft and yet it cut through with determination.

"I didn't send him away, for your information. He left, but I did not send him away." Marjorie fumbled with the latch on the large picture book. It opened, a couple of loose photographs and an envelope falling to the floor. "These are the pictures from Christmas 1953 that I never put into the book properly." Seeing that her sister's ghost was impatient, Marjorie picked up the fallen envelope and opened it carefully. The envelope was nothing special, but the letter within was written with a careful hand on a linen paper. It didn't take the brighter light to see that the penmanship was of almost professional quality. Marjorie looked at the letter a moment, heaved a sigh, and held it out to her sister. "Here. Do you want to read it?"

Theresa shook her head. "Since I can't hold it, I can't read it. Why don't you read it out to me?"

Marjorie pulled her hand back. She adjusted her glasses, looking with almost palpable trepidation at the linen paper. She then began slowly, reading line after line. As she read, her voice grew at first stronger, and then gradually faded, till, by the final line, even Marjorie could hardly hear herself say the words.

December 24, 1953

My dearest Marjorie Billingsley,

I am writing to you because I may not be able to speak to you in person. The reasons for that are many, but basically it involves your family gathering and my intended travel plans.

The last nine months have been the most incredible I could ever have hoped to spend with anyone. You are a wonderful friend and a beautiful woman. At various times I thought we might come to some agreement as to our future together. For some reason, this has never happened. At first I thought it must be your fault. You always went along with my ideas of shopping for houses, talking about possible marriage, and many other things. We could talk and talk for hours. I convinced myself that you loved me. Had I not thought so, I certainly would not have asked you three times to marry me.

Then I decided there must be something wrong with me. I knew you were full of love and compassion. You could be quick to pass judgment, but just as fast to forgive. You never turned away from me, and yet you held yourself away. It seems to me that something must be wrong between us. As I cannot at this moment understand what that something is, I am going away for a while in the hopes that I can figure this thing out more completely. If my plans go well, I hope to return in late spring. Even then, I am not particularly hopeful of your ever loving me.

To that end, I must tell you that my cousin in Trenton, New Jersey, has his eye both on a position I can take and a young woman he is certain I will find to my liking. I cannot hope to find anyone as warm and loving as you. But I cannot hope any longer that you will turn your attentions to consideration of marriage.

If I do return in the spring, I will certainly look in on you and your family. In the meantime, I hope you will give your sister my warmest love. I'm sure that she and Frederick will be happy together. I am sorry that we shall not be equally as happy together.

With warmest love and affection,

Paul Crestmont

Marjorie folded the letter carefully. "I loved Paul more than anyone could love another person not of their own family. Papa didn't like him though. And I was not the rebel you were. I couldn't just go off with him. Besides, I think he was right. It was all my fault. I found it impossible to let myself go and say yes to him.

"I got the letter at supper time. Papa had 'neglected' to tell me it had come. I tried immediately to go to the house where Paul was living. It was Christmas Eve, and there were lots of people in the streets. When I got there, I missed him by only ten minutes. I had the taxi take the quickest route he knew to the bus station. I was going to convince Paul that I would rebel against Father. He was just ready to board the bus. I tried to reason with him, to make him understand that I really, really **did** love him and that it was Father's fault. He just cupped his hand under my chin and kissed me lightly on the lips. Then with a tone in his voice I shall never forget, he said, 'In that letter, I tried to be nice to you. You see, I have tried to be patient, my dear Marjorie. I've tried to think that you would change. I even considered that it might be your father's fault. Ultimately, it came down to one thing and one thing only. You, my sweet little Miss Billingsley, are a cold fish who is incapable of true love. You'll dangle a carrot in front of your next bunny the way you have me, but you'll never agree to allow yourself free passion. I am a man of overwhelming patience and probably more passion than even I know. But I am not a fool, Marjorie, and I will not be made a fool by you or anyone else.'

"With that, he boarded the bus. Five hours later, in Upstate New York, his bus slid off the road and he died. He was right, Theresa, I am sure of it. He was right." Marjorie put the letter back into the book and wrapped the paper around it. She closed and locked the trunk again, retaining the picture book, sweater, and blouse out to take with her. She wrapped them all in the afghan. "Now you know why I was crying on the Christmas Eve so long ago."

Theresa stood, the attic lights returning to normal. She motioned, and the rocker rose in the air and floated down the stairs. The two sisters followed it. Once they were in the bedroom, the stair light flicked off of its own accord. "I'm sorry, sis. I did not know Paul had spoken with you in that fashion."

"Well, he did. Is it any wonder I dislike Christmas?" Marjorie deposited the things she was carrying in the middle of the bed, sitting on the end of it.

Theresa moved around and sat in the rocker herself now. "Did you remember those visions I showed you?"

Marjorie shrugged. "Of course I remembered the last one. It was the early one, when we were just children, that I don't remember." Marjorie was drying her eyes and trying to get calm again. The trip to the attic had been quite shocking for the elderly woman.

Theresa's voice suddenly sounded warmer, almost as if she was real. "I showed that to you for a reason. Did you notice that we were playing happily together, but that the moment Freddy entered, you backed away, refusing to greet him or to act normal with him? I noticed it at the time, but I never mentioned it to you. You and I were loving sisters, and nothing would change that. Yet here was Freddy, Christmas 1940, his first Christmas in town, and he came over from next door to greet us and wish us a Merry Christmas. You could not have been colder to him.

"The other scene was not quite complete. Or rather, I didn't tell you even then what I should have. You said upstairs that Father did not want you marrying Paul, and that his wish was the reason you always denied Paul's request for marriage. Father's denial was not in your interest—it was in Paul's. Marjorie, you have always loved me. You loved Mother and Father as long as they were with us. No one could ever complain about the love and affection you gave us. But there are other kinds of love. I never stopped loving you, but—"

"Yes, you did. You married Freddy." Marjorie lashed out almost before the thought had come to her mind.

Theresa's face became clearer but it also became cold, a kind of anger flaring in the semitransparent eyes. "You will not interrupt me again. When I married, I was yielding to a different kind of love. It is a good love, a pure love, and a very different love from what I held for you. I never stopped loving this family, but I loved my own family with great care and warm affection.

"On December 23, you and Paul went shopping in Cincinnati. He took you to see the bright displays in the windows of Shillito's and McAlpins, and the festive lights. On that day you bought at least half of the presents you were to give. When you got home, you ran upstairs to wrap them. I started to follow, but you told me you would be wrapping my present, and that I should stay down there. I did. I had chores, so I just thought we'd talk all about the lights later.

"Papa called Paul into the living room. I was setting the dinner table, so I heard everything they were saying. Apparently, they had talked before. Paul told Papa that there had been no change. He was very frustrated with you, Marjorie. He said he had tried everything he knew to draw you out, to get you to show a little affection for him. But—and he made this very clear—as many times as he told you he loved you, you had never returned the comment to him. If you loved him at all, he had no idea. He was actually crying.

"Papa told him bluntly that you had always been that way. I defended you with a firm 'No, she isn't like that.' Papa just looked at me, and his look told me that he knew I was just being a loyal sister. I knew, in my heart, almost at once that he was right."

Marjorie was sitting very still, her back quite straight and rigid. "You think I was cold and unfeeling?"

"No, you weren't to us, your family. But it was clear that you wanted to keep us to yourself. The next July, when I married Freddy, you didn't want to come to the service. 'It reminds me too much of my lost Paul.' No, Marjorie, I knew then, and I say it now that you didn't want to come because you felt I was betraying your love. Papa won out, of course, but you spoke to almost no one at the ceremony. We were all having a wonderful time, and you sat in the corner. You spoke to Jeremy Battle, but that's only because he practically made you. He would not leave you alone. He would have been a nice match for you. He quickly gave up too for the same reasons Paul did.

"Now I may not be Papa, and I am only a ghost, but I am going to tell you right now that you are going to go downstairs and open the door when the bell rings. It will be Freddy. He will take your overnight bag—it's packed—and you will stay at Mike and Margie's house overnight. You always said your heart had a great capacity for love. Well, you are now going to get the opportunity to open that heart and let that love out. There are gifts there for Freddy, for my children, and for my grandchildren. You'll even get some praise for those gifts being just what I would have given them. This is your chance, Marjorie, to let that love out. If you blow it, there will be no other chance. I won't come again at Easter or July 4, or any other day. This is my one and only visit to you." With that, she stood and walked over to her sister. Leaning down gently, she gave her a kiss. It was a kiss filled with such love and caring that Marjorie began sobbing. The kiss almost burned upon her cheek with such intensity that she felt it. Marjorie sat very dejectedly.

Theresa then backed away toward the window. There was a little light left there, but most of that came in from the few street lamps below.

Marjorie wanted to say something more and stood. As she did so, she could hear the doorbell ring down below. She turned and took a step toward the door. She knew she needed to tell her sister something else, but when she turned back to say how much she really did love her, Theresa was gone. The room was empty.

Marjorie went to the bed and picked up the sweater Paul had given her. She took off her gray one, placing it on the bed, and put on the far more festive blue and white one. Then she hurried into the hallway, shutting the door behind her. The doorbell rang again. She hurried, careful not to lose her footing on the stairs.

When Marjorie got to the entryway, she noticed her small suitcase and a laundry basket of packages sitting by the door. She opened the door at once and saw that Freddy was just on the steps, leaving. "Freddy, I'm sorry. I was occupied upstairs, and I couldn't get away quickly."

Freddy came back up onto the porch. Snow was falling, so he stomped his feet and scuffled them on the welcome mat. He went inside. "I was passing by, and I was wondering if you are sure you don't want to come to stay overnight and take part in our Christmas. Margie and Mike have promised a good meal, and of course their kids expect Santa to be good to them. They have extra room, enough for two interlopers." He was jovial.

Marjorie smelled the light smell of a cigar. Freddy had liked cigars since he was about seventeen, she thought. "I was just getting ready to call you or them. I was sitting here, watching it snow, and something just made me want to come over after all. I need to get to know Mike Jr. and Clara Marjorie—who, after all, is named after me."

Freddy looked down at the packages. "It looks to me like you had thought about it a little ahead of time."

"Well, I had thought about it. But it isn't something I thought about for very long. It was just a modest shopping spree in a hurry. Let me get my coat and come with you." She went to the hall closet and got out her black coat, but then she put it back into the closet and took out her red coat. She had not had it on for two years, but the dry cleaning bag had protected it. She put it on, wrapping a white wool scarf around her neck. She reached up for her old hat, but, as with the coat, decided on a little white hat, with pull down eartabs and a silly top knot. "I think Mike gave this to me three or four years ago. They've always brought over packages even when I didn't go to eat with them."

They went out the door, Marjorie carefully locking the front door. As they went down the steps, she looked across at the house where Freddy had once lived. "Do you ever wish you could see inside your old house again, Freddy?"

Freddy put the basket into the trunk and slammed the lid down. He had already placed the suitcase in the backseat. "No, Marjorie, I don't. That is a part of my life that is long past. It was a nice house to grow up in, don't get me wrong, but I have always felt such places are where you start to live. I couldn't wait to branch out and have a house of my own, with my own tastes and my own decor." A chunk of snow that had accumulated on a limb above Freddy fell down on him. Marjorie looked up and was sure she saw a smiling face in the upstairs bedroom. Freddy dusted himself off. "Of course, Theresa had some say in that decor too." He smiled.

They got into the car and started down the road. Freddy finally spoke, "Don't get me wrong, Marjorie, I know you live in the house you grew up in, but what works for one person doesn't always work for another."

Marjorie smiled, the thought of Theresa in her mind. "I think, Freddy, that if all you have is a house, then it isn't hard to leave it. If you make it your home, then it becomes your own. I've been thinking about modernizing my house—you know, updating and making it a twenty-first-century house, rather than something stuck in the 1960s. I know that means new wiring. Let's talk about it later tonight. I don't want to spend huge amounts, but I think the whole place could use a few coats of paint. And my stove has been getting rather cantankerous of late. I'd hate for someone to think my stove was like me: still cooking, but with not enough heat to get much of a life going." They laughed at the analogy.

Marjorie enjoyed Christmas Day at her niece's house, and the children dearly loved their Aunt Marjorie. In the spring, Marjorie had workers renovate the entire house. And the next Christmas, it was Marjorie who had Christmas dinner, with all the trappings. She even had a big tree. The lights were antiques, of course, but her niece's children found them "cool." After all, they had never seen anything but the little white, blinking lights, and the bubble lights that Marjorie had were much different from those. Marjorie found them in the attic while she was cleaning out some old things.

Marjorie even went to see Paul's sister in Cleveland. It was a difficult trip emotionally, but she felt much better about things after she went.

Curiously, every now and then, when Marjorie is alone, she'll call out her sister's name and hope that she will appear. Marjorie has yet to see her, but she knows somehow that she will.

And the love that Marjorie had held within her on such a tight rein was now released. Everyone loved Marjorie. Marjorie even goes to church now and sees her friends when she can. Some of her high school friends are amazed at the turnaround, but they say nothing. Having a happy Marjorie back is enough.

TALE 3
Celestial Greeting

Georgia Griffin had tried a number of ramifications of her name on for size. "Georgia Griffin" was too formal and stiff to be a pop singer in the year 2006. She had briefly toyed with a one-name moniker: Gigi (spoken in a distinctly *un*-French fashion). She wanted a single name hoping to distance herself from the new comedienne and the old talk show host with the name of Griffin. It was not until she spoke with the fourteenth agent, Jillian Richards, that they had decided on the name Celeste Griffin. Celeste was her middle name. (She hoped eventually to be just one name: Celeste.)

There was reason that it took fourteen agents. Even from the first amateurish audition, Georgia Celeste Griffin had been a diva in training. Her ego showed no boundaries, and her dismissive ways showed even the best agents that they could not work with her. Jillian Richards was a patient woman, however, and she knew talent when she heard it. She had warned Celeste even in their first conferences that she was to listen to her advice and not bank on just her own ego. "I may not be able to carry a tune in a basket myself, but I know quite well what makes this business work. That's something you don't know well, so let me advise you professionally."

Celeste listened to what Jillian had to say. Jillian arranged for coaching on all things musical, and for training in deportment on and off stage, and in dealing with the public. She was taught how to add as much charisma to her persona as it was possible for anyone to learn. Celeste Griffin began to emerge as a front-runner long before she tried out for that talent show on TV. She got into the top four, and many people became rabid fans. Her career was launched. Some said she was a professional and should not have been allowed on that show. She had only played four minor gigs as a professional, and, not to be forgotten, she lost the show to a guy from Atlanta with a phenomenal range and natural charisma. Some people thought she should have won.

All of this took its toll on her relationship with Chad Connors, an aspiring actor who was still waiting for his first break. He wanted Jillian to take him on, but she had to explain that she didn't handle actors. "I'll help singers get a job acting, but only occasionally and only if they really want a particular role in a TV show or in a movie." Chad was totally in love with Celeste. He even liked the name change. But he was also jealous of her fame and gathering potential for a fortune. This caused major friction at various moments backstage of the TV show.

Celeste's style was a strange mixture of country, pop, Broadway and even a little bluegrass. She could really soar into soprano range without sounding operatic, and she could lightly belt without sounding crass. On the talent show, Jillian made sure that Celeste did not even consider rap or hip-hop music, in which Celeste sounded out of her element: either bloated or just plain silly.

After the talent show, Celeste made her first album. It was called *This Is Who I Am!*, and it was a good first album. The single from the album, "Love Me Just the Way I Am," got on the charts, and, although it never got above number 5, it stayed between number 5 and number 15 for three months, almost unheard of in the business. Celeste heard the rumors around Los Angeles clubs that her album was a shoo-in for a Grammy, Country Music Award, or a couple of other honors. It was no wonder that Celeste was disappointed when there was not one nomination for her in any award show. Only her orchestrator was nominated.

Jonathan Devon was that orchestrator. He was only two years older than Celeste, but he was already an orchestrator with considerable respect from artists who considered using him. He had orchestrated single numbers for quite a few minor luminary singers, but even the majors were looking his way. The key to his success was that he stayed in the mainstream sound but gave lots of delightful little quirks to his orchestration that spiced it up without detracting from the singers. He also didn't have just one sound in his palette.

Celeste's first album came out in October, and, after its success, plans were put into motion to make a new album almost at once. Due to her "hometown girl" appeal, it was decided by Celeste and Jillian to make a Christmas album. Even at Celeste's first audition for Jillian, she had sung "Have Yourself a Merry Little Christmas," and Jillian had actually wept because of the way Celeste connected to the text. It was definitely going to be included in the new album.

Jonathan Devon, Jillian Richards, Celeste Griffin, and Eric Peterson (conductor for Celeste's first album and for all of her performances so far) met in early January while the holiday spirit was still in their minds. Eric said it was also a good excuse to avoid the plethora of football games that was clogging TV. By the end of the meeting, the entire album was planned. It would include ten to twelve songs, depending on how the arrangements and takes came out. The arc of the songs led from secular songs about Christmas through the joyful exhilaration (secular and sacred) into the spiritually uplifting "O Holy Night" and "Silent Night." Celeste said she could even do those last two in the original languages. The final idea was to open with "Silent Night" in English and then, at the end, do "O Holy Night" in French—all three verses (something Eric Peterson had wanted to do for years.) The final song would be a totally different arrangement of "Silent Night" in German. Jonathan would not say what it was, but he had in mind a strange and yet beautiful arrangement of that final number. "You're going to love it."

The working relationship of everyone at that first meeting was ideal. Jonathan asked Celeste to give him no more than three words to describe any given song. "It will give me the mood you want to create." Celeste tried hard but eventually gave up and, in a few instances, ended up with paragraphs instead of minimal word phrases. It helped Jonathan a lot, and they all went their ways.

Celeste had to hurry to the airport for a concert in Cleveland. Jillian wanted to go to the Cleveland concert, but attention to another artist prevented her from doing so. She wished later that she had changed her plans. The critic gave Celeste a stinging review, with phrases like "amateur," "imitative," "under-energized," and the final two sentences were worst of all: "Her final song was her hit single, but this critic couldn't help but think it was a plea to her audience for tolerance for her lack of talent. They clearly did not have that forgiving attitude."

Jillian Richards went to the next concerts, particularly the important ones in Los Angeles, Atlanta, and Riverside, New York. She could see exactly what that critic had seen. Without going to the negatives at all, Jillian began working with Celeste even harder to improve all aspects of her performing, including voice lessons. Celeste was a reluctant student. She was, after all, a "star." There was a reason for all of this turmoil appearing in Celeste's performances, but no one knew what it was. Only Celeste could tell why she was not connecting to the words in the way she once had.

Meanwhile, Jonathan started his work on the new album by listening several times to over twenty Christmas albums of all varieties. The variety showed Jonathan just how awful some arrangers could make things sound. It also showed how wonderful some of them could be. Still, Jonathan felt that many of them missed the mark by being too glitzy. They didn't trust the singer to carry the thought of each song across. That was something Celeste had done to brilliant effect in her first album. That was the reason that "Love Me Just the Way I Am" had been a great hit. Jonathan took no notice of the bad performance reviews.

The arrangements were written out with a music writing program on Jonathan's computer. It took till late March to get them done. Once they were finished and Jonathan liked what he heard, he saved an audio track of the arrangements on to CDs and sent Eric, Jillian, and Celeste each one. Eric Peterson was ecstatic. Even with the limitations of the electronically played arrangements, he could tell that this new album had major potential. Jillian Richards was in total agreement, suggesting only that they might reverse the playing order of two songs in mid-album. It was a point for discussion. Celeste did not respond.

With Celeste, the problem started when those nominations came out, and she was not nominated for anything. Jonathan was nominated for his orchestrations for Celeste's first album. Instead of being thankful for that, Celeste took it as a slap in the face, and she immediately resented Jonathan's success. Never mind that he lost in the Grammys and Country Music Awards, and never mind that nominations were nothing Jonathan had any control over. Celeste still held it against him.

So when everyone met in the second week of May to work musically through the arrangements with piano, things were in terrible shape. Celeste was singing with good voice, but everything was bland. There was no spark, no interest in the meaning. Even "Have Yourself a Merry Little Christmas" was just sung, syllable by syllable, showing not one ounce of understanding or compassion. Eric Peterson was quickly getting impatient. He had been fighting this malaise creeping into every performance for weeks. Now trying to coach Celeste on fine points of interpretation, she seemed unable to pick them up. Nothing changed. The frustrating point was that, even at her most amateurish, this had once been Celeste's strongest attribute.

At one point, Jillian Richards asked Celeste if she had even listened to the CD of the arrangements. Her response was hurled back at Jillian with a demeaning sneer. "Good God, Jillian, who in their right mind wants to listen to Christmas music in May? Don't be goofy!"

Jillian responded with the coldest tone in her voice that she could muster. She was not loud, but when Jillian spoke the words, Celeste could tell that she was really angry. "You were sent the CD in late March. I don't care if the temperature was one hundred in the shade—which it was not—it was your duty to listen and absorb the arrangements." Jillian was fuming.

Celeste was being petulant, and, despite her sometime-diva mannerisms, this attitude sat awkwardly on her shoulders. There was a facade there that no one was going to break through. "I don't like the arrangements."

Jillian snapped back this time. "You don't know! You haven't heard them!"

Jonathan was the only one who had an inkling what was wrong. At the end of the abortive three-hour coaching, Celeste left in a taxi, intending "to go home and sleep." She was tired. What Jonathan remembered from the first album, however, was that Chad had been at every rehearsal, taking notes for Celeste and even actively helping by coming up with extra words to bring out emotions in Celeste. Chad's absence was clearly noted, and Jonathan had the idea that things were not well with Celeste's personal life.

There was a different reason, though, that Jillian Richards was quite worried. In late April, she had been able to get a concert date in Sacramento where Celeste could actually sing the songs live for a Christmas in July concert. Now that she had heard Celeste's dispiriting renditions of the songs, she seriously considered cancelling. She said nothing, but she put in the back of her mind that she might have to cancel the entire concert and, while she was at it, her contract with Celeste.

The orchestra met in Los Angeles for the first time one week before the concert. They met in the morning at 10:00 a.m., reading and lightly rehearsing the various arrangements. Celeste was supposed to be there to listen and sing along in a place or two. She was not there. That made Jillian quite angry. Celeste arrived late, catching only the last twenty minutes of the rehearsal, and even then she paid no attention to the proceedings, preferring instead to stand just outside the rehearsal room door talking on her cell phone.

Jillian wanted to talk with her, but Jonathan suggested that she wait. "Things will probably be fine this afternoon." He was wondering anew about Celeste's deteriorating relationship with Chad.

The break was from noon to one for lunch. Jillian Richards calmly made sure that Celeste Griffin was ready to rehearse. Eric Peterson decided to rehearse "I'll Be Home for Christmas" first. The arrangement was straightforward, and Celeste had known it for a long time. That would be the easiest song to begin with. At least that was what he thought. Celeste was not in good voice. It was not that her voice was bad, but she wasn't warmed up and her voice came across as raspy. The orchestration sounded out with just the right simplicity and yearning. Celeste's rendition was as bland as breakfast food that still needs sugar and milk.

The second and third songs were no better. Eric Peterson was frustrated. With his increased insistence on more musicality, Celeste's temper rose higher too. She began to complain about the arrangements. This one was too high, this one too low, and a couple—notably "Deck the Halls"—were too hard musically to pull off. That arrangement of "Deck the Halls" was a quirky arrangement that changed meters, had humorous orchestral touches throughout, and included a chorus singing rhythmic passages instead of more traditional passages with words.

Celeste was also frustrated with herself. She knew she wasn't prepared. She had assumed she could coast through the music, and now she knew she needed to have put in some incredibly long hours to learn the arrangements. The prospect of a concert meant that she couldn't be singing with the music in front of her, as she might on a recording. After the third abortive attempt at the quirky carol arrangement, she snapped. "I've had it. This is just crap. The orchestra is playing beautifully, except that it's a concert where people will **come to hear me**, and all they can hear is the orchestra. Not one arrangement is any good." She threw her entire packet of arrangements on the floor and started to leave.

Jillian Richards was between Celeste and the door. "Young lady, don't call these fine arrangements crap just because you aren't prepared and can't sing them. *They* are fine. You were out partying with Britney Spears last night, and that has taken its toll on your voice."

Celeste spit her words back at Jillian. "The little you know about it! You don't know anything about anything." She wasn't making much sense, and yet what she was saying was coming across too strongly. She knew it and yet did not draw back. "I can't make any impression with all of this noise going on around me. You call it orchestration, but I call it crap."

Jonathan had intended to stay out of the argument. As he picked up the music off the floor, he couldn't help but say, "The fault is in the lack of any musicality in your singing and not in the orchestrations. A child of ten could sing with more Christmas spirit than you have shown."

"A child of ten would have made better arrangements, Mr. Grammy Nominee!"

Now at least part of the crux of it was in the open. It was not Jonathan who responded however. It was Jillian who coldly said, "We'll stop for the day. Jonathan and Eric, you two go into the green room of this theater. We'll talk about improvements or changes there. Orchestra, you'll get the pay for the entire rehearsal period, but for now, if you would please, file out quietly and with some haste. If you want to talk, please do so outside. Cory, could you kill the lights except for the ghost light?"

In three minutes, Jillian was alone with a nervous and defensive Celeste. Jillian motioned for Celeste to take the seat of the first cellist. Jillian sat in the chair of the first violist. She smiled. "You know, Celeste, this angle isn't right, but it'll have to do. I'd sit on the podium, except I'd have trouble getting back up. It's pretty low." She paused. "We have a major problem, and I want you to tell me how you think we can solve this."

"We need to have all new orchestrations," Celeste pouted. "They stink."

Jillian shook her head. "You don't know whether they do or not. You only heard three of the twelve arrangements. You were too busy to show up for the read-through this morning."

Celeste interrupted, "Well, I can't scream over all of that."

Jillian again shook her head. "That's not it. You're avoiding the issue. When you knew you had an important rehearsal today, why were you out till 2:00 a.m. with Britney Spears instead of home, studying the music and trying to get into the spirit of the music?"

Jonathan entered the room while Jillian was asking the final question. He needed to get the rest of the orchestra parts. Jillian turned from Celeste to Jonathan. "Could you leave us alone for a while, Jonathan? We're in private conference."

"I'll only be a minute. Celeste, I wanted to apologize for what I said a moment ago. I was entirely out of line." He picked up the brass music, saying as he did so, "Celeste, you might want to go to the little girl's room. Your mascara has run a bit. You can clean it up in there, regroup your nerves, and then listen quietly to Jillian. I just need these parts to make a notation or two in them."

Celeste went to the bathroom which was out in the green room. Jonathan stood next to Jillian and watched her leave. "You know, Jillian, today has nothing to do with Britney Spears. I also don't think Celeste is unprepared at all. There is some sort of major distraction that's bothering her."

"Jonathan, it's nice for you to stand up for Celeste, but I have my sources who told me they saw Celeste leave a club with Ms. Spears last night at 1:15 a.m." Jillian was clearly angry about that.

Jonathan leaned against the conductor's music stand. "There can be a number of reasons for being out late with someone. I was in that club earlier. I even spoke with Celeste. Chad was with her, and their evening was definitely a rocky one. They weren't loud, but the word 'strained' is way too mild for their conversation. Celeste was in tears half of the time, and Chad was in a foul mood. I left before dessert partially so I wouldn't be distracted. Britney Spears was just entering with her entourage. I knew she had met Celeste at the awards show, so I introduced myself. After she congratulated me on my orchestrations, I asked her to keep an eye on Celeste. If things went as I thought they might, I told Britney that she might be the perfect person to talk to Celeste. Without mentioning Britney's own public romances, I just thought she might be a close-enough professional acquaintance that she could help Celeste. The entourage usually can't take a hint when they should leave, so it probably took till

1:00 a.m. before Britney could have a chance to talk with Celeste on a one-to-one basis."

Celeste returned at that time, Jillian having no time to return any comment to Jonathan. He made a show of thanking Jillian for *her* advice and returned to the green room. Jillian patted the chair next to her, and Celeste sat there.

Jillian's new approach showed clearly that she had understood Jonathan's comments. "Celeste, I know that something is bothering you. I don't know what it is, and you don't need to tell me that it's none of my business. Strictly speaking, it *is* my business because it's affecting your work. So let me tell you a brief story. It's *my* personal story line.

"Do you remember meeting my twin brother Julian last January? He picked me up after our conference. He used to be a dancer. He could dance ballet or Broadway shows with equal ease. He was singing and dancing the role of Benjamin in **Seven Brides for Seven Brothers** and sustained an injury. The dancing demands of that show have kept ERs in business. By the way, the talent for singing went entirely to him. He's no opera singer, but he was fine for that and several other roles. Anyway, he danced on the injury for five days to complete the summer stock run. It cost him his career. He's been teaching dance at a college for five years. Two years ago, I was asked to talk at his college about being an agent and the ways you get started, the contacts you have to make. All of that stuff you've seen me do countless times was all new to the students.

"On the way to my class, I saw my brother sitting on a bench outside his dance studio. He looked awful. He was surprised to see me, but I asked him immediately what was wrong. He was trying to pass a kidney stone. 'Then why aren't you in the hospital?' I asked him. He had two more dance classes to end the semester, and he was going to finish them out.

"Well, my lecture lasted sixty minutes. After that, I thought I'd look in on the dance class. Julian was teaching and doing everything as if nothing was wrong. After the students had departed, I asked him how he did that. His answer is something I have always remembered. It's good advice for you too since you're now a professional. Julian said, 'Whatever pain or personal problems I have, I leave them at the door. They aren't part of my work. I don't even let personal joys interfere. Work is work. Outside life stays outside.' I learned a lot from my brother that day."

Jillian stood, gave Celeste a hug, and started toward the door. "I'll talk with Jonathan about a couple of spots in 'White Christmas' that are too overpowering. Otherwise, any real comments?"

Celeste shook her head. "Maybe something about 'Silent Night,' but it's only that three bassoons, a contrabassoon, and a harp might sound great, but it's a terrible expense to have two extra bassoons just for one song." Jillian nodded and left the rehearsal room.

Jillian Richards, Jonathan Devon, and Eric Peterson began poring over the scores. Celeste passed through the green room ten minutes later, quietly waving good-bye but otherwise saying nothing to any of them. She was quite subdued.

The conference lasted forty-five minutes. Finally, Jonathan picked up the last score and put it in his large satchel. "It's only 4:30 p.m., and that's too early for dinner. Is anyone up for a drink?"

Jillian looked a little worried. "What if Celeste saw us? Wouldn't that send the wrong message to her?"

Jonathan laughed. "First, by the look on her face, she's thinking about a lot more than drinking tonight. Second, we're not enemies. If she shows up, we'll ask her to join us. Now while we are there drinking and eating their free peanuts or popcorn, there is one important rule we have to follow. There must be absolutely no talk about this concert and recording. Agreed?"

They all agreed, and they went to a tavern two blocks away. After two drinks and talk, they actually ordered a light, early dinner. They all left at 7:00 p.m., just as others were starting to come in for the regular dinner rush.

Jonathan's head was spinning a bit. Three gin and tonics do that to you. He tried to work immediately, but he quickly realized that was going to do no good at all. He did the simple adjustments on three songs, and then, at 8:30 p.m., he set his alarm for midnight and went to bed.

Across town, surprisingly, Celeste was also going to bed early. She had fixed a grilled chicken salad supper. With that, she had a large bottle of water. She was exhausted from the night before, the tensions of the day, and from her attempt to study the arrangements anew. She was a quick study normally, but not this night. She also hit the pillow at 8:30 p.m., intending to rise around 4:00 a.m. to study the rest of the music.

There was still light in the sky when they went to bed. Their air conditioners were humming, allowing them to keep the windows closed more to keep the sounds of traffic out than to keep the heat out. It was actually mild outside.

It was at 10:30 a.m. that Jonathan awoke with a start. The room should have been dark at that hour, but he was aware that, in some way, it was too dark. Why didn't the streetlights cast their usual shadows on the ceiling? And why weren't the lights from passing cars and other neighborhood stores casting their lights either? He sat up on the edge of his bed. Across the room, where his writing desk should have been, he saw something sitting there. It was long and mottled in color, but that was all he could discern. Slowly, light fell more fully on the shape. It was a bed, a flowery sheet covering someone in the bed. That person too was waking up. She sat on the edge of the bed. It was Celeste whose pajamas were in a rather wild zebra stripe; but where white should have been, her pajamas were bright pink.

Jonathan couldn't help but laugh as he said, "Nice pajamas!"

"You don't notice the wild design in the dark. You're not much better. Did you forget your top?"

Jonathan looked down. "I was hot. Summer gets that way you know. At least I have on bottoms. I don't always. That could have been embarrassing!"

They paused. The silly small talk was over. Why were they really there?

"Jonathan, I'm worried about the arrangement for 'Silent Night.' First, I think you should use only two bassoons, string bass, and bass clarinet. That way, if we want to use the arrangement later, it won't be so expensive. Besides, the second clarinet is using his bass clarinet in "Have Yourself a Merry . . ." Celeste had been listening a lot more than Jillian gave her credit. "I would also like to add a recorder as an introduction to the German carol. The quiet, somewhat hollow tone should work well against the darker lower instruments. Maybe even use it for an obbligato in the last verse. That verse may be too full. I'd like to keep it almost entirely me. Let me pull the audience in to an intimate place. Do you think Eric would mind doing it only in German? I've known the German for years. Grandma Teresa taught it to me. I like your English arrangement, but we don't need it. It doesn't really fit the arc of songs."

Jonathan nodded. "I agree to that. I'll also print the words here in case you have trouble remembering them. You might tomorrow under pressure."

Celeste smiled. "There won't be any pressure. I'll leave it at the door. I think that tomorrow we work hard! I'll bring my guitar too. Maybe we'll try the German with guitar accompaniment only, introduced by the recorder. I always play it in the key of your arrangement, so you don't need to change anything if that's the way we decide to go."

Jonathan perked up. "Oh, by the way, I've taken out some of those intricate notes in 'Deck the Halls.' It will make you happier, and the flutist will find it much more to her liking. My sense was that the original arrangement was too busy."

Celeste's voice rose a little. "Jonathan, I'm scared about tomorrow."

"Nonsense, Celeste, you'll do fine. We still have another day too to get everything right before we head to Sacramento." He reached to the floor and picked up the vocal score. "Here's the revised score for 'Deck the Halls.'"

Celeste took it, glancing at it. "I'll study it on the way in to rehearsal." She put it on the foot of her bed and lay back down. Jonathan watched her do so. "Good night, Jonathan, and thank you. I was way out of line today. Your arrangements fit me perfectly."

Jonathan gleamed, "I hope so. They were tailored with your voice in mind."

Jonathan awoke at 2:00 a.m. The midnight alarm had not gone off. He somehow felt wide awake. He finished the tweaking of the various arrangements, printing off the parts for each. (Of course, he had to change his ink cartridge halfway through "I'll Be Home for Christmas," but that was the only delay.) Several of the arrangements needed only changes of dynamics, and that he did by hand.

Jonathan left his loft apartment at 6:00 a.m., heading to the local coffee shop for his favorite espresso. He had just entered when he noticed that Chad Connor, Celeste's sometime love interest, was putting his stuff at a table. The place was not full, but still Jonathan asked Chad if he could join him. Chad nodded that he could.

At first, the two said no more than cursory greetings, and then they went on about their work. Jonathan was studying the changes. Chad was still memorizing lines for a monologue. He was an actor, and the monologue was from a modern play. Although Chad wasn't speaking much aloud, it was clear what the play was like from the occasional blue words which slipped out. To Jonathan, it was more a shock monologue—one of those wonderful monologues that is more about saying blue words than about really good character exploration.

Chad finally closed his play book tentatively. "How are the rehearsals going?"

Jonathan swallowed a bite of his muffin. "Rocky! Celeste seems more than a little distracted." Jonathan paused, trying to swallow another morsel of muffin and also thinking how to broach the subject that was none of his business. "Do you know why she's upset?"

Chad stirred his refilled coffee. ("Too much cream," was all Jonathan could think.) Chad finally looked up. "We broke up a couple of months ago. We met for dinner two nights ago so Celeste could bring me a couple of books I had left behind. We should not have met. It ended badly. Oh, I guess you were there for part of it. It got much worse later." He shrugged. "It's probably all my fault anyway. Celeste thinks it is, I know that!"

Jonathan excused himself a moment to get more coffee. When he returned, he asked, "Why did you break up? You seemed pretty much a tight unit last summer when we finished the first album. You were there every day for the recording sessions and even made good comments for the editing."

Chad thought a moment, not thinking up an excuse—at least he didn't consider it so—but clearly defining his position. "I'm an actor, and I take pride in my work. When a friend does well, I take pride in their work too. I can be very supportive! Celeste and I were going together, so of course I wanted to support her. I still do. But for over a year, it has been all about Celeste and what she can achieve. It's never about Chad's successes, as if I even had any."

Jonathan clearly understood, and to him it was a valid but silly excuse. "Do you know that I went with a girl in college for three years? Everything revolved around her blossoming operatic career. It was never about my orchestrations or my composing. Even when I wrote a cycle of songs for her doctoral recital, she got all the praise. At the reception we threw afterward, only three people congratulated me on my songs, and two of those did so because they felt they had to."

Chad's face lit up. "So you dumped her, right?"

Jonathan pursed his lips and shook his head. "Wrong. She dumped me. She was above me. Her ego couldn't take little me anymore. I 'didn't understand what an artistic life was all about' so she fell in love and into bed—not necessarily in that order—with a baritone. Within a year, both of them were having vocal problems. She tried to talk with me, but I just told her I couldn't be bothered with her problems. She's dumped the baritone now and is trying to regain her voice. So your excuse isn't very valid to me. If you love Celeste, you should be supportive. You didn't want those books at all. You just wanted to screw up her next claim to fame, and messing with her head was the best way to do that."

Jonathan did not get farther into his rebuttal of Chad's excuses. Chad stood up suddenly and swung at Jonathan. Jonathan, seeing the punch coming in advance, ducked away from it, and Chad went careening into the next table, hitting his eye on the back of the chair and cutting his lip on the seat of the same chair. Jonathan helped him up. "Come on, Superman, let's see what damage you have done." He looked. The waiter brought over some water in a pail and several paper towels. After five minutes of work, Jonathan shook his head. "I'm afraid you won't look too good for your audition. I think you should go to the ER, actually. Do you feel okay? Your lip looks pretty bad."

Chad was crying, but Jonathan immediately knew it was not from his wounds. "Id's nod my mouf thad hurds . . . id's my heart."

The trip to the emergency room took quite a while. Jonathan left Chad there around 8:00 a.m. to get to the rehearsal hall. He needed to check out some new chords at the beginning of an arrangement. He had just seated himself at the keyboard when Celeste came in.

"Hey there! You look bright eyed and ready to work. What gets you up so early?"

Celeste held out a piece of paper. "I needed to go over this. Besides, you only gave me the first two verses. I hope you have the last one." She stopped talking a moment and then said, "Uh, Jonathan, just what happened last night?"

Jonathan bit his lower lip in studied pondering. "You know, if I could answer that, I might be able to answer why some people can sing well and why some can't. I might also be able to tell people not to bother even looking at a subject matter for a given musical. It'll flop anyway. Some things you just can't answer."

"But it did happen?"

"Celeste, you have that paper, and you know I didn't have on a top. You also know that I am fully aware how *bizarre* your PJs are!"

For the next hour, the two worked hard. They ended with the new arrangement of "Silent Night." They opted for recorder and guitar. It was then that Jonathan suddenly stood up, a look of horror on his face. "Celeste, I need to call Jillian right away. We don't have anyone to play the recorder."

A quiet voice came from the doorway. "I could play id for the rehearsal ad least." It was Chad. His lip was swollen even more, and his eye was quite black and purple.

Celeste got up and went to him. "What happened to you?" Her genuine love for Chad was still there.

Chad looked down first and then sheepishly over to Jonathan. "I took a swing ad a guy named Jonathan who writes music, and I hit a chair instead. I'm just a jerk sometimes, I guess."

Jillian had come into the hall and now stepped up behind Chad. "Maybe, but aren't you also a member of the musician's union? You could actually go on the tour with us, because I remembered last night hearing you and Celeste at a party playing guitars and singing 'Pat-a-pan.' It was your arrangement, and it was delightful. We could include it in the concert and album."

Celeste was delighted, and to everyone's surprise, so was Chad. Celeste then turned to Jonathan. "Jonathan, do you happen to have any arrangement that could give us an overture and an interlude? I'm worried about singing twelve songs, now thirteen, back to back without a break."

Jillian had to interject. "It might make the CD too long."

Jonathan shrugged. "We don't have to include them on the CD. I actually have just what you want on my computer here. I didn't mention them, because they weren't part of the plan. They could have voice or not. Besides, they can replace the English language 'Silent Night,' which Celeste and I agree is redundant."

The parts and scores were printed out, and Celeste went through a brief vocal for the overture, and then lightly sang through each song. Meanwhile, Chad reached into his attaché, shoving the playbook aside and pulling out his recorder. It was Chad's instrument of relaxation. His guitar (in a case for protection) had been strung over his back. At noon they all ate—no talk about the project! Chad was feeling better even if he looked worse.

At 1:00 p.m., the orchestra began to rehearse. The minor changes were explained for each number, and then Eric Peterson began the actual run-through of the program. Celeste was in top form, fighting no demons and making sure she was a professional all the way. Break came at the point of the interlude Celeste had requested. Part one ended with the "Pat-a-pan" arrangement. The orchestra applauded.

The orchestra was asked to sit quietly during the inspired transition from "Cantique de Noël" (O Holy Night)—sung as desired in French, with all three verses—into "Stille Nacht," the German "Silent Night." Chad's recorder solo floated in with a plaintive long note just after the end of the French song. The quiet cadenza that followed led gently down to the first guitar note, gently plucked by Celeste. The sound was soft and pulled the listener in. The sustained sounds came from two bassoons added in the second verse. When Celeste's last note faded away, the recorder took the note and floated it off into air. The orchestra was totally silent for a full minute.

It was Eric Peterson who broke the silence. "That, my friends, is artistry!"

Celeste turned to Eric Peterson. "It may be artistry, and I thank you for your compliment. I choose to call it faith. I want to apologize to all of you for my behavior yesterday. I was not able to leave personal problems at the door as I should have. Today I made a point of letting *me* take over instead of my emotions."

The next day was spent in rehearsing only a couple of the numbers. Then they all left the rehearsal hall and reconvened at the airport at 5:30 p.m. The flight to Sacramento seemed shorter than it was.

The crew there was already setting up the concert platforms. Early the next afternoon, Celeste walked around the set, trying out certain places to sing and making sure that everything felt right. The stage director was more a traffic cop for this show, but he did his job simply and efficiently, moving the chorus into place when needed and adjusting lights to suit the mood of the arrangements. He was more accustomed to rock shows, but he did wonders on this show too.

The place that evening was totally sold out. The concert was billed as **"Celestial Greetings—Celeste Griffin Celebrates Christmas in July."** The crowd was somehow subdued at first. Attendance was more a matter of being in a happening, but expectations for Celeste were minimal. The "fame" of her subpar outings had reached Sacramento. It was therefore unexpected when, after the lights had dimmed, Celeste's voice introduced the overture with a verse and chorus of "O Come, O Come Emmanuel." The rhythm reflected the original Gregorian chant of the song. The orchestra picked up that tune, and then went into a rollicking medley of "We Need a Little Christmas" and "Jingle Bells." The concert program went as follows:

1. Overture
2. Have Yourself a Merry Little Christmas
3. I'll Be Home for Christmas
4. O Come All Ye Faithful—with chorus
5. Let It Snow, Let It Snow, Let It Snow!
6. White Christmas
7. Pat-a-Pan (Celeste and Chad alone)
8. Interlude—based on God Rest Ye Merry, Gentlemen
9. Deck the Halls—with chorus
10. Count Your Blessings
11. Christmas Lullaby (Lyons) and Rocking Carol
12. Jingle Bell Rock
13. What Child Is This?—with chorus
14. O Holy Night (Cantique de Noël—sung in French)—with chorus
15. Silent Night (Stille Nacht—sung in German)—recorder and guitar, then bassoons.

The place was silent for almost a minute at the end of the German carol and then erupted. Celeste had successfully pulled the audience into her world, and her world was one of faith and happiness. "The Christmas Lullaby" by Ruth Lyons was a find by Celeste of a song written by a TV personality from Cincinnati, Ohio.

The critic who had so nailed her in Cleveland had traveled to Sacramento for the concert. He had hoped to get another scathing review in and to destroy Celeste's career. His report, like at least ten others, was ecstatic. He could not come up with enough adjectives to express his delight in the concert. His final line said as much as anyone could. "I expected to emerge from the theater and see snow. Instead, the glow protected me from the heat instead of the cold. It was an amazing concert."

She had to repeat it in Bethesda, Maryland, and in New York City. All the concerts were recorded, in case they needed to splice in a better take. But the Sacramento concert was intact on the CD—except for the quiet moment just before the French song, where someone in the audience let loose with a terrific sneeze. The CD won awards!

Chad Connors was part of Celeste's life only for this tour. Britney's advice for Celeste was right. If Chad couldn't deal with Celeste being successful, then she should just find someone who was happy with Celeste being successful. Celeste and Chad gradually cooled toward one another, and after the tour Chad moved to New York, where he auditioned for and got a lead role in the replacement cast for a musical. His expertise in both acting and recorder (he played it on stage) helped in that.

Celeste's career only lasted six years. After that, she seemed to lose interest not in singing but in the rigors of touring. Despite an occasional appearance on a TV show, she gradually left the public mania and faded away from the attention. Many still spoke of the incredible performance in Sacramento. One radio disc jockey turned to her album almost every year to play various tracks.

But the career became of little interest to Celeste. Instead, she took an interest in Chad's replacement in her life: Jonathan Devon. Jonathan's career, based on his success with Celeste's album and concerts, took off. He scored several albums—never in the hard metal sound, but always with a keen ear for texture and sound quality. This led to scoring opportunities for three movies (a series) and then to TV themes, more movies, and incredible notoriety as a major, hunky catch in Hollywood rags. Perhaps his greatest award, however, was Celeste.

They fell gradually in love during the tour. Eric Peterson was the first to notice it. At first, Jonathan denied any interest, but then he realized that he was truly interested and began more actively pursuing Celeste. For her part, she was already interested in Jonathan. They made several important "appearances" on the red carpet for movies—Jonathan was nominated twice for an Academy Award.

But when Jonathan's alma mater offered him a lucrative position teaching composition and orchestration, Celeste and Jonathan retired from active work in Hollywood and went to the smaller environs of the college town. They became part of the fabric of the campus life. Within three years, few even remembered their earlier notoriety, and that was fine with them. They had two sons, both of whom are destined for acting careers.

It was quite a surprise to Celeste, however, when a new freshman saw her in the grocery. She was dressed nicely, but she wore nothing fancy. He was dressed as many students are today, but he was most respectful when he addressed Celeste. "Excuse me, ma'am, but is your name Celeste?"

Celeste nodded that it was.

"I was in Sacramento a few years ago when you gave that incredible concert in July. I was bordering on declaring myself an agnostic. But when I heard you sing those songs, I just wept at how I could ever have doubted God existed."

Celeste mentioned the conversation that night to Jonathan. He just smiled. "Don't let it out now, but I too had my doubts. When we were in those early meetings for your Christmas album, something you said—and I can't remember what it was—totally moved me. Then I too heard you sing that concert. I loved the joy of the whole thing, but the last number took me to a new place I never knew existed. Even on the album, I can truly say that you're faith shines through. It is a **Celestial Greeting**, as the title says, but when I hear the album again, I consider myself the luckiest man in the world to call you my wife."

Happiness remains with them, but nothing ever rivals that moment in time when they were united at night for a strange meeting. And nothing will ever rival the fervent faith that Celeste showed that one hot night in Sacramento, California. There was no snow on the streets afterward, but the spirit of Christmas was still strong and moving.

TALE 4
Christmas in Baghdad

Sharon Gates wasn't sure she wanted to call the doctor's office, but the pain in her back was not getting any better. She also knew that her mother-in-law, Margaret, had not felt well for at least five days. At her age, sixty-five, that could be a worry. The Gates women were usually in extremely good health, so it was a rare moment when both were ill.

Finally, conquering her reserve, Sharon Gates dialed. It was 4:30 p.m., and she knew the office closed at 5:00 p.m. (She had once called at 5:05 p.m. to tell them she was detained in traffic, and the receptionist refused to answer, even though she was still there when Sharon had arrived five minutes later.) The telephone rang twice. "Family practice. How can I help you?"

Sharon cleared her throat. "This is Sharon Gates, Mrs. Nathan Gates. I have not been feeling well. I don't think I've got anything odd, but I think I should check it out. My mother-in-law is also feeling ill, and I need to make an appointment for her."

The receptionist put on her drippiest and most condescending manners. "I'm sorry to say, Mrs. Gates, that we have no openings for five days, and then we're into limited hours due to Christmas vacation. Could your trouble last till January?"

Sharon knew exactly to which receptionist she was talking. She hated dealing with her. It was always a tactic of making the patient grateful for the receptionist bending a little to "help" the patient.

"Look, ma'am, I need to see Dr. Mitchum right away. On an earlier visit, he insisted before that, if I'm ill, I am to contact him. I need to see him at once. This could affect my health permanently, and it could certainly affect the health of Mrs. Clarence Gates, Margaret."

"Well, I just told you that we have no openings, Mrs. Gates, so you'll have to live with that."

Sharon was fuming. "That's the point! I'm not sure I can 'live with that.'"

Suddenly, Dr. Mitchum spoke, "It's all right, Deborah, I'll take it from here. Sharon Gates? We're closing here a little early." To Sharon, that meant they weren't booked as solidly as Deborah had insisted they were. "Could you come to the emergency room tonight? I'll make sure they charge you my office rates. I have a feeling I can tell you why you have that pain in your back, but I want to check things out to be sure. And if Margaret Gates is ill, I want to see her for certain. She hasn't been shoveling snow, has she?"

Sharon laughed, "Absolutely not. Besides, we haven't had enough to shovel yet."

Dr. Mitchum was not laughing. "I'm serious! It is dangerous for older people to shovel snow."

Sharon Gates said she could be there at 7:00 p.m., and Dr. Mitchum assured her he would be there at that time or perhaps earlier. "If I'm late, it won't be by more than a minute or two." As she began to hang up, Sharon Gates heard Dr. Mitchum talking to Deborah, the receptionist. Sharon Gates was satisfied that Deborah was in hot water.

She immediately called Margaret Gates. The telephone rang three times before Margaret picked it up. "Hello?"

"Mother Gates, this is Sharon. I was able to talk with Dr. Mitchum just now, and he wants to see us both tonight in the ER."

Margaret clicked her tongue. "Well, Sharon, why would you do that? I'm fine."

"No, you are not! We've spoken every day this week, and you've felt 'punk' for most of that time. If you're not feeling well, it is better to see a doctor and for him to tell you you're fine than to stay away and find out too late that you should have seen him."

Margaret was belligerent. "Why don't you leave little Cathy here and let me watch her while *you* go?"

Sharon Gates had forgotten to arrange for Cathy. "Well, Mrs. Jacobs across the street will look after her. Besides, my mother comes tomorrow morning from Seattle for Christmas, and she'll want to look after her if we're detained." Sharon tossed it off as easily as she could, hoping Margaret Gates wouldn't notice the thought.

Whether she did or not Sharon plunged ahead, saying that she would pick her mother-in-law up at 6:40 p.m. Then she called Mrs. Jacobs. Mrs. Jacobs, as Sharon expected, was ecstatic about keeping Cathy. Her daughter, Donita Jacobs, liked to play with Cathy Gates, and this would be a great excuse.

Mrs. Clarissa Dougherty would arrive at the Indianapolis Airport at 3:00 p.m., and she would take the shuttle to within two blocks of Sharon's house. "If you aren't there, I'll be sure to have my key. Tell Mrs. Jacobs to keep an eye out, and Cathy can cross the street to stay with me. I'm sorry you're not feeling well, Sharon. Do call me if you find out what's wrong. I wouldn't worry much. It's probably nothing more than a sprained back from that yard sale you had two months ago."

Sharon didn't argue with her mother, but she somehow knew it was not in any way connected with her yard sale.

Margaret Gates was waiting for Sharon when she drove up, stepping carefully down the porch steps and out to the car. Once she was inside, she began her harangue. "This is a silly and needless trip."

Sharon shook her head. "I'll be happy if it is. By the way, I e-mailed Nathan that we were going. I also e-mailed Elliot."

Margaret pursed her lips tightly together. "A lot of good that'll do. You know Elliot won't respond to anything about us. We aren't one of his women."

Sharon drove carefully. "I don't know about any women, Mother Gates, but I want you to tell me just what has caused this impasse between Elliot and Nathan."

"You mean that you don't know? Well, the short answer is that I used to show as much interest in what each child was doing. Elliot was always the secure one, on top of everything that came along. Nathan was always good, don't get me wrong, but initially he needed help getting things done. Clarence and I helped both boys with scouting projects, model building, school work, and other such things. We **did not do** the work for them. But we helped. When Elliot was around twelve, he entered 4-H. For two years, he slaved away in electric. He got blue ribbons, but he never got a *champion* ribbon. Nathan liked watching Elliot work on making lamps and the like, so he entered too. His first year was Elliot's third. Nathan and Elliot both got blue ribbons, but Nathan got a reserved grand champion. He still didn't get to go to the state fair, but Elliot got jealous. After that, he would run down everything Nathan tried to do. That was something Clarence and I tried in vain to squelch. Elliot joined the air force right after college and made a steady climb up the ladder to lieutenant. Nathan joined up two years later, but he joined the Army. He's a sergeant. Even today, Elliot cannot give Nathan a decent word. Two years ago, as you may remember, Elliot said one thing to Nathan the entire day. That was 'Pass the gravy,' so I hardly think it counts."

Sharon nodded. She remembered what Nathan had said when they got home too.

The two women arrived at the hospital surprisingly early—6:50. Except for the above conversation, Margaret Gates had argued about how "silly" it all was the entire ten-minute trip to the hospital.

Dr. Mitchum met them at the door. He ushered them both into an examination room. "Mrs. Nathan Gates, I'd like you to take a seat there for a moment. Mrs. Clarence Gates, could you please follow Nancy into the adjoining room. She is Dr. Nancy Clover, she's on duty tonight too, and she's quite good. She can examine you, making you feel more at ease than you are when I examine you."

Margaret Gates followed Dr. Clover into the adjoining room, giving Sharon an exasperated look as she left. Dr. Mitchum took no time responding. "I saw your mother-in-law in the grocery a week ago and was alarmed even then how distressed she looked. Dr. Clover is a cardiologist, and I'm afraid Margaret's heart is simply giving out. But let's talk about you. How long has this back pain existed?"

Sharon thought a moment. "I think the first twinge came around mid-September. I thought nothing about it at first, until it seemed to get a little worse. At least it didn't go away, and I'm tired of putting up with it."

At that moment, yet another doctor entered the room: Dr. Bertrand. "Sharon, I'd like you to meet Dr. David Bertrand. He's an old friend of mine from medical school, and he works here every Thursday night. Why don't you leave your coat and purse here—they'll be quite safe—and come with me."

They went together into the adjoining examination room. Sharon stopped suddenly and pulled back. "I know that machine. It gives the image of whether you have a baby or not—an ultrasound. I'm not pregnant, Dr. Mitchum."

Dr. Mitchum just smiled. "Well, I'm not saying that is the reason for your back pain, but you *are* pregnant. When did Nathan leave? Wasn't it eight months ago?"

Sharon nodded rather uncertainly. "Doctor, I've been pregnant before. Don't you think I would know if I was pregnant again?"

Dr. David Bertrand shrugged. "I've had at least three or four women who didn't know until their last trimester. If you were not nauseous this time around, or if you didn't happen to show any of the prescribed signs, you might not notice the other more overt signs: enlarging breasts, weight gain, etc. As for the back pain, that's part of the reason I'm here. We'll look to see if your baby is far enough along, and it probably is, to bring it early into this world and get working on whatever is bothering you."

The two doctors began to work on the ultrasound machine, getting it ready to find out to what kind of a child Sharon Gates was about to give birth. They had just turned on the machine when Dr. Nancy Clover came in hurriedly. "Dr. Mitchum, Margaret Gates just took suddenly quite ill, perspiring all over, and now she has collapsed."

Dr. Mitchum went hurrying along. Sharon Gates started to follow him. "Wait a minute, young lady, you are also a patient here. We need to find out what we can about your baby right now."

Nathan Gates shut his computer down in total frustration. He had turned it on to get e-mail from home; instead, the computer screen turned a bright shade of orange and then shut down. He had received a worrisome e-mail two days before from Sharon, and he was sure she would have sent him a follow-up. If either his wife or mother was ill, he wanted to know—even if he couldn't do anything about it from afar. Understandably his computer was reacting to the extreme heat and dust that only Iraq could throw at intruders.

He walked slowly, aimlessly around, kicking the dust and trying to decide how to solve his dilemma. Without his knowing it, he had ended up by the headquarters of his squadron. He was hesitant at first, but he finally knocked on the door and then went in.

Sitting at a desk in the corner was Col. George Franklin. He looked up and could immediately tell that something was bothering Sergeant Gates. He saluted, a gesture that Nathan immediately returned. "Something wrong there, Gates? The look on your face is about as tied into knots as I've seen of late. Considering that we're in Iraq for what we hope is our last Christmas here, that is saying something." He motioned for Nathan to be seated.

Nathan began even before he was fully into the chair. "Sir, my computer just died. It isn't worth the plastic that surrounds it. I wouldn't care, I guess, except that I got an e-mail two days ago from Sharon saying that both she and my mother were feeling a little out of the ordinary. She said that she would call the doctor if it didn't clear up the next day.

Well, if I have heard anything, I can't tell. I couldn't get the computer to work right yesterday either. I'm worried, sir." The obvious distraction this dilemma was causing registered deeply with a catch in his voice.

Col. Franklin nodded, "I would say you have a reason to be worried. In fact, if you weren't worried, I'd think something was wrong with you." He paused a couple of minutes to think. He shook his head several times, finally explaining to the expectant Nathan Gates, "I was considering some way I could write an e-mail for you, but this computer isn't supposed to be used for private usage. There aren't any outs for personal emergencies." He let the last word trail out. "However, I might have a good solution."

Nathan Gates leaned forward. "I'd almost consider re-upping for another tour of duty in the armed forces if it wasn't that I have an offer for a cushiony job back home." He saw a look of pseudo alarm on the colonel's face. "Well, it isn't really cushiony, but compared to this place, it's pretty darn nice."

Col. Franklin smiled a mischievous smile, one filled with the knowledge of something he knew that Nathan Gates did not know. "Sergeant Gates, don't you have a brother stationed back somewhere in the Midwest?"

"Yes, he lives east of St. Louis, Scott Air Force Base."

Col. Franklin's smile grew. "And isn't he a lieutenant or something like that?"

Nathan Gates had no idea where this was heading, but he nodded his head. "Of course, you know he and I basically have not spoken in five years."

Col. Franklin did not let his smile fade. "That's okay, because I outrank him. I may be a different branch of the armed forces, but he would still be answering to me in some ways. Give me his e-mail address."

Within minutes, the following e-mail was heading to the Midwest:

Lieutenant Gates,

I believe we met three years ago at an officer's club. I am currently in the hot spot of the mid-East, and you're in the cold spot of the Midwest. Could you help my men and me greatly by sending me a full description of the cold weather there? Be as graphic as possible. We need it. It is roughly 120 degrees outside, and a cool 105 inside, with every fan we have going. As an example how hot it is here, a Sgt. Nathan Gates has just had his computer die due to too much heat and dust. Is he any relation to you? Anyway, his mother and wife have taken ill, and now he can't get updates on their condition. He's very worried too. Anyway, this is a gentle order to send the information requested to me as soon as humanly possible.

George Franklin, Colonel
U.S. Army

Nathan Gates nodded. "If he isn't totally a horse's behind, he ought to get the message, and yet it doesn't sound too personal."

"While I see if he responds 'as soon as humanly possible' as ordered, I wonder if you could help Cdr. Jenkins. He needs to do a patrol of the camp. His usual partner in such endeavors is in the hospital with dehydration. It won't be just two of you, but would you please join his patrol? I seem to remember that you've done it before."

Sgt. Nathan Gates knew it was given as a request but was really an order. "I'll do it right away. It doesn't take too awfully long."

"Not usually."

Within minutes of leaving the headquarters, he had run into Cdr. Jenkins. The two of them started out on the patrol, being joined by four other sharpshooters within the next thirty yards. The trek took them to the western fringe of the main enclosure, to the south, and then up the entire eastern barrier. The first part of the journey was almost pleasant. It wasn't that anyone took their duty so cavalierly as to be careless about what they were doing. But they spoke softly and almost whimsically about what at home made Christmas special when each child was growing up.

Nathan found the answers that each of them gave to be quite interesting. For his own sake, he had to relate how he and his brother used to wait up till midnight. "We were sure we would catch Santa, hearing him either sliding down the chimney—it went through our bedroom—or else coming in at the back door. We were sure we heard him coming in the back door one or two times, but neither of us dared tiptoe down to see him." The memory of those early years brought back surprisingly fond memories of Elliot. Nathan couldn't help but get a lump in his throat as he considered the terrible way Elliot and he had drifted apart.

Suddenly Cpl. Davenport stopped dead in his tracks. "Sirs, look next to that gray and brown shed over there at 0-200." All of the men followed instructions of the corporal. Sure enough, they could all see at least one man skulking around near a shed roughly forty yards outside the compound. Cdr. Jenkins pulled down his night-vision glasses.

As he did so, Cpl. Davenport stepped back and began to kneel behind a small brick wall. He knelt on a land mine which exploded. Cpl. Davenport was killed at once, as was Pvt. Upton. Pvt. Ellington had knelt directly behind a large rock and tree combination that protected him from any direct blast. As Cdr. Jenkins had taken a step forward to view the intruder, he had stepped out of the range and exact aim of the blast.

Sgt. Nathan Gates was not so lucky. The wall behind which Cpl. Davenport had knelt was blown directly at him, the cement blocks hitting his lower limbs with horrible, bone-crunching force.

Cdr. Jenkins immediately inspected Sgt. Gates, motioning Pvt. Ellington to examine Cpl. Davenport and Pvt. Upton. Comdr. Jenkins had little hope for those two men. As he examined Sgt. Nathan Gates, his hope for him began to falter. He was severely wounded. That much could be ascertained without aid of a medic.

The intruder was long gone, and others from the camp were running to give assistance, the blast having been heard from a good distance. The area was secured. The entire area would have to be scoured at least twice before the dead could be removed. Several men did their work with tears streaming down their faces. Sgt. Gates was taken to the hospital as soon as possible.

At the headquarters, Col. Franklin was sitting almost totally still, fighting off the horrid feeling that he had sent Nathan to his death. His impatience was not only with himself. Even figuring the time differences between Iraq and St. Louis, he couldn't help but think Lt. Elliot Gates should have replied by now.

Lt. Elliot Gates came into his apartment, stomping his feet. He didn't really like snow, and he sometimes almost chided those sick people who felt it wasn't Christmas if it didn't follow the old song. "White Christmas is not something to which I look forward. Too many people get hurt in such weather."

Elliot smiled at his image in the mirror. Since going to college, he had garnered the reputation of being a lady's man. It was an image he had worked at for several years. He was naturally handsome, but he made sure he also was as "put-together" as he could be—he wanted to have a touch of glamour. He never shunned the reputation, but he didn't exactly find it as comfortable as he once did. That reputation had once helped get the attention of female students. Now the women who paid him attention were, frankly, not that interesting. He liked a woman to look healthy, but far too many of the women who paid him any attention were scarcely above the level of bimbettes—bimbo being too kind a word for them. They had looks but no smarts. (He never admitted how biased that opinion was.)

He had roughly an hour before he was due to meet his current lady friend, Karen. She was only two years his junior, and she was exactly the sort of young lady he had wanted since he realized that he might actually be ready to settle down. He switched on the TV and his computer at the same time, stepping almost immediately into the shower.

As he showered and shampooed, he had a sudden memory of his childhood. It was a silly memory of the way Nathan and he had tried to catch Santa Claus coming into their house. The memory hurt Elliot far more than he had any idea it would. Something about the memory stung him, filling him with regret and even dread. A fleeting chill went down his back, as if someone was trying to whisper something alarming in his ear. He got under the shower and was almost immediately relieved of those tensions.

As he stepped out of the shower and was almost dry enough to walk across the room, the telephone rang harshly. He answered quickly. "Hello?"

"Elliot, this is Karen."

"Hi! What's up?"

"Listen, have you been watching the news?"

Elliot shook his head. "No. I just turned on the TV, but I was in the shower. What's wrong?"

"There's a big storm coming, probably bringing a little ice and lots of snow. The worst-case scenario would be a little snow and lots of ice. They aren't sure exactly where the rain-snow divide will go. Do you mind terribly if I beg off tonight? I hate snow."

Elliot laughed into the telephone. "Well, I always mind when I can't be with you." He closed his eyes in the knowledge that it sounded far too much like a pick-up line. "That sounded pretty shallow. I'm sorry. Listen, I had kind of a special outing planned tonight."

"I know, but I think it would be better tomorrow, after we know what hits." Something about the way she said that gave Elliot that cold chill once again.

"Well, listen, I'm off for the holidays, so why don't I pick you up tomorrow morning outside your apartment. If we can, we'll drive up to Indy and see my mom and sister-in-law." She agreed . . . if the road was okay.

He hung up and began to dress. He shoved his computer mouse once so it wouldn't go into sleep mode. Finally dressed, he thought about going out to get a steak at the local bar and grill. He loved their steaks. He decided to check his e-mail first. It was raining outside, and he didn't really want to go far anyway. A glance outside again showed that the rain was freezing rather heavily on the lines outside his window.

Elliot opened the e-mail and, to his surprise, he found that it had been over a week since he looked at his e-mail. The first two, dated December 14 and 15, were simple greetings. He answered them briefly, and then he opened one on the sixteenth from his mother. She was her usual newsy self, but it worried him a little that she mentioned feeling "punk," a condition that he would never associate with his mother. (He couldn't help but think how he had almost forced his mother to learn about computers enough to e-mail him.)

He eliminated the Spam that had gotten through the filter. "How do I keep getting all of this e-mail in Russian? I don't speak Russian, and I don't want a Russian bride!" He glanced over to his dresser. There sat a little red box, the one he had intended to give to Karen this evening.

Then he had an e-mail dated December 21. This was from Sharon, his sister-in-law.

Elliot,

> I thought I should tell you the most recent news. I am going to the hospital ER tonight with your mother. She's been feeling ill for at least four days. You know her. It's probably longer than that, but she didn't say anything at first. My back has also been hurting. I probably need to go on a diet. (Ha-ha).
>
> I haven't heard from Nathan lately. He was having a little trouble with his computer. I'll send you all updates as soon as I can. My mother will be here tomorrow and can take care of Cathy if anything is very wrong. You have our number. Give her a call.
>
> **Love,**
> **Sharon**

Now Elliot was truly frightened. There were hints in that e-mail that troubled him a lot. The e-mail was timed at 6:15 p.m. There was also another e-mail dated the twenty-second, but this one was timed at 4:54 p.m. It was from a colonel he knew vaguely. He started to delete it—"It's probably just a plea for seasonal prayers for his troops."—but something about it made him open it. Once he read it, he was even more worried. He glanced outside again, wishing to get the best weather report he could. After he was certain how to word that part of the reply, he started to formulate a good reply to Nathan.

Suddenly, the chill returned with a terrible pain in his left leg. The pain went away almost at once, but Elliot was bothered by it. He was never ill, and this didn't feel like the flu or anything. He shook his head to get the cobwebs out. It felt like some sort of ESP, something he believed in but had never experienced.

Elliot dialed the number for his brother. No one answered. He dialed Indianapolis Methodist Hospital. He knew Sharon's doctor worked through them. They answered, but before they could give him a report whether Sharon and Elliot's mother were there, the line went dead. He dialed again.

"Due to weather problems, we are unable to complete your call at this time. Please hang up and try again later." How can automated responses know about weather?

Elliot typed the weather report Colonel Franklin had wanted, and included a comment about trying to find out about his brother's family, but before he could send the e-mail, the lights went out. This meant that the computer was down too. He couldn't call by telephone, because it was too far, and besides electric outages frequently took out relay stations.

His battery-powered radio was sputtering like crazy, but the weather report was grim: doing anything important before 4:00 a.m. was not advised.

Elliot was stymied. What could he do? He could try his laptop instead of his desktop, but relay stations were still likely to be out. He finally fixed a large bowl of tomato soup (adding one slice of soft cheddar cheese to make it better), and ate some crackers with Brie cheese. The Merlot he opened was wonderful.

It was a pretty paltry way to spend December 23. He decided to go for a walk in the cold, fresh air, hoping that it would clear his brain. For some reason, he poured the remainder of the bottle of Merlot into a smaller bottle and slipped it into his pocket. He felt silly doing so, but it just felt right somehow. (This was absolutely not a normal thing for Elliot to do.)

He walked down the steps of his building and out into the crisp and wet outdoors. It was only as the door closed that he realized it would be impossible to get back in because the outer door was electrically controlled. He had a key that could bypass that device in such an emergency situation, but it was lying upstairs on his dresser. He had the little red box with the ring, his car keys, and his apartment key, but not that one key, which was on a separate chain.

He wandered aimlessly but carefully around town, looking at the low-hung branches weighed down with heavy ice. He slipped twice, once catching himself on an iron fence, and once grabbing a low-hanging limb to keep himself upright.

He soon noticed he was in front of a Presbyterian church. The pastor was just coming out the door. He hurried up in part to help the pastor, who was carrying two large packages. When he caught the package that was slipping from the pastor's hands, the pastor thanked him. "My name is Rev. William Tremont. My congregation calls me Pastor Bill. Were you hoping to worship with us? You're a day early if you are. Tomorrow night is Christmas Eve service."

Up to that moment, Elliot had no idea what he wanted, but he suddenly got an idea and asked slowly. "Not exactly, Reverend. I actually wanted to pray a while. I have some illness in various members of my family, and I wanted to sit and pray for a while."

The pastor checked his watch. "Well, I can't stay, and the church will be unattended. I'll tell you what we'll do. I know who you are. You're Lt. Elliot Gates. You signed the pad here about three years ago. I had hoped you would come back sooner than this, but delayed isn't avoided entirely. Go on in. The large candle is lit on the altar. With the power outage, I wasn't sure I should leave it burning, but it's a perpetual candle, so it should last. Just pray away to your heart's content." He paused a moment in consideration of what he had just said. "That's odd. I never thought about that before. Praying is supposed to give your heart contentment, isn't it? Well, I hope it does. This door will lock when you leave, so have a good communion with God, and Merry Christmas." His hands were once again laden with his two packages. "Can't shake hands, sorry. Oh, and the restroom is to the right, just beyond that corner. You'll see the door." He slipped once on the step, but then walked carefully to his car, parked in the church's driveway. After putting the packages in the backseat, he then got behind the wheel and drove away, not so much as glancing at the figure of Elliot standing in the church's doorway.

Elliot went inside. It was a new church, and it was dark everywhere within. The only light was the small light coming from the big candle on the altar. He went forward and sat in the second row. His heart was pounding. It's one thing to come to church for a service, but this was different. He looked up at the vaulted ceiling, the beautiful stained-glass windows. He had seen them all before, but at night and alone, they seemed so different. Spaces seemed infinitely vaster in the dark.

Elliot began to sort out his thoughts, but nothing would get right. Finally, he stood up and almost ran to the altar, throwing himself down on the steps in front of it. His prayer began without thought or plan. He prayed for his mother, whose heart he knew was failing. He prayed for Sharon, having no idea what might be wrong with her. He prayed for Nathan. As he did so, he suddenly had an image of Nathan being badly injured. Elliot's legs hurt again. He even prayed for himself, hoping that his relationship with Karen would last and blossom as he wanted it to.

Elliot had no idea how long he prayed, but he came to his senses once again as he realized that he was now kneeling at the altar, his head resting on the edge of it. He was in total darkness. The large candle was out. As he looked up, however, the devotional candles on and around the altar all lighted, not by a match or by a lighter but by some unseen force.

Elliot was just taking all of that in, when a hand touched him on the shoulder. It was a bearded man who was dressed in the vestments that pastors wear for service. He was dressed for a high service too. "That was quite a prayer, young man. You prayed for quite a while. It was a bit disjointed, but then God doesn't care about that. He's heard far worse."

The pastor proceeded to go behind the altar. Facing Elliot now, the pastor gently said, "You know, that Merlot in your pocket could serve a much greater purpose. These soda crackers I found in the pastor's study should suffice for our purposes tonight. We could have communion. I don't mean the formal remembrance of a typical church service. No, I mean communion in the deepest sense."

Elliot handed the pastor the small bottle of Merlot. The pastor took the bottle and opened it. As he did so, five goblets appeared. They were small goblets, but they were much larger than the typical communion cups churches use. He poured the Merlot into each of them, finishing the bottle off in his own. He then placed the crackers around at either end of the altar and in front of Elliot and himself.

"Reverend, there are only two of us. Why did you pour five glasses?"

To Elliot's surprise, his mother appeared at the left end of the altar. Her face looked gray and drawn. On the right end, both Nathan and Sharon appeared. Sharon looked tired, and Nathan looked almost worse than their mother. Elliot's concern was great, but his attention was drawn back to the pastor.

"Communion with God is more than just a retelling of a story of the Last Supper. It is about sacrifice. It is about glory in all its proper ways. It is about victory over death." The pastor held out his hands. "The master said it before me. This is my body, broken for you. Eat and remember what the breaking of that body did for you and your souls." They all ate the crackers. "Before you, in this goblet, is my blood, spilled onto the hard ground beneath my cross. Drink in remembrance of me." Again, they all partook of the communion together.

"I am the resurrection and the life. This communion rejoins your hearts and minds and souls to the world and to God."

Elliot looked around at his family. He was filled with a desire to go to each of them and to embrace them. Instead, with tears in his eyes, he looked up at the pastor. "Reverend, we all have ills that are physical, emotional, and maybe even psychological. Could you, as benediction to this communion, please give us each a healing blessing?"

The pastor smiled. He went first to Margaret Gates, placing his hand on her. He stood there for several minutes, saying nothing but being intent on his blessing. Then he proceeded to Nathan and Sharon. Placing one hand on each of them, the pastor closed his eyes and fervently prayed in silence.

Elliot was satisfied with that. The pastor was not finished with his blessings. He came to Elliot and placed his hands on the lieutenant's shoulders. Elliot did not hear the words, but he felt warmth invade his body, like a light that sought out the darkest corners of his soul and illuminated them. Elliot began to sob uncontrollably.

Just as suddenly as they had appeared, Elliot's family all vanished. The pastor was now standing behind the altar, facing Elliot once again. Elliot thanked him for the prayers, the communion, and the blessing. The pastor's face became quite serious.

"Lt. Elliot Jacob Gates, we are now to the difficult part of the night. You see, I am the angel of death. I have been instructed to choose one soul and take it to heaven. That soul is supposed to be someone from your family. You are to decide which family member that is. Let me tell you the physical condition of your family. Your mother has a very weak heart. In the emergency room, she had a massive heart attack. The heart was damaged and cannot continue to sustain life much longer. Sharon Gates did not know she was expecting, but just last night she gave birth to a sweet little boy. Clarence Elliot Gates is doing fine—his nickname will be CG. Sharon has, however, a growth around her spine that is the size of an orange. It has caused her much pain. Radiation treatment may help, but nothing is certain. Your brother was hit with debris from a wall that was blown toward him by the explosion of a land mine. You know your own maladies. So who do I take?"

Elliot had never been put in such a bind. For some reason, the motto "No man left behind" came to mind. It started his brain racing. His mother wouldn't live much longer, no matter what he said. But she had never seen or held her new grandson. She didn't know that Elliot wanted children now more than ever. Nathan hadn't held little CG either. He didn't even know he existed. Sharon didn't apparently know she was pregnant. Elliot felt that he was just beginning to live, to understand what life could really offer—a great deal beyond the frivolous and useless life he had been leading outside the air force regimental ways.

Elliot felt the stare from the pastor. Then as if a wave of angels had swirled around him, he looked up at the pastor. "You have told me what is wrong with my family. For that I am grateful. I'm sure you know more ills than that, though I sense they are vanishing now just as surely as my family did from this communion table. You say you are the angel of death. Yet only a moment ago you gave a healing blessing to each of us. Before that, you said you were the resurrection and the life. You cannot be both death and life. God does not work that way. The true resurrection and life never took lives. He changed them as you have changed the lives of my family tonight. Therefore, I choose the fifth person at this communion table, you, to be who I know you are. Let my family, all of us, live and prosper." Elliot was not in a challenging stance, but he made clear what his choice was.

The stern look of the pastor gradually changed into a smile. "Amen. So shall it be. You have chosen wisely, Lieutenant. I wish you a very Merry Christmas." The final words were not spoken loudly, but they seemed to echo around the church.

Elliot was alone. The candles went out and, to his surprise, the church lights did not come up again. Daylight was streaming through the beautiful church windows. It was a new church, and the images were symbolic of faith. One showed an open Bible. On the two exposed pages were two words, one for each page: Jesus Lives.

The door of the church opened. "Good heavens, Lt. Gates, are you still here? You've been here over twelve hours. It's 8:30 a.m., and if you haven't finished Christmas shopping, you don't have much time left to do so."

Elliot rose up from his kneeling position, using the altar as a support. He felt as if his knees would never unbend. Inwardly, he felt lighter and happier than he had in months. "Thank you, Pastor, for allowing me to stay here. As to gifts, I think I have given and been given more gifts than you can ever imagine."

Elliot went outside, turning his steps back to his apartment. He thought that, if the lights were on in the church, he might be able to get past the electric latch for the front door. Within a block, he ran into Karen. They walked toward his apartment together. "Karen, are you up for a little adventure? I still want to go to Indianapolis. I found out last night that both Sharon, my brother's wife, and my mother are ill. I think Nathan is injured too."

"How long will we be gone?"

"I have to call the base. I have the weekend, but I can't really have it next weekend. I can, however, get an extension for a family emergency." They were at the apartment.

Within twenty minutes, the base had been called, Elliot had packed a few clothes, and they headed off to Karen's house. She also packed a few things to take with her. They were on the highway within ten more minutes. When they came to the first rest area, Elliot pulled over to a corner of the parking lot and turned the engine off.

Karen turned to Elliot. "What's wrong? Are you having second thoughts about the trip?"

Elliot smiled. "Nope. I'm not having second thoughts about anything. I have something to give you for Christmas, and I want to give it to you right now. Close your eyes." She did so and Elliot reached into his pocket, bringing out the little red box. He took her hand and placed the box in it. "You can open them now. I'd get out and kneel down, but it's pretty messy to do that, particularly in a uniform."

Karen was in tears. "I was hoping, but you have hinted before that—"

"I wasn't always the smartest brick in the block. Now I want you to open my laptop and call up my e-mail. I need to reply to Nathan's commander right away." She had good signal, and she took the dictation from Elliot carefully.

Colonel Franklin,

I am sorry to have taken so long to return this e-mail to you. The weather here has been bad. You would, I'm sure, prefer my problems to those you have. We had an ice storm last night. The trees looked gorgeous, covered with ice and ready to break. Some of them *did* break under the weight of the frozen ice. Today I'm driving through snow- and ice-covered countryside, but the road is clear. It is white, but the ground isn't covered yet. We are supposed to get more snow tomorrow. I may get to build a snowman in the yard where I built my first one. That will be a thrill.

I cannot tell you how I know, but I am aware Nathan was badly injured yesterday. You may have taken X-rays to ascertain his condition. Please humor me and take new ones today. Something happened last night that I can't tell you about now. But it may have affected Nathan's condition. I will e-mail you again from Indianapolis. I am going there now to check on the condition of Nathan's mother—of my mother—she's had a heart attack, and his wife apparently has a small growth around her spine. That is pretty hefty news for you to tell Nathan. Something happy you can let him know is that he is a new Papa. Clarence Elliot Gates was born early yesterday. Apparently, he is quite healthy. When Nathan is brought stateside, I'd appreciate it if he could be brought to Scott Air Force Base hospital. It is well recognized as a medical facility, and I need him to be near to me.

His mother and wife and children will be able to get there much more easily than in some place like Walter Reid Hospital. As you know, having family around improves recovery drastically. Please tell Nathan also that I really do care about his rehabilitation as much as I care about my own. He'll understand.

**Sincerely,
Lt. Elliot Gates**

Elliot was satisfied with the wording, and Karen sent the message off. Elliot pulled out. "Now I have to tell you something that happened last night. You won't believe much of it. Come to think of it, I shouldn't either, but it seriously happened."

As he drove toward Indianapolis up various highways, he told Karen the fantastic tale of the night before. As he finished the tale, he drove into Methodist Hospital in Indianapolis; he hadn't even thought of going home first.

The receptionist was quite helpful. The two ladies of the Gates family were in adjoining rooms on the third floor. Elliot and Karen started to the elevator, but a voice called out to them. "Elliot?"

Elliot turned around. "Yes?"

"I don't know if you remember me. My name is Mrs. Clarissa Dougherty. I'm Sharon's mother. This is Cathy. I'll take you up to the rooms. I'm just getting here today. It is all just so much trouble. CG is in fine shape, however, and you'll be happy to see him. You are?" Clarissa Dougherty was looking at Karen.

Elliot spoke up quickly. "I'm so sorry. It's my concern over mother, Sharon, and Nathan. I'll have to tell you about that on the way up to the room. This is Karen Ackerbee, but don't get used to calling her that because she will soon be Karen Gates." They were up to the floor.

Mrs. Dougherty took them to the maternity ward to see CG. He was awake and kicking. "They'll take him in to Sharon in a little while.

Maybe you'll even get to hold him. Do you want to start by visiting your mother?"

Elliot nodded, and they started down a corridor, pure white and chaste as most such corridors are. Elliot remembered now why he hated hospitals. They had no personality. Near the end of the hall, in the cardiac wing, there stood three doctors. Their gesturing was overt and quite excited. Elliot was curious what could be wrong. The expressions on their faces showed surprise and elation, so maybe it was something good. Clarissa Dougherty walked directly up to the doctors. "I see you are all talking hurriedly. Is something wrong, Dr. Mitchum?"

Dr. Mitchum looked askance at Elliot. "May I ask who you are?"

"I'm Elliot Gates, Margaret Gates's older son and brother-in-law to Sharon Gates."

Dr. Mitchum smiled. "You've come home at last. Well, Dr. Bertrand?"

Dr. Bertrand looked down at the charts in his hands. "Elliot, is it? You will be happy and I hope surprised to know that your mother is doing amazingly well. Her EKG last evening was awful—I was surprised she was alive—and today it is normal, totally normal. Sharon Gates had a tumor the size of a grapefruit on her spine. We did radiation yesterday. Today, we can't find it in the X-ray or MRI. I just don't get it."

Elliot put his hand on Dr. Bertrand's shoulder. "You had help from a greater doctor than this hospital has ever hired. By the way, my brother is injured in Baghdad. As soon as I talk to the women Gates, I'll send a report to his commander. Would you say they are in guarded condition?"

Dr. Mitchum spoke up strongly. "Hell, no! I'd say they were in tip-top shape. They are about as healthy as they could be. They'll go home tomorrow, unless you upset them too much."

"I will have to give them news, but not until I get an update." Elliot opened the door to his mother's room and walked in with Karen right behind him.

Margaret Gates looked up and smiled. "Elliot, I knew you'd be here today."

Elliot put his arm around Karen. "Mother, this is Karen. As of this morning, we are officially engaged."

Margaret's smile broadened. "I am so pleased. You are a major addition to our family, Karen, and I promise to be a caring and interfering mother-in-law so you can enjoy a traditional marriage. Oh, Elliot, I'm feeling so much better. Do you think last night did that?"

Elliot was surprised. "Then it actually did happen. I wasn't dreaming it."

"Of course you weren't just dreaming it. I was there and received God's blessing. It tickles me to think we have the doctors here scratching their heads about my recovery. They don't want to let me go home yet, but I hope they will tomorrow. I may not last too many more years, but I'm fine for now. How is Nathan?" The mother's concern came to the fore immediately.

Elliot shrugged. "I haven't heard back yet from Baghdad. Let's hope I do before I go home. Is the key still under the troll in the flower bed?"

The medical assistant stood at attention. "I don't understand it either, sir, but if you come with me, you can look at the X-rays yourself."

Col. Franklin stood. "I'll do just that. I saw the original X-rays and, if what you say is true, the only thing I can say is that it is a miracle."

They started to the offices of the camp hospital. "Sir, if I may ask, why did you ask for the new X-rays?"

"Sgt. Gates's brother sent an e-mail and requested that I humor him and have the new X-rays taken. I don't know what's going on, but somehow he knew things might have changed. Oh, before I forget, Merry Christmas."

"Thank you, sir." They were in the office. The assistant took the X-rays and held them up to the light, holding the older ones up next to the new ones. Sure enough, the legs and hip bones that had been splintered and broken in the first X-rays were now only slightly cracked, only his left tibia being broken.

Col. Franklin stared at the images. "That's impossible! How can that be?"

"I don't know, sir, but you can ask Sgt. Gates yourself. He's awake."

Col. Franklin made his way to the hospital ward where Nathan Gates was lying. His color, so frighteningly gray only twelve hours before, was now looking almost normal, only a remnant of the pain he had felt lingering in his face and eyes. "Merry Christmas, Sgt. Gates. I finally have news for you. It was late coming because of an ice storm where your brother lives. He says that he is personally checking on your mother and wife. He did say, however, that you are a new father of a boy. His name is Clarence Elliot Gates, but you are to call him CG. Elliot sounds to me like he actually cares about you over here."

Nathan smiled up at the colonel. "Yes, he does. I can't tell you how I know that, but I do. Let's just say that his caring brought about a chain of events last night that I may not understand, but I believe in it totally. It's why those new X-rays are so different from the first. I'll just consider it his Christmas present to me—and for about the last ten years."

That Christmas was a joyous one. The Gates women came home on Christmas Day. Sharon went to her home with CG, her mother being more than thrilled at being the overseer and helper in her daughter's house. Margaret had Elliot and Karen to stew over her.

Nathan was moved two days later, first to a German hospital and then to Scott Air Force Base. He was wondering at first why he was sent there, but on the first day there he found out why. Elliot strode into his room with digital pictures of CG, Margaret, and Sharon. He was all smiles. "See what a little prayer can do?"

Nathan's face changed from the broad smile to one more serious. "Just how did you do that—on the twenty-third I mean?"

Elliot put the pictures on the table at the side of Nathan's bed. "I don't know, Nathan. I think it was a matter of a lost sheep returning to the fold and telling the shepherd that he was glad to be there. I don't ask questions too frequently when great things happen like they did that night." Elliot paused. "Nathan, I promise that I positively will be a better brother to you. Mom and Sharon will come soon. Now I'm not supposed to stay longer than five minutes, and my time is up. You get rest, brother, and do what the doctors say. It's important."

Nathan's recovery went much quicker than expected. He was given a medical discharge due to lingering problems that could not heal entirely. He went to work at the lumberyard that his friend owned. He could man the check out and earn a good living without major physical strain.

Karen and Elliot finally got married the following May. Nathan was able to stand to deliver a toast to his brother. As the reception meal continued, a waiter came up to Elliot at the table. "With your dinner, sir, would you prefer the Zinfandel or the Merlot?"

"Which do you think is best?"

The waiter's voice took on the smooth, resonant sound Elliot knew at once. "I'd say you should try the Merlot."

Elliot looked up into the familiar eyes of the pastor. "I should indeed. Thank you." His tone of voice told the pastor turned waiter that Elliot did not mean just for the wine that evening.

TALE 5

25 Percent Off: Just in Time for Christmas

Grenner's Department Store boasted that it had been family owned and operated in the same location since 1892. Such longevity in the retail business was not unusual in such a small city, but the idea that a store could remain in the same location was almost unheard of. It was beautifully located in the downtown district of 1892, but by the 1930s the main area of the downtown had moved three blocks farther east. By 1950, the entire area was ignored in favor of a section of town two blocks to the south. Twenty years later, the advent of shopping centers and malls had meant that the downtown merchants had to scurry around to make changes to pull people back to the central part of the city. As the year 2000 came in, the downtown—the entire street and that of two blocks away, plus several stores in between—had regained their momentum and people could park in garages nearby and shop to their heart's content, reveling in the atmosphere of the older part of the city and enjoying more secure parking as well.

This had meant some renovations for Johannes Albert Grenner. He had taken the reins of the company in 1978 (when he was merely twenty-five) upon the death of his father. For a long time, he was the leader in the movement to keep the downtown together and ahead of the mall contingent. It wasn't that he enjoyed such competitive actions. The truth was that he felt it was improper for such demeaning warfare. He reluctantly realized that he needed business to stay open, and he was gifted at the kind of publicity that would push his store to the fore.

Now in 2003, he was fifty and tired of the constant demand for pulling people back to the downtown area. He had toyed several times with moving out to Beaker Mall or to the Athenaeum Center (an enclosed mall that was even larger). But he hated both locations and did not want to move besides. There was something about "always in the same location" that tugged at his sense of honor. He just wasn't sure how much longer he could hold out.

Johannes Grenner knew the changing fortunes of older areas of town, and he did not want to consider that the downtown might ever become run down in that way. Yet he knew some specialty stores—Miracle Christian Music, Anderson's Sports Shop, and Tony's Guitars—were all having trouble, and several empty stores nearby were being turned into restaurants. They might help business a little but probably not. Such restaurants in other parts of the town had experienced great openings but had closed within eighteen months.

For all of that, "Joey" Grenner was not a person who liked to go out for special decorations for given holidays. It wasn't that he totally ignored Easter, Thanksgiving, and Christmas (or the national holidays). He even gave a nod to Chanukah, Kwanzaa, and a few others. At no time, however, did he want to go all out to decorate his store properly. His father's major concession was the installation of escalators, for which the public came back to the store. Joey was always getting them repaired; he had even had them replaced once and another replacement was looming.

It was Christmas 2003, and Joey Grenner had decided not to put up most of the decorations that normally went up in his department store. He felt that the presence of the artificial trees and the decorations in the windows of his store were going to be enough. Various areas, like jewelry, could have garlands and such carefully secured to the showcases or columns, but for the most part, he wanted to let the *merchandise* show everyone it was the Christmas season. "More than that detracts from the merchandise itself."

Some of the clerks agreed with him, but most of them felt it was a move to show that he didn't care about Christmas. That sentiment had been considered for the last two years anyway, and now, in 2003, it was clear. Joey Grenner had become a skinflint, unwilling to put out a small amount of money to harvest greater sales.

(For those wondering how Johannes became Joey, it dated back to his mother and sister and his childhood. The family was German, as the name might indicate. Johannes's mother, Gertrude, liked to call him Johanny, a sort of reference to the American Johnny. His sister, Annette, couldn't seem to get that right and it came out something like Joey. It was a nice alternative that avoided direct reference to his German ancestry, so it stuck.)

The date of our story can be pinpointed exactly for it all takes place one rather snowy night. It was December 15, and the traffic downtown was tremendous. People were flocking to the downtown because they had all agreed to a special rate. Exactly ten days before Christmas, the merchants agreed to lower all the prices by 25 percent. This, by consent of all of them, would only exclude those items that were not Christmas-type gifts, though who can predict what someone will give as a gift?

Joey Grenner had his salesclerks put up signs all over the store as to what was reduced. The signs were clear, they were big, they were red and white, but nothing about them indicated anything about it being a seasonal sale. He was just locking the doors for the night when a comely, middle-aged woman stepped into the store. "I'm sorry, miss, but the store is closed. Most of our sales people are already heading out the back door." Joey Grenner tried to be nice but firm.

The woman took off her scarf. "I know. That's unfortunate, of course, but I could not arrive sooner. My name is Angela Visitant. I live in Paradise, Maine, and I was told you had some things in stock I desperately need."

Joey Grenner was insistent. "I am glad we do, but you'll have to come back tomorrow. We really are closed."

Angela Visitant turned to Joey Grenner. "No, I don't think so. I have too many other places to go to come back. You will serve me now, or I shall abandon you for a store that is open and willing to sell me what I want. Considering your current sales for the season, and considering the amount I'm willing to spend, I don't think you want to do that."

Johannes Grenner put on his most proper manner. "Well, then, if you don't mind that I lock the door, I am sure I could wait on your needs." Ms. Visitant nodded and Johannes Grenner locked the door. "I won't set the alarm until you leave." He tried his best to be properly genteel and pleasant, but it was difficult. He really wanted to go home to a Scotch on the rocks.

Angela Visitant did not make things easy either. She began looking at winter coats. She was seriously looking through the racks, trying hard to find either a certain color or size. Grenner had no idea which, but, to facilitate her looking, he turned on the lights above the coats. She draped the coat over her shoulder and looked at herself in the mirror. She decided it was not right. As she hung it back on the hanger, she glanced up. She paused a long time, the hook of the hanger almost (but not entirely) on the rack. Finally, she finished putting the coat back and turned to Grenner. "Mr. Grenner, I am really quite surprised. I was told that you had some of the prettiest decorations in the city. My friend used to brag every Christmas about the moving figures that always graced your department store windows. But I don't see them here. In fact, I don't see many decorations at all. Where are they? Where are the garlands of red and green tinsel between the pillars of the store? You don't seem to bow to Christmas in any way except for stocking artificial trees. Even your stock of Christmas lights is terribly limited. How do you expect to attract people down here with no decorations?" She wasn't passionately arguing with Grenner, but she was quite dismissive of his paltry efforts at display.

"I feel," Johannes Grenner began, "that the true spirit is within. And besides, shouldn't it reflect more of the true spirit of Christmas as found in the gospels?"

Angela looked at him over the wire-rimmed glasses she had just put on so she could better examine the jewelry. "That, if you'll pardon my saying so, is a royal cop-out. Your Tinseltown has only the cheapest and ugliest Nativity sets. Besides that, the tinsel and bright lights are supposed to be reminiscent of the star and the gleaming brightness of that night years ago, when the baby Jesus was born." She put the necklace she had been absently studying back on the little necklace tree. "Frankly, Mr. Grenner, it just looks like you were being cheap, and that you were too lazy to put out the effort. That is such a pity. I'm afraid I'll have to go elsewhere. Nothing here puts me in the mood." She reached into her purse and pulled out a pair of red gloves. "I'll be going. I think D'Angelo's will serve my needs better." With that, she pushed the bar on the front door and went out, not returning so much as a thank-you or a "Merry Christmas."

Joey was stunned. He was also miffed. After staying open an extra forty minutes for that woman alone, and that because she had insisted, she had deserted him, not having purchased so much as a stocking.

He checked on the locked door. Then he reached for his coat, hat, and scarf. As he snatched them up, a small barrel of peppermint candy fell off of a countertop and rolled across the floor. It scattered candy everywhere. "Damn. That's just what I needed. Oh, well, I'll pick it up in the morning." He slipped out the back door, setting the alarm and locking the door as he did so.

His car was cold—it had been in the lot since 8:00 a.m.—and it fought Joey's effort to get the thing started. Finally after a growl or two, it turned over. As he was backing out, Grenner noticed a light on in the store. "I forgot to turn off that light over the coats. That's what it looks like. I'll take care of that in the morning too." He was quickly out onto the street and away.

The store was not quite as secure as it looked. Next to the coat rack was a small door that could be opened for deliveries. For that reason, it was not at all hooked up to the alarm system. Nor was it locked. It had been, but Angela Visitant had seen to it that the lock had been thrown. She stood across the street in the shadow of the recessed entryway to

Tony's Guitars. It was closed, but she made as if she was looking intently at a Fender Bass and a Martin acoustic guitar.

Once she was certain that Grenner was gone, she walked briskly across the street and slipped unobserved into the store. She locked the door behind her. She looked around and then went to the jewelry department. There sat one of the few decorations that went beyond a few basic garlands. It was a four-foot statue of an angel or fairy (she was unsure which it was) with wings and a wand. Angela took the wand. She glanced up and down the store and then flicked the wand carefully.

Grenner would have fainted had he been there. Out of the wand came a ray of light. This small ray suddenly flared out and into a brightly glowing halo around the tip, with glittering sparks flying from it too. This she waved at a manikin of a woman. The manikin was arrayed in a bright party suit of red and white. She immediately sprang rather stiffly to life. "Thanks, Angela. That's your name, isn't it?"

Angela nodded and smiled. "Angela Visitant, that's right. You might have thought Johannes Grenner would have caught on, but he didn't. How are you, Barbara?"

The manikin flexed her fingers. "I'm fine, thank you. Oh, I am a little depressed, but I guess that happens."

Angela indicated the store with her wand. "Yes, when there are no decorations anywhere, I'd say that happens a lot. Do you think you could help me?"

Barbara bowed her head slightly—well, manikins can't do much better than that, now can they? She indicated two other manikins. "Charlie and Louise would be good help too. I don't think Philip cares one way or the other."

Angela waved her wand, and Charlie and Louise came to life too. After a moment's consideration, she waved the wand at Philip, who came rather brightly to life. "Let's all gather around. This store needs considerably more decorations. Do any of you know where the decorations are kept?"

Charlie blinked his shiny blue eyes three times. "If I remember right, I saw them in the storeroom beside Mr. Grenner's office."

Angela waved her wand, and the lights all came up in a soft glow. "And where are the moving manikins, the ones that used to be in the window?"

Louise answered quickly. "There was a display delivered last month, but Joey Grenner just didn't want to bother putting it up. It's sitting just outside his office on the second floor." The troop all traipsed up the escalator and found the things that were needed. In the process, eight more manikins were brought to life.

Angela began directing the operations. They started on the top floor, which was woefully neglected. They had gone through about half of the Christmas supplies, and then they decided to display some merchandise more favorably. The Sale signs were now sporting holly leaves or wreaths. Once Angela felt the upper floor was good enough, they all traipsed down to the first floor again.

Beatrice, a lingerie manikin, put on a red silk bathrobe and went down the escalator. Bob followed a little too closely, but she put him in his place. "Keep your hands to yourself, Bob." Then eyeing the downstairs, "Oh, this is awful. I haven't been down here in six years. You'd think Mr. Grenner could afford a coat of paint at least."

Angela looked around and nodded. "You are so right, Beatrice. Stand here in the center everyone." She opened eight gallons of a soft, peachy yellow paint. This went whirling through the store, avoiding all decorations—there weren't many—covering the rather gray walls, white paint going to the pillars. Once that was done, Bob took the cans to the back of the store, while the others hung the tinsel, set up the better Nativity sets, and changed the windows to include the new and intricately animated manikins.

Angela bent down at last to pick up the peppermints Mr. Grenner had spilled. She put them all back into the barrel. Then she shook up the barrel and reached into it. She drew out peppermints again, but this time they were several times larger. She began tossing them to the various manikins, who attached them with a little magic to any surface that seemed right. The peppermints kept coming, almost as if Angela could pull them from the little barrel all night. The store was becoming more Christmas-y, and the manikins were really getting into decorating. When Angela called a halt, she placed the barrel on the counter.

To no one's surprise, the first rays of morning were just peeping in through the front window when the last glass ball was hung up beside the waving manikin woman in the window. Angela inspected everything carefully. "Good, I think that settles it. The store at last has taken on the festive look it deserves. Everyone! Return to your stations. In thirty seconds, I will send out a spell, and you had better be in the right places." She was as good as her word. In forty-five seconds—allowing for the stiff legs having trouble negotiating the escalator—she flicked the wand. Everyone became a manikin again.

She was just putting the wand back into the angel's hand, when a quiet voice whispered, "Thanks again, Angela." It was Barbara, who winked one last time and went rigid, still holding one silver glass ball securely in her hand.

Angela was faced with a small dilemma. She needed to lock the door again after she left. How was she to do this? The answer came. Cedric, a manikin who had exchanged a yellow hunting jacket for a green shirt and a red flannel jacket in honor of the season, stood five feet away from the door. Angela looked at him. "Now, Cedric, this is how to lock the door. I'm going to bring you back to life for one minute. In that time, you should just be able to secure the door and lock it after I leave. Agreed?"

Cedric winked an eye. Angela took the wand again and touched him, almost immediately slipping out the door. Cedric locked it after her, but, rather than returning immediately to his assigned position, he ran over to Barbara and gave her a kiss. "I have wanted to kiss you ever since I was uncrated two years ago." He turned to go back to his place, but the time was up. Instead, his arm got caught around Barbara, making it seem as if the two were walking together.

Twenty minutes later, Johannes Grenner drove into his usual spot. Today's sale began at 8:00 a.m. His clerks—at least half of them—were waiting there for him. He got out of his car, looking somewhat disgruntled.

The sun was brightly shining over the stores across the street. Had Johannes Grenner been able to see, he would have noticed Angela Visitant pulling out of the lot in her 1988 Chevrolet. But the brightness of the sun made it impossible for anyone to see. The cold made Joey Grenner fumble with his keys, trying to get the back door open. He flicked the alarm off.

Even when they were all inside, their eyes took quite a while to adjust to the darker interior. Joey Grenner and his clerks hung up their coats and started their way to their positions. The clerks could tell in the darkness of the store that quite a crowd was standing at the front door. They had not expected this, of course, and they kept looking that way to see if they were seeing correctly. It was as if they were all blind to everything around them, for not one person, not even Johannes Grenner, noticed the differences in the store. Only Nancy Christian thought she noticed a smell of paint. Paul Richardson passed this off as being silly, because all he smelled was peppermint. The time for the lights to come on had arrived, and Joey Grenner made his way to the switches. Only then did he see the two manikins standing side by side. He took a little extra notice of them. "Strange. I am sure they were not that way last night."

He threw the switch for the lights. The response from the clerks was to cheer loudly. This made Grenner turn around. "What on earth is wrong with you? We haven't let the customers . . ." He got no further. He saw the totally decorated store. The animated figures in the window had attracted a large amount of attention.

There was no time to think about it. He had to get the doors open. The effect of the decorations on the sales that day was incredible. The season had been rather slow, but this day made up for all of the downturn. It was a madhouse.

People kept complimenting Johannes Grenner and his staff on the decorations and particularly the animated window displays. One window had a woman handing packages from a bag to her husband, who was dressed like Santa Claus. He would put them down by a Christmas tree, and they would circulate again into the bag. The faces of two children were peeping around the doorway at the back, bobbing up and down in sheer delight.

The other window was a similar scene, but it was a large Nativity scene, with presents being given by shepherds and kings, all of which would circulate again.

It was about closing time—5:56 p.m. to be exact—that Angela Visitant came into the store. She acted as if she was quite surprised at the changes Mr. Grenner had done. He thanked her profusely, but he made no effort to tell her of the miracle that had happened. Several customers were waiting to check out at six, so there was no effort to shut the doors early.

Johannes Grenner noticed Angela proceeding in his direction. As the last person began to leave, he called out to the rest of his staff. "Thank you for a wonderful day. Open again tomorrow at the regular hour."

Angela stood directly in front of Mr. Grenner. "I wish to talk with you a moment, if I may."

Grenner shook his head. "Ms. Visitant, you wasted a lot of my time yesterday and did not buy anything. Why should I consider your request today?"

"Maybe you should listen to me because you profited a lot by my work last night. You see, I am fully aware that it was not *you* who wrought such a miracle in the decorations of this store. I mean, what with the beautiful garlands, peppermints, window displays, finely showcased seasonal specials, and even a new paint job, I should think you would be wondering just who had done this. You know *you* didn't!"

The clerks, instead of leaving the store, were all curiously gathering around Johannes Grenner. They wondered what the woman was talking about. "Well, I did not have time to consider the decorations. I certainly, during the day, appreciated them. As to how such work was accomplished in such a brief time, I confess I don't know. I am, of course, grateful, but I am not sure that I actually care how the work was done."

Angela Visitant sat on a chair in the shoe department. "No, you don't care. As long as you had no cash outlay and no energy outlay, it doesn't concern you. It does concern me! I am responsible for the improvements. You were not going to give witness to the miracles of the season, and it was important that someone do so. I am that someone."

Joey Grenner laughed. "And how could you possibly have done it? It would take an army of people to do this much work. Who do you think helped you, the dummies?"

"They prefer the term 'manikins,' I think." Angela smiled sweetly. She withdrew from her purse—which was rather sizable—the wand she had used the night before. "You see, they were all quite upset that you had done nothing before. Barbara and Bea and Bob and . . . well, all of them helped. Yet a few minutes ago, you were quite willing to take credit for the decorations yourself." Angela Visitant sat quietly and waited for a reply from Joey Grenner.

He looked around, and then he finally began to speak. "Ms. Visitant, this has been a very busy day . . ." He broke off. The various workers were all curious at how their boss would handle things. He also noticed that around them had gathered **the manikins!** "Just what the hell is going on here, Ms. Visitant?"

Angela Visitant stood slowly. As she did so, there was a bright light shining all around her. "Johannes Grenner, you have profited from the birth of the son of man. It is true, of course, that other merchants have seen sales jump this year. I have never seen anyone so willing to forget what this season is truly all about. It could be said all humanity profited from his birth. Yet you dare to stand there and to call these hard workers, all of whom, human or manikin, worked with the spirit of the Christmas season today, dummies. I can assure you that they are **not** dummies. Even those with man-made hands and faces have more heart for this season than you do. What to do with you, then, Mr. Grenner? Do we simply assume that you'll understand eventually? Your father and grandfather worked very hard during the Christmas season. They did not do so for the money. They did so because the spirit of the season demanded it. In the last ten years, you have done less and less for the spirit of Christmas. It has visited you every year, and you have ignored it. Well, now the spirit of the season shall ignore you. You need not worry, for you will be up in the attic, stored carelessly away. Someday, perhaps, you will realize how unfeeling you were. It is now too late for you, Mr. Grenner."

Angela Visitant waved the wand, and Johannes Grenner became a lifeless manikin, dressed rather shabbily in unseasonable clothing. Cedric and Barbara, however, did not return to being manikins. They became humans. "All of you here, clerks and staff, what you have seen is rather sad. Let it be a warning to you all. Cedric, you are now Joey Grenner. The rest of you will never remember that there was another person named Mr. Grenner. Only once in a while will you realize what has happened here. Now if you'll excuse me, I think I'll go on home. Cedric, er, Joey, you and Barbara will find clothing to fit you both at the Grenner residence. May you enjoy the season as much living as you did in your former existence."

It may seem strange that no one questioned Angela Visitant's actions, or that the change in bosses went so smoothly. Some miracles just work well all the way around. The Grenner Department Store went on for several years and was finally bought out by a larger chain. Barbara and "Joey" were quite the loving couple. Other merchants in the area never noticed the change in Joey Grenner's age or appearance either.

In case you wondered if Johannes was ever released from his imprisonment as a manikin, I can only say the story is inconclusive. Some years later, people began to say that the building was haunted. Strange sounds were heard by people forced to stay late. Eventually, when refurbishment of the building was mandatory, the attic was cleaned out, and Johannes, the older-looking manikin, was taken to the dump. "Joey" (or Cedric) went there hurriedly when he heard that they had taken the attic stuff there. He found some things that needed to be salvaged, but it took him a long time to find Johannes. The manikin had not changed.

Nearby, Cedric found the little angel and her wand. He thought it was sweet, but the angel was so discolored by the rains that day that Cedric didn't bother to rescue it. Almost as a lark, he waved the wand at Johannes and asked, "Have you learned your lesson well? Then return from living hell. Preach the joy of Christmastide to nations small and vast and wide." He laughed at his doggerel and threw down the wand.

Had he not turned at that moment, he might have noticed a jet of light streak out of the wand. No one knew if those rays hit Johannes or not, but the next morning neither wand nor Johannes were to be found.

It should be added that, one month later, in Southern Indiana, an itinerant preacher held a rally, and those who heard him said that he spoke with an intensity of spirit that they had never heard before. Only one comment was leveled against him. "I reckon he walked kind of stiff." Manikins do, you know.

TALE 6
The Spirit of Love

There was no one in the barnyard at 7:00 that December night, but at 7:04, two men stood silently in the shadows under the grape arbor. The dwindling light of the moon didn't penetrate through the tangle of vines. One of the men looked to be possibly twenty-one years old, while the other seemed more veteran—possibly in his late forties. It was the latter who spoke first.

"You are positive this is the house, Bryan?"

"I ought to know it, don't ya think? I grew up here." He pointed to a fence post that was leaning at quite an angle. "I did that when I was trying to put the brake on in my car and hit the accelerator instead."

The friends progressed quickly to the shadows under the living room window of the house. "And that woman is your sister?"

Bryan nodded. "Gretchen and Glenn married four years after I . . . after I left here."

"I thought it was the other house you needed to visit the most."

"I need to visit both houses. Gretchen has never forgiven me for leaving. I have to explain what happened." Bryan was standing on tiptoes, watching Gretchen and Glenn finish decorating the tree. "I'd love to know what they're saying."

"That can be arranged." Wolfgang, as the other man was named, waved his hand slightly. The sound of the voices inside the living room became instantly clear. "Don't worry. They can't hear or see you."

In the living room, Glenn reached down and picked up a long garland of tinsel. "I still like using this stuff, even if 'modern' places don't sell it much."

"You've also said that you prefer the larger bulbs to the twinkling ones. All of them have their place, you know." Gretchen took a beautifully decorated, golden glass ball and put it up higher on the tree.

"I know. I'm happy to have Jim over on Christmas afternoon, but why are you having the Dawsons?"

"Glenn! Why do you think I'm having them? If things had gone differently, Penny and Christopher would be proper family. Besides, Christopher needs our attention. It is something Jasper certainly doesn't give him."

"Then why is Jasper coming, too? The only thing he gives attention to is his bottle and his women." Glenn paused a moment. "Oh, yeah, and he likes being cruel to poor Christopher. His jokes make me embarrassed, and they are totally inappropriate around Christopher."

"Well, Christopher has a few demons to get rid of too. I feel so sorry for the boy. He has had a hard way of it." Gretchen stood back next to Glenn. "Is that enough on the tree?"

"Good heavens, Greta, if we put more on it, it'll droop over like Charlie Brown's tree." He started putting boxes back into the decorations box. "I'll try to do what I can to get Christopher away from Jasper. We still have the hoop on the barn."

Wolfgang motioned again, and the sounds died out. He pulled Bryan back to the place where they had originally observed the couple. "Does that tell you anything?"

Bryan nodded solemnly. "It's just what I thought. I have a way of stopping Jasper in his tracks."

Wolfgang held his hand on Bryan's shoulder. "I know what you're thinking. You're going to have to be careful what you say and how. It may be okay and normal for you to come back here after nineteen years, but some of the others won't take kindly to it. They also might find your excuse for not coming around to be a little hard to swallow."

"It's the truth. That's all that counts. They will have to accept it."

Wolfgang shook his head. "Some things, Bryan, are more difficult to accept than others. I'd say this is going to be a hard sell. I'm staying nearby at all times tomorrow. You're going to need my help. No, don't shake your head that you won't. I know you will. I'll see you right here in the morning. Are you sure you're okay?"

Bryan smiled. "I'm fine."

"Well, see ya then. Remember, you only have tomorrow to get through to them. After that, we leave, and you can't come back." Wolfgang left Bryan standing where he was.

Bryan watched for several hours, first leaning against the cherry tree and then sitting on the old picnic table. He watched as the lights downstairs went out and the lights upstairs went on. Gretchen closed the blinds to their bedroom and then turned off the lights as she and Glenn went to bed.

Bryan had a lot to think about. He had to plan how to talk with Gretchen first. Then he had to decide how to talk with Penny, Christopher, and Jasper Dawson. He couldn't help but think about the times he had spent with Penny. They had been joyful times, times filled with spontaneous good conversation and laughter. He remembered the one night they spent together too. That led to his dread of talking with Jasper. He hoped Wolfgang would be true to his word and be nearby when that happened. "I learned from the last time I spoke with him how futile it is to plan how conversations will go."

He slipped into the shed next to him. It was out of the wind, and he could think more comfortably without the fear of a snake coming along, or a raccoon, or a skunk. It was almost too cold for any of those. "Almost isn't good enough for me though."

Bryan Bannion didn't even notice when the sun came up. He was roused from his reverie by the sound of gravel scuffing along as Glenn pulled out of the drive. It was 8:30 a.m. Bryan squared his shoulders and stepped out of the shed. He looked across the drive at the front door of the house. "I might as well get started."

His knock on the door was almost timid, and Gretchen, when she answered the door, shook her head. "You look like you could do a better knock than that. I can't give you any handouts, if that's what you're wanting. The Methodist Church is open early today if you need money."

Bryan put up his hand. "I'm not here for that. I was just looking around the farm. I used to live here."

Gretchen looked at Bryan with a skeptical look that said she thought Bryan was both delusional and presumptuous. "I can assure you that you never lived in this house, young man, because it has been owned by someone in the Bannion family for 150 years."

"I know." Bryan knew he was at the first hurdle of the day. "My name is Bryan Bannion, and I used to live here." Gretchen looked at first shocked and then angry. "And you, Gretchen Marie Bannion George, are my sister."

Gretchen stood perfectly still for at least four minutes. Finally, she whispered violently, "If you are my brother, why did you leave us nineteen years ago? Were you so afraid of becoming a father that you couldn't face things like a man?"

Bryan closed his eyes, an action that stopped Gretchen momentarily from accusing him further. "I was not afraid of being a father, Gretchen. I wanted to be. I wanted a boy or girl. I loved Penny with the entire depth of my heart."

Gretchen lashed out. "The fact is, however, that you left her pregnant and our family with nothing to look forward to but heartache. Father died of it one year later, and Mother died three years after that. Where in blazes did you go?"

Bryan sat on the porch step. "In a very real sense, I didn't go anywhere. That is reality. The last time I saw you, I told you I was going to visit Danny and Ian. I wanted to show them my new car. Then, I said, I would visit Penny. I wanted to ask her to marry me. I wanted to make things right. Dad said I should, but I knew it anyway."

Gretchen shook her head. "Danny and Ian said you got there, but Penny never saw you."

Bryan nodded. "She was at the church, finishing the decorations for Christmas Eve. You know me, Greta, and you know that I would not have just gone away from you or the Dawsons."

Gretchen sat next to her brother. "Are you really my brother, Bryan?"

Bryan smiled, "I said I was. You asked where I went. I went to the Dawson house. Jasper met me." Bryan paused a long time. Finally he stood up, took two steps down the walk, and turned around to face Gretchen. He pulled up his sweatshirt. In the middle of his chest were two bullet holes. "Gretchen, this afternoon, Jasper Dawson will be forced to quit lying. He shot me that morning, hiding me and my car at the back of his property." Bryan expected some sort of horrible outburst.

Instead Gretchen rose up, supporting herself on the newel post of the railing. "That would explain why he's always been so cantankerous toward everyone. Bryan, if he shot you dead, then how is it you're standing here?"

Bryan shrugged. "I have been given a single day to come back. I'm supposed to try to make things right. As you said to Glenn last night, Christopher is in a lot of trouble. So are you and Penny. I don't care about Jasper." Bryan sat back down. "Could you tell me what, in your knowledge, is Christopher's problem?"

Gretchen made no show of emotion. She said nothing vindictively. Her voice simply ticked off the facts as she considered them. "He smokes, he does drugs, he is a great basketball player despite that, and he needs a father really badly to fix all of the above. Jasper Dawson ain't the one to rely on. You know him. He is physically cruel and shows no interest in being understanding. On quiet summer days, I've heard him ranting and raving clear over here. It's no wonder Christopher is in trouble."

Bryan nodded. "I think I'm going to have to play Christopher a game of one-on-one and straighten him out."

Gretchen looked up. "How long can you stay?"

Bryan's gentle smile slipped into a sad frown. "I only have this afternoon. Then I have to go back." As he said it, he looked across the drive. Wolfgang was standing there. "Can you see Wolfgang there?"

Gretchen looked up. "Yeah, I see him."

"He's my guide." Bryan gave Gretchen a hug. It was something both of them had wanted for nineteen years. "I have missed you, Gretchen, more than you can ever know." She nodded and watched Bryan and Wolfgang go down the lane. As they turned and went out of sight, she sighed, tears welling into her eyes. "You have no idea how much I have missed you too, Bry."

Wolfgang and Bryan stepped from the end of the Bannion-George drive to the end of the Dawson drive. They stood there a minute. Wolfgang put his hand on Bryan's shoulder. "You hoped to get these three separately, but I'm afraid you get them all at once."

"Lucky me!" Bryan made a strange semi-laugh and started up the drive. The ruts and tree roots hadn't changed much in the nineteen years he had been absent. The two of them were at the top of the drive—where it leveled off to become the parking area and basketball "court"—when they heard the strident voice of Jasper Dawson, railing against Christopher mostly, but swinging barbs at Penny too.

Wolfgang looked at Bryan. "I won't be far away. I've alerted the police about the car in the shed. I need to work something out in my head, so I'll leave you to your—uh—delights with the Dawsons. I'll only be on the other side of the garage."

As he walked quickly away, Christopher came striding out of the house, followed closely by Jasper Dawson. Penny came helplessly out the door seconds later, unwilling and unable to find a way of stepping into the fray. Christopher stopped when he saw Bryan standing there. Jasper was unseeing and uncaring, ranting away as if his voice and his alone could be able to say anything of importance. "I've done told you that you are not to smoke in the house. I've also told you that them drugs have got to go. D'you want the entire police force comin' here to arrest you. Uppers, downers, and God only knows what else you've been using. Why, you ain't nothin' but a . . ." Jasper finally saw Bryan standing there. He stared at Bryan for a long time. Finally he spat on the ground and said, "What the hell do you want? You're trespassing on my property."

Bryan smiled. Jasper didn't catch the superior nature and irony of the smile, but Christopher did. "I've been here before, Mr. Dawson. I am not here to beg money from you, or, for that matter, to do anything bad to you." Bryan put his finger up slightly, as if to interrupt himself. "Although there is one good reason I needed to talk with you. It is probably best if I talk with you first, because what I say to you will help make things clearer to Penny and Christopher when I talk with them."

"Yeah? Well, you ain't talkin' to them. I'm the head of this household, and I say you're getting off this property now, or I'll call the police."

Bryan looked over to Christopher. "What's this all about, Christopher? Why is he yelling at you?"

Christopher looked defiantly at Bryan. "I kind of tend to do bad things. I like to smoke pot. I've tried a little acid."

"That doesn't help you play basketball."

Jasper wanted control of the conversation back in his court. "I said to get off of my land. What part of that don't you understand?"

Bryan squared off on Jasper Dawson. "I don't pay much attention to people who live their lives based on a lie. Jasper Dawson, you've been living a lie for almost nineteen years now. Don't you think you should fess up?"

Jasper looked hard at Bryan. The look he gave him showed that Jasper was wondering just how much this stranger really knew. "You! You don't know nothing about nothing."

"Then call the police. Wait, I think I hear their sirens already on the way."

The sirens were probably still two miles off, but they were audible, and Jasper reacted violently to them. "Well, good! 'Cause you're gonna get arrested for trespassing on my property."

Bryan laughed lightly, noting as he did so that Wolfgang was coming around the end of the garage. "You can't do anything to me, Jasper

Dawson. What would you do to me? Do you want to shoot me? That'd be kind of hard, since I'm already dead."

Bryan lifted his shirt. The bullet wounds were red and bloody. Christopher took a step back in fright. Penny, however, took several steps toward Bryan and Jasper. Jasper, for his part, stared at the wounds. "Who the hell *are* you?"

"I'm your worst enemy come back to life. For these two people, I'm the lifeline that you tried to stop. My name is Bryan Bannion, and I'm back to do many things today. One of the things I have to do is make you realize that you are not going to live behind this lie anymore."

Christopher was standing beside his mother. "Are you my father? Are you the Bryan who ran out on her?" He ran forward and hit Bryan with a stick several times. Bryan finally caught the stick and wrenched it from Christopher's hand.

"I just told you, Christopher, that I didn't run out on your mother. Your grandfather killed me instead."

Christopher was trying to take it all in. Penny just slumped to the ground. Wolfgang caught Jasper's hand and put it behind his back. It forced Jasper to drop a knife he was drawing. Police came up the drive at that time. Three cars, seven officers, and quite a lot of turmoil followed for the next few minutes. Three men were dispatched to the shed.

While all of that was going on, Bryan motioned for Christopher to help his mother up from the ground. "Let's go around to the front hill of the house."

There were steps from the porch down to the first slope of the hill. The three of them sat on those steps. Bryan took a deep sigh. "Christopher, had I had my own wishes I would never have gone away from you or your mother. I loved her too much. I was absolutely overwhelmed at the thought that I could be a father. I came over here to ask your mother to marry me, but your grandpa intervened. He shot me in the driveway there, and then put me and the car in that shed. You're around on this side of the house so you don't have to look at that. It isn't a pretty sight."

Penny said quietly. "How is it you can come to us today? If you're dead, isn't that pretty odd?"

Bryan's energy suddenly left him. He looked down the hill, finally mustering the ability to answer. "I was allowed to come because there were three people who needed me, who needed to know what happened, and who might not survive if I didn't come." He looked down, hardly daring to say what he had to say. "I'm not given much time either. I have to go back in just a little while. I talked with Gretchen, and now I'm talking with you two."

Christopher let his young man's face look into his father's eyes. Before he could stop it, the teenager's eyes started filling with tears. "But, Dad, I need you! A few minutes aren't enough. I've missed you for eighteen years, and Mom has missed you for nearly nineteen years. I want you in a package under the tree. I want you here forever."

Bryan's eyes filled with tears too. "I was once told that 'Angels don't cry,' but I'm filled with as many desires for this family as the few minutes could put together." Finally Bryan stood up, wiping his nose on his white shirt. "Christopher, come here."

"No! You're just going to give me some lecture and then go away forever."

Bryan let his voice rise up. "Christopher, I don't have much time to argue with you. Please come here at once."

To Bryan's surprise, Christopher ran at his father, fists flailing and hurt spewing forth from every part of his being. Bryan let him have his fit. He wasn't surprised when, only moments later, Christopher stepped back. He had said nothing except for calling his father a few names. Bryan understood that. Christopher stood for a moment barely a foot from his father, but then he fell forward into his arms, sobbing into Bryan's chest.

What happened next is difficult to explain. Neither Christopher nor Bryan would have been able to say what was happening. The explanation Wolfgang eventually gave to God was that the embrace was like two computers downloading files so quickly that neither of them could explain what was happening. Bryan's every ounce of love and affection for his son, the whole of the wisdom he tried to have, and the terrible ache he felt in having to leave again transferred to Christopher.

Christopher's "files" were simpler. They were the desires of a boy for his father.

Penny came and joined the hug. It went on for several minutes. Nothing was said, and yet a lot was accomplished that words could not have told. They were just breaking from the embrace when Wolfgang came around the house.

"The police are taking the car, the body, and Jasper away. The sergeant wants to talk with you a minute." Bryan went to talk with the sergeant.

Christopher stood quietly, drained of anything but his need for his father. Wolfgang smiled at the boy and his mother. "I am sorry about these rules."

Penny spoke gently. "Are you Bryan's guide here?"

Wolfgang sort of shrugged. "I wouldn't call it being a guide as much as being a timekeeper. I make sure he gets done what he needs to, and I'm trying to keep him on his time schedule. I don't have many options in those tasks."

Christopher looked at Wolfgang with a wretched look of despair. "Do you think, sir, that a hug that's only a few minutes long is enough to make up for eighteen years of no hug, no words of encouragement, and no support in the things I do?" Christopher shook his head in disbelief. Suddenly, he looked up again, brightly smiling. "Does my father have enough time for a game of one-on-one? Can I sing him a song I have to sing tonight?"

Wolfgang looked at the sun. It was getting lower in the sky. "It's about 3:30 p.m. A short game of one-on-one is okay. The song is okay too." He smiled, hoping neither of them went on too long.

The police pulled away, Jasper's face scowling out of the rear door. Christopher came bounding out of the house and threw a ball to his father. "Here, Dad, let's play ball."

The father and son played a joyous game. It was as if neither of them wanted to think beyond the shot they were taking. Neither of them wanted to consider what would happen when they reached 21. When the game ended, they held each other like old friends . . . or like a father and son should.

Christopher beamed. "Now I have a surprise for you. I wrote this song for tonight's Christmas Eve service. You can't come, and I have to practice it. So let me sing it for you."

Bryan looked with worry at Wolfgang, but Wolf just smiled. "I'm sure your father will enjoy it."

Bryan and Penny sat together on the porch swing. Wolfgang sat on the porch railing. Christopher sat forward in the porch chair and put the guitar in front of him. He strummed a couple of chords. Then he plaintively started strumming some different chords, chord progressions that cut directly into the heart even before the words began.

> **Everybody always said that I should be a good boy.**
> **If I wasn't, Santa Claus would never bring me a toy.**
> **Eventually I understood what they meant,**
> **They were never clear, but I knew what they meant.**
> **And it was just my search to find a way to enjoy . . .**
> **The Christmas lights that shine on the tree,**
> **The Christmas lights that shine down on me,**
> **They are always trying,**
> **But I think they're lying.**
> **Those Christmas lights are nothing to me.**
> **They're s'posed to be a sign of great joy.**
> **They're signs of joy the angels employ.**
> **No matter how they're trying,**
> **There's no use my denying**
> **Those Christmas lights are nothing to me.**
> **What joy will come my way?**
> **How can God show the way?**
> **I've prayed to Him every day,**
> **But my words are not the best,**

At least that's what I guess,
Because God won't say yes
To what I say.
The Christmas lights that shine on the tree,
The Christmas lights that shine down on me,
They are always trying,
But I think they're lying.
Those Christmas lights are nothing to me.
God has never heard a single little word.
Why are lights so bright, when nothing here is right?
They're s'posed to be a sign of great joy.
They're signs of joy the angels employ.
No matter how they're trying,
There's no use my denying
Those Christmas lights are nothing to me.
God, I pray just one more time.
Answer me please this one last time.
Fill me with the light of love,
The light that comes from you above.
Peace on earth goodwill to men . . .
Yes, that too will please me when
I pray just one more time.
I pray this one last time.

Christopher's voice faltered. It had been strong and expressive the entire song, but just before he could finish the text, his voice gave out. He lowered his head, afraid to speak or even to think what should be said next.

Bryan stood up wearily. It was as if his feet were incapable of holding him up. He pulled Penny to her feet and kissed her on the lips and then on her cheek. Then he leaned down to Christopher and gently pushed the hair out of his eyes, giving him a kiss on his forehead. Without a word, he turned and stepped down to the walkway. Wolf dropped down on the outside of the railing. Bryan tried to look back to wave, but his whole being was crying out to find a way for reason and love to prevail.

Neither Bryan nor Wolfgang said a thing as they walked out to the drive and then down it. The long slope was gentle, and the house was still in view. Bryan couldn't muster the resolve to look back. His entire body, temporary as it was, could not let him take in that last look that Penny and Christopher were giving. He knew they were craning to see him go.

Wolfgang looked back once. As he did so, he saw Christopher fall to his knees, almost wildly looking up to the heavens. It was as if the message of his song was coming true. He was praying one last time, pleading with God for a positive answer just this once. It was a personal, private prayer, but it was as if Christopher knew it was something he needed. It was the last chance Christopher might ever have. His despair was so complete that his prayer could support no words. Only his heart could speak, and that had no words. Without thinking, he let his voice soar up, hitting a phrase of music that seemed to pull his very heart up with it.

> **Peace on earth goodwill to men . . .**
> **Yes, that too will please me when**
> **I pray just one more time. I pray just one more time.**
> **I pray this *one last* time.**

Wolfgang and Bryan were at the end of the lane. Wolf spoke solemnly to his friend. "I have a problem, and I need you to solve it."

Bryan hardly heard Wolf. Finally, he looked over at him. "Solve it yourself."

Wolf shook his head. "Well, you know God always proposes solutions to things in threes. It is his religious number speaking. I have already eliminated the first of the possibilities. I can see the road across this highway, and you can't. That road will lead me back to God. You aren't coming with me. The other two propositions are the ones I need help with. Do you explain to everyone else that you are your college roommate? Or do you tell everyone that you were in a hospital for nineteen years with amnesia? You see the problem with the last one? The police have your body. I mean, in any case, Gretchen, Penny, and Christopher will know the truth."

Bryan was looking at Wolf with a strange look, certain that the "guide" was crazy, except that angels can't be crazy. "How about I offer a fourth alternative? My college roommate—which I never had, by the way—came to visit nineteen years ago. I met him in town. Jasper fired at me but hit *him*. He was an orphan, so no one ever looked for him. I was so traumatized by it all that I ended up in a hospital. I only came out of my amnesia last month. I got here as quickly as I could."

Wolfgang tilted his head both ways. "I'd say that is the best. It will satisfy most of the people. Merry Christmas and happy birthday! As I said, only the few people need to know the truth. Don't tell the sergeant. He said he was a friend of yours."

"He'll figure it out quicker than most anyway. I can trust him. He'll see that I couldn't help my roommate because I was too busy saving myself. Besides, I was shot. See the wounds?"

He lifted his shirt again, but the bullet holes were gone. He looked up to exclaim something about it to Wolfgang, but he too was gone. Bryan looked at his shirt. It was no longer white, but blue. His light gray pants were now blue jeans. He knew what this meant. He turned around to look at the house.

Penny had slid down in dejection to the top step. Christopher was just trying to get up. It was the teenager who saw his father coming back up the hill. "Dad? **Dad?** ***Dad!***" He had quickly leaned his guitar against the porch and was almost flying down the hill and across the lawn to his father. They embraced. "Does this mean that you're going to stay after all?"

Bryan laughed. "Yes, it does. And I only hope Wolfgang put some clothes into the closet upstairs, or I'm going to be at the Christmas Eve service dressed very badly."

God looked up quickly from his desk. "What made you think you had that prerogative? You were supposed to bring him back with you. This is terrible. What kind of precedence does it make?"

Wolfgang bit his lip. "Sir, three years ago, when I brought that dock worker back, you told me I had the prerogatives to exercise there. You said I always had some leeway in what I had to do. I was the one on the spot and seeing everything. So when I heard what I heard and saw what I saw, I knew that it would be better to bend the rules on one than to lose both father and son. The son was that desperate."

God stood up slowly. "You don't have to tell me about the boy. Prayer receiving was so jammed with his emotional outburst that it took five minutes to get the systems running properly again." God paused at the door. "Wolfgang, I wish you had asked first, but I think you did the right thing. I just hope you have an idea how to clear up all the loose ends."

Later that night, Wolfgang woke up in a cold sweat. He was replaying the list in his head of everything and everyone who needed to have their minds altered. It was frightening how complex such a change of order could be.

The Christmas Eve service went very well. Naturally, people were astounded to see Bryan Bannion back in church. It took all the efforts he had to keep from correcting the preacher on some of his pronunciations and pronouncements. Bryan, after all, had met some of the people involved in the Christmas story. And he positively knew Gabriel, although they were hardly on a first-name basis.

Curiously, when they all awoke the next day the confusions of the day before seemed to be straightened out. Bryan could not remember some things he was sure he should, and they faded quickly as he became more and more embroiled in the business of living. He went with Penny and Christopher to visit the Bannion Christmas dinner. To say that Glenn was astounded was an understatement.

Bryan talked with Dan, Ian, and Sergeant Shrader. Dan and Ian were told the new story and accepted it just fine. As Bryan had said he might, Sergeant Shrader could see the truth shining through. It was Bryan's turn to be surprised. Shrader was once standing at the front door of heaven. He was sent back. He understood, and he kept silent when it came to prosecuting Jasper Dawson. The ballistics on the gun showed that Jasper had killed others before moving to his farm.

To this day, Christopher still writes songs.

TALE 7
Escape Button

Never assume that things are as they have to be. In this age of computers, that is simply not always the case. Take Topher Devlan for an example. He had hired on at Alphacorp when he was twenty-one. He was fresh out of business college, having graduated with honors. His typing ability was considerable, speed and accuracy being of equally astonishing quality. His understanding of business was quite high. He hit Alphacorp just when they went heavily into computers. At first, the new technology had baffled him. He did not like it. But he grew to like it, and that was the important thing.

When Topher had hired on, Harold "Harry" Henderson was the head of the company. He was a very good man, understanding the difficulties various employees had learning the new work methods. He had been an ideal boss. But that was fifteen years ago. He had died of a heart attack after Topher's tenth year, and since then the new head of the company was a terrible woman.

Banner Hilliard was a hard-driven woman, who drove her workers with equal fierceness. She had climbed the corporate ladder quickly with a ruthlessness that she didn't even try to disguise. In a sense, she was right. Her abilities were good and needed to be recognized. Her attitude toward her fellow employees, however, was that none of them were equal to her talent, and they deserved to be treated as underlings. Banner had always said, only half-jokingly, that her motto was to "raise the Banner high."

Such people don't realize the animosity these attitudes engender, and, truth to tell, many would not care even if they *did* realize it. Banner pushed her employees hard, and the result was higher productivity. Another result was quicker burnout. Danny Fortescue had quit "for health reasons"—he had come very close to a massive stroke—and he had taken on a much lighter work load elsewhere. Topher had always considered Danny a close friend and felt rather alone without him. Topher knew that Danny had done his best with no appreciation shown from on top. Banner Hilliard had considered Danny to be a weak link.

With Danny gone, Banner lit into both Janice Peters and Topher. There was no reason for this. They had both upped their output considerably, and both were bright and articulate workers. They were still not up to the fantasy level expected by Banner Hilliard.

Janice lasted under the renewed scrutiny only three months. Then one day Banner Hilliard lit into Janice extremely viciously. Janice held her tears back and spoke back to Banner with amazingly strong and verbal acuity. After she had had her say, she left the office terribly upset and nervous. In the elevator going down to the parking garage, she said to Topher (who had heard the confrontation from a distance), "I may get fired for that, but I'm not going to be walked over by that . . . that ***person.***" There were other words she wanted to say, but other employees were nearby, and she was afraid of being overheard. She got in her car and sped off for home. She crashed her car two miles later and died instantly.

The mood in the office was far worse after that. Everyone considered the wreck and death to be a direct result of Banner Hilliard's cruel assault on Janice. Everyone began to slow down. Everyone went into "meticulous" mode—which meant that they did everything with a thoroughness that was so extreme it took twice as long.

Topher did not go into this mode, however, because he knew that he was in Banner's sights already and could never slip under the radar. Oddly, he actually felt he was turning out more work than any of his colleagues. Still Banner eyed only ***his*** work.

The first Wednesday in December had been a hectic day. The office was to be closed the following day due to a flood that had occurred a week earlier. The flood had gone into the elevator shafts, and repairs were necessary in two of them. Thursday would mean a major repair, and that meant the building would have to be shut down. Even though Banner Hilliard had argued hard, the fire marshal would not allow people in the building when the elevators would not be functioning.

That morning, Hilliard had informed the staff that they would be required to remain in the building until 8:30 p.m. just to make up for the lost time on Thursday. "Expect a long day on Friday too."

Topher had to call the young lady with whom he was to have dinner and tell her that he could not come. It was not a pleasant conversation, because she had a festive dinner planned, and now it was going down the drain. Topher said he could come over on Thursday, but that didn't go over well. A friend was giving a Christmas party, and Julie was expected to make an appearance.

He had just hung up, when the looming figure of Banner Hilliard came up to his desk. "Was that a personal call, Mr. Devlan?"

Topher looked up at Banner. His first thought was to say something challenging, but instead he simply said, "Yes. I had a dinner date for this evening, and, since we need to stay late tonight, I had to call to let her know that I'm not coming. She wasn't happy about it either. I am afraid I may have just lost a very close friend."

"Really? I'm so sorry." Banner's cold and unfeeling voice said how "sorry" she was. "Perhaps you should realize that such calls are forbidden here in Alphacorp. If I hear of you making another such call, you'll be out." She started to walk away.

"Excuse me, Ms. Hilliard, but we are supposed to stay at our work stations until a given time. After that, we're supposed to be able to make plans of some sort. My goal in life goes a little beyond sitting at my computer and sleeping in my bed alone. I am not complaining about staying late tonight. I realize the difficulty this shutdown causes in this busy time of year. But my friend does not look at her computer on an hourly basis, and I had to let her know the only way I could. When I put the Ulster Report on your desk, I couldn't help notice that you were discussing your dinner plans for this evening. You were not canceling them either. I'm not complaining about working when you don't, so I have to insist that you not complain about my loyalty to the company when, without complaining, I take time to cancel plans that I have made."

The glare Topher gave Banner Hilliard was unyielding. She just looked at him a moment. Then as she turned to go, she slipped in, "I stand by what I said."

Topher answered, ever so slightly louder and with more point, "So do I."

The office became much quieter by 6:00 p.m. Half of the staff had gone home—their work ostensibly finished. Topher's cubicle was in the corner, and, although he could hear a few continued comments and sounds of work continuing, he felt isolated and abandoned. He began the final compilation of facts for three different accounts, all of them major contracts requiring considerable rewording. The contracts, as they stood, gave the company no loopholes with which to terminate contracts that went bad. They gave the contracting companies far too many openings for abuse of power. Topher knew the lawyers for those companies would see the loopholes clearly. He knew how to fix these, but it would take time and care.

He finished the first account and laid the contract to one side. Topher had just opened the Tremaine account (a minor account but one of considerable complexity), when he became aware of someone watching him. He looked around and was surprised to find a woman standing to his right. It was his girlfriend. "Julie! What are you doing here?"

"I brought you supper. The guard didn't want to let me in, but I convinced him I would only stay a few minutes." She handed him the lunch box. "It looks better to carry that than a brown bag, don't you think?" She stood up and prepared to leave. "By the way, I found the most curious Web site today. I was thinking about taking a vacation in early January, and I ran across a site called Escape.com which has all sorts of places a person could go. If you get a moment, take a peek at it. I'll see you Saturday morning?"

Topher was just opening the sesame chicken Julie had brought him. "Absolutely. I'm thinking maybe we should go to the museum on Thursday or Saturday, you can decide! Oh, pray that Banner Hilliard doesn't have other ideas to occupy my time. And thanks for supper."

Julie left and Topher went back to his account, eating with relish the broccoli, rice, and spicy chicken delight.

Julie went down the elevator. As the doors opened, she came face-to-face with Banner Hilliard, who looked her up and down. "And who the hell are you?"

Julie just smiled back. "I'm the young woman Topher Devlan was to see tonight. I brought him supper so he could continue working without delay for as long as it takes to finish his project. He has a really awful boss who extends hours at her whims. He may have to go to the bathroom, but at least he won't have to go away from his desk for any other reasons—no matter how important they might be."

"And just who let you in?" Banner was in her most high and mighty mode. "No one who is not associated with Alphacorp should be able to get in here."

"Well, I convinced the guard that I would only be a moment. In fact, you've had a much longer conversation with me than Topher did. Be sure to look out for Topher's boss. I hear she's a real ogre." She knew full well who she was talking to, so she turned and flounced out in her typically jaunty fashion, making sure she showed no sign of fear or respect for Banner Hilliard.

Ms. Hilliard went directly up to Topher's floor and charged up to his desk. Upon her arrival, Topher looked up, surprised and actually pleased. "Well, Ms. Hilliard, I'm surprised to see you here. Did you forget something? Or are you checking up on us before your dinner date?" Topher's manner was tinged with great respect, even if his words gave slight reason to feel the irony he tried to conceal.

Banner Hilliard began to reply, but Topher handed her two files. She stopped in midsentence and took the files. "What are these?"

Topher took a bite of sesame chicken and turned back to Banner Hilliard. "Those are the first two accounts that needed rewording. I still have an hour or so to go on the Jackson Springs account. I'm so glad you came by, because I didn't want to leave those lying just anywhere, and your office is locked. Of course, you're probably going out again, but if you could put them on your desk, it would be helpful. That way I only have one locked in my desk over our day off."

"I wanted to tell you," Banner Hilliard began, "that my presence here is a courtesy. I thought it better to talk with you in person. I want you here tomorrow anyway. I don't give a damn what the fire marshal says. And you will be required to be here on Saturday too, from 9:00 a.m. to 5:00 p.m."

Topher did not even flinch. He had picked up his last piece of chicken with his chopstick. He held it about a foot from his mouth as he answered her. "Perhaps you don't care what the fire marshal says, but I do. Alphacorp could be fined severely if I am forced to come in. I would not want that. And Saturday is not a normal workday, and, since I did not complain about staying late today and do not complain about staying late on Friday, I most certainly will not be here on Saturday. Julie and I have an outing planned."

Banner Hilliard let her reply ooze out with feminine venom. "Julie. Is that her name? I just met her. I'd think you could do much better than . . . her." She took the files and started away.

Topher finished chewing his last bite of dinner. "Maybe I could, but not when I work as many hours as I do." He turned back to his computer. The rest of the floor had gone curiously quiet. "You do know, I suppose, Ms. Hilliard, that the entire company has been on work freeze since Janice's death. Everyone has participated but me." Topher had kept his voice light and nonchalant.

Hilliard didn't even turn. "Considering your output, I'd say you more than anyone else."

Topher was furious. He wanted to take the two chopsticks and jam them into Banner Hilliard's head. Instead he looked at the file lying beside him. He picked up the phone and called the security guard. "Stanley, could you let me know when Ms. Hilliard has left the building? Oh, and I will be staying rather later than everyone else tonight."

Stanley chuckled back into the telephone. "You already have, Mr. Devlan. You are the last one here. How late do you think you'll be?"

"I hope to leave by ten."

"Well, work hard if you must. Too bad there isn't an Escape button on life, isn't it? I don't mean a 'check-out permanently' button. That might be kind of bad.—*Good night, Ms. Hilliard.*—She just left. I mean a sort of vacationland." He chuckled again and hung up.

Topher began working on the account. The original wording was good. But any corporate lawyer could knock holes in it with no effort. He had to put it all right. "It would help a lot," he said to himself aloud, "if Banner Hilliard would let some of us do initial wording. We wouldn't have to undo her mistakes if we did."

"That would make too much sense." The voice was that of a child and frightened Topher considerably. He looked around and then realized that the voice had come from his computer. "Yes, if you haven't planned for a vacation, it's your own fault. Don't sit and mope about it. You have to take the initiative. Do you think your boss will do so? Silly you. She expects you to work without a vacation. For a preview of the kind of vacation that could be yours, just click on the link marked Escape.com."

It was the Web site that Julie had mentioned. Yet Topher could not remember ever typing in the Web site. He knew he must have, because there it was. A smiling young boy looked out from the screen, a pretty young girl standing beside him. The boy was certainly no more than fourteen and the girl probably only twelve. They seemed to be waiting for an answer.

Topher was unsure why he did it, but he reached for his computer's mouse and clicked on the Web site link. Suddenly he felt a jolt, as if something had hit him hard in the back. He felt like he was seeing stars, but when his mind cleared, he was standing on a cream-colored walkway, with colorful flowers planted on either side. The walkway led down a hill and into a small town, so Topher followed the road.

Once inside the town, he saw various children wandering around doing small chores, like trimming weeds around the flowers, watering the flowers, shaking out throw rugs, and even taking their dogs for a walk. Topher was amazed to find that there was not one visible sign of an adult anywhere. He paused a moment, and in so doing he nearly ran over the young boy and girl he had seen in his computer. "Hello. We wondered when you were going to show up!" The boy extended his hand. "My name is Lars and this is Jenny. She's my sister. I'm in charge here—at least for now. I only have a year left to stay here."

"Oh, why is that?" Topher asked him.

"Well, when you get *so* old you can't stay here. Of course, I'm trying to change that. I want adults to start coming here." He pointed to a sign that said:

Welcome to Kinder Town

"You may pronounce that like English or like German. In English, it means we're always nice here. In German, it means we're all children here. I'd say the German is more accurate." The boy was very matter-of-fact.

Topher looked around. "You said a moment ago that, if I wanted a sneak peek, I should click on the link. Could you show me around?"

Lars licked the green sucker in his hand. "Sure. This is the main street of town. The road going that way leads to Children's Palisades, and that way it goes into the dark forest. We try never to get very close to that. I have heard that some rather nasty children have taken to living in there."

Jenny had a big swirl of cotton candy. As she pulled off a hunk and wedged it into her mouth, she spoke, "If we wanted bad, we would have adults here. We're still deciding on whether to let *you* stay or not."

Topher laughed. "Oh, I can't stay long. I have work to do and have to get back. But I **would** like the preview you mentioned." He was enthusiastic.

Lars suddenly became very offhanded. "If you aren't thinking of staying, why should we take the time to show you around?"

Topher's temper flared just a little. "Because you said you would. Isn't that a good enough reason?"

Lars shrugged and started walking, Jenny at his side, and Topher bringing up the rear by several paces. Lars was a well-built young man, athletic and wiry, and he had a lot of spring in his step. Topher couldn't help but think that he too should still have that kind of spring in his step. Lars and Jenny took Topher all around the town, showing him the candy store, the grocery store (few vegetables allowed), the toy store, the mill (for which the wheel was painted like a giant peppermint) that ground sugarcane into powder, and even the school. The school was the only thing that looked like it was in considerable disrepair.

"What do you do to support yourselves?" Topher asked.

"We don't need to support ourselves," Jenny answered. "Everything here is free—as long as you're a kid."

Just then two boys came out of the candy shop arguing loudly with one another. They looked like nice boys, but their language was filthy even by Topher's adult standards. The argument erupted into a fight that entailed rolling around on the ground in the dirt and some pretty fierce fisticuffs. One boy, whom Topher heard called Jack, got a bloody nose. At that, he could take it no more and stepped forward to separate the two boys. Before he knew what had happened, all of the children turned on him.

Lars pulled him back. "You blew it, Mister Topher. We don't allow adults here for just that reason. We came here to escape that kind of rule. I'm afraid you'll have to go back to your office."

Topher looked at him, and the realization suddenly hit him. "I don't know how to go back. I touched the link to get here, but how do I go back?"

Jenny finished her cotton candy and put the tube in an overfilled trash can—it obviously had not been emptied in quite a long time. "You just push that '**RETURN**' button there. You must not be very good at computers."

Topher saw then, to his surprise, a group of buttons arrayed in a row beside the little park beside which he was standing. The buttons read,

ENTER OPTION TAB RETURN ESCAPE SHIFT

He reached slowly for the **RETURN** button. "What happens with each of these buttons?"

Lars shrugged. "Silly question! If you push **ENTER**, you become a kid again and stay here for a long time. If you push **OPTION**, you find alternative places to go, but they're all here in Kinder Town—or in the forest. You could push **TAB** I suppose, but that just moves you suddenly somewhere else. **RETURN** will take you back to your computer. I'm not sure what difference there is for the other two because no one has ever pushed them that I know of. **ESCAPE** probably gets you away from wherever you are quickly, and the last one? I don't know."

Jenny laughed, her tongue being a peculiar shade of orange thanks to her cotton candy. "There are lots of these buttons all around this land."

Topher stood a moment indecisively. "If I push this, can I come back for a longer visit sometime?"

Lars looked very seriously at Topher. "You can return here one more time for a visit. After that, if you return again, you'll be here forever."

"You make it sound kind of ominous." Topher tried to laugh.

Lars did not change his expression. "Don't know if it is or not. We haven't ever had anyone stay who was an adult. Some of us want to, but we're scared."

"And what happens if someone pushes that other button over there, the one that says **DELETE**?"

Jenny became almost comically mysterious. "No one has ever had the nerve to try it."

Topher reached out again and pushed the button marked **RETURN**. At once he felt himself fall back into his office chair. He was a little stunned. Quickly, he looked at his watch and realized that he had only a few minutes to finish his work. But as he studied it, he became aware that it was already reworded and printed out. Topher Devlan was very good at finding loopholes, but the contract had some of the best wording he had ever come up with. He printed up the new contract and saved it on his computer. Then he put the entire printed-out contract in an envelope and turned it in, slipping it into the slot in Banner Hilliard's door. He then put on his suit coat and outer topcoat. He also put on a stocking cap, but, like most men, Topher did not like to wear hats or caps.

He said "good night" to Stanley six minutes later and was home at 10:35 p.m. He was tired and went almost immediately to bed. All he could dream about was the curious Kinder Town.

The next morning, he told Julie all about it at breakfast. She thought it was a funny dream. "The odd thing is," she noticed, "that it is just reversed from most dream states."

"What do you mean," Topher asked. He hadn't thought to compare it to anything else.

"Well," Julie began, "first of all, you had no trouble returning. More important stories like **Alice in Wonderland** or **The Wizard of Oz** are all children going to adult worlds. You were an adult going to a world populated only by children. And coming home was easy."

Topher and Julie went into the museum. They viewed some great masterpieces, most of which Topher liked a lot and a few that he hated. It was not the abstract art per se that he hated. It was the bizarre and difficult art, geometric in span and consumed with pretentious "meaning" that he choked on. It was, as he liked to label it, "artsy fartsy." Julie loved his expression, because she too thought the art to be less than interesting. The museum curator was quite offended when they thought a particularly obnoxious piece of art was offensive. "That is by the sublime Dutch artist Dromian." He was most ostentatious himself. Julie and Topher shuddered at some "normal" art too.

The two left the museum and headed home. Topher left Julie off at her apartment, promising to see her sometime on Saturday.

When he got home, there was a message from Banner Hilliard, who sounded quite upset about something. He called the return number. She was furious that he had not come in on his forced day away. "I specifically told you to be there. I read your 'improved contract,' and it did not have a single change in it."

"I beg your pardon, Ms. Hilliard, it was totally reworded. I happen to have a copy of it right here with me. Just a moment." He went to his briefcase and pulled the copy of the file out of it. It was perfectly reworded just as he had printed it. "Where are you now?" He demanded into the phone.

"Unlike you, *I* am at work!"

"Good. I'll bring it over immediately."

He went to the office. It was four o'clock, but the day crews had finished, so going into the building was legal. He went up to his desk and pulled up the file on his computer. It too read cleanly in the improved language he had given. He called Banner Hilliard to his desk. She brought the offensive file with her. It too read correctly.

Topher looked down at it and then up at his boss. "I want you to tell me what is wrong with this contract. It is totally reworded from your inadequate attempt, and it has no loophole for the contracted company at all. We have the proper escape clauses."

His own words rang in his head. He didn't hear what Banner Hilliard said.

"*Escape clause*" kept rolling around in his brain.

"Well?" Ms. Hilliard was insistent about something.

"I'm sorry, Ms. Hilliard, what was it you asked?"

Banner Hilliard was irate about something. "I said that my wording was perfect and needed only a little tweaking. It did not need total revision."

Topher just smiled at her. "Oh, yes, it **did** need rewording. Now since it is clear that the only reason you brought me here was to prove a point about working when you say so, I'm going home. I may even come in tomorrow. But if you so much as hint about calling me on Saturday, I shall be quite unpleasant about it."

He stood up and was ready to march out of the office, despite the ranting of the apoplectic Banner Hilliard, but then he noted that his computer was only on SLEEP mode. He pushed the mouse and the screen came instantly to life. In a moment, he was on the Internet. "Ms. Hilliard, I found a wonderful Web site I think you should explore. Look here. Sit down here and click the mouse on this link. I accidentally did it last night and found that it was quite a beautiful preview."

Banner Hilliard sat down at the desk reluctantly. "I don't have time for this."

"Why not? It is only a little something about vacations. You take vacations, I know." Topher was friendly.

Banner Hilliard clicked on the link but nothing happened. She did it again. Again nothing. Topher bent over her and clicked again. This time he felt the familiar punch in the back of his body and he found that he was, once again, in Kinder Town. This time Banner Hilliard was right beside him. He wanted her to see the joys of the place. He wanted a better look himself too.

"Where the hell have we gone?" Banner was quite angry.

So was Lars who stepped up rather abruptly. "Hello, Topher. Welcome back. As for you—Ms. Hilliard, isn't it?—we do not use such language here." He glanced at Topher, who knew full well that the fighting boys had used language that was far worse. "We severely reprimand those who do. You didn't know, so no harm done. Welcome to our little town." He went into the pronunciation of the town's name, but it was clear Banner Hilliard was not interested.

"Just what is this place anyhow?" She was looking around with considerable scorn. Her expression told her opinion of Kinder Town all too obviously.

Lars was extremely patient. "We are having a Christmas celebration right now, so if you'll take a seat, I can assure you I will be able to give you the guided tour in about an hour."

"An hour! Mr. Whatever Your Name Is, I am afraid that an hour is quite out of the question. I am a busy woman." Topher had never seen Banner Hilliard puff herself up quite as much.

Lars came ominously close to her, his smile taking on a steely fixation. "You, madam, are interrupting our celebration. Sit on this rock and be silent! Maybe you'll benefit by being *less* busy for an hour to take in the Christmas story."

Topher had already taken his seat, so he was in an ideal place to notice the reaction his boss showed to the fifteen-year-old Lars's threat. She was indecisive at first, but then she sat, glaring occasionally back at Topher with a hatred that would have melted his desk had they been in the office. He pretended not to notice.

The children were of all ages, from two or three up to fifteen. Topher surmised from what Lars had said on his other visit that sixteen must be the cutoff. Lars would probably have to join the world of adults or else push the **ENTER** button. But then Topher came up with an idea. What if he came back a third time? He would have to stay in Kinder Town. That's what Lars said. Would Topher become a child? If so, how old were some of these children actually? And if not—if he would not become a child—what would become of him? There were no adults here.

The children were enacting a pageant. It was a complete reenactment of the Christmas story. The children were very imaginative, with flying apparatus for the angels, real sheep, and costumes that were surprisingly well made. Banner and Topher had arrived just at the beginning. The story began with a child enacting the role of Herod. Then the travelers came into Bethlehem for the taxation, the scene of the inn with no vacancy, the shepherds and angels, and even included the Three Wise Men or Magi. The final scene was the flight into Egypt juxtaposed with Herod demanding from his throne, "I want to have them here! They must bow to my will. I rule here, and no king or peasant couple can ignore the great Herod."

Those children who were not in the pageant applauded frantically as did Topher. Banner stood up almost at once, but it was not in support for the effort the children had expended. "Now, young man, if you will, how do I get back to my office?"

Lars put down his helmet—he had been a guard for the three kings. "I have to give you the tour first. I also have to tell you that you are allowed two visits here. Upon your third visit, it is assumed you want to stay, and you can't return to your normal life."

Topher asked. "Lars, if I return for a third visit, do I remain an adult or do I change to a child?"

Lars cocked his head in thought. "I am not sure. Some of these children may be adults who decided to return a third time, much as you may do. Do you, Ms. Hilliard, think you'd like to return a second or third time?"

"Why on earth would I want to come here again? You must be daft if you think I would ever want to see this hellhole again. I didn't want to come in the first place."

Several children were gathering around Lars and Banner. Topher carefully drew back toward the **RETURN** button. He wanted to get out of the way of the children, who looked as if they were particularly angry at Banner's attitude.

Lars began his assault. "Ms. Hilliard, this place was established as a place for children to go to escape from people like you. We are all children, and we rule as we see fit. We eat what we want, and we do what we want. There are no bullying adults around to tell us that we are doing wrong." Lars was emphatic, while Banner did not back down one iota.

"Well, you are, I can assure you of that." Banner Hilliard was not giving an inch.

A bright-eyed young girl of about nine took up the tirade. "I knew a woman like you once. She was my mother, and I was extremely happy to have escaped from her and to have found Kinder Town. We don't appreciate people with your kind of nasty attitude coming here and treating us as if we knew nothing. Children know things adults can never know or understand."

Banner started to reply, "You know nothing about business or—"

A frizzy-haired boy with an olive complexion stepped up and interrupted her midbreath. "We know what real love is and real joy. We know that God looks down on us and he smiles. Jesus loves us, yes, he does. We don't need the Bible to tell us so. We know because we feel his love on a daily basis. It is something we can't ever take for granted. Neither should you, miss, if you know what's good for you."

Topher was rather happy at the surprisingly adept way the children could say things. Their thoughts were deep and telling. They had an inner piece that he had not felt in years. It made him love all the decorations and delights that he saw in Kinder Town. It was during this momentary reverie that he forgot to notice where the children were backing Banner Hilliard. She was being pushed verbally toward the **DELETE** button. Somehow Topher could tell this was not a good thing. He called out for everyone to stop, but the voices of the children were rising in such cacophony that no one heard him. Banner was yelling back in her normally strident tone of voice, not listening to a thing the children tried to say. Topher finally took a deep breath and called out loudly. "*Hey! STOP IT!*" Everyone turned toward him. "You aren't listening to one another. Listen, all of you, and come here so I can be included."

In the next moment, catastrophe struck. Lars pushed his way through the crowd to Topher. "No! We won't listen to you or any other adult. Now sit down and shut up."

Topher shook his head. "You don't get it, Lars. I'm on your side. I really am."

"And I said to shut up!" He pushed Topher in such a manner that he tripped over a curb and landed on the **RETURN** button. As his body pushed the curved button, he saw some children pushing at Banner Hilliard, who tried to get away, but who also tripped and landed on the **DELETE** button.

Topher was jerked from the back toward a solid darkness, landing roughly into his office chair. As he left Kinder Town, however, he noticed a strange blackness suddenly cover the town. He was afraid that the famous **DELETE** button, the one that had never been used, might have wiped the town from the face of the Internet.

He quickly shoved his mouse so that whatever had been there before would reappear. He saw the link staring at him. He did not want to go back there again. He would have to stay if he did. But he wanted to know if it was all right. He connected on the link and got the following reply: **UNABLE TO DISPLAY AT THIS TIME.**

Now he was worried. He started to pace, but he got only a few steps when a flash occurred and sitting in his seat was Lars. On his lap, looking somewhat worse for wear, was Banner Hilliard. Lars shoved her off his lap and into Topher's arms. Topher put her down in a chair. She was passed out cold.

Lars was furious and in tears. "That . . . that woman . . . that woman has destroyed Kinder Town. I have to go back to find out if anyone survived. Now I guess we know what it meant by **DELETE**." He started to push the mouse around.

Topher put his hand on Lars's shoulder. "I just tried it and got the famous line about not connecting at this time. I don't know how you're supposed to get back."

Lars looked up at Topher, a look of panic in his eyes. This changed immediately to defiance. "*I have to get back. Jenny is my sister.*"

He looked at the screen a moment and hit the link again. Nothing happened. This time there was not even a sentence. He looked at Topher. "What can I do? I don't know computers that well. I need help. I can't stay here. *My sister needs me in Kinder Town.* **I have to get back there.**" Lars was breathlessly upset.

Topher pulled Lars up from the seat. He tried a lot of different approaches. Finally, he noticed that the link could be pulled up in the history of his applications file. He told Lars how to do that move. Then when Lars was ready, he said, "First hit the link, and then, if what I think will come up does, hit **RESTORE**."

Lars clicked the Web site into place and clicked on it. A message appeared almost at once: **THIS SITE WAS DISCONNECTED IMPROPERLY LAST TIME AND CERTAIN DATA MAY HAVE BEEN LOST. TO SECURE THE SITE, CLICK ON *RESTORE*.** This Lars did, hardly having the nerve to click on it at all. Just as suddenly as he had appeared, he vanished into the screen—at least Topher would have sworn that was where he went.

Topher had to hope that Kinder Town would be restored to its pristine shape and colors. But he was not hopeful. He looked over to Banner Hilliard, who was smudged with grime but looked to be okay. She was breathing at any rate. Topher tried to waken her. It took several attempts, but he finally got her to respond.

When she came to, Banner was somehow distant. It wasn't so much that she was groggy as a strange darkness in her eyes. It was not something mean or nasty. Topher could see that much. What it consisted of was not clear either. She sat up and looked at him a moment and then around at the office. She shook her head in bewilderment, unsure what she was feeling or had experienced. She finally stood rather wearily. "Topher Devlan, I am going home. Don't bother to show me to the car. I'll be fine. Uh, don't bother to come in on Saturday. I'll call the others to tell them. Thanks for helping me."

"What about tomorrow? We're supposed to come in on Friday."

"What? Oh, yes, I lost a day somehow. Yes, come in tomorrow. I will want to talk with you a little bit. I think I need to go home now and be thoughtful for a while." She smiled at Topher in a way he had never seen. It was genuine! It was wistful! Something had happened in Kinder Town whether she had wanted it to or not.

Topher had dinner with Julie that night—a little late, but it was better than not at all. He avoided mentioning his excursion to Kinder Town until they were enjoying the crème brulée. He wouldn't have mentioned it even then if Julie hadn't. "Did you try that Web site I mentioned last night? I tried it today, and it said that it couldn't connect. I am so tired of that. It happens all the time on the Internet."

Topher just shrugged. "I got it to come up once, but not twice. Then I got the same message."

The next morning, he went to work. Banner Hilliard was there much earlier than her norm. She briskly called him in. Once Topher was inside her office with her, she sat down at her desk rather gingerly. "Mr. Devlan, I think it would be best if we not discuss what happened yesterday. In case you're wondering, it has had a marked effect on me. Perhaps you couldn't hear what those children were saying, but a lot of it hurt me deeply. Somehow, they picked up phrases I heard when I was a child and haven't heard since. It was very hurtful. Then I had that accident, and the boy Lars grabbed me and pulled me toward a form that read **RETURN**. How he got me there I don't know. I can't get that place out of my mind. It was beautiful, like a picture book I had as a child. My sister always thought that such places can never exist, but it did, right there in Kinder Town."

Topher looked down a minute and then replied haltingly. "It could be that you didn't destroy it. I don't know how we'll ever know. Lars landed in my office chair and was panicked about returning. He hit **RESTORE** and immediately vanished. If we're lucky, Kinder Town was okay after all."

"Do you think so?" Banner Hilliard's look was so filled with pathos that it was difficult to believe she had ever been an uncaring woman. Topher had no time to consider this. Eddie, the man from the cubicle next to Topher's, stuck his head into Ms. Hilliard's office.

"Topher. There's a kid at your desk to see you. He says he wants to apply for a job." Eddie was quite certain to address everything to Topher, ignoring Banner.

Topher looked back at Banner but said to Eddie, "Then why doesn't he come to this office?"

Eddie shrugged. "I don't know. He said his name was Clark, Lark, or something like that."

Banner Hilliard's eyebrows raised high up. "Could it be Lars?"

"Yeah, that was it." Eddie shrugged and left the office.

Topher raced to his desk. Sure enough, there sat Lars. Except that it didn't quite look like Lars at all. This kid was older and more businesslike. Topher motioned him to take a seat. The young man did so. "Your name is Lars?"

The young man smiled and nodded. "That's right."

Topher noticed no sign that the young man identified him. "I'm curious why you want to talk to me about a job instead of with the boss, Ms. Banner Hilliard."

Lars sat motionless for a moment. "Because she won't be here long, and you will."

Topher turned his head in a curious manner. "What do you mean by that? I have not heard that she's going anywhere."

Lars's eyes took on a very slight twinkle. "No, you haven't heard it, but she is."

Topher showed his surprise. "Really?"

Lars smiled broadly. "She is concerned about other things than this office. She worries about things she has said and done. She probably should be worried too. She's checking out a certain Web site right now. Jerry, the kid with the frizzy hair, will meet her. He is in charge now. She'll come back in an hour or so, but she won't resist the temptation to return there. That will be her third trip. She'll be forced to stay there until she has learned all that Kinder Town has to teach her. That will take a long time, and she won't be coming back here even if she does return to the adult world."

Topher noticed that Lars was on the verge of tears. He reached over to a box of Kleenex and took two, handing them to Lars. Lars did not want to let on that he was in any way on the brink of tears. He blew his nose and straightened up. Topher leaned back in his desk chair. "So how is it you are no longer in Kinder Town?"

Lars looked wistfully out the window at Topher's back. "I grew up. I found out what Kinder Town was all about. The name is really best if you pronounce it with just a hint of 'T' in the 'D' and chew the vowel a little—make it halfway between the two languages. It is a town for children. Children run it, and it exists through the joy and delight that only children can have. I'm sorry to say that when you grow up, you lose your capacity to care so much. That hit home with me yesterday. I found Jenny and she's fine. Her tongue will be permanently orange from all that cotton candy, but she'll be fine. She will stay there for a while. When I grow up a little more, I'll go back and get her. I can go back once more. Only once! If I try again, I'll end up in the forest and I'll never be able to get out again. At least that's what all the kids say, and I suppose I ought to believe them. I don't think I want to try it out. So do you have an opening for a mail boy or something?"

Topher sat smiling at the young man. Lars was so close to being a man and yet had the heart burning in him of a boy. "Yes, I think we can find a job for you. Your presence will be a reminder to Banner Hilliard of the place. You aren't thinking of tormenting her, are you?"

Lars shook his head, no smile tracing his face this time. "No. She'll thank me, I suppose, but she won't be able to shake Kinder Town from her psyche, and that will have nothing to do with me." He started to stand up. "I guess I had better go find a place to stay. I only left your computer ten minutes ago." He looked around the office and then started toward the door.

Topher stood up too. "May I ask you something first?

"Sure, I guess so." Lars turned and was casual now.

Topher put his hand on Lars's shoulder. "When you were a child living in this adult world, what was your last name?"

Lars thought a moment. Finally, he shook his head. "I don't remember. I was only five or six."

Topher shocked the young man by saying, "I was twenty-five or twenty-six, and I remember. It was North. Your name is Lars North. I wouldn't have made the total connection had you not said that Jenny was your sister."

Lars was puzzled. "You made a connection to what?"

Topher laughed. "When I was twenty-six years old, my two young cousins vanished from their home. No one had any idea what happened to them. They were six and four years old. Their names were Lars and Jenny, and their last name was North. Your father and mother, my Uncle Morgan and Aunt Terri, will be very excited to have you back—assuming you want to go there. They really want you back."

Lars looked worried at first, but then he nodded. "I think that would be nice. I've learned quite a lot since I lived with them. Will they baby me?" He sounded worried.

Topher laughed. "Not if you don't want them to. I'll call them and tell them that I'm coming over with a Christmas surprise for them."

"Don't tell them it's me." Lars seemed momentarily conspiratorial.

Topher laughed again. "Lars, I wouldn't think of it."

They passed by Banner Hilliard's office. She was sitting there, staring into her computer screen. Topher stuck his head in. "Ms. Hilliard, I'm going to take Lars to meet someone. I'll be back after lunch." She hardly noticed what he said.

Suffice it to say that the Monday after Christmas, the office was in turmoil. Banner Hilliard had vanished, leaving only vague references to going on a trip and to resigning her job. The new mail boy and Topher Devlan had trouble keeping their silence, but they managed. Topher was advanced up to the head position by the board of directors, one of whom said, upon strictest confidence, that he had been bothered by Banner Hilliard's methods all along. Topher thought that it might have been nice for the man to have spoken up earlier.

The North family was happily reunited. There were awkward times, of course, but things came around quite well. Jenny came back one year early. She had grown tired of the beauty of Kinder Town and wanted her mother.

As for Banner Hilliard, it was said by some of the employees that she was never seen again. Two or three of the staff, however, those who tended to travel more broadly, thought they saw her in Germany, on the Great Wall of China, and on a billboard advertising care for orphans.

Topher Devlan tended to believe that she had learned what Kinder Town had to teach and had gone into service for orphan children.

Lars stood up with his cousin one year later when Topher married Julie. At the reception, Aunt Terri asked yet again how it was that Topher had found Lars. Topher kept to his story that Lars had happened into the office to apply for the job. It was not a lie—exactly—and it was certainly easier than explaining about Kinder Town.

TALE 8
The Sled

Some people don't like to go out in the cold air of late December or January. They prefer to huddle next to the fire and drink hot cocoa with little marshmallows floating in it. That's fine too, but how much fun it is to be outside and making a snowman or skating on a pond. Skis are wonderful, if you have the right location. Downhill skis or cross-country skis give different exercise, and some people swear by each of those.

Skating, of course, sometimes involves rinks. Most of those arenas are enclosed, but the temperature is kept briskly cold. Some younger (and a few older) people can actually do little jumps and turns. One or two actually get good enough to do a double axel. Martina Polk actually got so she could do a triple, but then she fell and banged up her knee so badly that she never got to skate again.

Barry Norton never liked skates. He was always afraid of falling into the lake. "They never freeze as deeply as you think they will." He was a wiry teenager though, and he had lots of energy. He would usually build a snowman when the snow was wet and heavy. When it got packed down and dusty, he would prefer to take out his sled and slide down the hill.

Barry did not like using a new kind of sled. He thought the discs and long flat plastic sleds were uncontrollable and dangerous. He had a point, but then his old-fashioned Red Flyer was an antique. Barry's dad had used it for years, and anything his dad did was wonderful for Barry. Hal Norton had tried to buy a new sled in the old-fashioned design. At first he couldn't find one, and when he did find one, it was, at over $100, **way** too expensive. He harbored the idea of buying one for Barry though, a thought that kept gnawing in Hal's mind.

Barry was quite happy with his dad's sled. He kept the old sled in top condition, and if someone said it was an antique, he actually took great pride in that fact. It was never a fixation such as the man in that movie had. It was far more than some sort of idol or idle worship of the sled. Barry was a connoisseur of such things.

Barry was so intent on his observations about sleds that he organized and published them online in an article called **Sleds: A Study of All Existing Sleds, Their Good and Bad Points.** It had garnered the attention of Hasbro, who sent experts to talk with Barry. They spent a wonderfully wintry day with Barry going up and down a hill at the nearest ski resort trying out the different designs, Barry commenting on each and every problem or perfection.

Barry felt special with that kind of attention, particularly when they sent him a consultant fee. It wasn't much, but it was the idea that he was considered an expert. They promised to bring by any prototypes for new sleds. If he liked one, they would make certain he was given the first one to come off the assembly line. Barry could not tell them that it was the assembly line that was part of the problem. Hal's sled had been handmade, and the attention given to it was hands on and personal.

The Olympic bobsled team even took some pointers from his article. They sent him a thank-you note specifying which of his comments noted they had used to improve their team's performance in the tryouts. They sent a small check too.

Barry enjoyed the attention because in the eyes of many, and they were not Barry's friends, he did not deserve the attention that came his way. One teacher, who should have known better than to say it, suggested to Hal that Barry was not operating with a full deck. Hal responded with a rather cold, "Perhaps he isn't the brightest student at this school, but he has better manners than to speak in such a casual and hurtful way." The teacher was not back for second semester.

Barry could love baseball too during the summer. It was in the winter that he felt he was most in his element with sleds. His problems had been diagnosed as being a learning disorder bordering on autism. Hal and Connie refused to accept that judgment. When Connie and Hal split up, it was partially because of the tension that Barry had caused between them, but Hal positively refused to give up on his son. Barry had grown up to be a handsome, almost articulate young man of sixteen years, and even the doctors were amazed that Barry had done as well as he had.

It was now Barry's favorite time of the year—snow time! It was the first major snowfall in December, and he had just received two prototypes from Hasbro to try out. He was delighted with both of them. The first one was more like his old flyer, but with steering capabilities that made his old Red Flyer a pale second. The other sled was a really new idea, and at first he thought it was fabulous. He tried both of them repeatedly. He had Bobby and Teddy try them too, asking them what they thought.

They were not as used to verbalizing their ideas as Barry was. Hal was listening and recording with his pocket recorder the various opinions. He found it amusing that Barry could say in five words what was right or wrong, and it took the two "normal" boys at least twenty words to express opinions. Connie was visiting that day, and she understood Hal's enthusiasm for the progress he could see in Barry.

Connie was never the positive force in Barry's life that Hal was. She resented his attentions to Barry, and, even though she loved Barry very much, her love had its limits. It made her feel like she must be a bad mother.

The afternoon had worn on and the snow had begun to fall again. Bobby had to go home first—his cousins were coming in from Detroit for Christmas. Teddy got to stay about a half an hour longer, but he too had to go home. His grandparents were coming in around suppertime, and Teddy had to be there to welcome them.

Connie was getting chilled. She stood next to Hal as Barry pulled both sleds back up the hill. "I've got to go home. Craig is coming over for supper." Craig was her new love interest. "You are sure you don't mind coming over for dinner on Christmas?"

Hal hated the idea actually. He felt that he would be an odd man out, and he was not sure how Barry would take to the idea that Connie had a new man in her life. It was for Barry's stability and caring that he said, "Yeah, we'll be there. I'll bring the green beans with mushrooms in the Crock-Pot and the pies. You'll have so much to cook, why don't I bring the celery and carrots, the olives, and the pickles. They'll sit right over the pies in the basket just fine. Eleven a.m. okay?" Everything was set.

Connie called to Barry who came over to her and gave her a big hug. "I'll see you on Christmas, Barry. You be sure to have an appetite."

Barry kissed her on the cheek. "Will Craig be there?" It was an awkward moment that caught Connie off guard.

Connie looked at Hal. "I thought he would be. Don't you want him to be?"

Barry smiled. "Yeah, I'd like to meet him. If you think he's special, then he must be okay."

That night Hal, having put the pies in the oven, was watching TV and wrapping packages, while in the computer room, Barry wrote down his copious notes, listening again and again to the tape that Hal had made. At one point, he called Hal to see if he could make out what Bobby had said. That was the only thing at all iffy in the process. Barry sent off the e-mail to Hasbro, with the eighteen-page evaluation on the two sleds. He was surprised to get an almost immediate response from them. His contact was named Perkins, and he said that, obviously, he had not pored through the notes yet, but he said he was amazed how thorough Barry had been.

Hasbro knew about Barry's learning disorder, but as Perkins had confidentially said to Hal when he brought the two sleds, "Anyone who can analyze a product the way Barry can is not slow in my book, I don't care what doctors might say."

The snow continued all night, adding an additional seven inches onto the already impressive five on the ground. Barry decided that he wanted to go out with the two sleds one more time, this time trying them on the slightly bumpier and steeper back hill.

Hal looked up from his paper—he tested himself daily with the crossword—and said, "Just be careful. You don't know how slick this new snow is. I'd try the side hill first, the one you were on yesterday. You know that one so well that you'll be able to judge better how the new snow might affect the handling."

Barry said happily, "That sounds like a good idea. I can get a better feel for today's snow before tackling the stronger hill." He went down the easier hill several times on both sleds. He liked them both, and his eighteen pages held up under his renewed scrutiny. He decided to try the longer and steeper hill once with each sled.

Barry had gone up and down every hill within sight for years. The steeper hill was only a few degrees steeper—more of a skiing hill—and the "rough" spots were a couple of larger rocks in the middle. It was easy to avoid them. Barry had also developed a system that involved never taking an incline for granted. As he stood at the top of the long hill, he closed his eyes and visualized the trajectory of the hill. He knew the hill so well that he could think of the spots that the hill surface tilted slightly to either the right or left.

The hill, according to county maps, was called Creed Hill. No one knew why that was, and most people didn't care. The name most people used was Gopher Hill—a name that had made it onto newer maps as a parenthesis under Creed Hill. The hill was roughly a third longer than the other hills around. The bottom of the hill flattened out for about twenty yards before coming to a slight upturn toward the road. The road itself was an almost abandoned road that was used only occasionally by county trucks as an access road to some storage sheds. It was used, if at all, only in the summer. Beyond the road, the hill went down yet another forty yards or so in a steep incline, finally tabling out on flat land. Barry had only once gone down the hill so fast that he went over the road and down to that lower land.

It was a hill Barry knew well, but it still gave him a greater "rush" than any of the other hills. Not that he would ever admit it, but Barry was actually scared of the hill—just not so scared that he intended to avoid it. Barry's fighting spirit in all things would never admit defeat. Still, he certainly took greater care on this hill than on others he frequented.

Standing at the top of the hill, Barry was thinking about every bump and corner. The fresh snow would normally have made Barry think about getting a more solid snow pack, but the overnight snowfall had packed down rather well. He could tell that by the snow pack on the easier hill. In his mind's eye, he reached the bottom of the hill and went up the incline to the road, going over the road with just enough speed that he could get to the other side, then taking the long, curving slope down to the flat land.

Barry was ready to try it. He took ten steps back and was just ready to start his run when Hal called out to him. "Barry, be careful on that hill. You haven't gone up and down the hill to check for problem spots, have you?"

Barry took a deep breath. He had mentally been halfway down the hill, and Hal's remark had not only stopped him but had unnerved him a little bit. "Dad! I know this hill. I've gone through the track of it in my mind, like I always do. I'll be fine."

Hal came to his son. He did not want to interfere with Barry's self-confidence, but he didn't want him hurt either. "The road crews were working down there last month. Do you know what they were doing? I don't."

Barry had not considered that. "I—I know they were grading the road because it had rain wash problems. It's fine. I w-went down it two weeks ago, and I know they have not b-been there since."

Hal smiled, acknowledging that his son probably knew more about the hill than he ever did. "Well, just be careful." He stood back. In Barry's younger days, Hal would have given Barry a push, but Barry didn't like that anymore. It made him feel like a "baby."

Barry took eight running steps and jumped into a sitting position on the sled. It began to go down the hill with incredible speed. Barry leaned back a little, aiding the aerodynamic acceleration of the sled. This was the sled that Barry felt steered the best, and he was right. At one point, he was heading directly for one of the big rocks and slightly turned the front rudder, turning gently past the boulder. At the bottom of the hill, he slowed much less than normal and went up over the road. He was airborne for about two seconds. When he came to a rest at the bottom of the hill in the flatlands, Barry felt exhilarated. *This was a really cool sled!*

He traipsed back up the hill—that was always the problem with sledding. Hal and he had a wonderful couple of minutes talking about the best qualities of the new sled design. Then it was time to try the other sled.

Barry liked this sled too, although he didn't like its blue color. He was a little less comfortable on the sled because its design demanded that you go down on your stomach. Normally Barry liked that. On the big hill, though, that worried him. He didn't like going down face first. He sat down on the sled at the top of the hill. Maybe, if he sat on it feetfirst, he could guide with his feet and basically lie on his back. Even at the top of the hill, he realized this sled wasn't going to let him do that.

So he looked to his dad. Hal came over to see what Barry wanted. "I'll lie down on my tummy and put up my right leg. Then I'd like you to give my leg a push." Hal said that he would.

Barry lay down as he said, his right leg bent to make a starting handle. Hal gave the push, and Barry started down the hill. He was a little to the left of his last run, which was clearly marked in the snow. He maneuvered the sled to the right, landing in the old tracks. That made things a little worse though, because the tracks from the other sled were deeper, and this sent packed snow into Barry's face. He barely saw the rock to the right with enough time to avoid it. Even at that, he hit the outer reach of the bump, and it took him twenty or thirty feet to recover. He was flying now, and that many feet without control could be dangerous. He put his feet down into the snow, trying to slow himself down. It did no good.

Barry was coming to the upturn of land. He hoped he could slow down then. Instead he hit it at the fastest speed he had ever taken on it and was airborne for several seconds as he went over the road. As he landed, the rear of the runners caught on some brush and pulled Barry and the sled sideways. He was not going down the hill straight now but was heading to his right and toward a large copse of trees. He realized, too late, that between him and the trees were a small creek bed and three large rocks. Barry hit the first rocks at roughly forty-five miles per hour. The sled went into the creek, and Barry was flying through the air. His head hit a large rock on the other side. He did not move.

Hal saw all of this from the top of the hill. He started running down the hill, fumbling for his cell phone all the way. He tripped and rolled part of the way. He got the 911 operator and spent valuable time telling her how to dispatch the EMT unit.

Meanwhile, Barry woke up. He was not alone. A pretty young girl stood beside him. She had on a green parka, white fur around her face, and she was on bright red skis.

"You probably shouldn't come down the hill that fast, you know."

Great, thought Barry, *I am lying here injured and I'm facing a smart-alecky kid.* "Obviously, the sled got away from me."

"Obviously, considering where you're lying, I'd say you got away from it." She smiled and put out her hand. Barry sat up.

"Do I know you from somewhere?" Barry started dusting the snow off of his pants and coat.

"Well, yes, I used to sit by you in Sunday school. We all did."

It was only then that Barry noticed another girl and a boy standing behind the first girl. They were all dressed in winter coats and hats, but something seemed odd to Barry. "How come you don't come to church anymore? Luke, I thought you liked singing in the children's choir. You girls were always the acolytes. Then one by one you all stopped coming."

Luke got behind Barry and helped him get up. "If we're going to play, you have to get up off your behind."

The four of them played together making a snowman for nearly thirty minutes. Then Barry began to feel cold. He looked around, and the two girls were running off. Luke stood beside Barry. They both glanced toward the road, where there were lights flashing.

Hal was there helping as best he could. Three men were kneeling over something in the snow, and they were working furiously to strap the thing onto a stretcher. It was then that Barry noticed that *he* was the figure on the stretcher. He looked to Luke for an answer. Luke looked back at him with a strange maturity that Barry had not noticed before. "What's going on? How can I be here and there all at the same time?"

Luke shrugged. "You're here and there because *you* are your spirit and that is your body." The men were putting the body into the ambulance. "When you came flying down that hill, you flew over the road with way too much speed and hit that cement and rock culvert there. It's all that's left of the old roadbed, but you hit it with your head. You died almost immediately."

Barry was shaking. "I can't be dead. I'm supposed to go to Mom's house tomorrow for Christmas."

Luke sat down in the snow and motioned for Barry to do so too. As Barry sat down, Hal climbed into the ambulance and the ambulance drove away. "Well, because it's Christmas Eve, I was sent to get you and to offer you four options. The girls and I are all dead. Beth died of leukemia three years ago, Lily died in a fire, and I died in a car wreck. At least you had a little more style." Luke was laughing a little.

"Hey, Luke, it's not funny. I don't want to die."

"Well, as I said, there are options. I'm supposed to tell you what they are. Wait a minute." He reached under his snow jacket and into his blue-jeaned pocket. They were empty of everything except a gum wrapper. Finally, he reached up under his coat and pulled a piece of paper out of his shirt pocket. "Here it is. Let's see now . . ."

"Your first option is to die and go to heaven. You'll be fine in heaven. Any problems you had on earth will be totally gone up there. It actually isn't so bad. Beth, Lily, and I play together all the time."

Barry was getting very upset. He glanced over his shoulder and could just see the flashing light retreating in the distance. He couldn't hear the siren. "That's no good. You know already that I want to live."

Luke scratched his head and studied the paper. "Man, I wish I had written this better. It's really hard to read." He held the paper over to Barry. "Can you read that word?"

Barry saw nothing written on the paper at all. "Stop funning with me, Luke!"

"Okay, I got it now. You can go back and things will be as they were. You'd be slow to learn things, and your mom and dad would stay separated but friendly. A third option would be that you return to them in a state of vegetation—you'd be alive but you'd never be a boy again the way you once were—but your mom and dad would get together, partially because of you. The fourth option is that you'd recover and be an absolutely normal young man. You'd grow on up and be a wonderful example to the community. The downside to that is that you would never get to see your mother again. She'd get remarried and go off with Craig and they'd live happily away from you, never caring whether you got better or not."

Barry thought a second. Such options were difficult for him in normal times, but they all seemed clear to him this time. "That's it? Isn't there a better option?"

Luke shook his head sadly. "Nope. It is more options than I had! I died instantly, and Grandma came to get me."

Barry was sure what he wanted, but none of the options presented it. "Can I tell you what I'd like the option to be?"

"It won't do any good, but you can go ahead." Luke was a little offhanded with Barry, and that got Barry fuming.

"All right, what I'd like would be to wake up with Mom and Dad back together. If that means I'd have to be slow, okay. I've been slow all my life, so I can carry that burden. For me to die would break their hearts. Dad and I have great times together, and Mom always loves to spoil me with cookies and pies when I go to her house. They both love me a lot. And for me to die would tear them up.

"Going back the way things were would be okay, I guess, but I really want them to get back together, and you say that won't happen. At least Mom would still be able to love me. I'd be afraid of that next option. If I was worse than I was before, I think it would be worse for Mom and Dad than if I died. They would feel so hurt that they could not do anything to help me. And then I'd be afraid that they would put me in some hospital and forget about me—or else spend all their money trying to take care of me. I'd say it would be nice to wake up normal—but not if Mother moved away and took no interest in me. I love her too much to think about that, even if my whole life improved otherwise. I can't go through that without her there. Dad would start to resent me, I'm sure." Barry sat quietly a moment. Then with tears in his eyes, he looked squarely at Luke's face. "I think I've caused them enough hardship and pain. I think you had better let me die."

Luke nodded solemnly, a slight smile creasing his mouth. "You're sure about that choice?"

Barry swallowed very hard. "Yes, I'm sure. Will it hurt?"

Luke shrugged. "You've already felt the pain. Death won't hurt at all." He reached out to Barry's arm and started to draw him toward a large gate at the far end of the flatlands. Beth and Lily were standing just inside the gate.

After only a few steps, the world around them began whirling. Greens, blues, and lavenders, with light streaks of pink and glittering gold all swirled together. Barry decided that dying was really pretty neat.

Luke giggled happily. "Only a few more steps and you'll be in the clear."

Then Barry's world seemed to change. He felt pummeled by the swirling colors, all of which became darker and murkier. Barry could still hear Luke's voice, but he could not see him or the two girls. Barry felt himself tumbling over in space, his feet no longer firmly on the ground. Then he saw an immense down draft of air—in the shape of a hand—that lifted Barry up and then threw him down. If this was the hand of God, thought Barry, it was being awfully harsh.

In the distance, he thought he could just hear Luke saying again, "A few more steps and you'll be in the—"

"**CLEAR!**" The voice changed in an instant, and Barry felt as if a sledgehammer had just hit him in his chest. And then, the noise of the buffeting winds and the swirling and falling sensation ceased. Barry was lying very still. He kept his eyes shut, afraid what he might find. What if, he thought, God rejected me and sent me to hell?

"We have a strong pulse at last, doctor. Should I go tell the parents?"

"Not yet. We need to get the rest of the vital signs."

Barry didn't know who was talking, but he could tell them one thing. He felt awful! His body actually hurt all over. His head was all bandaged, he could tell that. His mouth was free, however, and he mustered every ounce of energy he could to say, "The lights . . . too bright." He didn't know why, but he could tell that those few words made an amazing impression on someone. Immediately, the lights were lowered. He opened his eyes.

To his left was a man in green scrubs and a green operating hat (Barry had seen that attire on TV). To his right was a pretty nurse. Behind her was another doctor who was putting away a defibrillator. "Where am I?" Barry whispered.

The nurse was checking the various machines that were beeping and squawking all around Barry. The doctor looked down at Barry and smiled broadly. "You, young man, are in County General Hospital, and you gave us a terrific run for our money." Seeing that Barry didn't understand what he meant, he explained. "Between the times when you went flying from your sled and now, you died three times on us. We were almost positive you weren't going to pull through."

The nurse looked over at the doctor. "Doctor Gerald, could you look at this please?" The doctor went to the other side of the bed. He began looking at the various lights and machines. His face was no longer smiling but was, instead, a knot of concentration on the graphs.

"Is anything wrong, doctor?" Barry asked, terrified that he might, after all, be going to die.

Doctor Gerald looked over at Barry. "No, young man, nothing is wrong. In fact, for some reason that I can't imagine, everything is absolutely fine. Your brain waves fifteen minutes ago were absolutely abysmal. Now they are all okay. You'd almost think you had never had an accident. Everything's fine, except of course for your broken collarbone and a mild concussion. Oh, and you still have a gash on your leg. Your little sledding experiment was pretty dangerous."

"I usually take more care and have more control than that."

Doctor Gerald looked at Barry again, a curious look on his face that Barry could not understand. "Would you excuse me a moment, Barry?" He went out into the hall. The nurse was checking on Barry's other wounds, making sure the wraps were good.

Only moments later, Doctor Gerald came back into the room with a doctor Barry knew all too well. Dr. Gwyneth Peters was his doctor for his autism. She came over to the bed and smiled the gentle smile that Barry loved so much. "Barry, Doctor Gerald says you were just telling him about your sledding accident. Could you tell me about it, too? I want to make sure you aren't injured in some way that doesn't show up on the machines here."

Barry didn't have a whole lot of energy, but as he told Dr. Peters the tale of the two sleds, he seemed to gain strength. It was, after all, his favorite subject. She listened attentively. Barry wasn't fooled though, because twice during the tale she looked over at Doctor Gerald with a raised eyebrow and a look of surprise. Finally, when his story was finished, he asked gingerly, "So when do I get to go home?"

Dr. Peters thought a moment before answering. "Barry, I know it's Christmas Eve and all, but do you mind if I let you sleep a little bit? You've been through a lot, and yet I want to run a couple of tests on you. Besides, they need to check you over a little more. When you came in, you were so weak that they couldn't do that. I promise, if I can, that you'll be away from here at the latest tomorrow morning. You'll still be able to have Christmas dinner with your mom and dad. I'm going to let them come in for a minute or two, and then you need to sleep. I'll wake you in the middle of the afternoon. Okay?" She smiled a big smile at Barry.

Barry returned the smile with a gentle "Okay."

Connie and Hal had been very upset. Barry could tell that. By the looks of them, they had been crying a lot. Connie did not seem to want to come close at all. Hal, however, came right up to Barry and put his hand on Barry's. "How ya doin', buddy?"

Barry could hear the catch in his dad's voice. He smiled back. "I'm gonna be fine, Dad, really I am. I'll be back to my old self in a day or two, I'll just bet you."

Connie finally came up to the bed. She was almost afraid of being too close, as if she might become contaminated by Barry's injuries. (The rationalization for that never makes sense, but it affects a lot of people.) In reality, she had been so afraid of losing Barry that she was afraid to show she really loved him. It was the major concern she had felt for the last year. It was what had caused the pending divorce.

"Hi, Barry! We have an idea. We're going to move tomorrow's dinner to your house. That way, you can go to bed anytime you feel like it. Okay?"

Barry shook his head. "Nope. We said we'd come to your house and we will. It's too much work to cart a bunch of food from one place to another. If I get tired, I can fall asleep in a chair the same way Dad does—watching TV." They all had a good laugh over that. Then Hal and Connie left with Dr. Peters, and Barry was allowed to snuggle down in his bed to sleep.

His dreams were strange. He was standing in the center of a large circle, surrounded by sweet-smelling red roses and Christmas cactus, poinsettias, and sparkling lights that seemed to have no plug strips attached to them. He looked around pleasantly, and then he saw three children standing in a doorway. He wanted to go to them, but they put up their hands to keep him from it. It was Beth, Lily, and Luke. Luke came forward just a little so he wouldn't have to shout. "Merry Christmas, Barry. I guess you probably hurt a lot now. Living can hurt a lot more than dying, but I've heard you're going to be fine. I guess God did not pay attention to the option you chose and picked one for himself. When you go to church Sunday, could you wish our parents a Merry Christmas? Thanks."

Barry woke up suddenly. Dr. Peters was standing beside him. "Barry, I want to tell you something. We've run a lot of tests—we'll run more next week. It's six o'clock on Christmas Eve, and you're going home. Now there's something you have to promise me. I don't want you to go sledding for at least a month, and only easy hills this year. You can tackle tougher slopes next winter—*with caution!* Your dad is here to take you home."

The male nurse came in and helped Barry dress. He had his arm in a sling, and his leg hurt really badly. The nurse then wheeled Barry out of the ER. Hal was waiting for him just outside the door of the room and he was talking to Dr. Peters. She turned around and kissed Barry on the forehead. "I have something I want to tell you, Barry, which you will probably find as amazing as I do. Do you remember when I said that we'd need to run a couple of more tests next week? Well, do you know why I said that?"

Barry shook his head. "No. Are you afraid I've done damage to myself upstairs?" He pointed to his head.

Dr. Peters just laughed. "No, it's hardly that. Oh, you did some damage, but that was just a cut and a slight concussion. You actually have something to be thankful for this Christmas, a present that none of us thought you'd ever have. Barry, I think you are actually cured. I think you're as normal as anyone could be. That being said, I still want you to come and visit me once in a while. Can you do that?" She helped pull the stocking cap down over Barry's bandages. He looked at himself in the hall mirror and laughed.

"Sure, Dr. Peters. But if I'm cured, why do you want to see me?"

She stood up rather straighter than normal. "Because I like you, Barry Norton, and I like visiting with you. And if need be, I want to help your mom and dad keep you from getting out of line."

Barry smiled impishly. "As if I ever would do that!"

The Christmas was the best Barry ever had. The ears of God had heard Barry take the most unselfish option he could have picked, and the hand of God had acted in the most perfect way possible. For the option that Barry wanted was what he was granted. He didn't want health for himself. He wanted his parents to love one another again and to grow older together as his guides in life. Craig did not attend the Christmas dinner. Barry's wish was fulfilled completely.

TALE 9
The Chimney Visitor

Though most people consider Christmas as a happy time each year, there are those for whom anger and depression rather than happiness fill their lives in December. Those people isolate themselves from the crowd; they do not want to enjoy Christmas. No one wants to be around such people, so the isolation grows from year to year. People avoid going near the person who would be a "downer" to their holiday spirit. The vicious circle continues.

Susan McFadden was a lovely young woman. Her blond hair, sunny disposition, and radiant smile always seemed to be inviting to everyone. People usually felt Susan was a positive and delightful person. There was the problem, however, in that much of her cheery attitude was false. She did not really have friends. Jennifer Hazelnut had tried to be Susan's friend, but after two or three attempts she backed off. She was quoted as having said, "No one is worth that much effort!" Susan was high maintenance.

At the day care center she owned and ran, Susan projected caring and eager warmth. The children could count on her to play with them. Parents could see that she was good with children. But children did not play with Susan very long. After a week or two, they would shy away from her. Children have an ability to see through facades easily, and they could tell Susan was not at all interested in them. They preferred Jennifer Hazelnut or Roger Hollander.

Roger loved the children, and they would flock to play with him. This got Susan jealous, but she was glad too that Roger was there. It meant she could tend to the children in her own way and not have to play with them. Susan could be good with the children when they needed disciplining. She had an uncanny ability to talk with them gently yet firmly, never faltering in the disciplinary lecture but also never causing them to hate her for being firm.

Susan also had a nice way with the parents. She could make them feel at home when they came to visit or to pick their children up. The children appreciated the polished persona she projected too. It just wasn't a very warm persona. And children do not gravitate to adults who aren't comfortable around them. It should be pointed out, however, that no one ever accused her of shaking a child or in any way endangering one. That would have been an impossibility for Susan McFadden. She loved children or she would not have opened the day care center.

Susan had had a lot of experiences with children because she came from a large family—six brothers and two sisters. Her mother died when Susan was eighteen. Only one brother was older. He was away at college. This meant that Susan had to help tend five boys and two sisters, all of them younger than she was. In those years she had dressed rather shabbily, and she still loved the sloppy look. She realized that such a look was not appropriate for her profession, and she had spruced herself up respectably.

Raising that number of children would not have been much of a problem had Max McFadden, Susan's father, been much help. He was a widower at fifty years of age, and he was not ready to stop enjoying female companionship. So he had quickly courted and married Mabel Denton, who proved to be lovely in many ways but not toward the children. She never actively hated the children, but she found that they got in the way of the attentions she wanted from Max.

Susan realized that the sooner she was out and on her own, the better it would be for her. It meant not only taking care of her siblings for a while but training them as well to be self-sufficient. They would soon have to do without her. Susan was pleased when one after another brother and sister found good jobs with futures and moved out of the house.

Max McFadden, for his part, was never one to shun his children on purpose. But he didn't realize how much Mabel's needs were taking him from them. Then he was suddenly alone with no one but her. The children were all grown, and he began to realize what an empty place the house was without his children. He also realized that he had missed something special in their lives, closing his eyes to the joys around him.

Mabel left him after a few years for a younger man more her own age. Max was eight years older than Mabel, and the difference made for considerable problems. The other children all made "Dad" feel wanted and helped him adjust to his new life alone. He dated some, but he was mainly a father and soon a grandfather with children to take an interest in.

Susan, although happy for her siblings, just could not bring herself to forgive her father for ignoring her and her siblings through the important years. One of her brothers had been a star basketball player in high school, but Max had only seen two games, and neither of those was the championship game they won. A sister had married an important lawyer and was probably going to be Mrs. Mayor of the city. Max had missed everything connected with the wedding to take a trip to Hawaii with Mabel.

One reason Susan hated the season was clear, and Roger told Jennifer so. "During the holidays, she has to close the day care because no one wants to bring children here. They all stay home. She knows she'll be alone."

Jennifer had been putting on her red scarf over her Kelly green coat. "Well, even if Susan is alone, I'm tired of trying to make her happy. I'm having my sister over for dinner. Would you like to come, Roger?" She adjusted the matching tam.

Roger shook his head. "I don't think so, Jennifer. My brother is going to call from Germany, and my other brother said he'd call from Burbank, California. So I have to be home. I'll have a quiet dinner alone, just Meris and me, and then I'll have Chuck and June over for dessert around four."

So Christmas rolled around, and everyone went their way for the extended weekend. Susan McFadden was left alone to watch TV and work on a needlepoint project she had. The young man next door stopped in to see if she wanted her driveway shoveled out, but since it was only two inches she opted to leave it alone. She gave him a $20 bill in case the prediction for eight more inches came true. It did and she was happy she had done so.

Still, on Christmas Eve, she began to feel rather lonely. It was, she knew, the prelude to a bout of depression. She always got depressed at Christmas, but she never realized that it was her own fault that people left her alone.

She had just brewed a pot of hot cocoa, far too much for herself, and she had her needlepoint lying beside her chair, when there was a tentative knock on the door. It was already 9:30 p.m., and she was in her bathrobe—over her dress, true, but she had hunkered down for the night, and now there was a visitor.

When she went to the door, she could see someone standing outside. She turned on the porch light and opened the door only a chain's length. "Yes, may I help you?"

The young man at the door was approximately Susan's age. "I hope so. I'm on my way home for Christmas, and my car just decided to quit on me down here on the corner. I managed to get it to back up and into the only open space I could find. Do you know any mechanic who could come by and, well, maybe tell me what's wrong?"

Susan was unsure of the young man. He looked nice enough, but he was a total stranger. "Wait just a minute." She got her portable telephone and dialed the number of her own mechanic. He answered almost at once. "Sam? This is Susan McFadden. Yes, Merry Christmas to you too." She tried to make it sound cheery, but from lack of practice it was rather lackluster. "Listen, there is a young man standing on my porch. His car just quit on him, and he's on the way home for the holidays. Is there any way you could come around and give it a look-see?"

Sam was not overly enthusiastic about the prospect of going out on a snowy night. The snow wasn't falling, but it was predicted to start before midnight and snow all night. "I'm supposed to go to midnight mass. Okay, tell your friend that I'll be around in about ten minutes."

"He's not really a . . . ," but Sam had hung up. Susan went back to the window that overlooked the porch. She could see that the young man seemed casually but nicely dressed. He certainly did not appear to be a criminal type. She opened the door again. The young man turned. "Listen, if you would like to come in, the mechanic should be here in about ten minutes. Meanwhile, I just made a little pot of hot cocoa that is way too big for just me and is getting cold. My name's Susan McFadden."

The young man smiled. "I shouldn't. I'm a stranger after all, and I don't want to inconvenience you more than I have."

"I know, but it's getting kind of windy out there. Besides, what says Christmas more than a cup of hot cocoa?" The young man followed Susan inside. He briefly thought that lots of things might mean Christmas more than hot cocoa, but he let it drop.

"Dan Morgan's my name." He held out his hand to shake hers. He took his gloves off and put them in his pocket. As he did so, he felt a little something in his left pocket. "Oh, look at that. I bet you don't know what that is."

Susan gave Dan a rather withering look. "It's a peppermint candy cane."

Dan gave a kind of buzzing sound. "*Bzzzz!* **Wrong**! It is a peppermint candy swizzle stick for hot cocoa." He tore the clear plastic wrapper off and immediately put the small cane into his cocoa cup, hooking the crook over the edge. He then reached into his pocket and brought out a second cane. "This is for you. You see, the peppermint melts in the hot chocolate and makes it mint chocolate. Now *that's* a Christmas drink!"

Susan took the cane Dan Gordon offered her, unwrapped it, and put it in her cup. Dan took his out and put it on a napkin on the tray where the little pot sat. "Don't leave it in till the whole thing melts, because that makes it a little too strong of mint. Give it a couple more stirs. That ought to be enough."

Susan put her candy cane next to Dan's on the napkin and took a sip. "Ooh, it is really good! Now why didn't I ever think of that?" They drank for a moment in silence. Susan thought to ask, "How is it that you're on your way home and yet are on this out-of-the-way residential street?"

Dan placed his stocking cap on the floor next to him. "I work in Akron, and I was going down to the south side of Columbus. I have always taken the Tuttle Crossing exit off of I-270, but this time there was a minor wreck that had traffic at the exit backed up. So I went on to Fisher Road exit, but it took me a little while to find my proper way. In the process, my car started acting up. I saw a bunch of lights to my right and figured they were a service station. They may be, but I didn't get that far. First of all, the lights are on the other side of a highway—no entrance—and my car pooped out right in front of here."

"Well, Sam should be here in a little while. What do you do in Akron?" Susan poured Dan a little more hot cocoa, and he picked up his 'swizzle stick' to remint his drink.

"I work for a firm that helps find people." He noticed a strange look on her face. "Oh, it's nothing sinister. We don't even do work for the government. It's mostly searching for an occasional person wanting to find a college friend or an insurance company wanting to find a potential recipient of an inheritance. It's kind of a boring job, but it pays the bills. I'm good at it too. I also volunteer for the local Make-A-Wish Foundation. By the way, I have heard the name Susan McFadden before, although I can't for the life of me think where."

Susan passed a little dish of corn chips over to Dan. "Well, the name is probably not that unusual, although I suppose you would know that better than me. I run a day care center. It also has its good points and pays the rent, but it isn't very interesting to babysit children day after day."

Dan finished his cocoa. "I don't know. I think it might be a lot of fun. Kids can be so inventive. The fantastic tales they come up with rival the best authors. I've actually started writing them all down, as many as I can, and I'm going to edit them and make a fantasy book out of them—for children of course. After I get the texts in some kind of order, I'll try to find an artist to illustrate some of the tales. Some will be difficult to include because they get so fantastic that they are scary."

Susan also finished her last corn chip and cocoa together. "How does that Make-A-Wish Foundation work? I've heard of it, but I've never really understood it." Susan was trying to convince herself that she was interested. She actually was, but not nearly as much as she wanted to make Dan think she was.

"Oh, you know," Dan began, "a kid gets sick, usually with a liver or kidney ailment or cancer, and they are diagnosed as being in a pretty bad way. They may not be terminal, but they need a big boost in morale. So the people attending the kid, and that can be nurses, parents, or siblings, contact us with the desire the kid has to meet someone or go to Disney World or to see something really nice, and we try to make it happen. It's a lot more fun than looking up names." Dan paused, obviously weighing something in his mind. "You know, I am sure I have actually seen the name Susan McFadden somewhere before."

He didn't get time to think about it. At that moment, the doorbell rang. Susan answered it, happy to see that it was Sam, her mechanic. Just as she opened the door, a white owl swooped down through the chimney of her fireplace. It soared around the hallway and living room, eventually perching on the living room chandelier. Sam, Dan, and Susan all looked up at it. Susan was dumbfounded. "How the heck did that get in here?"

Dan continued looking at the owl as he answered. "Well, this is an older house, and the chimneys had larger openings back when it was built. In order to let your gas logs send the fumes up, you have the flue open, and the owl flew down. It's amazing that he didn't get singed by the fire." Dan started laughing. "It kind of reminds me of that kids' book where the uncle hates getting messages by owls."

Sam finally spoke up. "I know how to get bats out of a house, but I don't know about owls." He kept looking at the owl, which moved very little other than to turn his head around and look at the three of them.

"Having a white owl fly into your house on Christmas might be a good omen. I mean, ya never know."

Susan was staring at the animal. "Well, *I know!* We have to get it out of here."

Sam answered. "Well, my son Jack is waiting in the truck. We'll see what we can do about fixing your car, mister, and if we don't think we can, we'll have to tow it in. Did you say you were going somewhere near here?"

Dan Morgan looked at Sam. "Yeah, but it's about twenty blocks south of here. I sure don't want to walk."

"Oh, you wouldn't have to walk. I could take you. If you drive careful like, you can get around. It's them semis that always try to go too fast and cause the wrecks. What kind of noise or such did your car make when it quit on you?"

Dan turned his attention from the owl to Sam and his auto. "My car's the blue 1993 Nissan out front, the one with a green fender. It started to sort of chug-chug, and I lost lots of power."

"I wondered about that. I thought I smelled a little burnt smell. It may be your clutch is burnt up. The chugging could be anything. You see what you c'n do about helping Susan with her owl. Jack and me'll take care of it. Oh, and Susan, you've had them lights up for four years and you haven't switched 'em on in three. Why don't you just turn 'em on and enjoy the bright spirit they give everyone else?"

Susan didn't have a good answer, so Sam sauntered out and closed the door gently behind him. His heavy tread could be heard on the wooden porch and even on the cement steps going down to the street.

Dan Morgan was trying to think what to do about the owl. "At least, Ms. McFadden, he or she hasn't pooped on your furniture." At that moment, of course, the owl flapped his wings three times and let fly with an amount of poop that luckily landed on an ornamental plate and a book, narrowly missing a basket of thread for Susan's needlepoint. "That was a close call. Hey, I mentioned that movie I saw, so I'll do what the kid did in the movie." Dan held up his hand like a giant perch parallel to the floor. He hoped the owl might fly down and land on his arm. He'd seen it in the movie, and the owl always did that.

The owl looked down at the two of them and blinked. He blinked again.

Dan moved his arm a little bit. The owl actually shook his head, as if saying no. Dan put his arm down.

"Hey, owl, are you being finicky? I wanted to talk with you. Is there a reason that you came down that chimney?" Dan glanced over at the still frightened Susan, and then turned his eyes back up to the chandelier.

The owl blinked again and then clearly nodded. Both Susan and Dan looked at one another with an expression of real surprise.

"Did you want to deliver a message of some sort?" The owl nodded again. "Was it to me?" The owl shook its head in a clearly negative way. "Then the message was for Ms. McFadden!"

The owl nodded, spread its wings, and floated down, landing on the mantle this time. The penetrating stare was placed on Dan Morgan, who stared right back. Finally, the bird gave a peculiar nick of his head as if motioning Dan from the room.

"What! Do you want me to leave? I don't think Ms. McFadden wants to be left alone with you." Dan held out his arm again, but the owl made the same gesture. Dan lowered his arm and looked over to Susan. "I guess I'll, uh, go out to see how Sam and his son are doing. If that owl causes you any trouble, you just scream and Sam and I will come running."

Dan made his way to the door, absently flicking the switch to turn the porch light on. But the porch light was already on, and the switch Dan hit was the switch for Christmas lights, which came on in a brilliant display of light on the porch. He went out slowly, unsure if he really wanted to leave Susan alone with the owl.

Susan looked up at the owl on the mantel. "Well, if you have some message to give me, what is it?" Her impatience was clear, but it was a facade to cover her being so ill at ease around the large, white bird.

The owl clucked its beak, the sound resembling to Susan some sort of sentence. "I'm sorry, owl, but I didn't get that. You may need to cluck slower." She couldn't believe that she was actually talking to an owl and expecting it to reply intelligently. Yet she had said it, and she really expected the owl to reply. Briefly, she thought how 'cool' it would be to take this owl in for show-and-tell at the day care, but she was afraid it might be too wild for the children.

The owl clucked its beak again, and this time Susan caught the word "closer."

"You want me to come closer? Why?"

The owl blinked again and quietly said, "Sooo I can talk to yoooouuu."

Susan stood almost paralyzed by the response. Her eyes were almost as big as the owl's eyes. Still she took three tentative steps closer. Every one of her senses was crying out that this was insane, but she stayed and she listened.

"That's better. Nowooo, we have some things to talk abouoooot!" The owl blinked again and then began to chatter in a fashion that was almost conversational, as if it was a domestic parakeet or a myna bird. "You have not been very open to friends of late. The good sign was that you opened the door tonight to a stranger, but your friends, the people you work with, and the children, are gradually giving up on you. Jennifer and Roger are actually talking about quitting and starting their own day care together. You don't want that." The owl paused a moment. The reader should be aware that every time the owl said a vowel that was even close to an 'o' or an 'oo' he elongated it just slightly. It was not anything he could control. Finally, he continued. "Do you know the way that children are the same as dogs and cats?"

Susan thought a moment. She knew it was not a rhetorical question, and the owl was clearly waiting for a reply, but she had no idea. "I'm sorry, but I really don't know."

"Toooo bad! You see, children and particularly dogs and cats give love unconditionally. It seems that, against all reason, they love the person they consider the one closest to them. In children this is their parents and their teachers or, in your case, their day care provider. In dogs and cats, they frequently love their owners only, and strangers need to be wary. Only when a person becomes so dismissive of the child's needs or the needs of the dogs and cats do the children or pets turn against the adult. That's when pets attack children with no reason, and that's why children turn against parents. I once knew a young man who had good looks, a fine physique, and a nice stage persona. He was an actor. But he was terribly moody. You see, his parents gave him everything that they could buy for him. What they did not give him was love. You, Susan, are like his parents in a way. Except, unlike his parents, you dooo have the capacity for love. Whooy don't you let it out?"

Susan looked at the owl with a mixture of uncertainty and embarrassment. "I do let my love out!"

The owl clicked his beak furiously, shaking his head at the same time. "No, no, no, no, no, you don't! Little Steven came up to you yesterday morning and was crying. Did you find out whooy? No. You patted him on the back and sent him off to Roger. Whooy would you do that? He came to yoooou! He wanted you to make him feel better."

The owl stood up very straight. It seemed to Susan that he almost doubled in size, though she knew that was impossible. Then again, she knew it was impossible for an owl to talk, and this one was chattering a whole sermon. It was then, however, that the owl made a loud squawk. He wanted an answer from Susan.

"I comforted him as well as I could. You don't know anything about it." Susan was defensive, only quietly beginning to ask herself how on earth the owl knew what she had done or thought.

"Nooooooo. You may think you do, but you do not. Roger was able to calm him down almost at once. The little boy needed a hug and a little love. That wasn't going to come from you. I ask again, whooy not?" The owl suddenly quit blinking and, instead, sat staring at Susan.

At first her method for dealing with the owl was to stare back, but she quickly began to wilt. It was only partially that the owl made her nervous. It was more that what she needed to tell him made her ill at ease.

"I come from a large family," she began, rather more defensively than she intended, "and I have always had to work to get the attention of my parents. They could look right past me with the greatest ease, and—"

The owl fluttered angrily and screeched, "Lies, lies, lies! That will get you nowhere! You have to be honest with me if you're going to be honest with yourself."

Susan's anger flared. "I am being as honest as I can." The owl turned his back on Susan, only occasionally looking back at her furtively and with suspicion. Finally, after two or three minutes of silence, Susan started to go toward the porch, but the owl called her back. "You think you're telling the truth, but you're not. Not at all! Here is the solution to the problem. You've already opened the door to a stranger. That leaves four more tests that you must pass. If you pass them, then you will be on your way to recovery. If you don't, then you'll be forever alone and lonely, and your depression will increase. Eeoo see, eeoo don't let the spirit of the season come in. Opening the door compassionately to a stranger was an act that had the seasonal spirit in it."

Susan was intrigued. "What will these tests be like?"

The owl clicked his beak in a kind of laughter. "Oooo, I won't tell you that, because that would make it too easy." At that, the owl flew up into the air. Susan began screaming in fright, but the owl simply flew around her head, until Dan, drawn by Susan's cries, opened the front door. Then the owl flew directly past Dan and out the door into the nighttime air.

Dan had ducked to avoid the owl, but then he stood up. "Are you all right?"

Susan nodded, somewhat stunned. "He said a lot of things that did not make sense to me. Some of it had to be guessing, but some of it . . . I just don't know."

"Said things? That's odd indeed. What made you scream?"

Susan looked up at Dan. "Have you ever had an owl fly around your head? It is no fun, let me tell you." She went to the kitchen and got a small bucket of water and some high-powered cleaner to clean up the mess the owl had made. But when she got to the table, everything was clean.

Dan, in the meantime, had followed Susan to the kitchen with the tray of cocoa stuff. As he was following Susan back into the living room, he let out a small "A-ha!"

Susan set the bucket down. "A-ha what? What did you just realize?"

Dan smiled. "I just remembered where I had heard your name. Don't you have a brother named Greg?"

Susan was surprised to hear her brother's name. "Yes, I do. They live up in Doylestown, which is near Akron. Hey, he's a good artist. Maybe he can help with your book."

Dan became enthusiastic for a second, "Yes, I know your brother. I didn't know he was an artist, but he coaches a Little League team near me." Then Dan's face dropped. "Oh, yeah, there's another reason I know your name. His little boy, Mr. G, Gregory Junior, is seriously ill with leukemia. The doctors haven't found a good marrow donor. Greg was telling me yesterday about it. It doesn't look good for Mr. G."

Susan was stunned. "What do you mean that it doesn't look good? He's a young kid of four years old. You can't mean he'll die!"

Sam came to the door at that moment. "We'll have to tow you in. If you come with us, we've found the problem. It isn't serious, so we'll take you in, fix it, and get you on your way. Opening up just for you is a Christmas present, but you'll have to pay for the services."

Susan put her hand on Dan's arm. "Wait a minute! What do you mean when you say that it doesn't look good?"

Dan looked at Susan with a look of exasperation. "Well, what do you think it means? The kid is sick! They've contacted Make-A-Wish, and you don't do that if you expect the kid to perk up in a day or two. He's terminal! That's what I mean." He realized that he had lashed out rather badly, so, as he pulled his scarf up around his neck, he softened his tone. "Look, call your brother here in town and ask him about it."

Dan left with Sam. He turned around only a moment to say, "I like the lights. They're really pretty." He left.

Susan waited until Dan had climbed into the wrecker and the Sam's Repair truck had pulled away. She was destitute. She tried to shut the lights off, but the switch seemed to have frozen. She could flick it on and off, but the lights remained fixedly on. She went back into the living room where she kept her cell phone. There she saw Dan's stocking hat lying on the floor by the sofa.

She dialed Sam's cell phone. Jack, Sam's son, answered the phone. "Yeah? Oh, hi!"

"Jack, could you please tell Dan that he left his stocking cap here?"

"Yeah, I'll tell him . . . He says he'll come by tomorrow night to get the hat. If you aren't there, he'll leave an address where you can mail it."

Before Susan could say more, Jack hung up. Susan immediately dialed Robert, her brother. It took several rings, but eventually Robert himself answered. "Robbie, it's Susan. Listen, I just heard something about Greg's boy. A guy had car trouble here and had to have help. He knows Greg and said Mr. G is sick. Is it really leukemia?"

Robert McFadden was extremely cool to his sister. After a perfunctory "Merry Christmas" to Susan, he said, "If you kept better tabs on the family you'd know all about it. Greg is devastated. They can't seem to find a match. Greg is a match, but he's had some illness that they say makes him ineligible."

Susan didn't think twice about her reply. "Greg didn't ask *me*. I have the same type of blood he does. We've known that since he needed that transfusion years ago."

Robert didn't think twice about his reply either. "Susan, I think we all figured that you have made it clear how little you think about us as a family, and Greg just did not want to bother you."

Susan was angry. "Bother! Robbie, we're family. It is certainly no bother to be asked. I have never said I didn't love you all. Don't shut me off like that. Did Greg come here for Christmas or did he stay in Akron?"

Robert's voice was hard edged. "Greg stayed in Akron, Susan, because Mr. G is in the hospital. And for your information, we have never shut you off. It's quite the other way around. You've shut us out. Now if you have a pencil and paper, Greg has a new cell phone number. I'll let you call him. I have a house full of company."

Susan could tell in Robert's tone that at least some of the people were siblings. She took the number down, and then, with her sweetest tone, she answered Robert with "Well, tell Julie and Matt hello." She hung up before Robert could have a chance to sting her again.

The next call was to Greg. He answered almost at once. He was amazed that he had reception inside the hospital. He seemed very upset when he spoke. "Yeah? What? Oh, hi, Susan."

Susan was desperate to explain how she knew that Mr. G was sick, but instead she simply said, "Greg, I've heard about Mr. G. Why haven't you called me? I could help. If it will help, I can leave in ten minutes and be up there in about two hours."

Greg was even colder toward Susan than Robert had been. "Don't put yourself out, Susan."

Susan blew her stack. "Damn it, Greg, first I have to find out from a stranger that my nephew is dying, and then you and Robbie treat me like I'm a wild beast, to be avoided at all cost. Stop it! I'm your sister, my blood matches yours, and I love you all, whether you love me back or not." It took Susan a moment or two to catch her breath. On the other end, she could hear Greg breathing, his silence almost strong enough to slice.

Greg responded coldly. "Look, Susan, whether you come or not is of no importance to me. Mr. G could probably use your help. But I'm not going to beg you or plead with you to come. You've made it far too clear over the last three or four years what you think about family. I wouldn't want to bother you with this little problem. You can bathe your conscience some other way."

Susan broke into tears. "Greg! That's unfair! I have never tried to be distant. If you think I have, then you can rest assured that I am sorry to have given that impression. Will you accept my help if I come up tonight?"

From Greg's end of the telephone, there was a long silence. At first Susan wondered if Greg had hung up, but she could hear him breathing.

Finally, when he answered, his voice was still unfeeling, but she could tell there was held-in emotion fighting to get out. "Sure. It's up to you."

Before she hung up, Greg told her that her nephew was in Akron Children's Hospital. She went hurriedly upstairs then and packed a few things. She noticed a table sitting there with packages on it, half wrapped and half not. She called Robert again and asked him to come around to her house right away if he could. Robert belligerently agreed.

She was just ready to leave for Akron when Robert arrived. "Robbie, it's cold out there. Come on in." She pulled him inside and shut the door. "Now I'm going to Akron tonight. I'm going directly to the hospital. I'm going to leave the Christmas lights on out on the porch. We've had our differences, Robbie, and I'm not about to say they don't stem from me. They probably do. But please do me a favor . . . pray for Mr. G and me that this procedure works. I've heard it can be painful for both of us, but if it works, I'm willing at a moment's notice to do it. Just keep us both in your thoughts."

They were on the top step of the porch, and the door was locked behind them before Robert finally answered her. "Susan, you'll do fine. I'll pass out these presents tomorrow. I guess I sort of wish you could be there. Give Greg my best, and here are three packages for them from us. As long as you're going, it will save time."

Susan took the packages and then thought about Dan's hat. "Do you, by any chance, know a guy named Dan Morgan? He apparently knows Greg from Little League or something, and he works with Make-A-Wish."

Robert nodded. "Yeah, I know him. He's a nice guy too. He usually comes home for the holidays, and his parents live three doors from me."

Susan sighed. "Wait a second." She went into the house and brought out the forgotten hat. "Could you take this down to them? He should be there shortly, and it's Dan's hat."

"Should I tell him you're going to Akron?"

Susan sat down behind the wheel and started the engine. "Why would you do that? He isn't interested in me. He just got lost and had car trouble directly in front of my house." She pulled away, leaving Robert to wonder if that was all there was to it.

He drove home and, before entering the house, took the hat around to the Morgan house. Dan had just arrived and was surprised to realize that the neighbors were actually Susan's family. "She was very nice to me."

Despite the beginning of the snowstorm, Susan sped up I-71 and then on over to Akron. She had to stop for gasoline there and asked how to get to the hospital. It had taken two and a half hours from starting out, but now, at about 1:00 a.m., she was in the hospital and asking for Greg McFadden.

The greetings were strained, but the doctor had been notified that a possible bone marrow donor was coming. Susan was asked what she had ingested within the last twenty-four hours, and she realized then that she had eaten very little. Of course she had drunk cocoa and eaten a dozen corn chips, but they decided to overlook that. Her meager sandwich at work had been it.

Work! She had forgotten to call Jennifer or Roger about the day care center. She handed her cell phone to Greg. "See those two numbers? Either the 5607 or the 3351 number will get you the people who work with me at the day care. Call them and tell them I won't be back for a few days."

Blood tests quickly said Susan was a perfect match. The real question now was not how good a match it might be but whether help had arrived in time. Susan went in to see Greg Junior—Mr. G—and was horrified how weak and helpless he looked. She smiled at him and gave him two presents. "Now you can think about what might be hidden in the packages! You can open them as soon as you recover."

Mr. G smiled back. "Do you think I will recover?" This was a question Susan had refused to consider before. It struck deeply into her heart.

"Of course you'll recover. I'm here to make sure you do."

The procedure was begun at 5:00 a.m. It was that important to get started on the healing process! Mr. G had two moments of near collapse, but he held on. Susan was unaware of the pain during the operation, but later in the morning, when she woke up, she felt as if she had been pushed through a sieve. The nurse was just opening the window and told Susan that the procedure was finished and had gone well. "As for your pains, only half of that is donating bone marrow. The other half will go away more quickly, because that is fatigue. I'm healthy as they come, but I couldn't drive that distance that late at night."

At that moment, Greg entered. Susan, despite her aches, had to laugh at Greg. "Brother dear, you look terrible! In fact you look worse than I feel."

"Thanks." Greg was not angry but took the ribbing well. "I guess that is what comes from spending the night in a waiting room. I, uh, had to come in and thank you. Why you felt compelled to bring presents too, I don't know."

Susan protested. "Some of those were from Robert."

"Still, Susan, it was a long and arduous drive. I didn't think you'd actually do it, and for that I apologize."

Susan felt a wave of fatigue come over her. "Well, we can discuss that later, I guess, after I take another nap. The nurse said the drive was a little draining. Oh, before I drift off, Merry Christmas!" She was asleep almost at once.

It was not until late in the afternoon that Susan woke again. She was alone, but almost at once Greg entered, looking much more rested than earlier. "I went home and shaved, taking the packages and putting them all under the tree. Mr. G is doing fine, although we won't know for sure about his remission for a while."

Susan was released from the hospital to go to Greg's the next day. Mr. G was kept in isolation for a few more days, and then he too was allowed to go home. It was awkward having so many people in Greg's small house, but it was still a happy Christmastime even if it was late.

Susan went home again on the tenth of January. It seemed that Mr. G was improving, but the doctors were still cautious. He had been **very** ill. Robert drove up to Akron, driving Susan and her car back while Robert's wife drove his car. They made sure Susan had ample groceries in the house and then left. Susan was sorry to see them go, and yet she was happy to be alone for a few hours.

The time alone was cut short, however, by the arrival of Jennifer Hazelnut and Roger Hollander. They were there to cheer Susan up but also to bring a business proposition. Would she like to sell the day care to them?

Susan had actually thought about this very thing lying in the Akron hospital and again while riding with Robert on the way home. "We'll discuss it on Monday. I have to think about it. I'm not sure what I'd do, but I'm not averse to thinking about a different line of work."

Jennifer and Roger left, leaving Susan to ponder their offer and to wonder about whether Jennifer and Roger were getting together as a couple. (They weren't, as it turns out, but they both married other people within the year.)

Susan was just enjoying the delights of her solitude when Molly brought Max McFadden around to see his daughter. The father was still a vital and vigorous man, capable of grasping many thoughts and concerns with almost no problem. He was getting older, but he still dated—no plans for marriage.

The conversation between Susan and Max was clearly strained. Molly sensed it and understood why—she was closest to Susan in age and had seen the difficulties Susan had endured. Finally she decided to break the ice. "I'm going into the kitchen to fix some hot cider. You both have a good talk." With her eyes, she tried to shove Susan into talking about what actually was bothering her, emotions Susan had steadfastly refused to discuss with anyone for years.

It wasn't Susan who broke the silence. Max could sense something was wrong. "Susan, I'm glad you went up to save Mr. G. Greg tells me that your gift probably saved Mr. G's life." He paused a moment, unsure how to proceed. "That operation isn't what's on your mind. I want to know what it is."

Susan wanted to rip into her father with all the venom and hatred she had held in check for so many years. She closed her eyes a moment, but instead of focusing her thoughts, the shadows of the closed eyes revealed a vision to Susan of the owl. It said nothing and it didn't move. But it stared at her as it had done on Christmas Eve. When she opened her eyes, she could see the concern and worry in her father's face. She began calmly and cautiously, unsure if her emotions would remain even or would jut out in an attack. "Dad, when you were married to Mabel, I deeply resented the attention that you gave to her instead of to us kids."

Max interrupted her. "I know. Don't think I don't realize all the things I missed. It was an aging man's fantasy to fall in love and to think someone would fall in love with him back. Sometimes you just have to realize that you can't do everything, and what should be important is sometimes pushed aside. I could have included Mabel in the things I should have been going to, but then she didn't care much for all you kids—or me, now that I think of it."

Susan shook her head. "I realize, Dad, that I was wrong. I held a lot of harsh anger inside of me because you abandoned us. No, don't interrupt, because it's true. My siblings just dealt with it and went on, but I harbored resentment all of these years. And yet, it's like you just said. You were young enough to fall in love and to seek a companion. Why shouldn't you? I'm upset with myself and not you, because I should have told you that I forgave your decisions years ago. I should be asking you to forgive me instead of the other way around."

It wasn't strictly true that she had thought to forgive him years before. She had just realized the error of her way of thinking. Max stood up and gave his daughter a peck on the cheek. He was crying. "Thanks, Susie, I appreciate that. Mabel wasn't right for me, and I should have realized that. You kids were too important for me to have ignored."

They talked freely for a few minutes and then Molly returned with the hot cider. Each of them found it perfect for the cold January day. After a light supper, they left and Susan was alone again.

There was much to consider. It was then that she saw something peculiar. Lying on a pile of mail that Robert had brought inside was a magazine with a picture of a boy holding a beautiful white owl. Susan thought back to her Christmas Eve visitor. He had promised her four trials. Had she had any of them?

She decided that she must have gone through three of them: Mr. G's illness, the offer of Jennifer and Roger, and the difficult meeting with her father. What would it mean if the difficult conversations with her brothers were somehow important, too? Had she already faced the four challenges the owl had told her would be hers? She just did not know for sure.

It was 8:30 p.m., and she was getting tired. She was about to climb the stairs to her bedroom when she realized that the porch lights were still on. "Oh, for heaven's sake, I don't want to push the season too long." She went to turn off the light but saw the figure of a man standing on the porch. It frightened her at first, but just as she backed into the shadows, the doorbell rang. She yelled through the door, trying to keep her voice even and calm. "Who is it?"

A familiar voice called back through the door. "I'm **not** having car trouble, in case you want to know. I just wanted to stop by to see you for a moment." It was Daniel Morgan, so she let him in.

"You have an amazing ability to come calling just as I'm ready to go to sleep."

Dan's eyes twinkled as he said, "Gee, I must have gotten my timing down pretty well then. Next time I'll call when you're already in bed."

Susan looked at his remark askance. "And just what does that mean?"

Dan shut the door, which Susan had left open, and sat on the bottom step that went upstairs. "It means nothing and a lot. I was wondering . . . uh . . . if you had had any more visitors flying down your chimney!"

Susan did not move. "I have not. But then I haven't been here long. I am afraid I took away your next Make-A-Wish recipient's need for a wish. He is probably healing just fine."

Dan's smile faded. "I know, and I'm glad for that. I actually have a better reason to come back for a visit. I told you that I help people find particular people. Well, I have a client who wants to find you." His face was not serious, and yet he was not smiling. "My client is sure he wants you for a good job up in Akron."

Susan was unsure how to respond. "What kind of job is it?"

"My client isn't quite sure. He thought about making it a job for a personal assistant or helping in his second occupation. He also thought about just finding a good job for you up in Akron. For that matter, he thought about moving his search down here and working for the Make-A-Wish people here in Columbus."

Susan shook her head, trying to clear the thoughts away. "What exactly does your client want? Don't beat around the bush. So far you haven't made much sense." She sat down on the desk chair.

Dan looked a long moment at Susan, his face playing a number of emotions but lingering on none of them. Finally he said, "I'm the client. When I left here two weeks ago, I didn't feel anything particular about having been here. The owl business was kind of funny—in retrospect at least—and I thought you handled it really well. Then I started thinking about you. You have a really nice disposition. I don't mean so much when you are talking to an owl, but otherwise yes. I went to your day care center just before returning to Akron. They said you were in Akron, so I went there and just missed you again. So I came back. I sort of had to. I suppose it helped that my sister kept nagging me all Christmas about not having a girlfriend, and, uh, well, I suddenly realized that I had met someone special and didn't do a thing to make that meeting last. I couldn't call you because I didn't have your number." He paused, inhaling to continue.

Susan interrupted him. "My number is listed in the book."

Dan finally smiled, but his face showed that he was really nervous. "Yeah, but some things shouldn't be, well, you know, conversed about over the phone."

Susan was unsure exactly where Dan was going with this discursive preamble, but if it was near where she thought, she wasn't going to make it easier. Besides, she was sure she was wrong.

Dan looked somehow really pale. "Susan, I don't want to fool around and . . . no, that sounds wrong! I don't want you to mistake my intentions . . . Oh, shit! Susan, I want to find a way that we can keep seeing each other. Jennifer and Roger—is that their names?—were not sure what you were thinking about for your future, but I was hoping—I am hoping that you'll consider doing it with me. Er, uh, that you'll want to go out with me and to find out more about me. I want to date you and, who knows, maybe even marry you. I . . . Oh, shit, this is hard to do." Dan had actually sunk down onto one knee on the carpeting of the entry just in front of the stairway.

Susan's face had been a tangle of crossed muscles. She looked at poor Dan, crumpled in front of her in fear of rejection and of commitment together. She started to giggle. She thought it was the wrong thing to do, but she couldn't help it; and the more she tried, the more it became imperative that she really let loose. Finally she could hold it in no longer and knelt down in front of Dan. He looked into her face with a mixture of dread and longing. She put her arms around his neck and pulled him into a kiss. It was the most spontaneous thing Susan had done in years. She held him there a long time too. Then she pulled back, gave him a light giggle again, and spoke quietly. "When I was in the hospital in your beloved Akron, all I could dream about was being on an open road, stuck in a snowdrift and you stopping by to push me out. Well, my poor Dan Morgan, the truth is that I **was** stuck in a snowdrift, and your friendly manner and handsome face managed to push me out of the snow when no one else, friends or family, could budge me. My dreams were very clear, and all I really wanted to do was to find you again and to tell you that. I guess I don't need to call now, do I? And you're very right: some things don't do well over the telephone."

They were kissing again when a loud metallic clangor sounded over near the fireplace. They both were certain there would be another owl flying into the room any minute. They weren't far from right. Lying just in front of the fireplace on the marble hearth was a little figurine. It was five inches tall, made of metal, and it was lacquered in mostly white, with black eyes. It was the figure of an owl.

Susan knew at once that she had met the four challenges. It didn't matter exactly which challenge was numbered what. She looked at Dan, whose inquisitive look was telling her clearly that he did not understand. She put her arm around his shoulder.

"Don't worry about this little owl. It's a Christmas gift. Whoever says gifts don't come down a chimney is clearly mistaken. They just don't always come from Santa Claus."

TALE 10
The Matchmaker

The snow crunched loudly under Ian Frank's feet as he walked from the parking lot to the church. He couldn't help but mutter to himself about the weather and the reason he was there. "Who in blazes thinks we have to have this meeting tonight? It could wait. We won't make a decision tonight anyway. My favorite program is coming on at 9:00 p.m., and I don't want to miss it."

He didn't get any further because he was already at the church door, and Rev. Mark Freeman was just unlocking the door. "Come on in, Ian. I stopped in just before dinner to make sure that the heat was turned up. This is unseasonably cold even for January!"

Ian Frank nodded and muttered again. "It's so cold it makes my teeth chatter."

They were inside, and Freeman was flipping light switches. They had gone into the addition to the old church through the side door. The pastor patted Ian on the shoulder. "Before we get really comfy, I want to show you the spot I'm thinking about that I think would be a good location. Ms. Gordon agrees, but not everyone else knows where we're thinking. In fact, some people don't even know we are contemplating a statue instead of a painting or a simple plaque."

Freeman switched on a couple of lights in the sanctuary as the two of them entered. He led Ian down the side aisle, speaking as they went. "Since you know about these things, I'm showing you because you will probably be the person who will contact the sculptor." He finally stopped next to the door that led back to the choir room and the stairs up to the organ pipes. Next to that door was a blank portion of granite wall that extended straight up twenty-five feet or so before it reached any beam. "This is a prominent place, it's easy for anyone to see what is placed here, and it has direct access without stairs to the front."

"What about getting any artwork through the front door? That won't be easy anywhere."

The pastor smiled. "I know. That's why I'm suggesting this location. The north doors over here are double, and the middle post can come out with minimum work. Since the doors are eight feet high, that would mean the biggest opening we can have. The other outer doors all lead into hallways or the narthex."

"It seems you have most of the answers to the questions. Now what we'll have to decide is what style of sculpture."

Ian Frank was a fixture in the Presbyterian Church. He always went to area conferences and had even gone to general assembly on the national level. He was active in the church, but he had no illusions that he was in any way indispensable or was in charge of the church. He served on committees because he could, not because he felt empowered when he did.

Ian's occupation outside of the church was with the school system. He had been hired as an art instructor directly out of college. He wisely had acquired his master of arts in education before applying anywhere. Although he had taken further studies, he saw no reason to get a doctorate and price himself out of his position. He earned plenty for his own needs. He had instituted various art classes and a history of Western culture class, something that had, over the years, become quite popular. As the arts were being threatened due to financial cutbacks, Ian showed an interest in becoming administration. He was already in line to become assistant superintendent.

Ian's only unusual drawback in anyone's eyes was that he was unmarried. It wasn't that this aroused undue curiosity or gossip. It was just that he was so bound up in his various aspects of work that he had no apparent time for dating. He would ask unmarried friends, women and men, to go with him to cultural and sporting events, but he never took any particular interest in any one person. His single status didn't bother him.

It bothered Ian's artistic sense, that the addition to the church was in the same stone as the rest of the church, but its architecture was less ornate and was only two stories. It didn't clash, but it didn't enhance its design either.

Back in the addition to the church, the pastor called the meeting to order. In addition to the pastor and Ian, Mrs. Virginia Peters (her husband had passed three years ago), Ms. Christine Gordon, Simon Paxton, Mrs. Ellison Fairbanks, and Ms. Meris Jason were in attendance. Meris was a senior in high school and was a lifelong member of the Presbyterian congregation. She would be attending college three hours away the next year. After the opening prayer, they got down to the discussion.

The sculpture was to be dedicated to the war dead from that community from the Viet Nam War and from the Gulf Wars. The committee had already decided to have a sculpture made, but it had not been decided what style or design would be best. They also needed to decide what materials would be used—bronze, granite, marble, or something else (possibly a combination of materials). Ian listened, participating in the conversation and fully aware that he needed to listen intently. He also knew that two and a half hours can go by quickly when discussions like this get started.

Mrs. Fairbanks wanted a traditional and inspirational statue, with symbols of war around. She also felt that, without naming the specific names, "The plaque should also include the phrase 'and the wars that have come before and will come in the future.' We will honor those from the world wars and from Korea, not to mention the wars before then."

Meris Jason shook her head. "I think that will water it down too much. I don't even know much about those wars."

Virginia Peters bit her lip before she spoke. "Well, my father and grandfather were quite active in those wars. Ms. Jason, you don't know much about them because your grandfather died in the Second World War, so he couldn't tell you about it."

Simon Paxton had been silent most of the meeting. "Ms. Fairbanks, the trouble with a realistic depiction of war things in the statue is that it will clash with so many other aspects of our church. I think that a realistic statue is a good idea, but it should convey the idealistic aspects of war."

Rev. Mark Freeman spoke up quickly. "But, Simon, I can't think that any realistic depiction of a person will be able to give us the inspirational message of hope for peace after all wars cease. Isn't peace, after all, our primary goal?"

Christine Gordon was usually reticent to speak. She suddenly sat up much straighter in her chair. "Are you suggesting that we commission some piece of modern junk that conveys no message to anyone except how weird the artist's ideas are?"

The discussion escalated from that point on into a fifteen-minute battle to be heard and to outmaneuver one idea over another. Few people noticed that Ian Frank said almost nothing. Finally he cleared his throat loudly three times—it took three times to get everyone to pay attention.

"I don't think it is up to us to design this artwork. Even I have no idea what will be best. I want to see pieces of art drawn out for us, and then decide from those drawings what would be best. From what you all say, I gather that the ideals of freedom and hope are important. I also can see that you want something to reference that this is a memorial for our community's war dead. It isn't just for those from our church—at least I don't think it should be. I move that I contact ten sculptors for designs. Then we can take these drawings and decide which three might represent our goals to the best. The three sculptors would then come in and explain their concept in greater detail."

Ms. Christine Gordon cocked her head with a strong sense of superiority. "Are you going to be the deciding person alone?"

Pastor Freeman interrupted. "We need a second before we consider any further discussion." Meris Jason seconded.

"Christine, if you had listened more carefully, I indicated that there would be ten drawings and that all ten would be presented to the committee for consideration. Only the top three sculptors, chosen by this committee, would be invited in to explain further their concepts, give bids, and so on. I will also elicit submissions through a local arts organization. You can never be sure where the winning design might come from."

The discussion had already taken place, so a vote came up almost immediately. It was unanimously passed.

Ian Frank had in mind several people he had known in college. He also knew some sculptors by reputation. The committee had already raised money for the project, so Ian had a good idea into what price range he could go. He picked ten artists, making sure to have varying styles and keeping in mind the nebulous nature of the commission. "Any style" wasn't quite right, but it was closer than saying any particular style mentioned by the committee members. The invitation was extended and worded with this phrase carefully worded. ***The sculpture is to enlighten and promote the ideals of the sacrifices made by our community's fallen soldiers, with a vision of the valor they showed and a hope for peace in the future.***"

It was an open invitation to anyone to submit an idea for the artwork. Ian expected to garner drawings from only the ten he contacted, although he had tried to be fair with the magazine posting. Ian set a deadline of March 1 for submission.

He actually got twenty-three drawings. Even the most amateur were considered. Some were drawings from people who could not have made the sculpture, but they had ideas that were worth considering. Ian called Christine Gordon for help. "Christine, I was wondering if you would like to come over to my house on March 4. I have twenty-three submissions for the sculpture. Not all of them can be made by the artist designing them, but I don't see any reason not to consider them. I just feel a little ill at ease making such a decision by myself. And I hate to go to the committee with all twenty-three and have no idea which ones might be better. That invites a marathon of squabbling."

Christine thought a minute. "What time on the fourth suits you best?"

"Seven o'clock in the evening is actually the best time."

"That's good for me. Do you mind if I ask Meris Jason? She has a good art sense too." Although Christine worked in the county welfare office, she was a gifted soprano. She had drawn program covers and set designs for high school plays for the last ten years.

The meeting was held. Ian had his ideas which he thought would work best, but he made a point of saying nothing at first. "My method of contact was this: I advertised and I also contacted through the web various artists. They were encouraged to e-mail me if they were interested. I then sent them specifications on height, including a picture of the place where the statue would stand—Pastor Mark was in those pictures for a reference point. Each person was to submit an explanation of their designs with their drawings. When they arrived, I numbered each envelope with the explanation and each picture. So now I want you both to look at these with an open mind. Consider what they might be trying to say and then decide if they achieve that goal. We can compare those notes with what they wrote when we're done. Also decide if what they are trying to say matches what the committee haphazardly narrowed the goals down to." Ian also showed them the wording he had sent out. They liked his statement of goal for the statue, and then they began to study the various works of art.

Ian kept the names and ages of the submitters covered so any accidental knowledge of the artists would go unnoticed. The two women studied each work separately, making notes to themselves about virtues and faults. Finally, after forty minutes of hard study, they sat down. Ian took out his own notes. "There is one drawing that moved me all by itself. I will positively not say which one. However, when I read the notes that accompanied it, I wept literally for about twenty-five minutes without stop. I think that emotion comes through in the drawing, but I'll let you critique each drawing. By the way, the numbering is totally random."

Christine began. "Shall we take each of them one at a time?" They agreed. "The first one is a nice, realistic sculpture design. It has good form and I'd say good size. It is drawn to blend in well with our architecture. I'm not sure I really like it, but it's a possibility."

Meris Jason held her notes in her lap, not even looking at them for the first drawing. "I agree that it blends in well with the decor. My problem with it is that it blends in a little too well. While I don't want it to clash with our church's interior, it should not fade away into the shadows. The design, if the statue was standing outside, might be a nice statue. But we don't intend to put it outside, so I'd say it's not right for our purposes."

Ian laughed. "Meris, would you like to read my notes? They are point for point almost exactly like yours. I also agree with you, Christine, however, in that it was drawn with our architecture in mind. I don't say I hate the drawing, but it isn't right for us."

The next four drawings were rejected out of hand with almost no discussion. The second one was considered so modern that it conveyed nothing that anyone understood, and the third was too grotesquely realistic. Meris shuddered at that one. "I can just hear Virginia Peters saying, 'I don't want to stare at that thing Sunday after Sunday. It's just ugly!'"

The fourth was to be in black marble, and the three agreed that it would fade away in the shadows. The fifth brought about a sense of revulsion from both women. Ian just laughed. "Just so you know, I looked at that one for ten minutes before I gave up trying to decide what the woman was about. Her notes are the biggest pile of garbage I've seen since I threw out my Christmas turkey."

The sixth drawing elicited the first really positive response. They agreed that far, and they put it aside as a viable candidate. They would reserve discussion till later.

Ten more drawings were quickly dismissed, although each of them was given due discussion. In each case the pictures conveyed quite well what was wanted, and yet each drawing seemed cold or harsh. Whatever the uncertain mood the committee, as represented by the three, wanted, those ten did nothing to move them. It wasn't that they were abstract. One was even a realistic depiction of a child looking up with hope, his arms raised. It was just that one after another fell into a feeling of generic lack of feeling.

Drawing 17 and 18 were immediately added to the pile of possibilities. Picture 19 made Christine giggle. Ian liked Christine's giggle, and he too began to snicker. Within half a minute, all three were laughing at number 19. It wasn't the amateur way it was drawn. It was more the fact that the subject seemed really silly. It was joyous, not monumental, and it hit something in each of them that, even though it was wrong for the occasion, made them laugh. Numbers 20 and 21 were just not right. The space was definitely vertical, and number 20 was horizontal. It would look awful placed in front of that portion of wall. Number 21 would just look awful, period.

Number 22 elicited a great deal of discussion before it too was rejected. The good points were obvious: it seemed to soar upward in a spirit of freedom, it had nice variety of textures (without seeming a jumble), and it was light enough that it wouldn't get lost in the space. It was just that too much of it was flimsy. Wires and other materials wound around aimlessly in the upward sweep. It was just a little too busy and smacked of being what Ian agreed was "artsy" for its own sake.

Number 23 changed their mood immediately. Ian watched closely as the two women began to express themselves. Christine, as in all previous discussions except for number 17, began the discussion. "There is something about this picture, this design, that is realistic and yet expressionistic. The birds flying upward from a bed of flowers are beautiful. They convey hope and joy while, at the same time, they have an urgency to them that is quite moving. It's as if an indomitable spirit were forcing them to fly up to the heavens."

Meris sat a moment in total silence. When she spoke, her voice seemed full of emotion. "I agree with you, Ms. Gordon, but I think what moves me the most are the two squirrels. The one on the stump is looking up with an expression that says he is at a loss to understand why the birds have flown away. The other nibbles his ear of corn with no concern about the future or the present. He's safe in his world—or so he thinks—and that is enough for him."

Ian pulled a letter from the bottom of the pile. As he took the letter out of the envelope that was numbered 23, he said quietly. "In addition to all of that, there is the bird on the other sapling. He's content to sing a hymn to peace. This is the picture I was talking about. The artist isn't a sculptor, but the style is similar to the one we laughed at, number 19. Listen to what the artist—and despite his age I call him that—says."

Ian cleared his throat, forcing himself to keep his emotions in line. "He writes, '*My father was deployed to Iraq last November. It made Thanksgiving really hard, even though Uncle Matt came over. I talked by Internet to my dad on December 20, when he wished us a Merry Christmas. We were all gathered again for Christmas, and we saw a car pull up in front of our house. A sergeant came to the door to tell us that dad had been hit by mortar fire on the twenty-first. Mother collapsed in tears. The sergeant told Uncle Matt that the details would be worked out in the next two days and that Dad would be flown home for burial shortly after that. The house was a storm of energy going every which way, and no one knew what to do. I finally suggested that, since Mom had fixed dinner, we should do what Dad told us to do: we should have a Merry Christmas, keeping him in mind and heart. We tried to be as normal as possible. Afterward, Uncle Matt and Aunt Jane did the dishes, while my sister and I kept quiet. Mom was lying down. I drew this picture then. I don't know why I did it, and I can't say I had a plan for it at all, but this is what my pencil drew. I include with these notes a photocopy of the original drawing. The design drawing was done by Uncle Matt and me. He had trouble drawing it because he got really emotional, so I had to help. I'm sorry that I can't carve, but I hope you will consider this drawing anyway.*' Then he signed it."

Christine had tears streaming down her face. Meris was composed but very quiet. She asked, "What was his name?"

Ian Frank could hardly speak. "Kevin Christian Marx is how he signed it. His father was Sgt. Harry Marx. He lives about thirty-four miles from here."

The accumulated money to fund the commission was $40,000 dollars, deemed sufficient for the time being. The three had an idea on what to present to the full committee.

On March 6, at 6:30 in the evening, the full group met again at the church. Ian brought with him all twenty-three drawings. He had them separated into two piles. The smaller pile had number 6, 17, 18, 19, and 23 in it. "It was originally thought that we would give you only three drawings. We narrowed it to five, and then down to two. You are welcome to look at any of them, but the three of us feel that the five are the only viable candidates. In fact, we feel only two are viable. One of the drawings we selected is not by a sculptor. The design so moved us, however, that we have contacted the designer of the other design, number 19, to see if he could deliver both designs. They are compatible designs. One made us laugh joyously. We thought at first that would be inappropriate. The other reduced us to tears and yet left us strangely calm, as if the peace of the earth was come again."

As the three had expected, Simon Paxton was filled with praise for all the rejected drawings. The others waffled back and forth from this one to another. It was Mrs. Ellison Fairbanks who looked at the two selected designs the longest. She looked from one to the other and then said, "Could we talk with the designers?"

Ian nodded. "They are both going to be here in five minutes." As he spoke, they heard the door of the church open. The young man who walked in was of college age. He was dressed in jeans, a white shirt, red tie, and a gray corduroy coat. He wore a parka over that which he removed as he greeted Ian Frank.

"You're Mr. Frank. My name is Darrell Jenkins. You wanted me to come here to talk about my design for a statue. I was able to get out of my university class for tonight. You mentioned some other design too. I'm not sure I understand."

Ian brought Darrell Jenkins into the meeting. "Mr. Jenkins, the design you submitted filled us with great joy, which I was pleased to note was your intention. It didn't quite fit the parameters we had in mind. Perhaps

I should clarify that it didn't meet them by itself. We actually laughed when we saw it."

"I'm not insulted by that. That's what I wanted."

"I thought it was. There is another submission, however, that left us all stunned. I would like you to read this letter. Since the others here haven't all heard it, could you read it aloud?"

Darrell Jenkins did so. He had trouble getting to the end of the letter. He handed the letter back to Ian when he finished. Mrs. Virginia Peters was dabbing her eyes. Simon Paxton blew his nose. "Which is the picture Kevin Marx designed?"

Ian had been afraid that the artist Jenkins would take the amateur's design with ridicule. Instead, he looked at it carefully, examining it first up close and then from a distance of four feet. It was from that distance that he stared at it the most. At first he seemed almost about to weep too, but instead, he just smiled, gently taking the picture again and putting it down on the table. "I haven't seen my competition besides this one picture. If you choose that picture, Mr. Frank, then you are choosing wisely. It captures something I can't define, but it says a lot in the simplest terms possible."

"The question to you, Mr. Jenkins, is this: Could you render both your design and this one into two statues for our sanctuary?"

Darrell Jenkins nodded. "It would be easy to do my own design. I would only hope to do justice to this one by Mr. Marx."

At that moment, Kevin Christian Marx walked into the room. "Is this where I'm supposed to go?" He was a young man, seventeen years of age, and his mother and sister were behind him. "Which of you is Mr. Frank?"

"I'm Ian Frank."

"Uncle Matt is parking the car." Kevin looked around at the curious faces of the committee.

"Kevin, I am glad your family came with you. I want to introduce you to Mr. Darrell Jenkins. He's an art student at Indiana University. He's going to sculpt his statue for us." Kevin's face sank. "He's also going to make a second statue, the one that actually won our little competition. Your statue will stand in the place shown in the picture, and his will be on the other side of the altar area. His is The Spirit of Joy. Yours is The Spirit of Hope and Peace."

That evening the contracts were drawn up. Darrell Jenkins would consult with Kevin Marx consistently throughout the carving period. The medium for both would be mainly metals, with some stone for the bases. The match had been made, the artistic goals met, and the congregation was informed of all of this the next Sunday.

Throughout the summer, the two areas were adorned with the renderings by the two young men. Little was heard from Darrell Jenkins until November. The desire was to have the installation of the statues and the dedication of the plaques before Christmas. Ian tried three times, once in September and twice in October, to call Jenkins. Darrell did not return the calls.

It was after "All-Saints Sunday," as the congregation was leaving the church, that Ian Frank was tapped on the shoulder by Darrell Jenkins. "Mr. Frank, I know you've been trying to get in touch with me. I'm sorry for being distant. I had a heavy second semester last year, and this summer I had to earn money. This semester hasn't been easy either. However, with all of that said, is there a time you could, well, come down to my studio to see the two statues?"

Ian Frank was almost agape. "Are they actually finished?"

Darrell Jenkins took a deep breath. "Yes and no! They are finished, but they aren't on the bases. I need to install the bases first, and then attach the statues to them. That has to be done in the church. Could I move the bases in on December 16, and then move the actual statues in on December 18 and 19? I don't want to try to move both statues at the same time. I have plenty of help and paraphernalia to move all of this, but it will take a little time for each, and I'll need the front row of pews taken out. The statues would fit through the aisle, but not the transports and the people to move them."

It was all arranged. During the service on the seventeenth, the congregation was amazed to find the bases in place. The plaques were in place but covered. Great secrecy was made about the moving of the statues. Other than the movers and Jenkins, only young Kevin Marx was allowed to see the installation. Pastor Freeman hovered around, hoping to get a glimpse, but by the time he was allowed into the sanctuary, the statues were covered and Kevin Marx was glowing with pride—and with glistening eyes.

The morning service on the twenty-fourth was a special dedicatory service. The Christmas Eve service would take place that night, so that portion of the Christmas message was held for that service. The sermon on the twenty-fourth dealt with the rise of the indomitable spirit, a spirit that is most noticeable at Christmastime but which rises in times of greatest contentment and in greatest sorrow or tragedy. Darrell Jenkins and Kevin Marx sat together in the second row, Kevin's family flanking him on one side, Meris Jason sitting next to Darrell on the other. His family was relegated to the third row. It seemed that, during the year, Meris was the only one of the committee to see the birth of the statues. She had let it be known, without details, that the art work was proceeding, "And it will exceed expectations like crazy."

At the end of the sermon, Jenkins was called up. "It is appropriate that this statue be unveiled on Christmas Eve. It isn't about Christmas, but it *is* about the rising spirit of joy that is so much a part of the season." He pulled a rope and the covering ascended up and through a high beam, revealing the statue of Darrell's creation. The congregation gasped in awe and then burst into applause.

Darrell then walked to the other side of the sanctuary, Kevin Marx joining him as he passed. Kevin stood resolutely in place, emotion filling his heart. He spoke, however, evenly and with great clarity. "It was one year ago tomorrow that my family found out that my father had been killed in Iraq. The design of this memorial to Hope and Peace was first drawn that day. I had no idea that it would ever become the statue you are about to see." At that moment, his resolve ebbed away. He tried to say something more, but instead he simply motioned to Darrell to pull the rope. Darrell understood the situation and showing almost as much emotion as Kevin, he made the covering ascend gently above the statue, to fall to the ground moments later.

The congregation fell silent, a sense of the beauty and simplicity of the peace filling them with sadness and joy simultaneously. They all stood then and applauded. No words were spoken, no cheers were sounded, and no one needed to do more than that.

The statues are still there, and Kevin and Darrell have become friends. In a sense, Ian Frank was a matchmaker, because Meris and Darrell married a year later. But perhaps the best match was the one made between Kevin, an amateur expressing a profound thought in a moment of sadness, and Darrell, a budding professional, whose design was good but who saw the beauty in another artist's work.

TALE 11
The Christmas Punch

The people of Traverton, a small town in the Midwest, had never known a time when Terri Templeton was not successful. In high school, she had been a cheerleader, president of her class (junior and senior years), and prom queen. She was a teacher to the nursery level children at her church and had a special way with children that endeared her to them (and their parents). She also took an interest in some of the local charities.

It was therefore no surprise that her venture into business took off immediately. Of course Terri had gone to college, majoring in English and business. Her eventual goal was to write children's books, publishing them through a firm that had nationwide distribution. A college friend of hers was the daughter of such a publisher. That friendship was not conceived around her goal, but it certainly would help.

The business she had opened was a crafts and knickknacks shop. The shop was across the street from the courthouse square, and customers frequently came to town for legal and other business and would stop in to buy things and to look at all Terri had to offer them. The shop looked festive throughout the entire year.

Terri had several young women under her employment, and they all thought she was a wonderful boss. Her way with them was always firm, but she was never severe. There was no reason to be. Terri was secure in herself and expected others to be as self-sufficient as she was. They were just that too.

The success she gained in business gave Terri a chance to write her books. She did not have lots of free time, but she had enough. She would take a half day now and then to work on her writing. He knew that her first efforts were too adult, and that her second try at any of those first stories came across as puerile in the wrong sense. They weren't written "down" for children. They were just badly worded.

That cool business savvy unfortunately translated into her relationships too. Her natural poise, personality, and organized manner made her attractive to one handsome young man after another, but no relationship seemed to go anywhere. Terri enjoyed the attention, but she never gave her heart to any suitor. She hardly noticed when their attentions generally began to fade away. The men she liked were growing up and moving on to either deeper relationships or to women who could and would satisfy baser needs.

Her college friend's father, the publisher, was gradually losing interest in Terri's elevated aspirations toward writing. He was beginning to decide that Terri, like too many authors, was all talk and that nothing would come to fruition. His daughter kept him interested as best she could, but her friendship with Terri had slipped some too.

Finally Terri caught an inspiration. The source was an unlikely one, but she would take inspiration wherever she could find it. Billy Mayfield had grown up in Traverton. He had been in Terri's senior class. He had run cross-country for the high school, but few considered him a catch. He bordered on being a nerd, reveling in scientific study. His attempt at college had floundered, however, because he was too interested in the study of minutiae and not in studying his classroom work.

Now Billy (who never took to Bill or Will as a nickname instead) was a local surveyor and mail carrier. He had his own house, true, but he spent much of his time at his parent's home or with friends, hunting, fishing, and enjoying a beer or two. He was what some people called a "good ole boy." The problem was that he wasn't old, was no longer a young boy, and was not nearly as good as he could be. He was wasting his time doing those things he "liked" in favor to those things he "should be doing."

Terri took Billy as the source for a story about a young man who, like Peter Pan, refused to grow up. Terri fashioned him into a character named Billy who wasted his time away in a car garage, "working" on cars, or as she explained, tinkering with them hour after hour, day after day. She got the story just right up to a point. But once she got his character down pat, perfectly written out in all details, she could find no way to take the character further. She had a character in search of a life. She tried to work that angle into her story, but she was stymied. She wasn't even sure why she liked Billy as her source for the fictional "Billy," but she did.

She passed the story idea around her shop. Conversation frequently centered on Billy anyway, and each of the young women had their opinions about him. He was certainly good looking. Everyone grudgingly agreed with that. There was general concurrence that he was smart too. Everyone felt he just needed a guiding star to focus his life. His hunting and fishing pals were not a good source of focus for him. Yet none of the young women, and that included Terri, would think twice about dating Billy. His "nerd" image remained too firmly in place.

All of that character stuff was interesting, but it still didn't add up to a story for children or adults. Terri somehow knew that children don't enjoy seeing a drawing, no matter how well rendered, of a man with his head stuck in a car or hiding in a blind to shoot a deer. She remembered her own reactions to the story of Bambi too much to go that route.

Finally, she concocted a story about "Billy" that took all of that into account, but made him gullible to something someone told him. That was a good angle. Now all she needed was to figure out what that subject might be.

Billy, for his part, began to realize that his friends were getting married and taking on responsibilities that he could take on. He knew he should take them on, too. But he had no one in whom he showed any particular interest, and no one paid him any attention either. In a way, he was fighting the need within to give up his childish comforts for deeper things. He liked hunting, fishing, playing cards, and drinking beer. He had given up cigarettes at least. (He hated the smell of smoke on his clothes when he came home from a card game or a bar.) His interest in tinkering in cars had never gone on to opening a garage on his own where he could earn money. His love of science waned away—too much effort to keep it up. He was too content in what he was and how he was living.

Billy Mayfield's idyllic life was shattered when his parents both died in a plane crash. The outpouring of affection from the community was overwhelming. He suddenly realized how much people really liked him. However, this only made those inner urgings grow. He wanted someone in his life. He knew who it was, but he had no idea how to get her. That person was Terri Templeton.

Here he was, Billy Mayfield, a simple young man, interested in lots of things that would not help him get anywhere, and he was in love from afar with one of the most popular young women in the community. He became depressed much of the time. Most people passed this off as being because of the death of his parents, but Billy knew otherwise. He knew he loved Terri and was too much of a bumpkin to ever appear in her radar. He tried to think of ways to make himself attractive to her, but short of winning the lottery or being given a sports car, he had no idea what to do.

Things got better for Terri and worse for Billy when a new recruiting office opened in Traverton. The recruiting officer, Sergeant Goodman, came to town with one or two soldiers to help him man the office. Billy never had any idea of joining; he thought joining was not about patriotism anyway. "It's all about taking time doing something for your country when you can't think of any better way to waste your time." This attitude did not endear him to any of his friends, but he was only being honest. At least he thought he was being honest. The truth was that he was seriously thinking about joining for just those reasons.

Billy was confused about where his life should go, much as the Billy in Terri's story (what little she had gotten right) was confused about his future. Billy needed help to get Terri's attention.

Billy went to the library now and then, usually to look at magazines on science (a passion he still held to—once in a while) or automobiles.

The library was where he frequently saw Terri. She was there usually, trying for inspiration in writing, and in fact she got her inspiration about Billy from there. They would occasionally speak, but they never got much beyond a casual hello.

Then Terri was returning a book, and Billy decided to use this as a way of opening a conversation. "Is that a good book?" Billy thought the book had an interesting title, one he had never heard of before.

Terri looked at the book she was returning. "***Tristan and Isolde***? Yes, it's good in a rather old-fashioned way. It takes place in the time of knights and fair maidens. I hoped it might inspire me, but it's too silly."

"Why is it silly?" Not knowing the story, Billy had no idea.

Terri thought a moment. "Well, it's a love story, and that's okay, but to have a love based only around a drink that induces love in the first person you see is a rather silly device for a story. We can't write that way now."

Billy thought a moment. "You mean the two only fall in love because of a drink? It might not be so silly if there was love unstated before they drank."

Terri adjusted her muffler around her neck. "Billy, if they loved one another, they would tell each other that they do. No one needs a love potion. I certainly don't, and I don't think you do either." She flounced out of the library, waving a cheery farewell as she went. Billy sat down.

"I might. Some people might not be able to get the courage to say that they loved the other person." He said this to himself. Then Billy checked out the book and went home. It wasn't a long book, and he read it cover to cover in one sitting. He dreamed that night about the love potion and how it could affect someone. He was a knight on a white charger.

The next day did not go well. He tried to talk to Terri, to tell her how much he really liked her. The problem was that his tongue got all wrapped around his mouth and he couldn't get anything out right. Then he had another problem.

Recruiting Officer Sergeant Goodman started making eyes at Terri. He was good looking, strong, stalwart in a typically soldierly way, and, to even a casual observer, it was clear he expected to get whatever he chose. And he chose Terri. She laughed his attentions off, but Billy, who was delivering mail to the shop at the time the sergeant was in it, could hardly breathe because of the tension in the air.

Once the sergeant left, Billy tried to talk to Terri, asking her how she could find the sergeant attractive. Terri laughed Billy's attentions off yet again. "I'm not in love with anyone, Billy. I'm certainly not in love with Sergeant Goodman."

Billy came back with, "Well, maybe you need Isolde's love potion!"

"Billy, would I need a love potion to fall in love with you? I don't think so, Tristan! For one thing, I'm not ready to settle down yet. Besides, the sergeant is attractive and fun to talk with. That's all. I like that in him. You are always so uptight and depressed. If you could remotely be as cool as Sergeant Goodwin, then you might have a chance with . . ." Terri paused and thought a second, "With any girl you might choose." She went on to wait on a customer. (She had wanted to say "with me" but didn't want to lead Billy on. She thought that would be cruel.)

Billy left, dejected as usual. Jeannie, one of the workers in Terri's shop just shook her head. "That is one whipped puppy."

The girls took lunch at a nearby restaurant. They were eating there when Billy delivered the mail. Unmercifully they lit into him, teasing him about being so silly. "Silly Billy!" They cried it over and over. The rest of the restaurant was laughing too. Everyone thought it was funny—everyone except Billy.

Billy could not have felt worse. His rejection and dejection did not go unnoticed however. A retired medical doctor, Dr. Rosario Aqua, saw him and had a wonderful idea how to cheer Billy up. It was an idea of deception, true, but it might just work.

The following Saturday was a community Christmas Party. It was to be held in the large, enclosed pavilion at the fairgrounds. It allowed for dancing (on a cement floor!) and decorations would be in place all along the walls and hanging from the ceiling to celebrate the season. It wasn't ideal, but it was the only place big enough to house the number of people who came to dance. Admission to the party was a present that could be given to a needy child. The local Community Chest sponsored it. Roughly half the town made a point of attending. The starting time was 7:30 p.m., ending at 10:30 p.m. so that cleanup could still get people home in time to get sleep before the morning church services.

Billy Mayfield got dressed up more than he usually did. He wanted to ask Terri for a dance. That was the least she could do. As he approached the pavilion, however, the shadowy figure of Dr. Rosario Aqua emerged from his automobile. "Billy, could I have a talk with you please?"

Billy nodded. "I don't want to be too late for the dance."

"You won't be. Besides, this might be important to you." He pulled Billy beyond the pavilion and over to the entrance to an animal barn for the summer fair. "Billy, I heard you speaking the other day with Terri about Tristan and Isolde. I know that story too, but unlike you, I know exactly what that potion really was. It goes by various names: Glory of Egypt, Tears of Christ, and A Knight's Love. But it can go by a much simpler name. It is an elixir of love so powerful that effects are felt within an hour after you drink it."

Billy stood there motionless, thinking hard about what the doctor was saying. "You mean you really know what it is? Do you know where I can get it?"

Dr. Aqua nodded (that was all Billy could see him do in the dark.) "I have it right here in this little bottle. I normally charge $20 for a bottle, but I'll give you this small bottle for free. Let's call it a sampler." He held it up in the slight light from the moon and the pavilion.

Billy could not believe his ears. He took the bottle and thanked the doctor profusely. Here was the chance he had been looking for to get in good with Terri. He hoped it would really work.

The doctor just put his finger to his lips. "Shush! Don't say a thing about it." He faded into the dark.

Billy took the bottle and tucked it into his pocket. He went into the dance, immediately seeing Terri surrounded, as usual, by quite a few young men, most of them younger than her, but a couple of them trying to renew old acquaintances. Her manner showed that she didn't really care for any of them, and her ability to maneuver them however she wanted was equally clear. She was in her partying element.

Billy went into the bathroom, took a small swig, and shuddered at the strong taste. He wasn't used to it. Then he went back into the dance room, heading directly for Terri. His intention was to ask her to dance with him, but, seeing him coming, she veered off into a dance with Sam Pennington. She even laughed aloud, giving Billy a glance that clearly told him that she didn't want to dance with him.

Billy was hurt by this, but emboldened by the little swig he had ingested, he went to Jeannie and asked her to dance with him. She looked around at the other girls at her table, then across the floor at Terri, so obviously dancing to tease Billy, and she said, "Yes, Billy, I'll dance with you." She was dreading the dance actually, but she wanted to make a point with Terri. To everyone's surprise, Billy turned out to be a gifted dancer. The other girls danced with Billy too. The talk at the table among those who were only watching any given dance was that Billy was light on his feet, could "lead" those dances that required it, and that he seemed to know no boundaries on his repertory of dances.

Billy had a little of the eggnog punch, "punched up" with his own elixir. Even that first swig had helped, and soon he was relaxed and enjoying himself. Anyone with experience at drinking might know that he was slightly drunk already—buzzed! But Billy didn't see it that way. He was garnering the attention of other women, even if Terri refused to acknowledge him.

There was a kissing arch, where couples could kiss under mistletoe. A couple of guys kissed there (their joking manner not allaying the scandal they instantly created), and Billy decided to post himself there to see who might come his way. He kissed Jeannie, Megan, Christina, and Caitlin. Terri looked his way but belligerently refused to come to the arch. The kisses Billy got meant nothing if Terri didn't come over to him. He went to the bathroom so no one would see him crying.

By 10:30 p.m., Billy had finished the little bottle. He had enjoyed the attention he got, but his heart was still low. Terri had flounced out of the dance at 9:50 p.m. The purpose of the little bottle had been achieved to some extent, but the intended target, Terri, had avoided him far too successfully.

Billy went home. The next morning, he was thankful that he did not need to deliver mail. His head was aching. He went to church—it was Christmas Eve morning—but all he could think about was the way Terri had treated him.

Terri went home from the dance too. She didn't fall into bed. She took the events of the evening and began fashioning a delightful story for children. She sat at her computer until 2:00 a.m. She had finished the tale, and it was actually pretty good. But such late hours made her oversleep church. When she got up, around 10:45 a.m., she polished the story off. She wanted to send it, but something stopped her. "I'll read it to the girls Tuesday morning. I'll see what they think. If they think it has the right tone and if they think the story is as good as I think it is, I'll send it to Gigi's dad Wednesday morning."

On Sunday afternoon, unbeknownst to Terri or Billy, another event made all their plans take on a futility they could never have imagined. Jeannie's father, a lawyer of some renown in the state, received a telephone call from a lawyer in Des Moines. The lawyer's name was Clive Cramer. Jeannie's dad picked up the phone and was surprised and honored to be talking to Mr. Clive Cramer.

"Mr. Cramer, of course I know who you are. Is something wrong? I don't usually get telephone calls from people on Sunday, particularly on Christmas Eve."

Clive Cramer came to the point immediately. "I wouldn't say anything is wrong. Something is quite pressing here, however, and we have to solve a question here soon or money will go into the unclaimed funds. That would be a shame, because the inheritance we are speaking of is 2.3 million dollars."

"Good Lord, Mr. Cramer, that's a huge sum. You can't find the recipient?"

Cramer sighed. "No. We have to get the paperwork done within the week, or the end of the year will come, and the money will revert to that fund I mentioned. Do you know someone named Alan Mayfield or his wife Paula?"

Jim McHenry, Jeannie's dad, sat down. "I **did** know them. They both died last September in a plane crash."

Clive Cramer hissed audibly into the telephone. "Damn it! I don't suppose there is an offspring."

Jim McHenry was glad Jeannie was not in the room. He didn't think it would be good for her to know the details of this conversation. "Billy Mayfield is their son. He lives here still and is a mail carrier and part-time surveyor. He's gifted with car repair too. He's a nice young man, smart but awfully shy."

"Well, he won't have to be shy after this. He's set for life. By the way, that amount is after the inheritance taxes are taken out. Could you set up a transfer of funds meeting for me, tomorrow preferably?"

"Of course I will. Tomorrow is Christmas. You can't get the paperwork done tomorrow. Why don't we set it up for Tuesday? I know where Billy will most likely be right now, and I'll go talk with him. Is three o'clock Tuesday afternoon a good time for you?"

Cramer checked his calendar. "That would be perfect. My flight is early in the morning. I'll be there." He gave Jeannie's father his telephone number, just in case there was a snag.

Jim McHenry hung up the telephone. He was stunned. He had no idea where this windfall was coming from, but he was sure he could find Billy and arrange for him to be at his office at three. Billy was usually working at the post office at that time.

Jim McHenry tried calling Billy first, but no one answered. There was no answering machine. He went to the post office. He wondered if Billy might be working overtime due to the season. Two men were in the post office, but not Billy.

Jim asked two or three people, but finally he saw Dr. Rosario Aqua walking back into his house. On a chance, he asked him if he had seen Billy.

"Well, I just left him. I gave him a little bottle of crème de menthe last night for the dance. I think he added it to his eggnog most of the night. I can't imagine that mixture! I was trying to get through to him to get him relaxed. He was hoping for a love potion. That was all I had. He just purchased another one from me."

Jim McHenry wasn't pleased about this. "Doctor, with all the depression in the world at this time of year, why would you give him something that will only get him more depressed?"

Dr. Aqua smiled. "I don't think it will have that effect at all. It is something to cheer him up. If that young man was any more tightly wound, he would explode."

Jim McHenry took a deep breath. Dr. Aqua was seriously unaware of how down Billy could get. "Well, do you happen to have any idea where Billy might be now?"

Dr. Aqua shrugged, oblivious to Billy's presence and not caring about it. "No idea, but I'd check down by the lake. He may have gone ice fishing."

Jim McHenry started to the lake, but, as he passed Billy's house, he noticed Billy's car out front. He stopped and went up to the door. He had to ring the bell three times, but Billy finally came to the door. He was holding the unopened bottle in his hand. He had been crying. "Oh, hello, Mr. McHenry, won't you come in? It's cold outside."

Jeannie's father went in. "Are you all right, Billy?"

Billy nodded but almost immediately sank into his chair, tears once again filling his eyes. "Mr. McHenry, why don't girls look at me?" Billy's whole face was streaked with the trail of tears falling down his cheek.

Jim remembered having seen his daughter dancing with Billy the night before. "Jeannie was dancing a lot with you last night? So were the other girls at her table. It seemed to me that you were one of the most popular guys at the dance."

"No offense to Jeannie, Mr. McHenry, but I think she was only dancing with me to taunt Terri." The next sentence poured out of Billy like a torrent. "I'm so in love with Terri Templeton I can't stand it. But she won't even listen to me try to explain it." He looked at the bottle. "I tried some of this stuff last night. It's supposed to be a love potion, but all it did was give me a splitting headache."

"Then why did you just buy that new bottle?" Jim McHenry was sympathetic to Billy's predicament.

Billy sat the bottle down on the table, not taking his eyes off of it. "It's the only hope I have."

Jim McHenry patted Billy on his shoulder. "First of all, you aren't giving Terri or yourself credit. I know she may be a social butterfly unworthy of attention from anyone, but she has a genuinely good heart. So do you. When you try to talk with her, what do you say?"

"I try to tell her how much I really want to be with her. She won't listen to that. She just laughs me off." Billy's voice was full from the profusion of tears. His words kept getting drowned by his agitation.

Jim McHenry picked up the bottle and put it on an upper shelf. "Why don't you go in Tuesday morning and ask her for a date? Just ask her out to dinner or to a movie. Tell her you want to celebrate something, and you can think of no one you'd rather celebrate with than her."

Billy let out a huge sigh-sob. "I don't have a darn thing to celebrate. Christmas this year means nothing. Mom and Dad are no longer here. I can't get Terri interested in me. Jeannie is sweet, Mr. McHenry, but I've been harboring this love for Terri for a couple of years now, and yet I just can't get her to notice me."

"Well, you do as I say, and then be sure to time your mail route to be at my offices at three o'clock. A lawyer is coming to town Tuesday to meet with you. He says he has an inheritance to give you. I don't know who it's from, but any amount of money inherited is something to celebrate, isn't it?" Billy nodded. "Good, I'll see you then. Oh, don't forget, you'll have even more funds once you sell your parents' house."

Christmas Eve services were lovely. The churches went together once a year, and this was the service. Joined choirs sang three anthems, while carols and scriptures filled out the program. The organist was in her element, supplying a prelude of regal majesty, an offertory of bright quirkiness, and a postlude (following the traditional singing of "Silent Night") that was a quietly luminous piece by Mendelssohn.

During the service, Terri was on one side of the sanctuary, and Billy was in the back row, enjoying the spiritual side of Christmas but definitely not feeling very joyous. He could see her, but he couldn't get close to her.

Christmas Day the town of Traverton was quiet. The coffee shop wasn't open, and the restaurant only opened from 10:00 a.m. to 2:30 p.m. Only the gas station was open, and that wasn't until noon. Families were staying home, opening packages and enjoying one another's company.

Terri's family—her parents and brother—were all happily enjoying their packages and enjoying the time together. It was when Terri was giving thanks for the food and the blessings of the season that she suddenly had a thought about Billy. She knew he was alone at home, and in her heart she felt as if she should have invited him to share dinner with them. It was too late then, but, to her credit, she considered it. It was a fleeting idea, but at least she had it.

Billy wasn't at home alone however. Wayne Philips, a hunting buddy and a bachelor, invited Billy over to share with his parents and brothers. Billy enjoyed the dinner but left partway through the football game. Billy was cheerful, but Wayne could tell that cheerful did not mean Billy was actually happy. Billy hadn't been truly happy since his parents died. Upon consideration, Wayne wasn't even sure he had been happy then.

The two talked a while on the porch, the brisk air keeping them almost dancing. Wayne halfheartedly asked Billy if he wanted to go out hunting later, but Billy declined. The cheerful conversation sank into a moody silence. Billy excused himself, and Wayne went back to the game—halftime was over.

Tuesday morning Billy roused himself at 6:00 to get to work. The workload the day after Christmas was almost as heavy as the workload the day before. Late mailed packages and cards were still coming through. Billy had a huge amount of mail, and he left the post office at 7:50, getting to the first house at 8:05. He hit the downtown stores after they opened at 10:00 a.m. He was a little later than normal hitting Terri's shop due to the masses of mail.

Terri had gotten to work early, as had her girls (all except Connie, who called in with a sick daughter). There was an After Christmas Sale. Terri was just finishing her children's story about "Billy" and the girls had just begun giving their opinions on it when Billy Mayfield walked in.

He could tell by the way that they suddenly went silent that something was up. At first he thought they were laughing about his dancing. But they had all been so genuinely nice to him! He knew his dancing was good too, so it couldn't be that. And then he noticed that Terri was clutching a bunch of papers in her hand with a big title splashed on the cover. The title was **Billy's Imaginary Friend.** He swallowed hard, trying not to explode while holding his hurt inside.

Then Billy's nostrils flared in anger. "Nice title for your story, Terri. The problem is that I have lots of friends and you don't have any. You think you do, of course, but if you weren't paying these girls they wouldn't be your friends. And despite being surrounded by a whole group of guys at the dance, how many of 'em ever come to see you on a regular basis? None of them! I'm the closest thing to a friend you have, Terri, and considering the way you treat me, I understand that lack of friends quite well."

Terri slammed the book down on the counter, knocking over a Santa Claus and sending it crashing to the floor and shattering into tiny slivers. "Billy, this is a fiction story. I only took your name because . . . well, because it seemed to be the right name for the story. Not everything has to revolve around you."

Billy let his voice rise higher. "No, of course it doesn't. And it won't as long as you can get it to revolve around you!"

"Oh, grow up, little Billy. Quit playing the tragic Tristan here." Terri was getting angry now too.

"Tristan? Oh, I have no intention of dying just because I can't get you to pay attention to me. I'll join the army with Sergeant Goodman!"

Terri laughed mockingly. "You wouldn't last a day in the army." The other girls did not laugh. "You'd have to grow up to last in the army."

Billy was furious, determined not to cry in Terri's presence. "I'm not the only one who hasn't grown up! You still think your charm and good looks are all that's necessary to get ahead. No, that's not quite true, but then neither is your estimation of me." Billy paused, picking up the book. He read the page that was open. "'*Billy was in search of a real life.*' Yeah? Well, so are you, Terri Templeton, so are you! I'm a heck of a lot closer to getting my life in order than you are." He stormed out and across the street. He went around the courthouse, finally sitting dejectedly on the steps on the far side. His heart that had been light and hopeful when he got out of bed that morning was now sinking into his stomach. It wasn't love for Terri that depressed him. It was the attitude she had taken, the silence of the girls he thought were his friends, and the sheer feeling of frustration that melted together to overwhelm him.

In the shop, it was Jeannie who broke the silence. "Terri, I have never seen you act like that toward anyone. I am afraid I can't continue working for you if you're going to be that way toward someone as nice as Billy. He's right. Everything *does* have to revolve around you. That is so shallow. I'm giving one week's notice and taking my week's vacation starting today." She got up, put on her coat, and left the shop, followed immediately by the other two girls.

Terri was alone and not sure what had happened. Then Jeannie stepped back into the shop. "I forgot my purse. I also forgot to tell you what we girls thought of your story about Billy. It was boring. It floundered around and went nowhere!" She flounced out, replaced by Dr. Rosario Aqua.

He was obviously not there to buy. "I thought, Ms. Templeton, that we should have a talk. You see, you are oblivious to the things around you. I helped your mother give birth to you, and ever since you were able to take in the changing world around you, you have ignored it. Oh, I don't mean entirely. But the niceties of little things pass you by. You don't take in the beauty of the world, the reactions of friends, or much of anything else. For your information, your Tristan took what he thought was a few swigs of a love potion Saturday night. Some girls paid attention to him, making him believe it was working. The one he most wanted to notice him pointedly did not. He was baffled. So was I. You made a noticeable effort to ignore him."

Terri looked at Dr. Aqua a moment, and then she hit him hard in the chin with her fist. He staggered back, but she answered his blunt criticism of her with a quiet rebuttal. "You, Dr. Aqua, don't know me much at all. Therefore, you have no reason to have the knowledge about me that you think you have. So I'll just suggest that you shut up and leave me alone. Isolde is not interested in your opinions. Go butt into someone else's life!"

Dr. Aqua bowed. "I shall do as you wish. But you'll be alone a long time. And you'll soon realize what you're missing out on." Before Terri could answer again, Dr. Aqua turned and left the store.

"Nosy old busybody!" Terri closed the store and started home. The sign on the door read,

I'm ill. I'll be back
tomorrow morning, usual time.

Meanwhile Billy rose slowly from the steps to the courthouse. He realized that he still had mail to deliver. He picked up his bag, turned, and ran almost directly into Terri. The silence between them was intense. Finally Billy simply smiled and looked down at the mail in his hands. "I forgot to give you this mail. Uh, I guess the old saying is true. Neither rain nor sleet—nor a broken heart—can keep the mailman from his route." He started off.

Terri called after him. "Billy, I wanted to tell you that the story isn't about you. Only your name was used. I thought it sounded properly

American. Don't be angry with me. I sometimes don't realize how awful I can come across."

Billy looked at Terri a moment. "Is your story any good?"

Terri shook her head. "Not if the girls are right. They all quit, by the way, over the way I treated you. I'm sorry if I offended you."

Billy laughed. "You did not offend me. You just ignored me. No one wants to be ignored. I guess I'm not good at putting things into words, but every time I start to talk with you, you shut me off and don't listen. Considering my affection for you, that's just rude. So no, I'm not offended. But I am hurt. You see, Terri, against all odds and reason, I love you. It would be nice if you at least acted like you knew I was alive. That's all."

"Billy, I wanted to tell you that I was sorry too that I didn't invite you over for Christmas dinner. I was asking the blessing and suddenly thought about you being alone."

Billy's lip protruded a bit, and then he answered. "Don't worry about it. I had dinner with Wayne Philips. It was a quiet Christmas. I opened the packages from Mom and Dad—I found them tucked in their usual hiding place in early November. I miss them." Billy suddenly perked up. "Oh, I'm going to join the Army. I figure no one likes me here, and I can get good training in the—"

Terri interrupted. "Why would you do that? You're wrong about no one liking you here. It's just that you are always sort of whining. I might expect it now that you're alone, but you did it even before your parents died. What reason do you have to be sad? If you join the Army, I'll just have to get you out again."

Billy had slowly made his way to the corner, intent on delivery of the mail. He turned slowly to Terri. "Is that all you have to say? I just said that I love you, and you don't react to that at all?"

"I don't know what to say." Terri was sure what Billy wanted her to say, and she was not willing to open her heart and tell Billy that she really *did* love him. Yet in that moment, she was sure that she loved him. That was why she had taken his name for her story. It had taken this long to realize it.

"Well, you might try 'I love you,' or 'belated Merry Christmas,' or any number of things. I would prefer 'I love you.' But do as you please. I have work to do."

Billy walked off. He was determined to keep his walking strong, no shuddering. He wanted to collapse with the pain in his heart, but he had decided, while sitting on those steps, that if Terri was going to be that way about it, she wasn't worth the suffering.

Terri watched him cross the street. Her heart was screaming at her to call out to Billy, but she somehow resisted.

Jim McHenry came across the street. He had seen Terri and Billy talking but had waited until the "discussion" was over. He came up to Terri rather briskly. "Jeannie told me you were upset and having a problem with Billy. Terri, he's a nice boy and not nearly as stupid as some of you girls think he is."

"I know that already." Terri could hardly whisper. "He could not be a mail carrier if he was stupid. I just—"

"He's just inherited his father's company after all. He's also garnered an inheritance from an uncle in Des Moines. Did you ever hear him speak about a sick uncle?" Jim McHenry made a point of not mentioning the millions Billy was to inherit.

Terri bit her lip. She was fighting back the tears. "He may have mentioned him. I don't know. Frankly, I am embarrassed to tell you that I didn't listen too closely when Billy spoke. My mistake! It won't happen again."

"Yes, it will, if you let him get away. Terri, he is everything I think you would want in a husband. I'm sorry to say that he isn't interested in Jeannie. Jeannie doesn't half see Billy's worth either."

"Then why did she dance with Billy so much at the Christmas Dance?" Terri only realized at that moment how much those dances had bothered her.

Jim McHenry laughed raucously. "Silly Terri, she was dancing with Billy for two reasons. First of all, she wanted to get you jealous of Billy in the hopes that you would see how delightfully normal he was. After the first dance, she realized how good a dancer he was and didn't want to let him go. At the dance, you didn't even let on that you knew Billy." Jim McHenry pulled his collar up around his neck, smiled, and left. Halfway across the yard, he turned. "Jeannie and the girls will be back tomorrow. I'll warn you, however, that I'm afraid she may have turned into a matchmaker."

Terri went home to a lunch of leftovers and milk. It was kind of a good lunch, but she wasn't really interested in it. Finally, she decided that a walk in the cold air would perk her up. The Christmas lights around town were bright, but the sky overhead warned of snow.

Without planning her route, she went down several streets and was walking by Billy's house just as he arrived home. His mood was strangely elated, not at all what Terri expected. She called out to him.

Billy paused on the steps to his house and then reluctantly turned. "What is it, Terri? I have a lot on my mind *besides* you. You're sort of in the backseat, in fact—you're not the primary concern at all."

Terri took an uncertain step toward Billy. "I just wanted to say that, uh, that I *do* love you more than I thought. I was wrong to have written that story. It was a pointless story. I really do love you, Billy."

Billy was on the offensive as he stepped toward Terri. "Sure, you think I'm wonderful now you know how much I've inherited!"

Terri was stung by Billy's reply. "I know you inherited a little money and a company. But that's not the reason I—"

"A little money? Terri, is 2.3 million what you call a little money?" Billy just looked at Terri coldly.

"No, Billy. I'd say that's a lot. I had no idea you were inheriting that much."

Billy shook his head. "Oh, sure, you had no idea. You expect me to believe that? Well, lie to yourself but don't lie to me."

"I'm not lying, Billy. I had no idea." Terri's voice was almost strident with her emotions. "I'm not that shallow kind of person. You know that. I swear I had no idea."

Billy stood very quietly for about two minutes. Finally, he said very softly, "Really? You really had no idea?"

Terri smiled. "No, Billy, I had no idea. Mr. McHenry said you'd had an inheritance, but he kept the amount completely secret. I was home eating lunch, such as it was. You must have just signed papers and stuff like that? Well, I'm happy for you, Billy, and I'll even say one more thing. I wouldn't care if you had not inherited a thing from anyone. I have been falling in love with you without knowing it. Today I finally admitted it to myself, but you had already gone across the lawn."

Billy nodded. He couldn't find anything to say. "I believe you." That was all he could muster. They were standing in the cold air, conversing as if it was summer.

Finally Billy said, "Would you like to come in for some coffee or cocoa? I'll even give you part of my supper if you like. Having just inherited a pile of money, I'd like to celebrate, and I can think of no one I'd rather celebrate with."

They went into Billy's house. Billy took Terri's coat and hung it on the peg by the front door. He hung his own coat there as well. They proceeded to the kitchen, where Billy's supper, a delicious-smelling beef stew, was cooking in a Crock-Pot. He took a large portion and gave Terri, who protested that she had eaten some at home, a smaller bowl. "What would you like to drink? Coffee, real or decaf, water, eggnog—I have them all."

Terri thought a moment. "Water is fine. But why don't we have a glass of eggnog to start with?"

Billy put a bottle of water on the table at each place. He then poured some eggnog into two festive mugs. He was about to put them at each place when he had a bold idea. "The other night, at the dance, I tried something Dr. Aqua called a love potion. It isn't that at all, I know, but it tasted kind of good in eggnog. What about it, Isolde, would you like to try it? Tristan is pouring."

Terri's smile was almost incandescent as she nodded yes. The tensions were still there between them, though they were diminishing. Once the "potion" had been added to each mug, Billy stirred them with a spoon. He handed Terri her glass, and silently they raised their mugs, a kind of unspoken toast between them. They drank. Something happened then to both of them. The moment they took their empty mugs from their lips, they leaned into each other and let those same lips touch.

It was a short kiss, but it sent an electric thrill between the two of them. It was like opening a dam. The floodwaters of emotion swept over them. The second kiss was much longer. Then they both started giggling, something neither of them ever did, as they ate their stew, biscuits with honey, and water. The Christmas love potion may have been a sham in the eyes of Dr. Aqua, and both Terri and Billy may have known it was not real, but that didn't matter, because it had worked for the two of them. Tristan and Isolde were together at last.

They were married three months later. Billy's house was plenty big enough for the two of them, but they began almost at once to fix up the house that Billy's parents had lived in. They wanted more size for the children, the first of whom came along in January of the following year. Of course Billy had plenty of money to put into the house, even though he spent a lot just pampering Terri. Once it was fixed up, they sold Billy's house.

Dr. Rosario Aqua couldn't believe they were getting married. Neither could the girls. Jeannie stood up with Terri. Wayne Philips stood up with Billy. Old friendships didn't stop just because they were together. In fact, Wayne began dating Jeannie shortly after the wedding.

For the most part, their lifestyles did not change. Billy gave up his mail route and surveying to take over his father's company completely, and Terri kept her shop, now renamed Terri's Boutique. She also rewrote the tale about Billy, and it became an instant hit in books for children. Billy and Terri were as happy as they could be. Christopher, Noelle, and Billy

Jr. (and Button, their dog) added to that happiness. When they referred to those rough times of the Christmas season, they just said that it took a little Christmas punch to get them to relax.

It wasn't quite true, of course, that the punch was a love potion. The love was there to begin with. It just took a glass of punch and a few punches (the other kind) from friends to wake them up to the love they felt.

Billy's life was focused at last. So was Terri's. It was as if two stars had come together to create a bright light.

Every Christmas, they renew their love by drinking a mug of eggnog (with the proper additive) and toasting the wonderful day that they realized just how wonderful each other was.

TALE 12
Christmas Vacation

Most Christmas stories try to be inspirational, frequently involving a person learning to accept something about the season. This story is similar to those, but whether it ends happily or not is not my call. I think it does, but I'm only the author. Tentatively happy may be better than not at all.

Melinda Hemming had always been a happy girl. From the time she was old enough to have a personality up to the time she was in grade school, she had the sunniest personality anyone could imagine. It was only as she entered junior high that Melinda's sunny disposition clouded over a bit. No one knew exactly why it did. Even Melinda wasn't sure. One of her teachers suspected problems at home, but that was not the case.

Melinda's mother was nurturing and helped Melinda learn domestic chores like cooking and mending. Melinda's argument with her mother was that other girls weren't learning these things, to which her mother kept saying, "Well, they'll regret it if they don't."

Her father was equally practical. From the time Melinda was twelve, she was helping in her father's clothing store. She had a good eye for matching colors, shirts to suits or ties to shirts. She even understood the colors some people should or shouldn't wear. This meant her father could take care of customers who needed pants or coats altered while Melinda took the easier customers.

There wasn't a Christmas season that came along that Melinda wasn't working in the store from the time she got out of school until closing, and that meant they usually stayed open until either seven or nine, depending on which day it was. They took Sunday off, but that was when Melinda got caught up on her schoolwork.

Easter season and other holidays did not create quite such a demand on clothing. Only Father's Day did that, and Melinda, not in school then, could work longer hours.

All of this may sound like Melinda did not like working for her father or that she did not like cooking. She did in both cases. But her childhood was somewhat lost on such labor-intensive activity. The parents tended not to see what they were doing to Melinda. They thought she was doing what she should to help out. They gave her many nice things to wear and other gifts like CDs and a TV for her room. They even thought they gave her love, but this wasn't always the case. *Things*, however nice, don't equal personal love. She was there for them, but they weren't always there for her.

She had a few friends but no time from work to have downtime with them. Once in a while something came along like a trip to the movies, a basketball game, or a concert, and Melinda would have to bow out. Because of this, some friends deserted her fairly quickly. This left Melinda feeling alone at times when she should not have been. There were three girls who were her best friends, and they understood her problem (begrudgingly, of course). They never let Melinda lose out entirely, sometimes even running interference between Melinda and her parents.

Melinda had reached her senior year in high school before she had a date, and even then her father wanted her to work that night. Melinda knew, despite being December 23, that it was a down night at the store anyway, and the movie was one she really wanted to see. Rod Chastain was a good boy too, guaranteed to be nice to her. Melinda had always thought Rod was someone she might like to know better, so when he asked her to the movie, she said yes. But it still took Amelia Redding a good bit of talk to convince Mr. Hemming that Melinda really needed the night off. Amelia was one of the three people Melinda considered to be friends.

After much him-hawing by Mr. Hemming, Melinda was allowed to go with Rod to see the movie at the nearest cinema complex fourteen miles away. It was two days before Christmas, and the roads were clear of any ice or snow, the sky was clear, and Melinda was heading for a wonderful night.

Rod Chastain was an excellent driver and a gentleman at all times. He had been raised by parents who had grown up in Georgia and were educated in "the proper way to treat a lady." He retained a bit of their Georgia drawl. Besides all of that, Amelia Redding was going to the movies with them, Chris Daniels being her boyfriend and date.

With such support, what could go wrong? With perfect weather, really good friends around, and a festive atmosphere everywhere they drove, it was destined to be a perfect evening. And it was . . . up to a point.

The movie was not as good as reports had said it would be. The four stayed through it, but their discussion was on how awkward scene-to-scene transitions were and how shallow the acting was. This discussion was held at a nearby restaurant where they ordered potato skins with cheese, soft drinks, and burgers. Two friends they had seen at the movie joined them. Chris Daniels and Amelia Redding decided to go home with them.

Rod had mentioned that it might be nice to go to the park and sit in the heated car and talk. He liked quiet places. Talking with people in a restaurant necessitated talking louder than you might like, and a quiet place like a park at night (or in the daylight even) was always more comfortable. Melinda wasn't sure she should go alone with Rod, but he assured her he would be on his best behavior.

He was too. They sat for about an hour. Their talk was about nothing in particular, but it got slowly more and more personal. Finally, Rod kissed Melinda. It was a gentle kiss, one she returned with the joy she felt in the attention. This was an awakening for Melinda, and she was enjoying it.

But the time came for her to be home. Rod reluctantly drove her home and kissed her again, gently taking his leave with a sweet brush of his lips across hers. He started home.

Once inside, Melinda had to face an interrogation that was terrible to endure. Her father was sternly crushing the joy she felt in Rod's acquaintance. His kiss had warmed her heart, giving her the strength to take this barrage from her father. Her mother said nothing in support of or against the date until George Hemming slapped Melinda across the face. Then surprisingly, Melinda's mother took sides with her father. The abuse, verbal and physical, continued until 3:00 a.m.

Finally, Melinda backed away from her parents and growled, "I'm going to my room now. I don't expect to hear anything from you after this. Is that understood?"

"You don't give ultimatums, young lady." Her mother's voice was raucous.

"Neither do you anymore!"

Silence took another hour to settle over the house, and even then the tears were still flowing in Melinda's room. Her pillow was her friend this night. She wanted to tell Amelia what had happened, but when she tried she found that the Hemming phone was off the hook. Her father had done that before, so she knew he had done it this time too.

The alarm clock showed it was 5:15 a.m.; after having almost no sleep, Melinda slipped down the stairs, carrying her shoes until she was on the front porch. She put them on then. She had left a note saying only, "I'm taking a Christmas vacation. I'll be back when I think you have gained some sense of perspective." Melinda felt like the spirit of Christmas had passed her by.

She walked to Amelia's house. She put a letter in her mailbox that clearly stated what had happened once she got home. She so wanted to go to Rod's house, but that would seem forward and ill-mannered. Still she paused a long time outside his house. She turned away and started toward the church. She knew Father Eldridge might help her. She was almost there when she remembered that the diocese had closed six months ago. The church was standing locked against the world on Christmas Eve.

Melinda had no idea where to go. Then she noticed that a little door was ajar down by the lowest steps to the church. Her curiosity was too much for her, and she made her way there, timorously entering the little hallway into which the door led. An indoor set of steps went down to the lower level or up into the sanctuary. Melinda went up. She was barely in the sanctuary when she saw someone kneeling at the railing. She was nervous about who it could be, afraid that it might be some vagrant. She walked very quietly up the side aisle, trying at every advantage to see if she knew who the kneeling person was. Suddenly, she gasped. It was Rod Chastain! Melinda stepped forward and said his name softly.

"Rod?" Rod turned his head toward her, pushing his hood back. He had a cut on his head. "Rod! What happened to you?" Melinda ran forward and knelt beside him.

Rod looked down. "According to Dad, I committed a great sin last night in taking you out. We're Catholic and you're not. I told him it was just a date. We weren't married. He kept pushing till I told him that marrying you would be a whole lot better than living in that house with my parents another day. That's when he got the kitchen butcher knife." Rod stopped, finally noticing that Melinda had bruises on her forehead, cheek, and neck. "What happened to you?"

Melinda sighed. "Well, if you are a sinner, then I am the sin. Except in my household, it seems more the other way around. Father lit into me like a gambler into a cheater. Mother sided with him too. Around three this morning, I told them I was going to bed. I am officially on 'Christmas vacation' from their brutality."

Rod kissed Melinda. "I'm sorry about your parents. It looks like they beat you rather strongly."

Melinda fought back a tear. "I reckon my bruises will go away, at least the ones you see. I'd leave for good, but I don't have much money, and I don't have any place to go." A shiver ran through her. She was just noticing that the church had no heat. "How did you get in here?"

Rod laughed. "I used to be an altar boy in this church. Father Eldridge once gave me a key to that side door. That way I could come in early to prepare the vestments without bothering him. When the Vatican closed this church, they didn't get quite all the keys back."

Melinda looked around nervously. The morning light was just beginning to stream in through the beautiful stained glass windows. There was Jesus knocking on a door, and across from that was an adoration of the Virgin Mother by the Magi. "This church is still gorgeous. I wish some other denomination could open it."

"I wish the Catholic officials would understand what a huge population this church had." Rod pulled his coat up around his neck. "Let's go downstairs to see if we can find some way to get warmer. I know they tried to strip the place, but we can hope something is still left."

Rod and Melinda went down the stairs to the basement offices, closing the outside door as they passed it. Downstairs consisted of a large fellowship hall with a kitchen and four offices—Father Eldridge (now in Chicago), the secretary, and two larger conference rooms, all empty. The fellowship hall had a large fireplace. It had never been changed for use with gas, so all Rod and Melinda needed were some pieces of wood and a match.

Rod forced the back door open and found, to his delight, eight large logs. He was just starting to pick three of them up when a man stepped up beside him. "Can I help you with those logs?"

Rod wasn't sure whether he was in trouble or not. "Uh, I guess so."

"It's a pity they closed this church." The man said this with a twinkle in his eye, but picked up four more logs and put them beside the fireplace. As Rod and Melinda rummaged around in the kitchen for a match and some paper, the stranger brought the last log into the room and began stacking three of them in the fireplace. He seemed to know how to make a good fire.

At this point, a few descriptions of our people might help. Melinda was tall and slender, with light brown hair. She was not properly dressed for weather that was as cold as it was outside. Rod was tall too, with an athletic build. His thick hair was brown, and he could have a "five o'clock shadow" by eleven in the morning. His hooded sweatshirt, in faded red, was also far too thin a fabric for the frigid temperatures. Under his sweatshirt, he wore another sweatshirt and a long-sleeved undershirt. It was still not enough.

The stranger was tall and lanky. He sported a dark brown Van Dyke beard. He was dressed in a green parka, brown jeans, and snow boots.

Once inside, with the door closed, he took the parka off, revealing a turtleneck shirt (white) under a red sweater.

The three of them worked for about fifteen minutes, but they got a good fire going. No one had said anything the entire time they were working on the fire. Finally, with the fire crackling, they heard the audible sound of melting the ice off of the logs. The stranger finally asked, "Why is it you guys are in here anyway? On Christmas Eve day, shouldn't you be home with your families?"

Rod answered with a blunt explanation. "Our families have strict rules that prohibit us from seeing one another. We like one another though and want to go out together and have a good time. I don't mean that we want to act crazy, but just have fun. But she's Baptist, and I'm Catholic. Her father is vehemently against me and mine is against her. What are we to do?"

The man thought very briefly. "Well, what are you doing? You're here together, but what plan do you have?"

Melinda just shook her head. "We came here separately. I don't suppose anyone will believe us that we did, but it's the truth."

"Why wouldn't anyone believe you? Have you given them reason to distrust you?" The man was trying to be helpful, but he was more frustrating with every question. "If you have always been truthful with them, your parents should believe you were acting honorably, unless they are totally unreasonable."

Rod answered a little more vehemently than he meant. "They are! Here's why they're angry. We went to a movie. It was the late afternoon showing at 3:50. We got out around 6:10 and went to a restaurant. We had two people with us and met two more just as we were leaving the movie. They had seen the same show so we ate together, the usual foods teens like."

The stranger chuckled. "What was worse, the movie or the food?"

Melinda shook her head, continuing the story. "The food wasn't bad, but when we were finished Rod wanted to drive out to Royalton Park. So our friends came home around 7:45 and we went to the park." Melinda thought she had picked up the story well and had explained things equally well.

Again the stranger raised his eyebrows. "To a park? I don't wish to be indelicate, but did you park?" He wasn't smirking. He was just clarifying things.

Rod caught the stranger's drift before Melinda did. "Not in that sense we didn't. The others had gone on home. We just sat and talked. I've seen Melinda around school for a long time, but I've never been able to get to know much about her. We kind of quit talking for about five minutes as we kissed, but then we came straight home. Melinda was to be home by 9:30. We were on the porch by 9:20. It's just that I kissed her once or twice more and then drove away."

The stranger shrugged. "It doesn't seem like such a terrible date, unless one of you is a bad kisser. I suppose that wouldn't have gotten you both injured. How did that happen?"

Melinda's face clouded over. "I've tried to do everything my parents have asked, working with Dad at his store and learning from Mother about sewing and stuff. She says it's to help me find a better man. But if they aren't going to let me date once in a while, if they're just going consider me a slave, I'd say all of that is useless. They've made it clear they don't want me to go to college. If I don't, I'll never get away from home. I'll never break their entrapment."

The stranger was quite sympathetic. "And that led to bruises like that?"

"Yes, and to an argument that went on for over five hours."

The stranger turned to Rod. "Are you similarly held at home?"

Rod could hardly speak. "Not exactly. You see, I was raised Catholic, something my parents say they put great stock in. They don't want me seeing anyone other than a Catholic. Well, first of all, without dating Melinda, I had no way of knowing what her religion was. Besides, Baptist isn't exactly being agnostic or something. But Dad and Mom hit the roof. Dad was physically after me with a knife. I'm just sick of it. If they had quit going to church because this church closed, maybe I could see their attitude, but they didn't go much even before it closed. I'd say if more people had come regularly to this church, the Vatican would not have closed its doors." Rod stepped closer to the fire, trying to get warm.

The stranger took a deep breath. He stood and stretched his back. "I found a few more logs out back. I'll bring them in. Keep the fires burning for a while! No one can see the smoke. I'm going out to talk to a few friends—and to your parents. I will positively ***not*** tell them where you are. Shut the door and lock it. Lock the other one too. I have a very distinctive knock and I can get your attention, even if you're sleeping."

The stranger was gone. Rod and Melinda wandered through the offices to see if they could find anything helpful. They found one abandoned bottle of unopened wine, a corkscrew (without which the bottle would have been useless), a few altar cloths and, to their delight, a supply of clothing that should have been shipped out for a clothing drive but which got left behind. It was all clean, and they used coats and hats to get warmer. They covered their legs more with oversized pants.

Then they just sat in front of the fire and enjoyed their time together, talking about each other and telling each other Christmas stories. It was the middle of the afternoon before the stranger returned. They had opened the bottle of wine, but with no food they had only had a swig or two. There were two cracked cups to drink from, no glasses.

Rod ran to answer the door when the stranger knocked. When he entered, the stranger was noticeably silent. He handed the two teens a deli sandwich and a pear each. Melinda was the first to notice the stranger's silence. "Did you talk with the people you wanted to see?"

The stranger nodded quite solemnly. "Oh, yes, I did, Ms. Melinda Hemming. They were church friends of mine. Then I went to visit *your* parents first. I have known a Baptist or two to be narrow minded in my day, but I have never known a more infuriating pair in my life. No, I take that back. I know one other pair, but they're Catholic. I told them that I knew exactly where you were, that you were safe, and that you would not come home unless I could bring them proof that they would change. They offered money and said they would write a check for anything. I assured them that money and affidavits weren't the ticket with me. I needed something much more concrete. I needed them to take an avowal on the Bible, under punishment from God if they reneged. I had their Bible in my hand, and those . . . those parents of yours would not take the oath. They said I was coming between them and their daughter, and that they had a right to punish you as they saw fit. I pointed out to them, however, that slavery in this country was abandoned 150 years ago. Uh, that did not go down well. I lifted the Bible and told them that the teachings of God did not allow for that kind of imprisonment. They threw back at me the notion that new translations do not supersede the King James Bible in their minds. I couldn't help but yell back at them, 'I'm thinking more the original Hebrew and Greek Bibles!' That didn't go over well either, so I left them.

"I thought I would surely make more headway with your parents, Rod. I was quite wrong. They were the Catholic couple I referred to. Vatican Council was way back in the 1960s, and their knowledge of what is acceptable goes back beyond that at least to the Dark Ages. After your father, Rod, finished barraging me with terms like Baptist heresy and Calvinism or Lutheran hypocrisy, I saw his Bible lying there and picked it up. I held it out to him and asked him if God had written that book. He answered in the affirmative.

"My answer to him is too exhaustive to go into now, but I hit him with every answer and argument I could that all Christian religions use the same book, the same Bible. The differences are in the politics that run each religion. Well, that didn't win them over, I can assure you. You see, I am right, but diplomacy isn't my strong suit.

"So I went to the police. I know the sheriff well. I told him what was going on, and he arrested both set of parents. By the time they start arguing in front of him, he'll light into them and they'll never see the light of day."

The stranger paused. He looked sadly at the two teens. "I'm really sorry. I used to be able to get through to everyone. Not today, not with them." The man's face showed a weariness that moved Melinda.

Rod had been looking at the stranger oddly. "Were you a minister?"

The stranger shrugged. "Some congregations said that I was their best preacher."

Rod shook his head, "But aren't you Jewish by birth?"

The stranger smiled sadly. "Yes, I am. I preached to Jewish synagogues and to protestant congregations and to Catholics parishes alike. I usually start by pointing out that all Christians worship a Jew. The Muslims don't approve of my message much. However, I've even gotten through to a Mormon or two. Why do you ask?"

Rod looked back at the stranger with something between fascination and dread. "I am just wondering if you think our case is hopeless. Being here alone with Melinda makes me like her more and my parents less."

The smile which had lingered on the stranger's face fled from the faintest onslaught from Rod's direct questioning. "It shouldn't be hopeless, should it? Wouldn't you think saner minds could prevail? I'm not sure I have the heart to return to that jail and to confront them again."

Melinda was watching Rod intently. "Rod, what is it? What's wrong with you?"

Rod stood up. "Follow me both of you." He pulled them back up into the sanctuary. The afternoon shadows were making seeing in the church difficult in places. The bats enjoyed it, but the three were not so sure they agreed. Finally, Rod stopped in front of one of the windows and pointed. There was Jesus knocking on the door. He turned to the stranger, pointing at the window. "Isn't that you?"

Melinda at first wanted to laugh at Rod, thinking he was being silly. When she looked at the stranger, however, the glow on his face wasn't coming from the window. His winter clothing seemed whiter than it had earlier in the day. She could hardly ask her question. "Are you . . . him?"

"Let's go back to the warmth downstairs, and I'll tell you."

When they were back in front of the fire, sitting on two office chairs that had been left behind, the stranger, who remained standing, answered. It almost immediately seemed to Rod and Melinda that his voice was more resonant, his speech was less American, and his face was kinder.

"That window was a source of major controversy when this building was built. The parish had met for a while in the old Methodist church, and they loved similar windows to the Adoration of the Magi and Jesus Knocking at the Door in that church. When this building was begun, ninety-seven years ago, the Vatican had to approve each and every aspect. The archbishop at the time suggested that tall, slender windows show the various saints. Their somewhat-abstract design was considered a plus. The Adoration of the Magi was considered, surprisingly, an iffy project. They acquiesced readily, since Catholics do deify the Madonna. Their objection to the other window was stronger. *Christ does not have to knock on the door of Catholics because they are already worshippers.* The parish insisted, and the window became a reality. Donators for each window were listed on the plainer glass at the bottom of each window. The Vatican didn't like that either, but it was a moot point. The parish was **going** to put the names there. They have faded away, most of them, with the washing of the windows, around forty years ago.

"A highly respected young man in town at the time was Josiah Steiner. He was Jewish, but everyone liked him—even the anti-Semites. He was a tailor. He was the model the window designer used for the face. I ought to know because he was my great-grandfather. That probably explains why I look like him."

Rod shook his head, hardly visible through his shivering. "I wasn't referring only to the similarity of facial structure. You're whole demeanor is so friendly, and you can find logs that don't exist for a fire that should give out smoke but doesn't."

The stranger smiled. "Don't go building me into an edifice like this church. The logs were there. The smoke goes out, but at this end of the garden, no one sees it. People passing by don't bother to look at this church anymore. If they did, the church wouldn't have closed six months ago. Oh, by the way, I know all about this congregation because the history records of this parish were going to be thrown out! I rescued them last June. Someone had no idea how important some records can be. Melinda, do you know that your grandfather was the one who left this congregation to join the Baptist church? Your family was originally one of the founding forces for this parish. What does that say about your father's hatred of the Catholic church?" He laughed softly to himself.

The stranger reached over and picked up his hat. He spoke again as he tied the eartabs down and buttoned up his coat. "I think I'll go back to the jail and tell both of your parents that. It may not help, but then again it might. You two just have to have hope, and you have to have Christian love and charity for your parents. They aren't right, but I have to hope they can at least see light and reason." He started toward the door. "Keep this door closed, and don't open the door again into the sanctuary. It'll just let all the heat from this fire go up. Oh, and the bats might come down." He left.

Rod looked over at Melinda. "I wasn't aware there was that much heat down here." They laughed, but in the sound of their laughter there was a hollow bitterness. They neither one thought that their parents could be swayed by anyone pointing out to them how out of proportion their reactions had been to a simple date. They also were beginning to feel the cold sinking deeper into their very souls. It was a beginning to despair.

Rod snuggled nearer Melinda for warmth more than love. "Melinda, where are you going to college?"

Melinda looked down. "I—I don't know that I will go to college. I may not get to finish high school after this."

Rod tried to laugh, but he was so cold he couldn't muster more than a snort that turned into a cough. "You're one of the best scholars in our class. You might even be valedictorian."

"Don't hold your breath on that. I might not either."

"Well, still you have good enough grades to get scholarships to any college." Rod put his arm around Melinda and pulled her in to him.

Melinda put her head on Rod's shoulder. "Where are you going to college?"

Rod cocked his head and shrugged. "I've applied at Ohio State, Yale, and Princeton. I might get a sports scholarship to one of 'em. I just d-don't know." He was shivering.

"Well, I applied at Ohio State. They have the curriculum I want. Of course, Dad is dead set against it. I just need to get away. I don't disobey the law of God, because I do love my mother and father—I honor them. I just wish they would honor me a little bit in return."

Rod stared a moment into the fire. "They love you, I'm sure. Maybe they just don't realize how overprotective they are." He paused. "Aren't you in the choir? What voice type are you? I wanted to join—I'm a tenor—but I couldn't fit it into my schedule."

"I'm a soprano." They sat a moment longer and then started singing, almost together, *The First Noel*. It was followed by several other carols. They felt better singing the carols, although there was no new warmth. They invented harmony that showed how well their voices blended together.

Melinda suddenly broke away from Rod. "Get up. The fire's getting really low. Listen to me. Pay attention, Rod. We're only three blocks from my home. Let's go there. I don't care what that stranger said."

Rod shook his head. "He said we were safe here. He said we could remain warm. Besides, if your father and mother come home and I'm there, what do you think they'd do to me? *That's* dangerous."

Melinda fought harder. "So is freezing to death in the basement of a church. I don't want to fall asleep here waiting for the stranger. He's gone and can't know what's going on here. I know things would be warm at home. We can sit in the kitchen and have hot cocoa—or coffee. I make it every morning. If my parents come home, they'll be able to see we haven't done anything wrong. We can even explain."

"If they let us explain!" Rod looked around. He nodded and stood up. As he did so, the stranger came in.

The stranger dusted fresh snow off of his parka. "You are right, Melinda, go home. Take Rod with you."

Melinda gave the stranger an odd look. "Is something wrong, sir?"

The stranger smiled. "There's no need to call me 'sir.' Just call me friend. I think you can be safe there. Your parents have come around nicely—if still a little stubbornly. Your parents, Rod, are so straight-line that I can't budge them from their Catholic stance."

"I knew it. Stranger, could you tell us your name?" Rod was simply curious, but he was also still transfixed by the nature of the stranger. "My parents will never come around unless . . . Could you go back and tell them that we're going to Melinda's house, but that we've spent the entire time in the Catholic Church."

The stranger nodded. "I will tell them why you were here too. I know that you were seeking a blessing from the season. You were seeking God in his place. What could be better than that? My name is Christian. Strange name for a Jew, I suppose, but my father insisted. He felt the light around him and in him of the Christmas spirit every year more than most Protestants or Catholics. I'm afraid the police will want to see you, though, about those bruises and that cut." Christian held out his hand and led Rod and Melinda out of the basement. The door slammed shut and locked behind them.

They made their way slowly through the back alleys and side streets to Melinda's home. The back door was unlocked, and they went in. Christian checked to be sure that the place was secure—no intruders. He then turned to them. "I wish you both a Merry Christmas. I need to go. You know, tomorrow is my birthday."

Melinda was just starting the coffee. "Are you sure you don't want some? It'll only take a moment."

Christian shook his head, but before he could leave, Rod called out. "Are you sure you aren't really Jesus Christ? I think you are!" He looked intently at Christian's eyes to see if they would answer before Christian did.

Christian's eyes became very tired and filled with tears. "Let me answer you this way, Rod: when it came to both of your parents, I knocked on their doors. Melinda's parents came out to meet me. Your parents, Rod, have kept the door closed. I'm disappointed. They don't realize that all I wanted to do was to enter their lives and make them happier for this wonderful season." He shook his head sadly and walked down the driveway.

Rod noticed that Christian had left his scarf and rushed out the door. When he got to the street, no one was there.

Melinda Hemming poured the coffee just as Rod came back in. They had just seated themselves at the kitchen table when Amelia came in with Melinda's parents. She hugged Melinda and then, with warmth that Amelia possessed more than most, hugged Rod.

Melinda's father and mother hugged her, but it was her father who spoke first. "I'm sorry about yesterday, Melinda. It was a trying day at work. That's not a good excuse, but it is the truth. You won't have to go back to work after Christmas unless you want to. A letter came for you today, by the way. It was from Ohio State University. They are offering you a full-ride scholarship." He still wasn't warm, but he was trying.

Mrs. Hemming was standing by Rod. "Where did you go, may I ask?"

Although Mrs. Hemming had asked Melinda, Rod stood and offered his hand. "My name is Rod Chastain. I live over on Sycamore Street." Mrs. Hemming did not take his proffered hand. "I went to the old Catholic church to pray. I have a key from when I was an altar boy there. I went in and left the door ajar. Melinda came in after I'd been there for at least an hour. We watched the sun come up in the church, shining brightly through the stained glass. Then we went to the basement. There's an old fireplace there. A stranger came along and helped us find firewood. It kept us a little warmer. I'm still freezing." He took a swig of coffee.

Mr. Hemming looked coldly at Rod. "You were alone there for quite some time. Did anything happen between you two?"

Melinda abruptly laughed, something her parents and Rod were not expecting. "Dad, you do realize, don't you, how cold it is outside. Where we were was almost colder than outside. We dressed in extra layers of clothes and huddled under a blanket or two we found there and watched the fire in the old fireplace. We're chilled to the bone as it is. We certainly weren't about to do anything that might involve taking our clothes off. And I didn't go there to meet Rod. I just went there. I had to clear my head so I was walking. The weather was so cold I looked for shelter. The church door was ajar."

Mrs. Hemming just nodded. "Then I'm glad you found the shelter and that you weren't alone. Thank you, Rod, for looking out for Melinda." She paused a moment. "Do you happen to know where you'll be going to college?"

Rod swallowed a swig of coffee. "Yes, ma'am, I'm going to Ohio State University. I'm offered a scholarship there too." His decision to go to that university had been made the moment he knew Melinda was going there.

The telephone rang. Mr. Hemming picked it up and quietly had a brief conversation. When he hung up, he turned to the others. "Melinda, you might want to make more coffee. We're going to have company from over on Sycamore Street." Amelia departed quickly then, wishing them a Merry Christmas.

Three minutes later, Rod's parents drove into the driveway. They started to the front door, but Rod went to the kitchen door. "Come in this way." They came in rather nervously. They weren't sure how the ordeal of the past twenty-four hours would sit on the minds of those sitting in the kitchen.

All six people sat rather stolidly at first around the kitchen table. Nothing much was said. Priscilla Chastain finally smiled. "This is rather silly, isn't it? Rod, you were right. There is no reason to disparage others their beliefs. The Bible is the Bible. The differences don't amount to that much. Nor do doctrines. Believing in the glories of the message, particularly of this season, is the most important thing."

A woman knocked on the kitchen door, interrupting the revelation. She entered without being asked. "My name is Phillipa Jones, and I'm with child welfare. I want to see the injuries to your children. Police business demands that I do." She took a few minutes with the cut on Rod's head and another two or three on the bruises on Melinda's neck. "Does anyone want to explain these?"

Rod nodded. "I will. Believing in God can make people follow certain doctrines strongly, perhaps more strongly than the churches those doctrines represent intend. Melinda and I had a date yesterday afternoon. I got her home on time but a little later than expected, and my tardiness became an issue that escalated into a few words that came about from fatigue, zealous beliefs, and overprotectiveness. I think it's all ironed out now."

Phillipa Jones wasn't sure she believed them. "Well, don't make me come back to any of your houses." She left.

The late afternoon lapsed into evening, and those in the Hemming house had a nice conversation in the living room. Melinda and her mother made a delicious soup that sent everyone away with warmth in their stomachs. Rod gave Melinda a hug, but thought he might do better not to push it by kissing her. As he stepped out through the door, however, he said, "That silly comedy is opening at the Cineplex. Do you want to go on Friday?"

Melinda looked back at her parents. They just looked on good-naturedly. She turned to Rod. "I'd like that a lot. We have to be back here by 8:30 p.m., because Mom and Dad are having a New Year's Eve party. Mr. and Mrs. Chastain, would you like to come to that party, too?"

Mr. Chastain smiled. "I'd like that. Something else, too—Since our church is closed, aren't you having a service tonight at ten? My family and I'd like to sit with you, if you're going."

The service was beautiful and lasted roughly forty-five minutes. Then everyone went home filled with the spirit of Christmas.

It was only as the Hemming family started up the stairs to bed that Melinda said, "We were visited by this stranger named Christian. He helped us get through the day. He was so nice. I wish I knew where he lived, because tomorrow is his birthday."

Mr. Hemming gave his daughter a hug. "You're always thinking about others. You teach us all, Melinda. I don't think this stranger named Christian will be without presents. I'm sure a lot of people will help him celebrate."

After Christmas, Rod and Melinda went back to the church. The temperature was warmer. The fireplace showed signs that they had been there. As they were leaving, Rod carefully relocking the door, a man in a clerical collar came up to them. "Ah, Rod Chastain, I see you kept a key to the old church, too. Good."

Rod looked at the man a moment. "Father Eldridge? What brings you back to town?"

The priest smiled. "I was asked by a local man to consider reopening the church. I've consulted the Vatican. I'm retired, but I could restart the parish up. I've often thought you might make an excellent priest. Now that I see you with this young lady, I have a feeling those goals won't happen."

Rod laughed. "Probably not. We're just very good friends—at the moment."

They helped Father Eldridge search throughout the church to see its condition. As they were about to leave, Christian (the stranger) came around the corner of the church. He was carrying two large boxes. "Father Eldridge, as they were closing the church, someone saw fit to throw these out. I thought you might like them."

Father Eldridge clearly did a small bow to the man. "Some of us are blind, Christian, to the real treasures in our lives. Thank you for these. They will be safe with me, and they will take their lawful place again soon, hopefully within the month. Rod, I hope you will keep in touch with this church. Perhaps you can have a service here even if you're not a priest." Father Eldridge's eyes twinkled brightly.

Christian talked briefly with them all and then left as did Father Eldridge. Melinda quietly said to Rod, "You know, I still think you're right about Christian."

TALE 13
A Day of Hope

Serena Albert was normally a happy eighteen-year-old. She loved school, and she loved Danny Groverland even more. They had gone together since sophomore year in high school. And it was Danny who helped get Serena through Thanksgiving that year.

The family had gathered for Thanksgiving in 1967 like it did every year, but this time was definitely different. Connor Roy Albert was not there. He had left in mid-October to serve in the military in Viet Nam. This left Serena and her mom alone for the holidays. Serena's mom had invited Danny over for dinner. Although his family didn't much like him not being home for the meal at *their* house, he promised to be home for supper—and to suffer the consequences of eating two big meals in a row.

Serena had a beautiful soprano voice. It was clear and focused, not like other senior girls, and she could sing pop songs and classical songs with equal ease. She was encouraged to get lessons and try for a professional career. That did not really interest Serena. She liked singing. She did not intend to quit singing. But she was interested in being a normal wife and eventually a mom. It wasn't that she was poor and content (or condemned) to stay there. The Albert family was wealthy enough. But Serena was not sure what she wanted to do.

One thing she had an idea about concerned her dad. Right after Connor Roy left for Viet Nam, Serena put into motion her little plan. Why not make a tape of Christmas music and send it to her dad in Viet Nam. He had given them his address, so that should be no problem.

Serena got Marty, her best friend, to play piano. They went to the church, where the acoustics were just reverberant enough, and made a cassette of carols, hymns, "O Holy Night" and, as a thrown-in added bonus, "My Heart Belongs to Daddy." The taping took two hours, but the tape came out really well.

Serena made a copy of the best takes and was about to send it off, when she had a new idea. Serena had a theatrical side to her, and she enjoyed showing off—within taste, of course. Her idea was to go to Viet Nam and appear as a surprise to her father in *The Bob Hope Show*. So she went to the nearest recruiting office and asked if they could give her an address for Bob Hope and his entertainment tours to war-torn areas. The guy took twenty minutes to find it, but he finally got the address. Serena sent the first copy of the tape to Bob Hope, including her senior picture as well. The second copy went to her dad. She didn't mention the tape to anyone else. She was afraid of being laughed at for doing something stupid. Besides, as she later thought, why would they ever dare let her go into a danger zone? That wouldn't make sense.

December 15 rolled around and there was still no word from Bob Hope. She thought he would at least send a rejection letter. *"I'm sorry, Ms. Albert, Mr. Hope heard your tape and liked your picture, but has to refuse you due to the extreme security risk of the region. We can't allow normal citizens to visit their relatives in Viet Nam."*

Such a letter didn't come, and December 15 was the school Christmas dance. Serena took an hour fixing her hair and donning her beautiful gold dress. It wasn't a formal—the dance was not a prom after all—but it was very dressy and quite impressive. Danny Groverland arrived at 7:05 p.m., wearing a dark gray pair of pants and an off-white shirt with balloon sleeves and a lace-up front. The added leather vest (in oxblood) made his whole appearance look very romantic. He pinned a corsage of white roses on Serena without being self-conscious at all. Serena and he were on such familiar terms that his touching her shoulder or brushing her bosom was no concern at all to him. Besides it was later this night that he wanted to kneel down to ask her to marry him.

They were just getting in the car, when a red-white-and-blue truck pulled up. It was from the post office. A man got out and started up the Albert walk with a legal envelope in his hand. Serena called out to the man. "Is that a letter for Serena Albert?"

The deliveryman turned. "Yes, it is."

"I'm Serena Albert."

The man brought the envelope over to her, and she signed for it. It was just a little bigger than a normal business envelope, and it was quite thick. As he left, Serena said to Danny, "Let's take it back inside the house to open it."

Danny frowned in frustration. "But we'll be late for the dance!"

Serena laughed. "Now, Danny, you know Jack and Graham will both come in an hour late. I just don't want to leave this in the car."

They went back in. Janine Albert was surprised to see her daughter back so soon. Danny and she were even more surprised to see what the envelope contained. In it was a letter.

Dear Ms. Albert,

Thank you for your request. We have had to make several calls and make quite a few arrangements on your behalf. Mr. Hope was quite impressed with your tape and with your picture. Enclosed is a plane ticket from your native Indianapolis to Los Angeles International Airport. The plane leaves at 7:55 a.m., December 16. Once you reach LA International and get your luggage, proceed to the American Airlines counter and ask them to page Paul Howe. He'll then escort you to a waiting plane to bring you and some other entertainers to Viet Nam.

You are to bring two changes of clothing only, plus a clean and crisp—but not too fancy—entertainment outfit. Without being crass, I'll suggest that showing a little leg or cleavage is an okay thing, but don't go overboard. It is a war zone after all. The arena for the first concert is the one where your father will attend.

> Once that concert is over, you and some other staff people will be heading back to the U.S.
>
> I look forward to seeing you in Viet Nam.
>
> Sincerely yours,
Jonathan Young

Serena was ecstatic. Of course, she had to explain the whole thing about the tape. Her initial idea was to stay home from the dance to pack. She finally changed her mind but not because Janine had gone on for ten minutes about going to the dance. It was Danny's forlorn face, ever so slightly bitter, that made her decide to go after all. Her mother would get her passport out of the desk and pack her things so she could fall into bed and crawl out a few hours later with no problem.

The dance was beautiful. Danny realized, of course, that his intended desire to "pop the question" was now *out* of the question. Instead he informed Serena about **his** good news for the day. He had been given a full scholarship to Chicago University. Serena wanted to go there too. He also was given an internship at Stratton and Stratton law firm. If all went well, about the time Danny was ready to become a lawyer, the elder Stratton would retire. The younger Stratton would hang on a few more years and then, if Danny proved himself, Danny would take over the firm entirely.

Serena was very happy for Danny, although her brain was still whirling about her upcoming trip. She was kind enough to say, quite sincerely, "Your news is wonderful and so far reaching. My news only covers a week at best. And we'll be together at the university. That's fabulous too." Danny understood her preoccupation with other things and didn't press the issue.

At one point, however, while Serena went to the restroom with Marty—girls must talk about things—Danny found a piece of paper and pen and wrote a little note on it. When Serena came back, he gave it to her. "Don't open this now. Give it to your father for me. It's a little greeting and an encouragement for his tour of duty."

Serena thanked Danny and tucked it inside her purse. Danny and she began to dance again, managing to dance eight of the next ten dances. At eleven o'clock, the dance began to unwind rather quickly, and people went their separate ways.

Danny took Serena home, feeling the box for the ring in his pocket. He so wanted to ask Serena to marry him, but he needed her full attention, and that would not come that night. He reminded her about the note and then kissed her good night.

As he drove off, Serena went into the house, taking the note and tucking it inside her passport in her carry-on purse. She slept soundly, but her dreams were filled with conflicting images. Balancing against the beautiful lights from the dance and Danny's romantic image were the images she had seen on TV of injuries to men on the field of battle and of newsmen running for cover under mortar fire.

Morning rolled around way too soon. Janine Albert called upstairs to Serena at 5:15 a.m. Serena couldn't believe how early it was, but she knew it would take time to get to the airport and checked in. She also knew she could sleep on the plane.

Once she got to Los Angeles International Airport, she went to the American Airlines counter, as she had been told, and asked them to page Paul Howe. Paul Howe appeared almost immediately at her elbow. He was a tall, good looking but slightly balding man who obviously was tired and needed rest as much as Serena felt she needed it. He escorted Serena down a long corridor and then down a second one. This did not lead to American Airlines but to a private boarding spot. There were some entertainers there whom she knew. She couldn't remember their names—they were from her mom and dad's generation—but she knew the faces.

It took several hours of flying (and sleeping) to get to a landing strip in Viet Nam. One of the young women talked with Serena on the way, a dancer and singer who had several records to her credit, and who had appeared in *Bonanza* on TV. That impressed Serena a lot.

Finally they were ushered off of the plane and into a hangar, quickly traversing the tarmac so that prying eyes would not find them interesting. The first person she met was Bob Hope. He was gracious to her, but he had so much to do that he couldn't give her more than a pleasant nod and thanks for coming. She felt a little disappointed, but she realized that it was her doing that she was there at all.

The producer and director for the show both caught up with her and led her through the paces of what she would do. She would sing "My Heart Belongs to Daddy" and then lead the group in "Silent Night." No dancing and only movement during the secular song. This was all she had to do.

Then a young woman wearing army fatigues came around and escorted her to a little room where she would change into her outfit. The show would start in one hour's time.

The show went beautifully. Bob Hope was his usually great self, introducing new and old acts alike as friends and acquaintances of his. When it came time for Serena, she was introduced as Cdr. Connor Roy Albert's daughter. Most of the people gave a few whoops and cheers, but Serena and Bob Hope both noticed a small assemblage in the front row immediately start talking among themselves, nodding to one another and making agitated gestures.

Serena couldn't tell what that was all about, but she pulled herself up and turned on the charm. Her "innocent" portrayal of her song warmed everyone's heart, not just "Daddy's," and the ovation was quite strong. She went back into the corner while the rock star gave his rendition of "Rockin' Christmas." A couple more acts followed, and then Bob Hope introduced Serena again for "Silent Night."

Her quiet rendition of the first verse pulled the crowd of mostly men right into the stage. She let her voice sore a little more with the verse about the shepherds, and then the others all joined in for verse three. Some in the crowd were crying, thinking about loved ones at home. Bob Hope led "White Christmas" after that.

Then as the orchestra played "Thanks for the Memories" (Bob Hope's theme song), the whole group left the stage to a standing ovation from the appreciative guys in the crowd. They took two more curtain calls and that was that. Bob Hope gave Serena a little peck and said that she had done a wonderful job. Then he left with the crew.

It was at that time that two men came up to Serena. She had remembered seeing them in the front row. "Ms. Albert? We need to speak with you a moment." They ushered her into a side room from the hangar. Her luggage, she noticed, was already there. "Your father, Cdr. Albert, was shot down yesterday in an attack near here. He was seriously injured and was taken to another airbase south of here. We have a plane ready to take you there so you can see him. Mr. Hope insisted that we do this, although it is quite unusual. After you see him, we'll fly him to a hospital in Hawaii and you back to LA and then to Indianapolis."

Serena asked, "What's wrong with him exactly?"

The younger man, who seemed a lot gentler, put his hand on Serena's shoulder. "We aren't exactly sure, Ms. Albert. We know there is shrapnel involved, and he has a bad wound to his left leg. But something is keeping him from rousing. It is almost like he doesn't want to get better. Is there anything at home that could make him not care whether he gets home or not?"

Serena shook her head. "There is nothing that I know of. I think Mom and he had a few unhappy words in September, but I don't think it was serious." She began to worry that they might have decided on a divorce—she had heard them mention it once or twice in years past.

Serena was ushered onto a small shuttle airplane with a big cross on the side of it. She reasoned to herself that it was supposed to keep Vietnamese from attacking the plane. Bob Hope actually saw her off, thanking her again for being such a special part of the program. (He did say that her participation would not make it onto TV in America—but that was due to union rules and the length of the broadcast time slot, and Serena understood that.)

It was nearly dark when they took off. The ride took about forty-five minutes. When they landed, they went immediately into a hangar and the door was closed behind them. The young man came forward again and ushered Serena to a jeep. They would keep her luggage there, because she would depart from that airport when her visit was over. Ten minutes later, the jeep pulled into the hospital compound. It was only here that the young man explained that he had been in the plane with her father. "He was the only one hurt seriously. The rest of us have rallied. He just hasn't. Uh, he won't look too good, so try not to get too upset."

He pushed the door open, and Serena stepped gingerly inside. Her father's head was bandaged quite heavily. She could tell by his chin and hands that it was Connor, but he was all filled with tubes and wires. It made her hurt just seeing him. She pushed down the fear that filled her heart and mind, stepping slowly up to the bed. She whispered, "Dad, I'm here. Serena is here." He did not respond. "Daddy, I'm Serena, your little girl." There was still no response.

She did not know why it was, at that moment, she thought about the note in her passport, but she suddenly remembered it and that Danny had asked her to give it to her father. She pulled it out and clutched it. Instead of opening it at once, however, she started to sing her song from the show, "My Heart Belongs to Daddy." It seemed that he stirred. It wasn't much, but the young officer who had been so kind to Serena noticed it immediately.

"That's more movement than he's done in the last twenty-four hours." He quietly slipped out the door to get a doctor.

"Daddy, I sang with *The Bob Hope Show* tonight. It was supposed to be a surprise just for you, but you couldn't get there, so I'm here. I want you to open your eyes. I have a note from Danny. He asked me to give this to you, show it to you, and I think get a response from you if I can. I'm not supposed to read it, so you'll have to open your eyes."

The young sergeant stepped back into the room. "I don't think he *can* open his eyes yet. The light hurts them, and he can't focus. If you give me the note and then step out into the hall, I'll read it to him. If he gives a response, I'll tell you what it was."

Serena stepped out into the hall. She heard doctors talking about a serious patient. When they realized she was standing there, they stopped talking and moved into the next room. She knew then that her father might not make it.

The sergeant stepped out just in time to see Serena start to slump to the floor in tears. "Here, now, you can't do that. Your dad answered me. He said he'll be there, no matter what. You need to tell your dad good-bye now, 'cause we have to get you on a plane back to LA and him on a plane to Hawaii. They were reluctant to move him before, but maybe you've helped him more than you know. I hope so."

The two doctors who had been talking came back into the hallway. Serena went into her father's room as the doctors began talking with the sergeant. She saw the note lying on the stand at the side of the bed.

Mr. Albert,

You remember me, Danny Groverland. I have been going with Serena for several years now. We're both accepted into Chicago University. My prospects for the future are bright. So I want to marry her this coming summer, and I want your blessing. If you can manage it, I want you to be there too. I don't know how long you have to serve there, but I really want you at the wedding.

Danny Groverland

"Dad," Serena began after reading the note, "Mom and I need you at home. Whatever the reason that you've been not responding to treatment, you need to put that aside. We need you to be a part of our lives for a long time to come. I thought this was a Bob Hope tour, but now I realize it is really just a tour for hope—your hope. If you give your permission for me to marry Danny, I will. But I want you at the wedding."

The sergeant ushered her out, and within minutes Serena was on a plane back to the United States. She could hardly believe, when she got home, that she had been gone only four days. It was a whirlwind tour, and it left her exhausted.

Once she got home, of course, she had to tell her mom about her dad's injuries. That didn't seem to worry her mother. "I dreamt about him three days ago. Danny had told me about his note, and he came to me to tell me that he would not miss your marriage to Danny for any reason."

Christmas Eve came far too soon. Danny had finally officially asked Serena to marry him—she answered yes of course. At about eight o'clock that evening, the telephone rang. It was Bob Hope wishing Serena a Merry Christmas. He was praying that her father's recovery was progressing.

The call that came at 8:30 was from the sergeant. He wanted to know if Serena was there, but she had answered. "This is Sgt. Wilkins. We met in Nam. I just wanted to tell you that your father is making a wonderful recovery. He keeps talking about his angel who saved him. I guess that'd be you."

"Thanks, but I just spoke to him like I always do."

"You can tell him that." The line went dead for a moment, and Serena was afraid she had lost the call completely.

Then a weak but steady voice came on the line. "Serena, I'm sorry I couldn't talk to you. You came all the way to Nam, and I couldn't squeak out a word. I heard your voice. Your singing reached down deep into the spot that needed touching. I guess it always has done that. Thanks for coming. I'll see you soon. Could you put your mother on?"

Janine spoke for five minutes and then hung up the phone. "He'll be home in a month or two."

The sergeant sent Serena progress reports weekly.

Summer came, and Connor had yet to get home. The reports had become vague and, as Serena began to read between the lines, more troubling. Perhaps her father had lapsed again. By May the reports stopped altogether, and writing and even calling didn't seem to help.

The wedding was set for August 1. With reception hall, church, and cake arranged for, they couldn't postpone the wedding. Besides, both Serena and Danny were headed to college. Serena was fretful and anxious about her father's absence.

Serena told her Uncle Gerry to be in the front vestibule of the church to walk her down the aisle. The time was so hectic that she had no time to give her father a thought. Her mother left her and went out to be ushered to her seat. Serena stood at the door of her room, trying to breathe deeply. The air outside was heavy and humid and inside it wasn't much better. She heard the strains of the Purcell Trumpet Tune starting and could watch as her first bridesmaid stepped into the vestibule.

In her mind, Serena could see the ushers pulling back the runner, and Danny and his three attendants coming through the side door and into their place. Then she pictured her neighbor's daughter strewing pink rose petals down the aisle, followed by Gerry's son Todd carrying the pillow with the two rings tied onto it. She then watched as the second bridesmaid (Marty) stepped into the vestibule and then her maid of honor, her cousin Theresa.

The wedding planner pulled the veil down over Serena's face and led her forward to the vestibule. As she stepped into the vestibule, she heard the organist change to the traditional wedding march. The trumpet quit playing, and the string quartet joined in.

Serena was almost numb from nervousness. It was only as she started down the aisle that she thought, "Oh, if only Daddy could be here!"

Danny looked like a knight standing at the end of the aisle. His eyes were filled with love for her. Did he like the dress? Everyone had stood up and several people were weeping and smiling happily. Danny stepped forward and put his arm out to Serena. She took it, but the other arm was still held by her Uncle Gerry.

"Dearly beloved, we are gathered here to join Serena and Danny in blessed matrimony." The comments were made about objections—there was silence. And the questions began. "Do you, Danny, take this woman to be your lawfully wedded wife, to have and to cherish from this day forward?" Serena could hardly hear the preacher. He also asked her the same question, and she answered somehow. Her head was almost swimming in anxiety. "Who gives this woman to this man?"

Serena was so thinking about her dad that she hardly heard the reply. "Her mother and I do." Wait! That wasn't Uncle Gerry's husky voice. It was a sweeter voice, one filled with a depth and beauty she hadn't heard since . . .

Serena turned and looked into the eyes of her father. Connor had a cane in his left hand. He leaned down and kissed Serena on her cheek. "I told you I wouldn't miss this day, no matter what. Look on the altar."

As he sat down next to Janine, Serena turned slowly to the altar. Sitting on it was a beautiful bouquet of flowers, in the midst of which was a small figure of a girl, dressed exactly as Serena had been back in Viet Nam except for the presence of wings. Serena understood the gesture and nodded gratefully through her tears.

Serena got through the ceremony, though she had no idea what had actually been said. At the reception, everything went as it always does—cake in the face, drinking wine with intertwined arms (despite the age of both the bride and groom), and even garter and bouquet toss. The most special moment was when Connor Roy Albert came forward haltingly to Serena, held out his hand, and took her out onto the dance floor. His legs had been crushed, and they looked crooked. (Connor would never walk normally again and received a medical discharge two days later.) Halfway through the dance, Danny stepped forward and danced with Serena as Connor danced carefully with Janine.

Then they went to the dinner. The best man gave his toast. It was the unusual moment of Connor standing to give *his* toast. Fathers seldom do that. But this time everyone fell very quiet.

"There were those who said in December that I would never make it through rehab and get to this wedding. There were days I almost thought I wouldn't too. I made a promise to Danny and to Serena that I would be here. When I make a promise, I keep it, just as I made a promise to my men that I would not desert them in combat. Danny, you once made a promise to me. I expect you to keep your promise as I kept mine. At the moment, I could not be happier. So I too want to offer a toast: to my Christmas Angel, the shining light who led me through the long time of rehabilitation."

The Christmas angel smiled up at her dad. It was something that perhaps no one else understood, but they were happy to have come through the darkness as a united and happy family.

TALE 14
The Orphan at Christmas

Few people can remember Egan Swift. Those who do frequently say that they wish they did not. George Temper was the head of the orphanage, and he knew Egan Swift far better than he had any desire to know him. By age fourteen, the orphan Egan Swift was already known by the police, and he had not even as yet left the orphanage.

That was, of course, part of the problem. He had come to the orphanage when he was eight months old. His mother was unwed and had tried to keep him, but she just could not manage. The father was from the road show of a play that had performed in a nearby theater. Although George Temper knew the name of both, he had never told Egan. It was not a matter of privacy or anything like that. Temper knew that the mother had died in a house fire only weeks after bringing Egan to the orphanage. She had picked the name of the baby, and Temper always knew it was too odd to be good for the kid.

The actor father had gone on to a couple of lead roles on TV, including two guest shots on Rod Serling shows. His career ended suddenly when he was found overdosed on drugs in an apartment building in Queens. Temper had made sure he told Egan Swift that much, and that there were no living grandparents or uncles or aunts or cousins. He was the last of the line as far as Temper knew or cared.

George Temper told the young boy this when he was eleven years old. "He's old enough to know the truth now." The news had hit Egan hard. His troubles had started before then, but they certainly escalated after that.

Egan was blessed with an incredibly handsome face. His smile could capture the hearts of anyone who saw him. His vivacious personality burst from his eyes at every moment. Such spunk is cute in a two, three, or even a five-year-old. But it does not always get you adopted. Something about Egan's appearance became hard the older he got. His mouth could be smiling and yet the observer would see malice. Egan never tried to be anything he wasn't, and that meant he continued to live in the orphanage.

Oh, he would occasionally go on an outing to someone's house for a holiday dinner, or he would go with some officials of the orphanage to a movie. But no one ever came to take Egan home with them for good.

Egan dealt with being passed over each and every time as well as he could, but he would clearly be upset for days. Some of his best friends in the orphanage would be playing with him one day, sure that they were going nowhere, and the next day their beds were empty and they were gone. Even young boys and girls whom Egan liked and considered friends would go away and never write to him.

Egan began acting out his frustration early on in two ways. The positive way was that he began to work in the shop. The janitors and Mr. Temper had seen to it that Egan and a couple of other children would learn skills that appealed to them. Egan loved working with wood. I don't mean just building basic birdhouses and letter holders, but fabulously designed compotes and pieces that had inlaid wood. He could build intricate miniatures of national monuments too, with carving of quite advanced skill—and all of that by the time he was fourteen years old.

There was, unfortunately, the other side of Egan Swift too. Egan would use his innocent and sweet face to cover up some fairly brutal attacks on the younger children, usually but not exclusively boys. He would push and shove them, badger them, say nasty things to them, and, in the case of a girl called Susan, he tore up a book she had just been given for Christmas.

George Temper was taken in by the sweetness of Egan's personality at first, but it was not long before Egan was a regular visitor to Temper's office. Legally, Egan had broken no real laws, and, even when he came close, the orphanage was bound to care for him at least a little longer. Temper had asked Family Services in the courthouse, but no one there knew what to do.

Egan needed a family, and not just any family would do. He had developed into a bright but manipulative young man. He smoked—although the orphanage tried to stop him—and had somehow even gotten drunk on beer. They knew it was beer because Egan was sick all night.

He was old enough that he could go out and do some hired chores for people in the neighborhood. That did not usually work out. He had gone to Mrs. Dickerson's house to do yard duty. He was to be there two hours. She complained angrily that he wasted time and didn't do nearly what he should have. She would not pay him, for which he complained bitterly to Mr. Temper. "Look at this list. She has the stuff she wanted done broken down into two groups, and each group would have taken three people over an hour. The old bitty just didn't want to pay me, that's all." George Temper looked over the list. He had to agree—grudgingly. Mrs. Dickerson had expected way too much of a fourteen-year-old boy.

The orphanage always tried to celebrate birthdays of their children. Egan's birthday was November 27, and he always looked forward to the orphanage having to treat him nicely. This year, as he turned fifteen, there was no cake and no celebration and, worse yet, there were no presents. He knew George Temper had not forgotten but had ignored him on purpose.

Tommy, a ten-year-old who was quickly following in Egan's worst habits, made it clear what his opinion about that was. "They're tired of you. They just figure that if someone doesn't adopt you soon, you'll have to be thrown out and the city will be rid of you. They hope you run away." They were in the garage, and both were smoking. Temper was out and had left the door up. He would not be gone long.

"Yeah, well, don't think I haven't thought about it. I have a project to finish in the shop, and then you may just see the back of me going out the fire escape." Egan cocked his head and blew out a smoke ring into the air. "I'm going to go back to work on it just as soon as I finish this cig."

Tommy smiled. "This project, is that how you hurt your hand?"

Egan held up a finger, which sported quite a bandage wrapped around it. "Yep! I was carving some wood around the little . . . well, I was carving and the chisel slipped."

"Whatcha carving?" Tommy tamped out his cigarette on the sidewalk, carefully putting the extinguished butt in an old coffee can and putting the lid back on. The can was half full of butts.

"You'll see it eventually, but not yet."

Tommy stood up and brushed his behind off from any dust. "I bet you're just saying that to make me think you're something big. Well, I don't. I'll get adopted long before you do. You just watch and see if I don't." He sauntered out of the garage.

Egan's cigarette was finished too, and he put the butt in the can, putting the can on a lower shelf in the back. The lid was on, and no air would mean that the cigarettes, if they weren't quite out, couldn't burn.

Egan stepped into the shop area. Dan Yeager was the janitor. He was there cleaning out a sweeper. "Darned thing worked fine two weeks ago, and it's gotten worse every day since."

Egan stepped over to Yeager. "Let me take a look. What's wrong with it?"

"The stupid brush won't turn around in the way . . . What! Do you think you can fix it when I haven't been able to for a week?" Dan wasn't angry, but he was a little astonished that Egan would even try.

Egan looked all up and down the sweeper. He had no idea what he was looking for, but he really wanted to figure it out. It wasn't a matter of wanting to be better than Dan, but more a matter that he wanted Dan to help him finish his project. Egan noticed an odd groove in the middle of the brush. He looked closely at it, finally noticing a similar groove on the upper portion of the motor, a round wheel that turned when the sweeper was turned on. "Should there be a rubber belt here?"

Dan looked. "I don't know. Yeah, it looks like there should or at least could be. I don't see it."

Egan looked further. "I think you'll have to go to the hardware store on Monday and get one. Be sure to take the model name and any number you can find. The bag size won't help any."

George Temper came in at that moment. "*Egan, were you just smoking in the garage?*" It was, as usual, never preceded with anything like a greeting to either of the two workers.

"Yeah, I was smoking in there, about fifteen minutes ago. The door was open, so Tommy and I went in there. We put the butts in a coffee can that we keep there. We usually smoke outside, but it's raining."

"I have told you not to smoke at all, and you know you are not to smoke in any enclosed space." Temper was livid. Dan Yeager was actually surprised to see his boss so upset.

"You know, Mr. Temper, if the door is open, the real effect of smoking in an enclosed space is mitigated a lot by—"

George Temper rounded on the janitor. "Shut up, Yeager, or you'll celebrate the upcoming holidays by losing your job."

Dan had a burning desire to quit right then and there, but instead he stayed quiet.

Egan spoke very respectfully, trying to hold in check his burning and growing hatred of the head of the orphanage. "I'm sorry, sir. I don't smoke a lot. I've cut back as much as I can. I hope to quit entirely in the next couple of weeks. But there are times, when I'm tired or have a lot to think about that I just need a cig."

George Temper sneered. "And what bloody hell do you have to think about that is of the least importance? The only thing you have to think about is why no one has ever adopted you."

Egan looked directly into Temper's eyes, unflinching at the stare that came back at him. "Oh, I don't ask myself that question any more. I know the answer to that one." The way he said it made George Temper suddenly diminish.

Temper had never promoted Egan as a likely candidate for adoption. It wasn't that he discouraged people from considering Egan Swift, but more a matter of suggesting any and all other children over the young man. He may not have wanted Egan around, but he certainly took some consistent pleasure in degrading and tormenting him. "You need to be in the house in five minutes." He turned to go.

"Sir . . . Mr. Temper? Could I please have thirty minutes?"

"No, Egan, you may not!"

Temper turned to go again, and again Egan stopped him. "I swear I'll be in there in thirty minutes or less, but I really have to finish an important project tonight. It's really important to me. I even think it's something you'll find interesting."

Temper's eyes narrowed. "I will give you thirty minutes from right now—6:14 p.m. But I can assure you, Egan Swift, that there is nothing that you could ever do, say, create, or think that I would ever find interesting." He left the janitor's shed.

Without looking in Egan's direction, his eyes still watching the departed boss cross the lawn, Dan Yeager controlled his voice into an almost catlike purr. "Could I help you finish your project, Egan? It could speed things up."

Egan considered a second. "Yes, I think you can—if you promise not to say anything to anyone about what you see." Egan motioned the janitor over into the shop section of the shed. There, in a corner, under a workbench, sat a wooden box filled with excelsior shavings. Lying on top, somewhat askew, was a lid. "Can you help me get this lid hinged onto the actual wooden box? I can do it, but if we both work, I might still have time to burn the writing into the top."

Dan was curious. "What is in the box under all of that excelsior?"

Egan shook his head. "Can't show you, but you'll know if you put the writing on the top. I have never used that little wood router you have, and I need to put the writing on the top somehow. My preference is with router or else inlay."

The hinging took almost no time, and yet when the lid was firmly affixed to the box, the time was already 6:35. "Listen, Egan, what do you want written? I can write it and even darken it with wood stain. Unless you need to give this gift tonight, the box would look even more beautiful with a satin finish on it, all rubbed down and nice. I could do the writing tonight or tomorrow morning, and the finish won't take too long to put on. It won't dry tonight. Besides, it would be best to rub it down with steel wool and put another coat on. You've done such a beautiful job of inlaying this wood, why rush it?"

Egan made a desperate look in the direction of the house. Finally he blurted, "Okay." He reached into his pocket and pulled out a piece of paper. Before he unfolded the paper, he reached behind the workbench and pulled out a piece of tiger maple. "I really want it written on this, which will fit right down in this carved-out area. What I want written on it is this." He handed Dan the piece of paper. "I have to go, or Temper will be furious with me." He ran away to the house.

Dan could tell that Egan didn't want to relinquish his project to anyone. He could only wonder what Egan had been working on. He had not noticed the boy working at anything special, other than occasionally finding a little wood glue or a jigsaw lying on the bench, not put into their proper places. He opened the paper and read,

Nativity Scene
Hand carved by Egan Swift
Begun 2004—Finished 2006
Gift to the Hillcrest Orphanage 2006

Dan was amazed. He secured the piece of tiger maple to the flat surface of the bench and took out a ruler and magic marker, carefully indicating exactly where the wording should go. Then with his most careful strokes, he routed the letters out, taking a light-colored wood Egan had purchased and cutting out letters to inlay into the tiger maple. He secured the wooden letters into the place Egan had indicated on the top panel.

Dan then took out the satin finish he had and covered the entire box. The lettering stood out against the precious maple. Then since the finish had to dry overnight, he pushed the box back under the bench. He was about to go, but curiosity got the better of him. He looked into the box more closely and saw evidence of a structure around the walls of the box. He had no intention of viewing everything, but he was curious. So he reached down into the excelsior and pulled up the first piece he could find. The piece was a kneeling man with a large shepherd's crook in his hand (made, Dan surmised, of a carefully bent dowel). The man wore a shawl of different wood and had the look more of Joseph than a shepherd. He gently put the figure back into the box and closed it.

Dan climbed into his car and started to drive home to his family. As he sat at the first stoplight, he dialed his cell phone. "Tracey Fenby? Hi. This is Dan Yeager. Yeah, we went to school together. You're the County Welfare officer now, aren't you? I thought I had read that you were. Do you know Mrs. Regal? Yes, she's also with Child Welfare. I was wondering if you could both come to my house tonight. I have some questions, and I definitely have some comments. I'm the janitor at the orphanage . . . Yes, I've been there for six years. No, my salary is fine! It's, well, I have someone I want to talk with you about. No, it is not one of the children."

Egan had entered the door of the orphanage with twenty seconds to spare. Even at that, George Temper was in a verbal mood and lit into him. It was only intervention of Mrs. Evert, the cook and night steward, that everyone sat down to a tense but quiet dinner. Egan was on kitchen duty to clean the dishes. After that, everyone went to bed.

George Temper lived alone in a separate part of the orphanage. His suite of rooms was spacious. He was always alert to unusual noises or uncalled-for talking after the appointed hours. Once in his apartment, he read fifty-four pages in a book of short stories. It was two stories, and he found the first one quite good, but only finished the second because he wanted to see what happened. It was, otherwise, a maudlin tale that he hated. He went to sleep almost at once, sleeping much more soundly than was his norm. This was fortunate, because upstairs in the orphanage Egan was quietly packing.

Tommy, always the snide voice of dark cynicism, whispered, "You know you won't get away with it. George Temper will find you and bring you back."

"George Temper only wants me here so he can browbeat me. I am sick of that, and I have my own plan on how to handle him. I'm going to go out on my own. I can make a go of it." The two froze a moment as they heard distant sounds of feet moving about. Finally Egan finished packing in silence.

Tommy was concerned and caring about his friend. "How do you intend to get out of here? You can't get out of any door without an alarm going off."

Egan went to the window and opened it. The night air was cold and crisp, the earlier rain having turned to icy crystals in the air. "I'll go out this way and down the fire escape. Then I'll jump the last five feet so I don't go past Temper's window. I'll have my clothes on my back, so I won't have to worry about making noise. I'll write you when I get somewhere." He stepped out. Tommy shook Egan's hand for luck and then closed and locked the window behind him.

Egan very slowly and quietly worked his way down the escape. It was slick with ice. He could see George Temper's window, and, as he watched, the light in the window was switched off. Egan opted to stand where he was for nearly twenty minutes. Freedom might take time, but it would be worth the wait. He finally walked down to the desired landing, not even thinking that he was going past the windows of some of his other friends. Then he leapt with a sprightly grace into a bush below. He quickly stood up and backed against the wall of the orphanage. He wanted to be as invisible as he could for a moment.

Finally, certain that no one had heard him, he made off down the driveway. A bright moon or a galaxy of stars might have helped to light his steps, but the weather masked all the stars, and the moon was almost a new moon. It would have been a sliver of light in a clear night. Considering that the ice in the air had turned to an actual snowfall, and a heavy one at that, in next to no time, there was no auxiliary light by which to see. Only the few lights that lined the driveway and the two large globes at the end of the drive just before you turned out onto the highway gave enough light for Egan to see. The snow was rapidly filling up the footprints left in the snow by Egan's heavy boots.

"Please be seated, Tracey. Mrs. Regal, if you would sit here." Dan Yeager offered a dish of Christmas candy—Divinity!

Mrs. Regal wanted very much to decline, but she had to take one. "There are few foods I just cannot refuse. Divinity is one."

Tracey Fenby took out a pencil and a pad. "Now, Dan, what seems to be the problem you wanted to talk about?"

Dan Yeager put the dish on the coffee table ahead of him. "Well, I assume you know the name Egan Swift." Both women said they were familiar with his file—it was rather frequently added to. "Yes, well, there is a good reason for that. George Temper is the head of the orphanage, and he has taken delight in tormenting Egan Swift for almost Egan's entire life there. George never puts Egan's name up for adoption either."

Mrs. Regal took another piece of Divinity. "Well, Mr. Yeager, you surely know that Egan Swift is considered a young man who would be difficult to adopt. He has emotional problems."

Dan Yeager shook his head. "I don't think so. Egan Swift has talents in woodworking like I've never seen before . . . ever! He also solved a problem with a vacuum sweeper tonight that's bugged me for about two weeks. It took Egan five minutes, and instead of buying a new vacuum at $300 or so, I bought a belt for $1.50, and I will install it tomorrow."

Tracey Fenby smiled. "Dan, I'm sure those are admirable traits in their way, but they don't point to being adoptable. He's hirable, perhaps, but not adoptable."

"Wait, Tracey, there's something I found out tonight that surprised me more completely than I've been surprised in years. George Temper was verbally beating Egan again. Egan had done nothing wrong. George did not want to give Egan a chance to do something he urgently wanted and needed to complete. Once George had gone fuming into the house, I told Egan I could help him finish whatever it was he wanted to finish. Egan reluctantly showed me his project. I want the two of you to know that Egan has carved in various woods a complete Nativity scene. I don't know how many pieces there are because they were in excelsior. The one figure I saw was amazingly beautiful. He's been working on it as a gift to the orphanage for two years. He somehow knew he wouldn't be adopted in that time."

Mrs. Regal leaned toward Dan. "Do you mean a freestanding group of figures?"

"I think so. I saw one figure—Joseph, I think—and I could tell that the box, which is not small, contained more figures and a background of some sort."

Tracey Fenby shook her head. "Dan, it still doesn't mean that he's not a troubled child. I can't think what kind of family could possibly want to adopt him."

Dan Yeager smiled and looked his classmate in her eyes. "I think I know exactly who could adopt Egan Swift. He needs a family who are willing to give him the unconditional love he has lacked for years. George Temper has fitted his approach to Egan to George's last name. I firmly believe that if someone loved Egan for who he is, those bad traits of smoking, drinking, and attitudinal problems would all fade away."

Mrs. Regal's face was filled with caring. "You seem to have given this some considerable thought."

Tracey Fenby's cell phone rang. It was into its third ring when she finally answered. "What is it, John? I told you I was in a meeting. Is there a good reason that you're calling me? . . . Really? Are you sure that is the name? They were asking about that specific name?"

If Egan turned left, he would be in town within an hour. He might go to see Dan Yeager. He had been there the Easter before, so he knew where he lived. But it was now 10:30 at night, and he was sure his family would be in bed. Egan was equally certain Dan would just bring him back to the orphanage. He didn't want that. He didn't know anyone else in that town. There was the church, of course, but he was fairly certain they would return Egan, too. "They all work together." It was a problem. Of course, he could turn right. Then the walk would be more like two hours. He had been in Clayburn once before, but he had paid no attention to much that was there. It was not much different than Hillcrest. They were decent attempts at smallish sized towns, and neither offered a support system for runaways. At least Hillcrest boasted having a hospital facility. The church there also had an open-door policy. People went inside to pray frequently. Egan could go there and stay overnight—"praying" sometimes takes a long time. He had a little money with him and could get a bus the next morning.

So Egan turned left. The traffic was almost nonexistent. Travel, however, was still difficult. The shoulder of the road was narrow, and the increasing rain-snow mix was already making his feet wet. Egan hurried as much as he could, but his footing was slippery and visibility made knowing where he was stepping hard. Bright headlights from the occasional car made seeing his footing even worse. For that reason, Egan hardly knew what caused him to fall.

He was on the bend of the road, he knew that, and the oncoming car's lights were on bright. Egan tried to shield his eyes from their brightness, but in so doing, his eyes missed the presence of a culvert. Egan tumbled down into the wet and cold ditch, hitting his head as he did on the culvert itself. For a moment, he lay there in a half-conscious state. Then he felt his head go black and he passed out.

When he awoke, he was surprised to find himself on a sofa in a large log house. A heavyset man in brown pants and a blue shirt was stirring something over a fire, the orange-yellow light of which danced off the man's white beard. The man was talking to someone, but Egan did not see at first who the person was. He was surprised to realize that he was naked under the covers.

About that time a woman came into the room. She also had white hair that was piled up onto the top of her head, held there with innumerable pins. She was carrying a large hot-water bottle and was dressed in a long sleeve white blouse, gray sweater, and a plaid skirt with leggings underneath. She brought the hot-water bottle directly to Egan. "Well, I am so pleased that you're awake. Klaus and I were worried. Here, put this on your tummy. It will heat your entire body from there. You gave us quite a concern."

Egan gasped—the water bottle was hot. "Where am I?"

Klaus, the man with the white beard, turned around and smiled at Egan. "That is a little difficult to answer. I'll start by saying that I was on my way to the orphanage to talk with you when I got held up for several hours with transportation problems. I couldn't hope to get into the orphanage at that hour, so I don't know why I kept going. I was just behind a blue pickup truck and saw you tumble down the shoulder into the ditch. The driver of the pickup was in a hurry to get to his family and kept on going. I stopped to help you. You passed out about the time I got there. You aren't hurt, but that water was really cold. Your clothes are in the dryer. The bag you were carrying lay at the top of the ditch, so it didn't get wet."

Egan was no fool, and he had heard a couple of things that made his curiosity rise. "How did you know the guy was on his way to see his family?"

"Oh, I just know that sort of thing. No problem in that."

For some reason, Egan let that answer stand. But he actually sat up a bit when he asked, "And why were you coming to see me?"

Klaus tasted what he was stirring and then swung the pot off of the fire. He took a large ladle and dished up some of the brew into a white ceramic bowl. This he brought to Egan with a large spoon. "Here, eat this while I explain." Egan began slowly to taste the stew. "It is my own special blend of vegetables, apples, chicken, and stock. It is wonderful at a time like this because it has so much flavor but it's not heavily spiced.

"My name is Klaus. I almost never use my last name—neither does anyone else. As for my coming to see you . . . I've been told that you are quite handy working with wood. My friends seem to know that you are capable of real craftsmanship. Is it true that you know how to inlay wood? I don't mean kind of but really inlay wood—in a nearly professional way?"

Egan was surprised at the vehemence with which Klaus was questioning him. "Well, how professional I am is debatable. I'm only fifteen. But I have learned how somewhat, and what I wasn't taught I've figured out . . . sort of."

Klaus laughed. "You're too modest. By the way, in case you wondered how I knew that you were the person I was seeking, let's just say your wallet told me your name. I was pretty sure anyway by the sweatshirt you had on with the insignia of the orphanage. My fear that you would run away was apparently well founded."

Egan paused midsip of his stew. "You knew I would try to run away?"

"Of course I knew. It is my job to know." Klaus laughed.

"Oh! You're with Child Welfare Services?" Egan was almost finished with the stew and was scraping the bottom of the bowl.

Klaus looked suddenly quite serious and more than a little worried. "No. I would not put it quite that way. I care a lot about what happens to children the world over—call it a mania with me—but I am not with any particular organization or county service. Why don't we say that I keep lists, checking them on a regular basis to see who is still in need of my assistance." He reached inside his vest pocket and pulled out a pipe. He lit it and took a delight in the smoke rings he could produce. "My full name, by the way, is Nicklaus Geschenker. Don't let the name fool you. I speak several languages besides German and English. Let's see, there's Norwegian, Swedish, Finnish, Chinese, Russian, Italian, and a couple of others. It's so confusing that I still have people looking up my true ancestral lineage." He sat down next to Egan. "I have a position for you that would last three weeks, December 1 through December 21. My company makes many things that people tend to want. We make toys, dolls, golf clubs, electric trains of all sizes, and the list goes on and on. This year, twenty-two people have asked for wooden things ranging from humidors to cuckoo clocks to candy dishes to statues. One person even wants a full-sized writing desk in Victorian style. Now I have people who can help you make them, and they can do almost anything you tell them to do. But they can't do it alone. They don't entirely understand how to work with wood. You do! Can you help me?"

Egan was eager for such a challenge. He was certain it would be rewarding to his spirit actually to have a place to go and a purpose when he got there. The belligerent side of Egan just had to come out. "You haven't mentioned a price. Maybe I'm too expensive."

Klaus looked down into his pipe, taking his tamper and messing around with the positioning of the tobacco. When he finally answered, the momentary frown on his face was gone and a twinkle had returned to his face. "Let's not talk about the payment right now. I can assure you that I know what you want, and you will most definitely get it. Is that satisfactory?"

Egan looked askance at Klaus. "What if I ask for a million dollars—or three million?"

Klaus laughed heartily. "Well, if you do, you'll be out of luck. I make things, but I don't pass out checks for money. Besides, that is not what you most want. This is Christmas season, so plan your payment well. Whatever you want, I will give you. Of course I'm already sure what that is, so don't screw it up."

Mrs. Geschenker brought in Egan's clothes. "They're finally dry. Good, you finished your stew. As soon as we get some pudding down you, we'll be off."

Egan sat up, clutching the blanket to his chest. "Off? Off to where?"

Klaus was already at the door. "You get dressed, and then we'll be off to my workshop—that's where my people make all of those things." The door swung shut behind him.

Egan half walked and half stumbled over to a more secluded section of the room. There he let the blanket fall as he quickly put his clothes back on. They were still warm from the dryer, and they felt wonderful. No sooner was he finished dressing than Klaus and his wife came in, bundled up in parkas and carrying Egan's bag of clothes. Klaus also carried a gray, fur-lined parka for Egan.

"Here, put this on. It won't take long to get where we're going, but it will be a very cold trip. It *is* winter, you know! We'll skip the pudding if you don't mind."

Egan put the parka on, and, as he was picking up his bag, asked, "Isn't this your house that we're in? It's really pretty if it is."

Klaus looked at his wife with a slightly conspiratorial look in his eye. "Well, actually it's the house of someone I'm working for. We'll try to explain when we get to our home."

Egan followed the other two out the door, but he was not at all prepared for what met his eyes. There sat a large sleigh. Some of you who are reading this may have been expecting that, but you must understand that the pictures everyone sees are all wrong. This sleigh was larger, sleeker, and more aerodynamic. The sleigh was drawn by ten reindeer. "Sorry, Egan, about the number of reindeer. The old sleigh used to be smaller, but with the population explosion—well, you know how things can be."

Egan started to climb into the sleigh. "Er, uh, do they have names?"

Mrs. Geschenker laughed. "Of course they have names! Their names are Marbles, Dillyhead, Corn Bread, Flyboy, Dasher III, Excalibur, Tango, Hop Scotch, Dancer IV, and Haley's Comet. And in case you want to know, Rudolph III is at home, and he most certainly does have a red nose. I don't suppose it is quite as bright as his grandfather's nose, but then his brother Romanoff's nose is quite bright and makes up for him."

Egan laughed. "Then you are really Mr. and Mrs. Santa Claus?"

Mrs. Geschenker closed the door to the sleigh and pulled down a wind protector from the overhang. "We are Klaus and Rebecca Geschenker, and there is nothing that saintly about either of us. We do good things, but sainthood is not our exact providence. There were in history a couple of people who were confused with us. Go ahead, Klaus, we're comfortable."

Egan was stunned at the speed with which the sleigh took off, gliding first over the newly covered ground and then rising effortlessly (but somewhat bumpily) into the sky. He was thrilled and a little scared to look out the side of the sleigh as the ground slipped quickly by beneath them. The sleigh gained momentum, and Egan actually enjoyed it more, his apprehension growing too at their extreme speed. He closed his eyes a moment and then, almost before he had taken a breath, he could feel the sleigh slowing down.

The landing was as smooth as if they had landed on a glass surface. In fact, the snow was so deep and compact—and so very flat—that it was basically just that. The sleigh went slowly (for it!) into a large barn, and several scurrying figures closed the barn door behind him. Then they opened the door of the sleigh. The people greeting Egan were all elves—pointed ears, turned up noses, in brightly colored attire elves! Egan could suddenly feel the warmth of the place. He stood a moment looking around. Then he asked Klaus, who had just stepped up beside him, "Where do I sleep here?"

Klaus lifted his eyebrows. "Sleep! Good heavens, Egan Swift, we don't need sleep here. Besides, we have too much work to do." He motioned three elves over to stand in front of them. They bowed deeply. "This is Dan, Tommy, and George. Do you think you can remember their names?"

Thinking back briefly to the orphanage, Egan smiled. "I'm sure that I can."

Klaus turned to the elves. "George, you're in charge of the crew. Egan, however, after you tell him the rules and regulations, is in charge of getting these things done and done right. There will be no skimping on techniques just to get it done faster. We have enough time to get everything done right. But there is to be no delaying. Now go."

George led the way into a large room where literally everything was being made. Egan could not believe his eyes. The room was huge and elves were working in all corners of the room, making fantastic toys and things. "My God, this really does exist. I feel like I'm in a fairy tale or a made-for-TV movie."

George turned sourly to Egan. "Well, you're not. And put that cigarette away. We do not allow smoking here at all. There are far too many flammable things here that could send the whole North Pole, Ltd. up in smoke. Oh, and we do not take the Lord's name in vain here!"

Dan put forth his hand to shake Egan's. "We are glad you could come to help. This is a terrifically hard three weeks. We usually get to help in the easier areas, but this year there are so many difficult things to build from wood."

Tommy looked much younger than the other two. He smiled a kind of goofy smile at Egan. "Hey, I like to smoke too, but I can put it off for three and a half weeks—I guess."

"Guess or not, you will." George was quite nasty. "There aren't any other real rules, except that we are already late getting started. Where do *you* think we should start, Mr. Swift?" The way he said it showed that George was most uncomfortable having Egan around.

Egan wanted to show he was in charge and yet not insult the others. "Where is the list of what needs to be done?"

George quickly showed Egan the list. Egan was horrified. "I thought Santa, er, Klaus said there were twenty-two things to build. There are four thousand here."

Dan just laughed. "That's no problem. We just have to make the prototypes, and our duplication machines make the remainder. Most of the things are in multiples of a minimum of eighteen or twenty. Only that one desk is not to be duplicated. I personally think it's beyond us and that we should scrap it."

Tommy shook his head rather bluntly. "You know that's not an option according to Mr. Geschenker."

George just sneered at Tommy. "If it has to be scrapped, we'll scrap it."

Egan put his bag under the workbench and started looking through the twenty-two designs that were laid out before him. "Do you actually have the wood for all of this? And the hardware?"

George was suddenly alert. "Hardware? What do you mean by hardware?"

Egan pointed to the drawings. "You will need hooks, and pull knobs, and screws to put things together, and here a screen for the bottom of the birdhouse. The desk is the biggest, but I'm not sure it's the hardest." He studied the plans again.

Dan said rather quietly. "I think we could divvy up the jobs. If you make sure we do things right—telling us exactly what to do—we can do anything. I'm only worried about the desk."

Egan put the papers down. "I'll do the desk. Now this is how we'll progress. I'll take pieces of wood and draw each and every piece that we need on them. Then I'll give them to you to cut, bend, or whatever. George, you should do the cutting. Don't you agree?"

George was pleased that Egan had picked him first. "I think so. I'm the most experienced at that."

"Good. Then Dan, you can be in charge of drilling holes. I'll mark exactly where they go. Then you and Tommy can do the assembly. We'll start with the easiest ones that also need the most duplication. I don't know how that is done, so you guys will have to show me." Egan had shaken off any sleepiness he might have felt.

Tommy spoke up. "What about painting? I usually paint things."

George spoke rather hastily. "Yes, he usually paints things. Sometimes he even does a good job."

Egan felt a pang for Tommy, as if Tommy was always the whipping boy. "Don't worry, Tommy, there are enough of us to get the job done, and you won't have to hurry. Are there any more people who will be working with us?"

George smiled a kind of nasty smile. "Don't you think we're enough?"

Egan didn't want to seem doubtful. But he didn't want to get behind either. "Well, to be candid, I've never worked with elves before, and I don't know how speedy you can work. I've never done quite such a big job of stuff so quickly either. I just want to get a good running start, and I was wondering if any other elves would be helping? It isn't so much that I doubt your ability. I'm just new here."

The next few hours went hurriedly by. Of the twenty-two different designs, they had to tackle, the doghouses, birdhouses, and feeders were scheduled for the most duplication. The prototypes were easily finished. Even Tommy did a wonderful job of painting. Egan enjoyed working with the three (even George), and he modified each design just a little to make each have a slight dash of whimsy. Klaus even came by at one point and liked very much what he saw.

The first batch of five prototypes was sent off. Next Egan had decided to tackle the cuckoo clocks, wooden toy trains, wagons, and specially designed beds, particularly those of the bunk beds being intriguing to him.

The duplication process was of interest to Egan as well. They could change the colors of the prototypes at will, and they still came out looking fabulous. Egan kept most of his attention on the work at hand.

It seemed that they were making great headway and that only a day had passed and they were through eighteen of the twenty-two designs. Egan leaned back. "I think we're doing pretty well for the first day."

Dan looked at George in a worried way. "You forgot to tell him, George! You didn't fill him in on all the facts. You **want** him to fail, don't you?"

George looked daggers at Dan. Tommy just stood up and walked between the two feuding elves and went to Egan. "Egan Swift, the problem is—what George neglected to tell you is—we haven't been at this for only a couple of days. We've been at it now for fifteen days. And we have almost no time left for those really difficult projects."

Egan looked horrified. "That's impossible. Time hasn't gone by that fast!"

George looked coldly at Egan. "Time always flies by faster than you think when you have a project to complete. Now, Mr. Big-Wig executive of design and construction in wood, how do you think we'll get the rest done?"

Egan stared at the remaining designs. "We have to cut out all the pieces of the desk right away. What will that take? Two days?" Tommy shook his head. "More or less?" Dan put his thumb up. "Three?" They all nodded. "Then here's what we'll do.

"I'll draw the designs for the desk, while Tommy goes to get the hardware. Then while I'm drawing the pool table, the bookcase, and the stereo speaker enclosures, you guys can be cutting out the desk pieces. There are lots of them. Dan, I'll put an indication where holes are to be drilled. This will have some wood construction, not all screws." He quickly finished his description of what was needed.

Incredibly the desk pieces were all cut out accurately and laying all around him by the time the other pieces were drawn. It was going to be a mad dash to get everything assembled. Everything had to go like clockwork. No one could take time off or get hurt.

The pool table and bookcase were finished at the same time. This left the speaker enclosures and the difficult desk. It was in the haste around installing the speakers that the accident happened. The speakers were being obstreperous about fitting where they should. Attaching them was causing inattention to things around them.

Two outer drawers for the desk were sitting on their ends, the finish drying, while Egan was putting together the final drawers for the inside. Tommy, when he was finishing attaching the speaker enclosures, bumped the two drawers. The sizable drawers fell over and hit Egan's head hard, putting a deep gash there. He passed out for a moment. When he came to, the room looked very odd, as if all the color had drained from it. Klaus was bending over him though. "You'll be fine now. Just rest comfortably while we do a few more things. You'll need to stay tonight yet just to be sure there are no more problems." He walked away.

Egan couldn't figure out where he was. Then he looked over and Dan the elf was standing there. "You took quite a bump on the head, Egan Swift. You've been out quite some time. I finished your project just the way you wanted me to. It'll be under the tree on Christmas Day."

Egan looked around again and back at Dan. But Dan no longer had elfish features. His ears were normal. He was Dan Yeager. Next to him stood Tommy, his buddy, and there, in the doorway, talking to two women in business suits, was George Temper. They were giving him quite a difficult time. When the doctor came back, Egan read his name tag: Klaus G. Schenker.

Egan motioned to Dan to come closer. "Where am I right now?"

Dan patted Egan's shoulder. "You're in Hillcrest General Hospital."

"What's Mr. Temper so upset about?"

Dan whispered into Egan's ear. "Someone, it seems, has been discussing his treatment of you with Child Welfare Services. I can't imagine who that person could have been." He had a twinkle in his eye. "I think he just got fired from his job as head of the orphanage."

Everyone left Egan alone, and Egan snuggled down in the warm bed. He was very confused. He felt as if he had been working twenty-one straight days at the North Pole, and yet here he was in a hospital bed in Hillcrest and had apparently been there the entire time. Dr. Schenker came back to the bed. "You sleep, young man. You've had a rather stressful couple of weeks."

"Dr. Schenker," Egan began, "what is today's date?"

Dr. Schenker paused. "It's the twenty-first of December."

"What? Have I really been here for three weeks?"

Dr. Schenker cocked his head oddly, stroking his white goatee. "Well, I'd say so, basically, although you've certainly been muttering about places and things somewhere far away." He gave Egan an odd look, filled at once with vague whimsy and serious mystery. Then he laughed and left Egan alone to think and to sleep. The room was quiet, and Egan began to get sleepy.

Egan's brain was not tired. It kept asking questions, questions that kept coming even when Egan was sleeping. Everything was too real to be a dream. Then a lingering thought gnawed at his brain. "If it was real, Klaus did not keep his promise to pay me what I want."

The next afternoon, December 22, Egan went back to the orphanage. Dan came to pick him up at the hospital, and it was Dan who helped him into the orphanage itself. Tommy helped him up the stairs. After lying still for so many days, Egan felt a little weak and light-headed. Mrs. Evert told Egan that dinner would be served at 5:30 p.m., with gifts afterward.

Gifts were always passed out in the orphanage on the twenty-second, so that children who were going out to stay with a family for Christmas could leave at any time on the twenty-third or twenty-fourth. It was a plan that always worked.

Egan unpacked. Tommy sat watching him and eventually said, "I'm sorry you didn't get very far. I was hoping for a note from you saying that you were basking in the Florida sun."

"Thanks. I wish I was. But hey, at least we'll be together at Christmas."

At 5:15 p.m., Egan descended the stairs and went quickly out to the janitor's shed. Dan was there. He smiled at Egan. "I thought you'd be here any minute. I hope you don't mind. I put a small lock on the front and some handles on each side—all in brass. It will help us carry it inside. Oh, and I made this." It was a large bow on a piece of cardboard that perfectly fit over the inlaid plaque. Dan gave Egan a conspiratorial smile. "No use everyone knowing what it is ahead of time. This should block nosy children in a satisfactory way. I hope the inlay suits you. I'm not as good as you are at it."

Egan smiled a warm and genuine smile. "It looks beautiful. Did you look at any of the pieces?"

Dan nodded. "Curiosity got the better of me, so of course I did! I only looked at one, I promise. I think it was Joseph, but it might have been a shepherd."

The two carried the box inside the orphanage, putting it just behind a corner of the tree. George Temper had never allowed a tree before. He had even resented presents and minimal decorations. Child Welfare had seen to those for years. Once the box was in place, the two went in to dinner.

Mrs. Evert had spared no effort in making a really wonderful meal, and yet she had saved the best for last. It was an ice-cream roll, in which the ice cream spiraled into the center of a piece of chocolate cake. It was topped with whipped cream and a maraschino cherry. Everyone took their time eating it, savoring every bite that they took. They were in no hurry to move—in fact they felt that moving was almost impossible. It was an almost painful delight.

Thirty minutes later, even though they were stuffed from food, they were opening presents. As one might expect, they were mainly clothes, although the little children got toys and dolls. Egan was given a pale blue dress shirt and a dark blue suit. He was sort of stunned. It was the nicest gift he had ever been given. He was in the process of opening his cards too when Dan stood up.

"I have an announcement for you all. I have resigned my position as janitor for this orphanage." There was considerable uproar at this. "Oh, I am not leaving you. My wife and I and my children will be moving into the headmaster's suite as soon as it is painted and cleaned up a bit. Egan, shall we open the gift you made?"

Egan nodded and went forward. The two lifted the box and brought it into the center of the room. Dan asked Mrs. Evert to come forward. "What is in this box is going to fit very nicely on this window seat. You are all going to think it is pretty, but I don't want you to play with it. It is to look at and to feel the Christmas spirit."

Mrs. Evert removed the big bow from the top and read aloud what was written there. Then she looked at Egan. "You made this?" Egan nodded. "You really are a dear boy."

The Nativity scene had a cow, a mule, Joseph, Mary, Baby Jesus, five sheep, one goat, four shepherds, three kings, three camels, and two angels. They were all in different woods and had been carved to fit together in a perfect way. The differing woods made painting unnecessary. The workmanship was astonishing. The scene, finally set up in front of a kind of barn Egan had also made, looked magnificent in the window. Egan helped put the pieces where he had envisioned them going.

Then he sat down to finish opening his cards. The first one was addressed in a bold hand.

Mr. Egan Swift

Inside the card read simply: *I keep my promises. KG*

Egan was puzzled. Who was "KG"? He didn't think he knew any one with those initials. Then he opened the last card. It was equally simple. It read,

Thanks. D., T., and G.

Again Egan was baffled. Everyone had finished their packages by this time and the little children were heading off to bed. Tommy was examining the wood carvings closely and smiling at Egan's achievement. "You did do it after all!"

The telephone rang, and Dan, who was just putting on his coat to go home answered. He spoke only briefly and then hung up. "Mrs. Evert, may I speak with you a moment?" She went over to Dan Yeager, and he whispered a sentence or two into her ear. She seemed surprised and even pleased. Dan seemed a bit perplexed, as if the news was not so very good.

Egan passed it off and went upstairs. Tommy came in shortly afterward. They talked for a little while, but both were soon asleep. Egan's brain still thought about those cards. He had an answer for the initials on both cards, but since he had decided everything was a dream while he was in a coma, he allowed those answers to fade quickly.

The next morning it was Mrs. Evert who knocked early to rouse the young men. "Egan, you need to hurry. Dan needs to see you."

Egan was getting ready to dress in his usual sweat pants, T-shirt, and sweater, but suddenly he had an inspired idea. He wanted to try on his new suit. The shirt had a tie, so Egan dressed up the best he had dressed in his life—at least what he could remember of it. Tommy woke up just as Egan was finishing and was amazed how good Egan looked. Egan even brushed his sometimes-mangy mop of hair into a neat look. He had a pair of dress shoes, and these he polished as brightly as he could. He was just finishing when Mrs. Evert's voice came through the door again. "Hurry, Egan."

He opened the door, and she fell back almost stunned. "My, oh my, you do clean up well. Dan, er, Mr. Yeager will be pleased that the suit fit so well."

At the bottom of the stairs, Egan could see Dan standing and talking with a man and a woman. Dan was facing the stairs and a broad smile broke out on his face when he saw Egan. "Well, young man, you look pretty good at that. I won't say this is Christmas wrapping, but it is certainly a wonderful surprise. And I have one for you too. Come on into the office." The couple and Egan all went into the headmaster's office. "Egan, I'd like to introduce you to Carl and Bonnie Swift."

Egan did a double take. The name Swift was not that common. "Swift?"

Carl spoke up. "Yes, Egan, our name is Swift. My wife and I have been searching for quite a few years to find you. My sister, Monica, was about three years older than I was. We knew that she was expecting a child, and when she had him—er, you—it was a wonderful event for her. Except that she could not support you and herself too. So she put you up for adoption. She always wanted to return to get you or to find you, but she never could. She died in a fire shortly after she left you here. Your father fell during a theatrical event and died of those injuries. I did not know where Monica was when she gave you up. It took this long to find you, despite the fact that we live relatively nearby.

"Bonnie and I have a young son who is about your age and a daughter two years younger. We would very much like you to come live with us. You won't even have to change your name. I'll even teach you my business if you want." He seemed pleased, and yet he was looking Egan over carefully.

Egan was intrigued. "What do you do?"

Carl smiled. "I make fine furnishings for people. And in my spare time, which I almost never have, I'm a wood carver. I saw your gift to the orphanage. It was quite good. Better than I can do."

Egan suddenly became panicked. He had dreamed all his life of actually being adopted, and now that he had a family to go to, he was scared. "Where do you live?"

Bonnie answered in a jovial manner. "We live in a big log cabin about forty minutes on the other side of Hillcrest. You'll be able to come back to visit Mr. Yeager if you want. I'm sure he'd like that."

Twenty minutes later, they were on the road, all of Egan's meager possessions stored in the trunk of the car. The trip seemed to take far less time than fifty minutes. Egan was surprised, however, when he arrived at the house. It was a beautiful log cabin, with several rooms that sprawled off to the sides. Egan's surprise, however, was not because it was log, but because it was the house where he had awakened after his accident.

His surprise was even greater when he went inside. After meeting Bobby and Julie, Egan followed Carl into his office area. "I don't want you to say anything to Bobby about what I'm going to show you. A man spoke with me about making a desk for me, and this is the desk." Carl opened a door to a large workroom off his study.

Sitting there was the desk that Egan had built. He took two steps toward it and gently touched the smooth surface. "It has a bright green writing surface inside. The inner wood is mahogany—the outer woods are the same, inlaid with rosewood, Cyprus wood, ebony, and even white pine."

Carl stood stunned. But he was even more stunned when Egan pulled out the drawer. "What are you doing?"

Egan examined the pulls. "Good, they went with the polished brass pulls. Carl, I don't want you to think I'm bragging, because I am not saying this for that reason. But I'm sure Dan Yeager told you about my accident."

Carl nodded seriously. "He mentioned it. He said you had been in the hospital for about three weeks."

"Well, I was and I wasn't. That's where they say I was. My brain tells me that you were dealing with a man named Klaus Geschenker. He picked me up from the ditch and brought me here to this house. He said the owner was a client. I was resting on that gray couch in the living room, and he fed me a stew that Rebecca his wife had made. I think she put the remainder of it into the freezer. Then we flew to the North Pole. He was Santa Claus in disguise. At least I think he was. I was totally amazed at what I saw there. Then three elves and I spent the whole time there making things in wood. While I was finishing up the last piece, this desk, a drawer fell over and gashed my head. The next thing I knew I was in Hillcrest Hospital, and—"

Carl's face had gone very dark. "Now listen, Egan, Bonnie and I want you here. But I will not have you lying like that in front of Bobby or Julie."

Egan turned the drawer over. There, on the corner of the drawer, was a large smear of red. "That's blood. It's my blood. If you look on the windowsill in the little study off the living room, you will find half of a hook. It goes on my winter coat. And if you look on the back of the middle drawer of this desk, you'll see the initials ES. My initials." He put the drawer back into the desk.

Carl opened the writing desk and pulled out a long central drawer. Sure enough, on the back was carved ES. "It is true that I was dealing with a guy named Klaus Geschenker. But how on earth can this be?"

Egan just shrugged. "I have not the foggiest idea. I can tell you this much—Klaus Geschenker promised me that my pay for helping at the North Pole would be whatever I asked for. I never got to ask for anything, but I got what I most wanted in the whole world, so I'm not asking stupid questions."

Carl looked puzzled as he put the desk back together and led Egan out into the office. "Well, what was it you were wanting?"

Egan stopped and stared at a picture sitting on the desk. It showed a younger Carl and a pretty, blonde-haired young woman. "I wanted to know about my parents—who were they? And I wanted someone to adopt me. I don't know if you're really adopting me or just letting me live here but I don't care. I'm happy. I've just been given the best Christmas gift I could ever get."

"Dinner!" It was Julie's voice.

They went in to eat. They were about to pass things around the table, when Bonnie Swift said to Egan. "Would you like to ask the blessing?"

Egan reached out his hand and took one of Bobby's hands and one of Carl's. "Sure. Heavenly Father, bless this food and let it nourish our bodies. Help us to see the glory in the birth of your son. And thank you for this wonderful family. May we grow to love each other and appreciate each other in all ways! This is the best Christmas ever!"

They ate rather heavily and went into the living room to unwrap presents. Egan loved the gifts he was given, but he felt somehow sad. He had nothing to give them. Then Carl stood. "Egan, can you help me bring that other present into the living room?"

Egan and Carl went to the workshop and lifted the desk. "Gee, I had no idea it would be so heavy," Egan huffed. They carried the desk into the living room, and Bobby went ballistic with happiness.

Carl went back to close the workroom door, but came back to motion to Egan. "Can you come with me a moment, Egan?" Egan went again with Carl. Behind the desk had been tucked another present. Egan could tell immediately what it was. Carl was astonished, but he helped Egan take it into the living room.

"I will explain this present sometime, probably as soon as I can figure out how it happens to be here. For now I'm just ecstatic that I can actually give you what I hope will be a little of the Christmas joy I'm feeling." Egan took the pocket knife Carl offered him and cut the big blue ribbon. Julie was given the privilege of lifting the cardboard that covered the box. The writing on the top of the box said it all.

Nativity Scene
Hand carved by Egan Swift
Begun 2004—Finished 2006
Gift to the Swift family 2006
Duplicated by K. Geschenker and elves.

Explanations would, indeed, have to follow at some time, but for now, no one cared. They simply marveled in the gift Egan Swift had made.

TALE 15
New Road, Old Destination

There were many adjectives that people used to describe D. Drummond Wilkinson. The complimentary terms were "handsome," "quick-witted," "role model for Afro-Americans and whites alike," "upwardly mobile," and many other wonderful phrases. Unfortunately detractors also had phrases that they used. Those were "slick," "woman chaser," "pushy," "an ego the size of Texas," and "coldhearted." Drummond Wilkinson knew both sets of words, considering that all of them were too extreme to be accurate.

He had been considered "handsome" when he was a football quarterback in high school. The other positive terms had started then too. He told a friend that, if "slick" meant that he could be highly efficient, he did not mind the terminology at all. He thought the same about "pushy." He had an ego, true enough, but used it only in a positive stance in working with people. He was usually right and did not intend to listen to arguments from people who did not know all the facts—particularly if those facts contradicted his own feelings of what was right.

The "ladies' man" moniker was "just inaccurate!" He flirted outrageously at times, but he had "never cheated" on his wife, Angie. Actually, he kept the secret trysts from her for a long time. Their argument Christmas Eve morning had been about that. It started when he got up and found Angie sitting in the kitchen, drinking a cup of coffee and pondering a bra that was clearly not hers. She had gone out to the car to get a scarf she had left there two days before and had found the bra tucked under the seat. There was no defense strong enough or "slick" enough to get him out of this one.

So now he was backing out of the garage into the rain. Angie was looking out the living room window, her bathrobe pulled tightly around her. The Christmas lights that encircled the window cast odd colors onto her face. Drummond was glad he couldn't see the tears from that far away. The argument had not ended. It was merely a truce. She would go to her mother's for Christmas. Where *he* was going even he didn't know. But he knew that he too was going to his hometown. His mother was in a nursing home there, and, despite the forty-minute drive, he hadn't seen her for a couple of months. He had intended the trip anyway, but he had also intended for Angie to go with him. "This is not going to be a very nice Christmas Eve!" The drive was through awful weather and gray skies.

There were other people he always looked in on when he went home, and he would catch up with them too. They were classmates from his high school. Some he knew would be in the local restaurant or at the grocery, buying a ham or turkey and making believe that they would get through a veritable mound of food on Christmas Day.

He would be sure to look in on Maggie Robbins. He had walked with her daily all during high school, and they had been in the same English class as freshmen in college. Yet he had not seen her since college graduation until he saw her at the opening of the new high school library. He had seen Maggie there, and his fixation had been on her ever since. She had glowed in the evening light, her short blonde hair pulled back and looking quite chic. Her satin pantsuit was deep red, and more than a few people from the class had commented on how great she looked.

Drummond drove out of town on State Highway 25. If he went the way he normally did, that road would take him beyond Buckland by three miles, and he would then have to double back. He knew there were other roads that went from 25 through to Buckland Pike (also known as old 25), but the only one he knew well was Trover Lane. It went about two miles through to link up with Buckland Pike. The lane had been repaved five years before, but he had never taken it. Today, despite the snow and rain in the air, he thought it would get him home sooner.

Just after entering Trover Lane, he crossed a culvert that was just overflowing with water. It should have been a warning not to proceed, but Drummond Wilkinson did not even consider turning back. He went straight up the incline in the road, reaching the main level of the road after a rise of fifteen feet or so. He sped down the road, noting as he went how much smoother it was than before. The bridge at the other end was totally flooded, and traversing the bridge might be possible but terribly unsafe. Drummond turned around and went back toward 25. Now the water was higher over that culvert too, and he was trapped.

Drummond knew there were no crossroads that might help him navigate around the blockages. He surveyed the names on the mailboxes: Daggett, Peters, Wilkins, Myers, and Corcoran. Two boxes did not have visible names anywhere, while a third house had a FOR SALE sign on it. Wilkins was the only name he thought he recognized, and even then he wasn't sure whether it was because of his own last name or from some earlier acquaintance with someone with that moniker. He drove into the driveway of the Wilkins house. The house was a well-kept, small house in light blue, with white shutters and trim but with a bright lavender door. There were festive lights on the other houses, but this one seemed possibly empty. Perhaps the owner was away for the holidays. "I'm certainly not going to knock on the Daggett door. They had five cars in their drive. I'd be intruding on some family get-together, and I'd rather not do that."

Momentarily, the idea of a family gathering bothered him. He suddenly missed Angie, even though he still was fixated on Maggie Robbins. He harbored ideas based on things she had said years ago, and he wanted to see if he might be able to coax her into an affair with him.

Drummond stepped slowly from his car, wondering who might live at this pretty but clearly unfestive house. Drummond was only partway up the walk when the door opened. In the door was a man with short white hair and a white mustache. He wore wire-rimmed glasses which he removed as he opened the door. "As I live and breathe, Dondee Wilkinson! Welcome to my humble abode. What brings you out onto Trover Lane?"

Drummond quickly stood quite erect. "I don't use the name Dondee anymore. And just who might you be? Don't say you're Mr. Wilkins, because I read that much on your mailbox."

Mr. Wilkins motioned Drummond inside, closing the door behind him. "Clearly you don't recognize me."

"Clearly I have never met you in my life!"

Mr. Wilkins held out his hand. "Michael Ellis Wilkins. And as a matter of fact, you met me three days a week for an hour-long session while you were in your freshman year in college. I was brought in as a replacement for Deidre Philips, whose fiancé was killed in a car wreck the second week of September that year, sustaining injuries herself that took eight weeks to recover. She lasted to the end of the year—barely—and then left teaching to open a bookstore in Indianapolis."

Drummond looked at Michael Wilkins for a moment. "I vaguely remember all of that, but I don't remember a thing about you."

Michael Wilkins laughed and reached into a drawer of a desk by the door. "Would this old picture help remind you what I looked like then?" The picture showed a man with light skin, short brown hair, and a Van Dyke beard. In his hand, he held a cigar. These helped Drummond, but it was the carefree, too-casual stance that he remembered.

"I recognize you now, at least a little. I certainly remember the cigar. Why didn't you take over permanently for Ms. Philips?"

Michael Wilkins put his photo back into the desk. "Your mother was a trustee, or I would not have had the opportunity I had to teach you. She was a friend at a time when I needed one badly. There was an incident at my former college that, despite tenure, fifteen years of hard work, and good results, made the college release me. Tenure only holds good until you step over a perceived line of misconduct. To be sure, I had done nothing wrong, but perceptions persisted, aided by the malicious gossip spread by a young coed. So I was dismissed just one week before classes were to begin. All the contacts I had with your college as an alum would have meant nothing if it hadn't been for your mother. She knew the course of study was right up my area of expertise. So I taught."

"But that must have been eight years ago!" Drummond was trying to be helpful and to further the story along.

"More like ten. You were the only Afro-American in my class. My skin may be lighter, but Mom was black and Dad was white. I went between the cultures pretty easily. I tried hard to get you a scholarship in English. Your revelatory reading of the lines from *Canterbury Tales* brought more than a few experts to my home, marveling at the natural way you read that prologue. When I think what you might have done with that, the scholarships you might have gotten, I just can't believe you turned it all down."

Drummond smiled. "I'd almost forgotten that. I wasn't into English as a full-time career. Do you still have the recording we made of that and the two tales?"

Michael Wilkins nodded. "I don't listen to it much, but at least I transferred it to compact disc three years ago. The discs sound as if you recorded them yesterday. If you stop by on your way home from Buckland, I'll have made a copy of it for you." He entered the kitchen, Drummond following him almost aimlessly. "So what do people now call you? Dee-Dee? It seems like kind of a sissy name."

Drummond laughed despite his pique about discussing the name. "No, they do not call me Dee-Dee. Nor Dondee. They call me Drummond or Mr. Wilkinson. I sign letters and merchandise orders with D. Drummond Wilkinson."

Michael Wilkins shrugged. "I guess that sounds better, but I'll always be partial to Dondee. It is simple and has nothing pompous about it. So why are you going to Buckland?"

Drummond sat in a kitchen chair. "I usually go to Buckland to visit Mom in the nursing home. I'll also catch up on some old friends from high school."

"How's your mother doing? Do you get there frequently?"

Drummond looked down, a momentary cloud crossing his thoughts. "No. I can't get away much during the week, and Angie is just as busy on the weekends as she is during the week."

Mr. Wilkins stirred the soup he was cooking. He looked straight ahead at the wall, however, as if afraid to turn around and glance at Drummond. "Dondee, when I was your age, my mother was in the nursing home too. She was an alcoholic, and most of the time, she wasn't sure who I was. I went twice a week or more. I knew all she had done for me, and I was not about to let her think I was not grateful."

Drummond thought a moment. "You mean you didn't want people to say that you were inattentive to her needs. I suppose that's a good—"

Michael turned around furiously. "I meant what I said! I loved my mother a great deal. She deserved to have me beside her every day, but I just couldn't get there. It was not some lame-ass excuse like you just used."

"I wasn't making up some excuse . . . Ya know what I'm saying?"

Michael looked for a full minute at Drummond. "Oh yeah, I know exactly what you're saying. I've heard every evasive word. Let me tell you a story. You'll like it because it's about you!

"There are certain students I've tried to keep track of. You, obviously, are one of those. After all I did to get scholarships for you, I thought you might even keep in touch with me. I did not see you frequently. I only knew where you were by the pictures in the newspaper, the TV ads, and, of course, your high-profile commitment to helping people in your community.

"Last March, the high school opened their new library. As an alum, I gave a whole set of new books—Chaucer, Shakespeare, and Marlowe. I arrived at the opening early and had a lovely chat with Maggie Robbins. She looked great. She had been with you in high school, walking with you daily—just talking—and then she was surprised to see you in college, too. She filled me in on all of her meanderings since she had been in my class. About the time she finished, I saw Angie entering on your arm. You were immediately the center of attention. Maggie Robbins shied back.

The inexplicable look in her eyes was strange and most unpleasant. I immediately wondered what you might have done during high school or college to awaken such a strong reaction from her.

"Hers was not the only reaction I saw, however, and that other one I understood quite plainly. It was your reaction to seeing her. And now, at the other end of the year, you are running off to catch up with her and see where your persuasive powers can lead you. Why do I think this? Well, despite Angie always coming with you before, she is not with you now."

Drummond's face had gone blank and expressionless. "She wanted to celebrate Christmas with her family for a change. She hasn't seen her brother on Christmas for the five years we've been married. We've always been with Mother, and nursing homes can be a bit of a downer at this time of year, so we just thought that—"

Michael Wilkins allowed his voice to rise above Drummond's accelerated chattering. "Would you **like *some SOUP?*** " He dipped up some soup and placed it in the bowl, setting that bowl in front of Drummond. "Dondee, I can't care much about your activities. They don't pertain to me. I might have cared more had you pursued the natural talents you had in English. As you did not, I won't worry about them now. This flippant jabbering irks the hell out of me, mainly because it is all lies."

Drummond's face was suddenly creased with tension lines. "I am not lying."

Michael Wilkins sat slowly down at the table. "And I say that you are." He broke up two saltine crackers and put them into his soup, passing the box of crackers over to Drummond. "I forgot to tell you about three other reactions at the opening. Mayor Theodore saw you enter and gave a violent gesture. I'm not sure its exact meaning, but it wasn't kind. Mark Cuthbert had been talking to me, and stopped dead in his tracks. His one-word reaction was something pretty strong. I don't say such words readily. Then Mary Hickox was talking to Maggie Robbins, a mere six feet from me, and her string of expletives was not something a gentleman should repeat—in fact I shouldn't even have heard it. So much for the positive image you thought you made."

Drummond took a sip of the soup. "This is good soup. Why were you so concerned about what people thought about me?"

Michael chuckled, his mouth retaining a serious set. "A teacher invests heavily in his or her students, and it hurts that teacher when a student proves to be less than an ideal alum. After all the work we did on that recording, I thought you'd understand that by now."

They did not speak much more until the soup was finished. Michael put the bowls into the dishwasher. He then got some peach Jell-O with real peaches in it, scooped out two helpings, and sprayed whipped cream on it. "Here! This is an ideal dessert."

Drummond took a bite and liked it. "Despite the whipped cream, the dessert is light. By the way, the new road is nice, but why are the bridges covered over? Wasn't that part of the reason they put in the new road?"

Michael Wilkins smiled. "Yes, that was why, but the engineers who built the road 'knew better' than any of the rest of us. Hal Peters, Chris Daggett, and I argued with them for two hours. We even went to the courthouse. The county had set the parameters of the work. So we got a good remake, except for each end. Those pretty much negate the blessings of the whole thing."

Drummond finally got around to insisting that he needed to get into Buckland. Michael had, by this time, put the dishes into the dishwasher. He covered the soup to cool in a large bowl and pushed the button on the washer. "*Wanting* to get into Buckland ain't *getting* into Buckland, though, is it!" He motioned Dondee into the living room.

The fire had burned low, so Michael added two more logs. "The rain should stop within the hour, and then the water recedes almost immediately. You'll be in Buckland within two hours tops." He unfolded the screen in front of the mantel. "Now am I right about Angie and you? Your protection around the subject is so strong that I would have to guess that you had a squabble of some magnitude either last night or this morning. Do you care to tell me about it, Dondee?" He started to sit, but, pausing, he added, "Without the baloney! I'll know if you're making it up."

Drummond nodded. "I guess. I can't go anywhere anyway." He thought a minute. "Angie and I got married right out of college. We had intimately enjoyed each other's company for most of college, and we decided to keep the relationship going. It was a sensible idea, just not a very bright one. There was at least a little sexual chemistry but not enough to sustain an entire relationship for years on end. I felt something was wrong in our marriage, and Angie felt the same. I never put a face to it until I walked into that opening. There was Maggie, standing basically as I had always known her. She opened up in her typically friendly manner, and I knew that was what was missing."

Michael nodded. "An' now, you want to go and find out if you're right. I won't speak for Maggie, but I'm pretty sure she won't welcome you with open arms. I suggest you go to the nursing home to see your mom first. After that, just judge by the hour that it is and don't be late in heading home. Buckland hasn't grown, and there aren't that many people for you to see."

Just as Michael finished his assessment of the situation, the sunshine suddenly poured through the window. Drummond stood. "I think I'd better get there if I can. People to see, ya know." He started toward the door.

"And hopefully people to maneuver, too?"

Drummond just shook his head. "Mr. Wilkins, naughty, naughty mind!"

Within two minutes, Drummond had backed out of Michael Wilkins's drive and headed toward Buckland. To his surprise, the bridge was just barely open, so he crossed it, vowing never to come that way again.

Michael Wilkins watched his protégé go. As he did so, a woman came up beside him. "Should I have told him more?"

The woman shook her head. "Nope! I don't think so. You said enough that he'll be able to connect the dots when the time comes."

Drummond went to the nursing home. He felt a little guilty about not having been there in a couple of weeks. To his surprise, however, the first person he met at the door was his football buddy from high school, Larry Thurmond. He greeted Drummond warmly but in a very businesslike fashion, motioning him into the nursing home office. Greta Hammer, director of the nursing home, was there already. Not only did she not leave, but instead she closed a file at which she had been working and turned her full attention to what Larry Thurmond had to say to Drummond Wilkinson.

"Dondee, I am very glad to see you. You don't know it, of course, but I'm the lawyer for Buckland Nursing Home." His affable tone began to change almost at once. "There is little reason to beat around the bush. You have not been here in several weeks, and our repeated attempts to reach you have been ignored. Do you not understand that, without the advice of family and friends, we are terribly bound in what we can do?"

Dondee shrugged. "It's only been two weeks, three at the outside, and my business is quite filled at this time of the year."

Mrs. Hammer opened the file in front of her again. "It has been over nine weeks, not two, and you have been phoned three times this week, three last week, and two each of the preceding weeks. Does your secretary never see fit to forward our messages? More important, when you personally tell us you will call us back, why don't you?"

Dondee sat back, his manner relaxed and offhand. "Nothing sounded very urgent to me. And besides, as I told you, my work has been really hard, ya know what I mean, and I can't always—"

Larry Thurmond put his face directly in front of Dondee's face. "Well, perhaps you'll understand our concern when I tell you that we became worried about your mother's condition two days after your last visit—again, *nine* not *two* weeks ago. Her physical capacities were already limited, but then her mind started slipping. She asked for you almost daily, eventually several times an hour. She wept a lot. She stopped asking ten days ago, and she died three days ago in her sleep. Her wishes had been dictated to Corbin Heck, her attorney, and he saw to it that her possessions were disposed of before she died. She was cremated yesterday, as per her instructions, the ashes being scattered in the woods at Tracker Park. The bill will be sent to you this next week. I suppose that leaves only this box to give to you." Larry Thurmond unceremoniously thrust a shoe box into Dondee's hands. It contained a small devotional Bible, two gold chains, three rings of precious stones, and a deck of cards. The rest, pencils and a pad, seemed random and meaningless.

Dondee looked up, anger flaring in his eyes. "And just who the hell gave anyone power of attorney to do these things without my permission?"

Greta Hammer took a blue piece of paper from the file and handed it to Dondee Wilkinson. "You did! You signed this paper fourteen months ago. We had been having difficulties with your visiting or returning calls even then, so we had you sign this waiver. You were eager to read it, so I assumed you understood it when you signed it." She then reached into the file again. "I also have one more thing from your mother. It is this letter. You are not to read it here. Corbin Heck took the dictation the day after you left the last time. I have no idea what it says."

Dondee Wilkinson tore open the small envelope. "I'll read it wherever I want." He started to read it silently, while Mrs. Hammer and Larry Thurmond looked at each other. They knew the slant of the words that had been written, even if they had no idea of the exact wording. Dondee shook his head. "This doesn't make any sense to me at all."

Greta Hammer said quietly and with compassion, "It didn't make any sense to Mr. Heck either. Read it aloud to see if it still doesn't mean anything."

Dondee took the letter to the window to get the best light he could. It also kept the others from seeing the tears forming in his eyes.

Dondee,

Remember that the road is always bumpiest at the beginning and at the end. You might consider stopping and thinking about this on the way home. Go home the way you came. The answer

will come to you then and there. Don't expect more of yourself than you have. If you still don't understand when you arrive home, let Angie read this too. She understands all that I mean. She understands you too better than you know.

With eternal love,
Mom

He folded the letter. "I don't get it."

Larry had far less sympathy for Dondee than Greta Hammer. "She apparently loved *you* more than you loved *her*."

Dondee Wilkinson stepped forward and picked up the box from the chair, where he had left it. Once he reached the door of the room, he turned back to the two remaining in their places. "You two may think I'm just some uncaring boob, but I loved my mother very much. All of your fancy-dance airs and high-handed talk means nothing. You are not as wonderful as you think you are. For the record, I'm considering suing you both."

Greta was ready for that phrase. "Dondee Wilkinson, just so you know . . . I have a detailed record of each and every attempt to contact you. So your strategy won't work."

Dondee barely heard her. He was out the door and into the parking lot almost before he knew where he was. Once in his car, he started it and sped out of the parking lot, almost smacking into the side of an oncoming automobile. He did not get far. Buckland was not a big town, and, as with many small towns, the bar was centrally located, easily accessible to anyone. He pulled into a parking stall and went in. The bar had only been open ten minutes, and he was already ordering a tall beer.

"Ain't it a bit early for that, Dondee?" The voice came from behind him. He turned and found himself face-to-face with Maggie Robbins. "I'd call you Drummond, but I never have, so why should I start now?"

Dondee was astounded. He had so wanted to see Maggie Robbins, but the woman who stood before him was not the Maggie he expected. Her shoulders were broad, and her legs were muscular. She wore cowboy boots, jeans, and a golden-yellow shirt. A fancy blue and red tattoo decorated her right arm. "Maggie! You are just the person I need to see. You are the only one I can even think of to ask about this." He held up the letter.

Maggie nodded her head to one side. "Let's sit in that booth."

Once in the booth she took the letter and read it. She hardly thought about it, but instead handed it back. "I ain't the one you should ask, ya know. It's Angie who can answer it. She was always better at that shit than I was."

Dondee folded the letter and put it in his suit pocket. "You don't have a clue?"

"I didn't say that. I saw in the paper that your mother died. What did she leave you?"

"A Bible, some notepads and pencils, uh, I don't know, two gold chains, a couple of rings, and a deck of cards." He showed her the contents of the box. "I'll get what little money was left."

Maggie Robbins looked down at the box for five minutes, saying nothing but tilting her head from side to side. Then she glanced at the letter again. Finally, she picked up the Bible and opened it where a folded page marked a place. She glanced first at the folded paper. "What the heck is this gibberish? It isn't quite English, and it for sure ain't some foreign language either."

"It's the prologue to Chaucer's *Canterbury Tales*, but just the first few lines." He glanced at them. Then without so much as a reference to the paper again, he recited the lines.

> "*Whan that Aprille with his shoures sote,*
> *The droghte of March hath perced to the rote,*
> *And bathed every veyne in swich licour,*
> *Of which vertu engendred is the flour;*
> *Whan Zephirus eek with his swete breeth*
> *Inspired hath in every holt and heeth*
> *The tendre croppes, and the yonge sonne*
> *Hath in the Ram his halfe cours y-ronne . . .*"

Maggie shook her head. "Man, I hope you know what it means, 'cause I sure as hell don't." She held up the Bible. "That paper marked this page. It's the opening of Genesis."

Dondee stood very quietly thinking a moment. "I understand the Chaucer, but I don't get the reference. Give me the Bible.

"In the beginning God created the heavens and the earth. The earth was without form and void, and darkness was upon the face of the deep."

Dondee put the Chaucer back into the Bible and then turned to another passage marked later.

"You shall not make unto yourself any graven images . . ."

Again he turned, this time to Habakkuk. He looked at Maggie, "Now who on earth reads Habakkuk?"

"Your mother, obviously, did."

"O Lord, how long shall I call for help, and thou wilt not hear? Or cry to thee, 'Violence!' and thou wilt not save? Why dost thou make me see wrongs and look upon trouble?"

Maggie chuckled. "At least she didn't say that God gave his only begotten son, that whosoever . . ."

A small blue piece of paper fell from the Bible. Dondee picked it up, glanced at the paper, and then showed it to Maggie. It gave the quote exactly as Maggie had started it. They both laughed, not with raucous laughter but with subdued laughter and palpable sorrow. Dondee put all of the papers into the box and closed it.

"Maggie, let's leave me alone for a while. What a change has come over you! You were so sexy at that library opening, and now you seem, uh, maybe a little tough?"

Maggie let the smile fade from her lips. "It's been a long time, Dondee, since we really talked. I'm not sure we ever really did. I'm tough because I have to be. I'm not in a cushy job like you've got. I can bounce the hardest thug out of here, like Randy Potter, and I can honey up to any of them, too. I don't do men though, if you know what I mean. I ain't no lesbian, but the way men are ain't my way. I can clean up once in a while when I want to. I let you get away, ya see, and I regret that sometimes. But I ain't about to say I regret my life. I am not turning back. It ain't my way. I know why you done come here, Dondee. You wanted to reclaim the old ways. Well, you don't fit the old ways any more than I do. You can't turn back the clock. Didn't your momma ever teach you that? Your dad taught you a lot, I reckon, but he wouldn't have taught you that." Maggie got up to go behind the bar, but Dondee caught her arm.

"What do you mean that my dad taught me a lot? You know I ain't got a dad!" Dondee was more than a little anxious, sure somehow that Maggie had almost told him something she should not have.

Maggie realized her mistake. Instead of denying it or telling Dondee the truth she knew, she just shrugged. "I reckon you'll find out soon enough, Dondee. I mean all guys got dads. They just don't always know who they are. That info ain't gonna come from me. Now go on home to Angie. I need to wait on customers." Hardly catching a breath, she turned and called out, "Clyde Carpenter, what the hell are you doing in here with your wife in the hospital?"

Dondee left the bar, having drunk the last half of his tall beer in one gulp. He got to his car but threw up almost at once, beer coming from his mouth and nose. Once he felt well enough, he fell behind the wheel. He wasn't drunk, no matter how many ounces that beer had held. Most of it had landed in the gutter. He was sick from the knowledge of what he had become.

Without knowing it, he almost immediately found himself on the steep climb up to the road where Michael Wilkins lived. As the road leveled out, D. Drummond Wilkinson, Dondee to all his friends, pulled to the side of the road. He looked down the steep hill he had just climbed. He thought about the culvert at the other end. Then he thought about the paper his mother had written to him. How could his mother know about the road weeks ahead of that day? Yet even before he thought about the letter, he had stopped to think about events and the road, just as she had told him to do.

D. Drummond, Dondee forever in his heart, started to drive past Michael Wilkins's house but stopped abruptly. There was an old FOR

SALE sign in the yard, weathered and clearly from some year other than this one. He pulled into the drive.

He knocked on the door. No one was there. He peered in through the windows. There was no furniture inside except for a small table in the center of the living room. He tried the garage door, but it too was locked.

"I could let you in, if'n you're interested. It needs some work. No one's lived there since April." The man stepped into the yard. "Daggett is my name."

Dondee's spirit flared up. "What do ya mean? I visited with a guy here this morning. Michael Ellis Wilkins had been a teacher of mine, and damned glad he was to see me."

Daggett gave immediate lie to the opinion of some that black men can't blanch white. "You did not talk with Wilkins this morning, I can tell you that for sure."

"Take me inside." Dondee more ordered than asked this, but Daggett took no notice of it and opened the door at once. There was no evidence of soup being cooked and served, dishes, or indeed of any habitation having been there in at least three or four months. There was only one thing in the entire house: that small table in the middle of the living room floor. On it were pamphlets describing the attributes of the house.

Daggett could see that Dondee was confused. "Hey, man, don't get upset. You won't be the first, and I doubt you'll be the last to go by this house and be greeted by Wilkins. Ya see he was a loner, a man left to his own for too many hours of sadness. The woman he loved was out of reach for him, he was never allowed to tell his son that he was his father, and Michael was never allowed to claim his rightful place among a hierarchy of great minds. Some thought he pushed too hard, but I reckon that was racial backlash." He stopped a minute, and then he corrected himself. "No, it might not have been. But Mike was sad. He went for as long as he was able, living on the meager settlement he got from a slander case back somewhere. I never knew much about it. It made the papers, and there were lots of lies proven to be nothing more than willful slander.

His girlfriend's dad didn't like Michael, so she couldn't marry him, even though she was pregnant.

"Michael lived here so he could be near his girlfriend. He went to visit her at her house now and again, and I think he went to the nursing home after that. He died of a stroke in the spring. She held on as long as she could, but then I reckon she done got lonesome for him. She died a couple of days ago, so the paper said."

Dondee suddenly sat down on the windowsill. Things were becoming clearer and yet more befuddled. "What . . . that is, do you know what the woman he loved . . . what was her name?"

Chris Daggett sat down next to Dondee. "Well, now you mention it, I ain't sure. But if you c'n wait a minute, I have the paper. Do you want it? I ain't fixing to keep it."

"Yes, please." Dondee could hardly breathe. Daggett rushed off to his house to get the local paper. Dondee sat totally whipped. He was about to rise to get some air outside, when his eyes caught something in the kitchen, glistening on top of the refrigerator. He ran there, unsure what it could be but sure it had to be a clue, something to light his way through this murky day. It was a house key on a keychain. The chain was what had glistened to him. It was gold, and it matched perfectly the chain that was in his box in the car. He didn't hear Daggett come back.

"Ya know, ya don't look too good! Come over to my place for a little to catch your breath." He led Dondee out the door, locking it behind him. Dondee handed him the key. "What's that? Oh, that's the key to the cellar door. I wondered where it got to."

Dondee looked at Chris Daggett, and his eyes got wide. "Show me the basement now!" The urgency in his voice prodded Daggett to reopen the house. They went to the basement door and inserted the key. The steps were in good shape. In the basement there was very little that might have been called interesting. Daggett didn't think much of it anyway. Dondee found a scrapbook. It was tucked down in the folds of an old folding lawn chair. The pages were protected by plastic that was wrapped around the book. Dondee could hardly get the plastic off. Inside, as he somehow suspected there would be, were hundreds of pictures of himself, carefully preserved and progressing from a smart, wide-eyed kid of about seven years old up to his garnering the PhD. At the bottom of the last page were carefully lettered three simple questions:

> But what will he become when he grows up?
> How much more can he do than he has done till now?
> Must a father always worry?
> Tucked into the book at the end were three CDs, carefully labeled,
> **Chaucer—read by Dondee.**

Chris Daggett helped Dondee back up the stairs. Dondee's face was stained with tears. Finally outside again, he leaned against the oak tree as Daggett closed up. He started to help Dondee to his car, but Dondee squared away his shoulders. "Thank you, Mr. Daggett, but I don't need help. You don't even need to tell me who Michael Ellis Wilkins loved. I know. That's why my name is Wilkinson. I'm his son, and his love was my mother. I now know a great deal. This day has been a real trial for me. And I'm not to the end of the learning I have to do. I'll get there. You bet I will."

Daggett nodded knowingly and let Dondee drive out. As Dondee's car descended the road by Chris Daggett's own house, Daggett remarked to himself, "I hope you know what you're talking about, Dondee Wilkinson, because I sure as hell don't."

Dondee got almost into his own town, when he remembered that he had not purchased milk for breakfast or, in fact, anything to eat. His ability at cooking was limited, so he had to think what he could possibly fix. As he pulled into the grocery lot and parked the car, his mind raced through the Chaucer and the phrases from the Bible.

The grocery was crowded. It was Christmas Eve afternoon, and people were stocking up on oysters, ham, rolls, green beans, sweet potatoes, and lots of other things. Oranges were plentiful but going quickly. Bananas were down to a few. Dondee had just picked up the few fruit he knew he needed, when a major altercation broke out in the check-out line, not more than twenty feet from where Dondee was standing.

"If you have money to buy fancy hams like that, you've got money to pay me my back rent for the last two months." It was a man Drummond knew well. He had been ruthless toward Dondee once upon a time, and Dondee had delighted in thwarting the man's efforts to oust him from his apartment by making a major sale in his business, paying the man and then making sure that he himself moved within days. He didn't like the man, and he wasn't going to stand around and let him bully the young woman.

The woman was a white woman he also knew. They had spoken frequently in line at that same grocery. With her was a little boy, his blond hair almost white under the fluorescent lights. He rode in the cart. The little girl was a year or two older than the boy, and she clung hysterically to her mother's skirt, afraid of the man yelling at her mother.

"My husband is over in Afghanistan. He isn't home yet. His checks were delayed in the mail. You know how difficult times are for everyone. It's a dry spell that we're all trying to get through." The woman was tumbling all over herself trying to make excuses.

Dondee stepped up to the man, brusquely spinning him around. All the people within hearing distance went silent. The man's foul mouth started spewing epithets at Dondee, but Dondee put his hand over the man's mouth, and, with his most resonant voice said quietly, "That will be enough, Mr. Peters. This woman is going through enough hell in her life with her husband deployed in the Gulf, and all you can think to do is bellyache about your precious purse. Well, I have a solution to that." He reached into his wallet and drew out two hundred dollar bills. "Now I have to keep one for myself. I know your oversized prices for your meager apartments. That pays you up for one month and a little over. If you must have the rest, we'll go to that ATM and get the rest. But you will not say another thing to this woman in this store, not today!"

"Well, I have a right to expect money. I have expenses at this time of the year too, you know. And for the record, I'm getting tired of you damned black men throwing your weight around, bullying us into doing what we don't—" He did not get any further.

Dondee stood up very tall. He had been a quarterback in college, but in high school he had also been center in the basketball team. He looked down on Mr. Peters. "I have not touched you. I have not spoken loudly to you. I have spoken emphatically and clearly, but not that loudly. Come with me and I'll get you the money you need."

They started toward the ATM, but there, standing in the door of the grocery, was a man Dondee knew well: the woman's husband, still in his travel fatigues. He motioned the soldier to his wife. Their reunion brought the grocery to a cheering standstill. Belligerent, Mr. Peters saw it all and started to back down. "Well, since her husband is home, I suppose—"

But Dondee had pushed the button at the ATM. The hundred dollars came out in five twenty dollar bills. "Here, Mr. Peters, now leave them and their joy alone. You may not remember me, but you were once just as angry with me. I was scared of you then, but I'm not now."

The store owner shook Dondee's hand. "Thank you for averting a catastrophe. What an ass Peters is."

Dondee shook his head. "He was right. He deserved his money, and so do you." After paying for his groceries, he caught up with the young couple and their children. The soldier was thoroughly overwhelmed. "I'll repay you when I can. I get a good salary from the government, but—"

Dondee put up his hand. "I have a way you can repay me. I want you to help me distribute a bunch of food to needy families."

The soldier looked at his wife a moment and stammered, "Sure, but when? It's Christmas Eve. Christmastime is here."

Dondee smiled. "I know. And I hopefully have someone waiting for me at home. I'll bring her. If your wife can take care of your children and can spare you for a mere two hours, then meet me back here in one hour's time."

The meeting was arranged, and they all set off.

At his home, Dondee was ecstatic that Angie met him at the door. "Angie, I'm so sorry about this morning. I've been a louse and a lousy husband. That's changing now, tonight, right now. I'll explain on the way what has gone down today, but I have found out a lot of things I had no idea about."

"Your mother died!" Angie slipped in the words quickly.

"Yes, and so did my father. I know who he was! And he has always been a kind of hero to me. I just didn't know the entire reason why."

As they changed their clothes and turned off the various things that were cooking (and as Dondee called the nursing home to set up a memorial service the following Sunday), Dondee filled in Angie on the events of the day. He didn't stint on his true intentions regarding Maggie either.

After hearing the events of the day, Angie shook her head. Nothing much was clear, and she didn't know why she was putting on her coat. Leery of his motives, Angie kept her distance as they went to the car. "Okay, so we're going to distribute food and stuff to needy people. Do you know who? Who will pay for all of this food? And why are you so damned happy? Are you planning another rendezvous with some bimbo?"

Dondee stopped at the light. "Mom wrote me a note, and Dad—uh, I now know that was Mr. Wilkins—left me clues. It just took me putting them together, and suddenly my life unkinked. As for bimbos, well, they are in the past—forever. Let me explain about what I'm planning.

"I'll pay for the food. I'm hoping Mr. Gradisson can help by giving me a little break on the price. He'll need to close in about five minutes. I think I can persuade him not to. I'll explain a little now, but most of it will have to wait. Mom left me that box I mentioned. It had a Bible in it, and various quotes were marked. One of the pieces of paper marking a Bible quote had a quote written on it too. It was one I knew really well. Then there was the letter Mom left me. It started with a cryptic quote about a road being rough at the beginning and the end, but that the middle was smooth. At first I thought she meant the road that goes beside my father's house. But that wasn't what she meant at all. It's hard to get started on the road to finding yourself, but, once you get started, the travel is easy. It is hard to finish. You think, 'Hey, I've done great stuff.' That's when you can easily revert to your mistakes of the past. I won't be reverting." They could see the grocery lights from the stoplight where they sat. Once the light was green, he started to drive on slowly.

Angie nodded. "I get that. Are all the quotes that hard?"

"I'm afraid they are."

"Then answer me this, and no evasion this time: Who did the bra belong to?"

Dondee steered the car into grocery lot. The help was just leaving, and Frank Gradisson was just about to lock up. Dondee blew the horn and pulled up next to the exit door. "Let's just say that the bra belongs to the past, and the lover-boy image I have so well deserved in that past is gone forever. I'm going to live in the now. You have no reason to trust me except that I've already told you I've been a louse. Read into that what you want and know that I'm into a new chapter of my life, and I don't reread chapters or reenter them." Without Angie giving any assent as to whether she would trust him or not, they both got out of the car.

Mr. Gradisson was standing at the door. "We're closed, ya know."

Dondee motioned Angie forward to be by his side. Sgt. Bill Craft was just pulling up behind Dondee's car. They all entered the grocery. "Glad you could make it, Sergeant Craft."

"Like I said the store is closed, so don't expect me to reopen for you."

Dondee answered with a gleeful retort. "But you don't have to reopen for us. All we want to do is purchase about twenty large bags of groceries. I want nothing less than $100 worth of groceries in each bag. If that means two, three or four bags times twenty, so be it. Let's hurry. We'll do the shopping. I want you, Mr. Gradisson, to go to your files. You have food stamps, and you'll probably have the names for those people. At least I'm sure you must have addresses for some people who are down on their luck. All I want you to do is get me the names of twenty families who won't be having such a happy Christmas tomorrow. Bill—I hope you don't mind if I call you Bill, sergeant is a bit unwieldy—you go to the Christmas toys over there and pick out about forty stuffed animals. Price is no object—okay, it is, but nothing there is too expensive anyway. Angie, you and I will do the power shopping routine."

They started by getting twenty turkeys, twenty bags of potatoes, other vegetables, stuffing, bags of oranges, and pies (when the pumpkin pies were depleted, they chose cherry and apple.) They even included some soups. Staples like milk and cereal were picked up as well.

While they were filling basket after basket, Frank Gradisson was checking each basket out, dividing the food into twenty baskets. Sergeant Bill Craft was sacking stuff up as fast as he could, but Dondee and Angie still got ahead of both of the others. Finally, after three large bags were filled for each family, Dondee paid Frank Gradisson over $2,000. "We're done here. Now if you want to come with us to help, Frank, you can, otherwise you're free to go home, and thank you. Sergeant Bill, you take these twenty-one bags. I think these families are near where you live. Once you get them delivered, give me a call on my cell." He handed him a card. "I was wondering if you might be able to come tomorrow for dinner."

Sergeant Bill Craft shook his head. "Sorry, we're having my brother, his wife, and my mom over. It's a family time. And I just got home."

"I understand. You don't need to say further. Where do you live exactly?"

"We're in an apartment. It's kind of cramped." Bill explained the area.

"I know it well. I lived in apartment 14 several years ago. Could you take a little time away from football to bring everyone over? I don't mean for dinner, but, let's say, midafternoon—four o'clock. I have a house for rent that might suit your family even better than where you're living now. Mr. Peters isn't my favorite man, you know. He has a right to money, but he doesn't have a right to deliver such terrible services for the little apartments he rents out."

Bill Crafts scratched his head. "Well, I guess we can. We normally eat Christmas meal at five o'clock. Could we come at 11:00 a.m., just Peggy, the kids, and me?"

Dondee glanced at Angie, who was dumbfounded at all Dondee was doing. "Sure. That's even better. As I said, I have a house to show you. Once I do that, I also have an offer of a job. I need to make the offer soon, or you'll do something stupid and re-up in the army for less money. I'll be out the help and you'll be out the job."

The surprised sergeant went his way. It took seventy-five minutes for him to deliver to his seven families. Dondee and Angie were just finishing with their eighth family when Bill called. He came over to where they were and helped deliver the remainder. The elation Bill, Dondee, and Angie felt was overwhelming. "I've seen guys in the army show great glee after doing this kind of thing, but I've never been able to help. Now I know why they do it! What could be better than this?"

Dondee reached into a little bag, extracting a red Santa hat. "This, Sergeant, is better still. Now you go home and enjoy the night. I'll see you late tomorrow morning."

Once Angie and Dondee were home and relaxing in the hot tub, Dondee began. "The numbers of my philandering ways don't matter. I've been a schmuck, and that's over with. Now let me explain the Bible quotes." They each sipped their Chardonnay. "First of all, I was like that quote from the Creation—I was a void, empty, and without meaning in my life. I realized I had filled my life with the worship of money, and if that's not a graven image, I don't know what is. I felt like Scrooge, except I soon realized I only had two ghosts to help me. I suspect that Mr. Wilkins and Mom were helping me together. I just hope they're together now forever.

"The quote from Habakkuk was about crying out, but no one hearing. It was not that I was crying out to God—it was, instead, that he was crying out to me, and I wasn't listening. Well, I got the message quite well this time. God giving his only son did not take much thought from me to understand—even if I am, for sure, not godly in the least."

Angie passed the tray of chips and dip to Dondee. After Dondee carefully took a couple of chips, she put the tray back down, reserving the chips (without dip) for herself. "Well, what about that obscure quote from Chaucer? That's a Wilkins trick if there ever was one."

Dondee nodded. "So was leaving a scrapbook of my entire life in the basement. He always wanted me to be a Chaucer scholar. Maybe I should have been. That kind of mania, poring over ancient publications and noting the tiniest differences between editions, can be just as mind-numbing as being in business. That quote was one I had to memorize years ago. It spoke of the rejuvenation one feels after April showers have watered the parched ground of dry March. It spoke of the healing winds. The moment I heard Mrs. Craft mention having a dry spell, the quote clicked into my mind. I had to water her dry land."

"It's nice to offer, but do you really have such a position for Bill Craft?"

Dondee took another sip of wine. "I don't know if I do or not. Between Joe Dangler, Edie Corbin, Phil Johnson, Jackson Jones, and me, I'll bet we can find him a good job. He's been a good soldier, and the honor and sacrifice that entails means he should be given a good job stateside. That's something I couldn't talk about tonight. I can't give him a medal personally from me, but I can be sure he gets some proper rewards—starting with a house and not a cramped apartment. We'll offer them the house on Canterbury Road, or we can go up to the Wilkins house and offer that to them. I'll buy it and then rent it to them. Now you and I should just relax and enjoy the hot water. I've had a long day."

"Canterbury Road? It keeps coming back to Chaucer, doesn't it?"

Dondee laughed. "Well, there are worse authors to base a life on."

Angie leaned back, allowing Dondee the freedom of putting his arm around her shoulder. The joy he was showing was something she had not seen in a long time. So she would enjoy it too. Doubts still crept into the corners of her mind, but she kept them there, vowing to avoid them at all cost. They would go away if the transformation was truly complete and lasting. And such transformations were what Christmas was all about. So she decided to enjoy the new Dondee as much as he was. Then they clicked their glasses together and sipped more of the wine. Christmas would be a whole lot better than she had thought it would. The hope, however, was that they would not awaken with a headache tomorrow.

To this day, neither of them know whether it was Santa Claus who came early or if there were a pair of ghosts watching out for them. The two were happy from that day forward, and the spirit of Christmas—give it what name they would—remained with them for a long time.